the
scarlet
macaw

A MYSTERY

S.P. HOZY

DUNDURN
TORONTO

Editor: Gillian Buckley
Design: Courtney Horner
Printer: Webcom

Library and Archives Canada Cataloguing in Publication

Hozy, Penny, 1947-
        The scarlet macaw / by S.P. Hozy.

Issued also in electronic formats.
ISBN 978-1-4597-0598-2

        I. Title.

PS8615.O99S22 2013   C813'.6   C2012-904647-7

1   2   3   4   5   17   16   15   14   13

We acknowledge the support of the **Canada Council for the Arts** and the **Ontario Arts Council** for our publishing program. We also acknowledge the financial support of the **Government of Canada** through the **Canada Book Fund** and **Livres Canada Books**, and the **Government of Ontario** through the **Ontario Book Publishing Tax Credit** and the **Ontario Media Development Corporation**.

Care has been taken to trace the ownership of copyright material used in this book. The author and the publisher welcome any information enabling them to rectify any references or credits in subsequent editions.

J. Kirk Howard, President

Printed and bound in Canada.

Visit us at
Dundurn.com
Definingcanada.ca
@dundurnpress
Facebook.com/dundurnpress

Dundurn	Gazelle Book Services Limited	Dundurn
3 Church Street, Suite 500	White Cross Mills	2250 Military Road
Toronto, Ontario, Canada	High Town, Lancaster, England	Tonawanda, NY
M5E 1M2	LA1 4XS	U.S.A. 14150

For my mother

If I keep a green bough in my heart, the singing bird will come.

— Chinese proverb

Singapore

2010

Chapter One

At the time Maris didn't realize she was witnessing a murder. Peter seemed fine at first. Then he began slurring his words, which she thought was odd because he hadn't even finished his first drink. Peter always liked a glass of Campari on the rocks before dinner. She had tried it once, years ago, but didn't care for it. She preferred a gin and tonic. They would be having wine with dinner, probably white, maybe a nice Riesling. Peter's face seemed to be going rigid and he was having a hard time speaking. *Oh my God*, she thought, *he's having a stroke.*

"Peter," she said, "smile. Can you smile?" It wasn't really a smile. More like he was clenching his teeth. "Put your hands up in the air!" she shouted at him as she reached into her bag for her mobile. "Up, up." *This is serious*, she thought. He was staring at her just the way the sea bass he was going to cook for supper had stared at her: a wide-eyed, fishy stare.

"What's your name?" she asked, as she dialed 9-9-5. *Don't die*, she thought. *Please don't die on me*.

Those were the three things you were supposed to do when you thought someone might be having a stroke, weren't they? Ask them to smile, to raise their hands in the air, and to tell you their name. Something about facial muscles, arm strength, and memory.

"Hurry," she said when someone answered. "I think he's having a stroke. He's not responding to any of my questions." She gave them the details, trying not to panic. There was white, foamy spit dribbling from the corner of Peter's mouth. "Please hurry," she pleaded. "I don't know what to do."

In the ten minutes it took for the ambulance to arrive, Peter sat slumped over on the tan coloured sofa that he prized above all the other art deco pieces he had collected over the years. It was made of a silky suede — the original covering — and worth twice what he'd paid for it. He had discovered it in a photographer's studio just off Orchard Road and had offered to buy it immediately. The owner, an elderly Chinese man who was in the process of closing his business and retiring, was only too happy to sell it to Peter, along with a lamp and an end table that he had owned since the 1930s.

Maris didn't know what to do. *Why am I thinking about his furniture?* she wondered. Peter appeared to be unconscious, his chin touching his chest, his hands palms up at his sides. He was still wearing his wire-rimmed Armani reading glasses. She couldn't tell if he was breathing; there didn't appear to be any movement of his chest under the butter-yellow silk shirt, but it was hard to tell because his head was blocking her view of the upper part of his body. It reminded her of the way penguins buried their heads in their chests to sleep. But she knew he wasn't asleep.

Shouldn't I be giving him CPR or something? she thought. But she didn't know how to do that. She seemed to be riveted to the spot, on the opposite side of the low, curved coffee table (another art deco find of Peter's) staring down at him, completely incapable of thinking of anything except art deco furniture. She was still clutching the mobile in her right hand, and her left hand was half-raised in a reaching gesture as if she were just about to give him benediction. She'd seen the Pope make this same gesture from his balcony in St. Peter's Square.

It was so quiet. As if the power had just been cut and every humming appliance — refrigerator, air conditioner, laptop computer — had suddenly died. Maris realized she'd been holding her breath. She exhaled softly through her mouth and half expected Peter to do the same. But he didn't. He didn't move.

Where are they? she thought. *What's taking so long?* Singapore was the most efficient city in the world. Why hadn't the paramedics arrived yet? Would they be too late?

She heard a commotion in the hallway outside the apartment and realized that she hadn't opened the door. *Oh God*, she thought, *are these few wasted seconds the ones that will kill Peter?* Was she, ultimately, going to be responsible for his death? She ran for the door and turned the safety lock to release the spring. She was fumbling with the cellphone, the spring lock, and the doorknob, and cursing her stupidity when the door swung open and two men with a gurney pushed past her.

"He's in there," she said, pointing to the living room. She ran after them. "I haven't touched him. I didn't know what to do. I didn't want to do the wrong thing."

One of them had pushed Peter's head back and was pulling his eyelids up to look at his eyes, which appeared to be staring up at the ceiling in surprise. Then the paramedic ripped Peter's shirt open and the buttons flew onto the sofa. *He's going to be mad*, she thought. *That's his favourite shirt.*

She heard one of the men say, "No vitals," and then they were laying him out flat and rubbing his chest. The paramedic closest to her was pulling something out of a suitcase and she saw it was those paddles they use to get people's hearts going when they're flatlining. She'd seen it on television on *ER*. Then the one who'd been rubbing Peter's chest stood back and the one with the paddles drove his hands into Peter's chest. She heard a buzzing, crackling sound, then nothing, then the buzzing, crackling sound again.

"He's had a stroke," she heard herself say, but they didn't appear to be listening to her. The buzzing, crackling sound filled her ears again and then there was silence.

She looked at Peter's bare chest. The red marks from the paddles were like two patches of sunburn on his pale skin. Then she looked at his face. He wasn't wearing his glasses.

I'd better find them, she thought. *He needs them to read.*

Are you his next of kin? they'd asked her at the hospital. No, she'd said. I'm a friend. We need to notify his next of kin. Well, she'd said, he has an ex-wife who's in Germany right now and a half-sister here in Singapore. *Dinah*, she thought, *I should have called Dinah*. She searched for the number on her mobile and gave it to the hospital administrator, a no-nonsense Chinese woman in a severe grey suit with the jacket buttoned. The pointed collar of her white silk blouse laid flat against the worsted material of the suit. She wore no jewellery other than a pair of small pearl studs in her ears.

"Please take a seat over there," she said pointing to a row of yellow plastic tub chairs bolted to the floor. "I'll make the call from my office."

There were very few people in emergency, maybe because it was dinnertime. Hospitals had their ebbs and flows of activity just like everything else, she guessed. She thought of the sea bass lying on Peter's kitchen counter, staring at the ceiling the way Peter had stared at the ceiling when they'd pulled back his eyelids. Peter was lying on a gurney behind a dull beige curtain.

Maris hadn't had time to find his glasses or pick up the buttons from his shirt. She'd have to go back to the apartment and do that later. And put the fish in the fridge. She tried to make a mental list of the things she'd have to do in the next day or two. She should call Angela in Berlin. It was only fair. She and Peter were no longer married but they were still business partners. *Angela*, she thought, pronouncing it in her head with the hard "g" so it sounded more like angle instead of angel.

She tried to figure out what time it was in Berlin. How many hours difference was it? And were they behind or ahead? *No, no*, she thought, *they had to be behind. It would be earlier there, late morning*, she figured, *or lunchtime.*

God, she was tired. She tried to remember if she'd locked the door to Peter's apartment and then she remembered it had a spring lock so it would have locked automatically. *Thank God*, she thought. Peter had a lot of valuable stuff. He only bought top of the line. His laptop was only a couple of months old and it was fully loaded. The plasma TV that hung on the wall facing the sofa was less than six months old. The Bang & Olufsen sound system was state of the art and included in-home theatre surround sound components. They were going to watch Scorsese's *The Departed* after dinner. "Not the pirated version," Peter had told her. "I paid full price for the real thing, with all the extra interviews and stuff." That was one of the things that she and Peter had shared — a love of movies. They sometimes saw two or three a week, either on DVD at his place or in one of Singapore's ultra-modern movie theatres with widescreen, THX sound, and super-comfortable seats with nobody in front of you blocking the screen.

That was one thing they did well in Asia: movie theatres. There wasn't anything comparable in Vancouver. Not even close — and for a quarter of the price. And shopping malls: luxury shopping malls that sold all the designer labels, the real ones. You could get the knock-offs on the street and who could tell the difference? Of course, you knew that the shopgirl with the Gucci bag and the Prada T-shirt was probably not wearing the real thing. Maris looked down at her Versace handbag. Thank God she'd remembered to grab it on her way out the door. She'd paid about twelve bucks for it ... worth every penny, too.

What was she sitting here for? Wasn't she supposed to be doing something? Then she saw Dinah and she remembered.

"Oh God, Dinah," she said, getting up and moving toward the small, slender woman with the Chinese face who was Peter's half-sister. Maris put her arms around her and hugged her tightly for a few seconds before letting her arms drop to her sides. They felt like dead weights. She had no energy, as if she'd run all the way to the hospital instead of coming in the ambulance with Peter and the paramedics.

"Peter's dead," she said, but Dinah already knew. Her eyes were red from crying. *I haven't cried yet*, Maris thought. *What's the matter with me?* "He had a stroke," she said. "I couldn't save him. I didn't know what to do." And then she sat down on one of the yellow plastic chairs and cried.

CHAPTER TWO

She and Dinah had gone back to Peter's apartment that night so Maris could find his glasses and put the fish in the fridge. She couldn't stop thinking about that fish. She'd half expected to smell it when they opened the door. Luckily Dinah had a copy of Peter's key; otherwise they wouldn't have got in.

"I wasn't thinking too clearly," Maris told Dinah. "I meant to bring Peter's glasses because he'd been wearing them when he had the stroke. I should have brought his wallet and his keys, but I didn't want to waste time looking for them. They didn't tell me he was dead until we got to the hospital. It was all such a big rush, like maybe the paramedics thought I would hold them responsible." She knew she was babbling, but she had to dispel that awful silence that still filled the apartment like stale air inside a balloon.

The apartment didn't smell of rotting fish; instead, it had the cool, dank smell of the sea: slightly salty and a bit chilly. The air conditioning, she remembered. Peter always kept it a couple of degrees below her comfort level. Probably because he was always on the move and couldn't sit still for more than a few minutes before he'd be jumping up to do something or check something in the kitchen. Or he would show her his latest find, a book or a piece of furniture or some artifact he'd scooped in Chinatown or Little India. He was always shopping, always looking for something different, some hidden treasure. It was probably why the gallery had been so successful, right from the beginning. He had an eye — he always said he had a nose for a bargain — but it was his eyes that did the work. They never stopped searching.

They found his glasses on the floor behind the sofa. The paramedics had probably thrown them there when they'd pulled back his eyelids. What value did a pair of reading glasses, even Armani, have compared to a human life? Maris picked them up and felt grief grab her heart like a fist. One of the arms was bent and there were fingerprints on the lenses. Peter would have been furious. He valued his possessions and took such good care of them. He didn't take anything for granted. He'd worked hard for what he had; he'd never felt entitled to any of it. It had all been earned.

Maris looked over at Dinah, who was picking up the yellow buttons from where they'd scattered across the sofa. She counted them, then looked to see if there were any wedged between the cushions.

"I'd better put that fish away right now," Maris said, "or I'll have nightmares about it."

"Maybe you should take it home," said Dinah.

"What am I going to do with a whole fish?" she said.

"Then throw it out. It'll only go bad in the fridge."

"I can't throw a whole fish away," said Maris. "It'll stink. Maybe I should freeze it."

"Good idea," said Dinah. "We can deal with it later."

Maris went into the kitchen and looked for some plastic wrap. She found it right where it should be: third drawer down on the right. Peter was so predictable. She stared at the fish. *Why can't you just disappear?* she thought. The fish was beginning to exhaust her. She tore off a length of the plastic wrap, which immediately began to cling to itself at the corners. She laid one end against the fish and realized it wasn't wide enough to cover the whole fish so she picked up the wrap and laid it lengthwise. She tried to pull the corners free so it would lay flat and then thought, *Why?* She shoved the wrap under the fish, unrolled another metre and wrapped it around the fish. She did this three times until all of the fish was covered in plastic wrap. It looked like a postmodern acrylic sculpture of a fish. Then she put it in the freezer.

"Goodbye," she said. "I never want to see you again."

She tidied up the counter and put the sliced lemon, ginger, and onion Peter was going to poach the fish with into the fridge. She noticed he'd already made a salad and she put that in the fridge, too. A nice meal that nobody was ever going to eat. But she didn't have the heart to put any of it in the garbage. Not tonight.

She went back into the living room and saw Dinah sitting on the sofa, staring at the buttons in the palm of her hand.

"We have to call Angela," Maris said.

"Oh, God," said Dinah. "Do we have to?"

"Yes," said Maris. "It's still daytime in Germany. She'll have to arrange a flight and all that. It's going to take her a couple of days to get here."

"Peter wanted to be cremated," said Dinah.

"How do you know that?" asked Maris.

"He told me. We talked about it after our father died. He said he definitely didn't want to be buried in the ground in a box." She shivered. "He was adamant."

"I guess you and I will have to take care of all that."

"Yes. Angela won't care one way or the other whether he's buried or cremated."

"They are divorced, aren't they?" Maris asked.

"Yes. But legally she's still his business partner," said Dinah. "I'm not a partner. I just work for them."

"Do you think she'll want to keep the gallery going?" Maris thought of her own paintings that had sold so well under Peter's careful auspices.

"I don't know," said Dinah. "I hope so. She makes a lot of money from the gallery and we have such an established customer base. Although, I don't know. Without Peter ..." She didn't finish her sentence. She looked down at the six yellow buttons in her hand, and then slipped them into her jacket pocket.

"Why?" she asked softly. "He was only forty-five. He seemed so healthy."

"I don't know," said Maris. She sat beside Dinah on the sofa and ran her hand over the soft suede. "They're going to do an autopsy. Apparently they have to when it's a sudden death like this."

Dinah shook her head. "He wouldn't like that," she said. "People cutting him open and looking at his insides. You know how fastidious he was about everything, especially his body."

Maris thought of that damn fish again. *Shit*, she thought. *Shit, shit, shit.*

CHAPTER THREE

By the time Angela arrived from Germany, they had the results of Peter's autopsy.

"Poisoned?" said Maris. "But that's impossible."

"Not Peter," said Dinah. "Nobody would poison Peter."

"Ridiculous," said Angela. "There must be some mistake."

In time the initial shock wore off, but not the astonishment. Who would want to poison Peter? And why? The investigation soon told them how it had been done. The poison was in Peter's Campari — not just his glass of Campari, but the whole bottle. It was chloral hydrate, a depressant used in sleeping medications — usually harmless, but lethal in an overdose, especially when combined with another depressant, alcohol.

"I was so sure he was having a stroke," said Maris.

"Of course you were," said Dinah gently. "Why would it occur to you that Peter had been poisoned? I probably would have thought the same thing."

"You are both too kind," said Angela. "I would have thought he was playing a trick to get attention. I probably would have told him not to be stupid and then I would have ignored him." She crossed her arms in a self-satisfied gesture that was meant to absolve her of any compassion for her ex-husband.

Dinah smiled nervously at her and Maris glared. Angela worked hard at being uncompromising, and Maris supposed it had served her well in the cutthroat world of art and antiquities. But on a personal level, Maris thought her unkindness was despicable because it was so deliberate. She worked just as hard at it as at the other disagreeable aspects of her personality.

"You know," she began, "you could show an ounce of compassion, Angela. If not for Peter, then at least for me and Dinah. We loved him, even if you did not."

"Sorry, sorry," said Angela, in a way that showed she was not. "It's just my way of showing grief: by burying my true feelings under a mountain of rock. Okay?"

Maris wanted to say, "No, it's not okay," but she didn't — more for Dinah's sake than for her own. She was more than willing to take on Angela, but the time and the place weren't right. It was true, she knew, that people often behaved in uncharacteristic ways in the face of grief or shock, or the truly unexpected, like murder. There was something about a situation like this that brought out either the best or the worst in people.

And this had to be murder. Peter wouldn't poison his own Campari. There were easier ways to commit suicide. Besides, he'd only have to put it in his own glass, not the whole bottle. What if Maris had decided to have a glass with him? Would she be lying on a slab in the morgue along with him, with a Y-shaped incision in her chest badly stitched together with thick black twine?

It was an ugly picture. She excused herself and went to the washroom to splash cold water on her face to try and expunge the mental image. When Peter's lawyer had called to give them the results of the autopsy, they had been at the gallery trying to decide what to do. Should they re-open and conduct business as usual after a suitable period of mourning? Should they sell off the inventory and close up for good? What about relocating the gallery to Berlin where Angela spent most of her time when she wasn't travelling? Maris and Dinah preferred the option of leaving the gallery open. Surprisingly, so did Angela. All three were amazed at how easy it had been to agree.

"Of course," said Angela, "it means I'll have to take a greater part in the day-to-day operations. Peter was the one in charge of all of that." The prospect was clearly distasteful to her. Angela preferred the role of globetrotting procurer. She liked the hunt; it suited her predatory personality. Angela had instincts, Peter used to say. He knew where to send her, but it was Angela who knocked on doors and shook hands with people, and then got whatever she wanted from them. She and Peter had been a good team where the business was concerned; but the marriage had failed after eight years. Neither had remarried in the seven years since the divorce and the business had benefited from their redirected passion. The gallery was their love child.

"You know," said Dinah tentatively, "I've been Peter's right hand for the last five years. I know the customers. I know the books. I know how Peter liked things done."

Angela stood up and straightened her black silk skirt. Then she adjusted the matching black silk jacket. Maris thought, *She's built like a boning knife: all precision, balance and sharpness.* Her highly polished, red-painted fingernails were perfectly manicured. Her blonde hair had just enough platinum highlights to catch the sun but not so many to make it look like a dye job. She was forty-five, Peter's age, but looked thirty-five. Nothing drooped, nothing sagged. Give it another five years and she'd be getting the eye job and the Botox injections, probably in Bangkok where she could disappear while the swelling went down and the scars healed.

Maris looked at her own hands, an artist's hands with strong fingers and flat, spatulate fingertips. Paint thinner had left its mark on them, cracking them around the nails and roughing them up on the backs. No amount of Vaseline Intensive Care for Extra Dry Skin could undo the damage. She was almost forty and had been painting for half her life. *I look forty*, she thought, catching her reflection in the glass cabinet that held the gallery's most precious pieces. *I'm low-maintenance*, she thought, glancing at Angela, *and it shows*. Her brown hair used to be shinier, used to be thicker. When did that happen? Her skin already had a web of fine lines around her eyes and her mouth. It was hard to avoid the sun in Singapore, and she'd been here nearly four years. *Who cares?* she thought. *I'll age gracefully. I will become an "original," like my mother. I won't cave in to the youth cult thing. I won't turn myself into a Botox Barbie like Angela. Right,* she thought. *Blah, blah, blah.*

"I can't pay you any more than Peter was paying you," Angela told Dinah, thinking she would nip in the bud any plans Dinah might have to take advantage of the void Peter's death had left. Maris saw Dinah flinch, ever so slightly, her head jerking back about a centimetre as if a mosquito had grazed her skin.

"I think we should discuss finances another time," said Maris. "We're all a little raw right now."

"I have to go anyway," said Angela. "I'm getting acupuncture treatments for these damn headaches." Maris pictured Angela with a head full of long, thin needles, like a pincushion. It was perfect. She looked at Dinah, who was pursing her lips and staring off to the side. She knew that expression. It meant that Dinah was doing her detached thing so she wouldn't laugh. Or cry.

After Angela left, Maris said to Dinah, "Are you back?"

Dinah nodded. "I just needed to zone out for a minute," she said. "I was actually thinking about killing her." Maris smiled. Dinah was probably the most gentle, least violent person she knew. The fact that she was small — maybe five feet tall — and slender — maybe ninety pounds — had nothing to do with it. Dinah was like a jasmine blossom. You walked by them every day without a second look. They were tiny and white and plain. But one day you might walk by when the wind was blowing a certain way and something would catch your attention.

A subtle fragrance or a shiny leaf might get caught by the sun and you'd stop and take a second look. And you'd notice how beautiful it was, how essential. Because if all the jasmine disappeared from Asia, it would be a different place, bereft, less welcoming. And you'd be glad you stopped and took notice.

"So now what?" said Maris.

Dinah sighed. "I guess we try and pretend it's business as usual."

"I'm not keen on Angela being in charge."

"Neither am I. But that's the way it is. For now." Dinah ran her fingers through her straight black hair. "I, for one, intend to…."

"What?" said Maris.

"I don't know," said Dinah. "I suddenly lost my train of thought."

"Ah," said Maris.

They had the funeral five days later. The police had released the body but said the case was still open. There were no clues other than the poisoned Campari and that wasn't really a clue. It was just a fact. It didn't lead anywhere. It would take a month to canvass all the pharmacies to find out who had purchased chloral hydrate in the past — what? Two weeks? Two months? — then it would take several weeks to track down and interview them all. The investigation was going to be long and slow. It would be about legwork rather than luck. Without any sworn enemies to step forward and confess, there wasn't much to go on. A disgruntled client? They would check out the possibility, even though Dinah and Angela both denied such a person existed. But who knew? If they were dealing with a psychopath, it could be someone who was charming on the outside and seething with thoughts of revenge on the inside. Like Ted Bundy. And Peter's clients were scattered all over the world. You didn't have to live in Singapore to buy your art from Peter Stone Antiquities: You could go to Peter's website and do your shopping online. It would be like trying to find a pedophile in cyberspace — a forty-year-old man masquerading as a teenager. It was just too easy to be invisible online.

They tried to keep the funeral simple and elegant, the way Peter would have wanted it, but a lot of people showed up because of the publicity and because of their morbid fascination with the way Peter had died. People who barely knew him tried to pretend they'd lost a dear friend. The ones who had lost a dear friend were offended and upset by the curiosity seekers, who thought that to be at the funeral of a victim of murder had some kind of status attached to it. Something they could dine out on for months. "It was a closed casket," they'd say. "He must have been hideous," they could tell an enthralled audience. "All purple and bloated. He was poisoned, after all. So dreadful. And he was such a lovely man. So smart and sensitive. I feel as if I've lost my best friend. I miss him terribly." Cut to a series of faces with downcast eyes, nodding sadly and sympathetically. Murmurings of "You poor thing," "I know, I know," and "I feel the same way."

Maris tried hard not to let anger interfere with her grief. Peter had been good to her, and had supported her and her art when she believed she had nothing to offer. She had come to Singapore when a gallery owner in Vancouver noticed that local Chinese people were buying her art. He recommended she contact Peter Stone in Singapore because he might be interested in carrying her work. She had emailed him some photographs of her paintings and he'd said, "Send me something. I'm interested." She was thirty-five, single, with no real prospects in Canada. So she bought a plane ticket, packed a few of her paintings and a bunch of her drawings, and flew into her future.

She and Peter had become friends, even though they were as different as coffee and coconuts. Peter was meticulous, discerning, careful, and successful. She was impulsive, intuitive, messy, and success was not even in her vocabulary. She was an artist. He was a businessman. But he knew art when he saw it, and she aspired to create art. Their relationship was symbiotic. Peter began showing her paintings in his gallery, and people started buying them. In a way, she owed him everything. It wasn't just the money she was able to make that allowed her to continue painting; it was the fact that Peter believed in her. He told her she was an artist and so she started to believe in herself.

Now what will I do? she thought. She knew what she wanted to do, but crawling into a hole and shutting out the world wouldn't solve anything. Besides, it wasn't fair to Dinah, who had lost much more than she had. Dinah had lost a brother — at least a half-brother — and her best friend. Maris felt as if she were starting all over again, only this time without Peter to pick her up when she fell down. She couldn't imagine painting again. When she looked around, she felt tired rather than energized. Nothing inspired her. *It's temporary*, she told herself. This is what grief can do. It fools you into thinking the world has ended, when it's really just holding its breath for a while. Soon it will be time to exhale and start again.

Chapter Four

Maris hefted the old leather trunk onto the airport conveyer belt along with the suitcase that held her clothes, a few books, and some mementoes of her four years in Singapore. Her carry-on bag contained her brushes and sketch pad, the only things she would be upset about losing. The rest would follow in a month or two on the first available ship from Singapore to Vancouver.

I'm going home, she thought. But it didn't feel like going home. It felt like taking a giant step back into a life of failure and defeat. She hadn't been able to paint a thing in the months following Peter's death. Instead of the vivid colours she was used to seeing, Maris now saw things only in shades of grey. Not really, but it seemed like everything was grey. It was like looking at wet concrete through a misty rain.

There had been no progress in the case of Peter's murder. She had been the only witness, and the police had questioned her several times, asking the same questions and hearing the same answers.

"What time did you arrive at Mr. Stone's apartment?"

"Just after six o'clock."

"Was the bottle of Campari open when you arrived?"

"No. Peter uncorked it and poured himself a glass in front of me."

"Was it a new bottle?"

"Yes. I noticed that it was full when he opened it."

"What made you notice?"

"I don't know. I guess it just registered. I probably would have noticed if it was half-full or almost empty, too. I just noticed."

"Was Mr. Stone in the habit of drinking Campari?"

"Yes. He liked a glass before dinner."

"Why didn't you drink the Campari?"

"I don't like it."

"What did you have to drink?"

"A gin and tonic. Peter mixed it for me at the bar before he poured his Campari."

And on and on. They couldn't link her to the bottle of Campari or to the poison that had been put into it. And she had no motive. Her life was better with Peter alive. He encouraged her work and he sold her paintings. Why would she kill him?

There had been no suspects, although clients and customers had been questioned. No one seemed to bear a grudge against Peter, and they could connect no one with the poison. The bottle of Campari apparently was not a gift, but there was no way to be sure. Peter was in the habit of buying Campari for himself. It was his favourite.

Finally after four months, during which she could not paint, could not even think, Maris decided to go back to Canada to see if a change of scene would snap her out of the funk she was in. She knew she had been fond of Peter, but his death was more than the loss of a friend. She had lost her way, her bearings. Her focus was gone, and her eyes no longer saw things that spoke to the painter in her. She saw neither beauty nor ugliness. She saw only drabness and mechanics. She saw people walking with their heads down just to get somewhere, unsmiling and faceless; traffic rolling through the streets of Singapore in the same way every day; grass growing and being trimmed; and flowers being planted and opening and dying on schedule.

I'm looking at the world through a Plexiglas shield, she thought. Like watching planes take off from an airport lounge without the sound, the smell, or the vibration of the powerful engines: an endless loop of cogs meeting wheels, engaging the gears of nature, society, life, in a stupefying rhythm. She found herself sleeping more than usual, taking naps in the afternoon, and sleeping a dreamless sleep.

"You're depressed," said Dinah. "Maybe you should talk to someone."

"Take Prozac," said Angela. "Everybody does." They were in the storeroom behind the gallery, unpacking a shipment that had arrived from Chiang Mai in northern Thailand.

"I'm not taking Prozac," Maris said, "and I'm not depressed. I'm just sad and tired. And aimless."

"That's depression," said Angela. "We're all sad and tired. But you don't see me or Dinah sleeping in the afternoon. We have too much to do. We're running the gallery without Peter and it's hard work. You need something to do. You need to work."

"Maris is an artist," said Dinah. "You can't just tell an artist to work and expect them to put their nose to the grindstone. Honestly, Angela, you're in the art business. You should know that."

"Yes," said Angela, "I'm in the art business. And that's what it is: a business. If artists don't make art, they starve. They have to eat. Just like everybody else."

Dinah rolled her eyes. "This conversation is clearly over," she murmured to Maris as Angela left the room, muttering about some people never putting things back where they belong.

"That was a conversation?" said Maris. "I thought it was a sermon. From the high priestess of the Church of Business."

"As soon as the words were out of my mouth, I knew I shouldn't have said them," said Dinah. "I'm sorry."

"Don't be," said Maris. "Maybe I needed to hear it. I have to do something to stop this inertia. I'm not going to take Prozac, that's for sure, but I have to make a change." Dinah handed her a penknife and pointed to some boxes that needed opening. "Angela's right in a way," Maris continued. "Art is my work and without it I'll starve. And not just from the lack of money. It sounds corny, but I've lost something, some part of my soul. Peter sort of re-invented me as an artist. He made me believe in myself. Before, I had only seen myself as a painter, someone who put colours and shapes on canvas. Peter made me think about art. I mean really think about it as a medium for ideas. He believed I had something to say." She slid the knife across the tape sealing one of the boxes. "And now I'll have to learn to live without that — whatever he gave me — and find it somewhere else. But what are the chances of finding another mentor like Peter?" She sighed, lifting the flaps on the box. "I guess I'll have to create my own internal ego-booster. Can people do that?" She smiled at Dinah, but just thinking about it made her tired.

"I think they can if they want to," said Dinah. "You can't go on waiting for someone or something to come along and do it for you. In my experience that doesn't happen." She started unpacking the opened box, stuffing Styrofoam popcorn into a plastic garbage bag. "But it's easy for me to say," she continued. "I'm not an artist. I don't have to be inspired to work. I'm just the hired help. 'No tickee, no washee,' as my ancestors used to say."

They looked at each other and they both started to laugh. "I have no idea where that came from," said Dinah, wiping a tear from the corner of her eye. "What a stupid thing to say."

"Yes, but it was funny," said Maris. "It's probably because Angela makes you feel like a coolie. She makes you run around and do grunt work all the time. I'm sure if he could have, Peter would have left his half of the business to you. I don't see why a half-sister should have fewer rights than an ex-wife."

"I know, but they had an ironclad agreement that if anything happened to either one of them, the other would own the business outright. Though I doubt that Peter envisioned anything like this happening. Still," she said, looking into the box, "I'd rather be working for Angela than not working at the gallery at all. It's what I love."

Maris sighed. "You know, art isn't just about inspiration. It's also about putting pencil to paper and brush to canvas. Even if the result is bad or mediocre, it keeps the juices flowing. It's like practicing the scales if you're a musician. You have to be doing whatever it is that you do. And I haven't been doing anything, not even looking at other people's art or doodling, for months. I think I have to do something drastic before it's too late."

Dinah looked alarmed. "How drastic?" she asked.

Maris laughed. "Don't worry," she said. "I'm not going to jump off a bridge. I've been thinking about going back to Canada for a while. Maybe a change of scene will help. I could stay with my mother. She has a house north of Vancouver where she makes pottery. Pretty good pottery, actually. She's been doing it for years."

"Maybe you could send me some," said Dinah. "I could put it in the gallery and sell it. Authentic Canadian handicrafts."

"That's not a bad idea. Why not?"

Just then, Angela came back in the room, a large pair of scissors in her right hand. "Haven't you finished opening these boxes yet? Do I have to do everything?"

Dinah looked at Maris. "Don't worry," she whispered. "I'll deal with her." She lifted an ebony carving of a woman's face out of the box. An expression of beatific tranquillity on the face suggested she had seen Shangri-La. "Isn't it exquisite?" she said.

After the funeral, Maris and Dinah had sorted through Peter's stuff and decided what to do with it. Angela had flown back to Germany almost immediately to attend to the business that had been interrupted by Peter's death. She told them not to get rid of anything without consulting her first.

In his will, Peter had left instructions for certain things to be given away, and they attended to them first. To Maris he had left an old leather trunk that at first glance appeared to hold nothing more than some old books and paintings — probably from his childhood and not the kind of thing he chose to display in his elegant apartment. Peter was not sentimental, but he wouldn't have kept the old trunk if its contents hadn't been important to him.

To Dinah he had left his precious art deco furniture, but with the stipulation that she could sell it or dispose of it in any way she chose if she didn't want to keep it. She had cried when that part of the will had been read. Later she told Maris, "I've always loved that furniture but I never told Peter. It wasn't as if I had to have it. I was just happy to look at it whenever I went to his place. He must have known."

"Peter was pretty good at reading people," Maris said. "I'm sure that's why the gallery was so successful. He had a knack for matching people with the things he knew they'd love."

"Is that why he gave you his childhood mementos in a trunk?"

"Maybe. He never did something without a reason."

"Then I'm sure all will be revealed," said Dinah.

Maris hadn't examined the contents of the trunk before she left Singapore. She believed Peter's decision to leave them to her had been deliberate and she would have to figure out why. But for now she wasn't in a frame of mind to figure anything out. She was beginning to wonder if she really was depressed, as Dinah had suggested. Maybe she should talk to someone. But even the word "psychiatrist" made her uneasy. She knew a shrink would prescribe some kind of drug, and she believed that it would suffocate any creative impulses she might have. *I have to find a way to work this out through my art*, she thought. *Words are not a good way for me to express myself. I never quite say what I mean. But a painting is either right or it's not. It's not finished until its meaning is clear. To me, at least, if not to anyone else.*

She was looking forward to seeing her mother again. *She'll know what to do*, Maris thought. After Maris's father had left them for both another woman and a completely different life, her mother had been forced to re-invent herself in her mid-thirties. She had married Maris's father, a California draft dodger, when she was twenty-one years old and they had moved to a hippie commune northwest of Vancouver. There they had raised three children: Maris, her sister Terra, and a brother, Ra. Maris had been thirteen, Terra twelve, and Ra nine when their father left to marry an heiress whose money had been made in automotive parts. Arthur Cousins had so transformed himself after marrying his second wife that he was now a successful businessman and owner of a BMW dealership in the posh Vancouver suburb of Kitsilano.

Sheila Cousins, or "Spirit" as she was called in those days, had been devastated. Arthur's betrayal had gone way beyond breaking her heart. He had cast aside everything they had believed in and moved into the enemy's camp. Had he just been playing a role all those years? And if that was the case, why had he loved her? Or had he loved her? Sheila Cousins *was* Spirit, in her heart and in her soul. She had not been one of those costume hippies who wore gypsy skirts and beads and feathers. She had been a believer. Meeting Arthur, who'd introduced himself as "Freedom Man," had been pure destiny. She knew they were meant to be together. He'd heard about a hippie commune somewhere on the Sunshine Coast of British Columbia.

"Pure Earth," she'd said. "I know where it is. Near Roberts Creek."

"Then be my lady and I'll be your man," he'd said. "And we'll live on the land and be free."

And they had, for nearly fifteen years. They'd cleared land, planted fruit trees and a vegetable garden, and raised goats for milk, butter, and yogurt. There were twelve other people on the commune in the beginning. After six years there were just eight of them left, but by then the children had started coming. The kids had run free, and they had names like Free, Moonbeam, and Meadow. Spirit had named her children for the sea, the earth, and the sun: Maris, Terra, and Ra (who later decided he would rather be Ray). She'd believed, and so had Freedom Man, that children were born filled with truth and goodness, and they should be allowed to grow without the restrictions and rules that society placed on people. They would learn to read when they decided they were ready and they would study what and when they wanted to learn.

Maris's interest in art had begun early. Both her parents had encouraged her and sometimes she would draw pictures all day. Then she would give them to Terra and Ra to colour. The walls of their house were covered with drawings of animals, trees, flowers, people — anything Maris could see in the sheltered world around her. One day Spirit had taught her about still-life drawing. She had taken one of her own pottery bowls and filled it with fruit. Placing it on the kitchen table, she had added a candle and an open book, and told Maris to draw it. Then she had rearranged the objects, putting the fruit on the table, and the candle in the bowl. Another time she placed a sleeping kitten on the book.

By the age of ten, Maris began to develop a style of her own. But she hadn't yet started to work in colours, except for red. She loved red and usually included something red in her drawings. They were quite dramatic in their own way, especially after her father gave her a bottle of black ink and some Japanese brushes. The commune operated on the barter system as much as possible, and Freedom Man would drive up the coast in an old pickup truck and trade fresh eggs, chickens, fruit, and vegetables for staples like flour and sugar. At the hardware store in nearby Gibsons, he traded some of Spirit's pottery for small cans of paint and brushes for Maris. When Freedom Man left a few years later, Spirit started to sell her pottery for cash so she could buy art supplies for Maris. She got a library card and borrowed books on art and art history so that Maris could study and learn from the masters.

By this time, twelve-year-old Terra had developed an interest in pop music and wanted to learn the guitar, and Ra, who was nine, was obsessed with reptiles and spiders, especially the poisonous ones. Spirit refused to accept money from Freedom Man, who was no longer Freedom Man, of course, but Arthur Cousins, businessman, but he opened bank accounts for each of the children and deposited an allowance each month so that they could have some "extras," as he called them. He was not without a conscience, even though Spirit told him he was a shallow, unscrupulous shit. But he was determined to provide an education for his children, however they wished to get one.

A couple of years after Arthur left, the three kids were still being home-schooled on the commune. Arthur wanted Maris to go to high school, so he drove out to the commune (in his BMW convertible) several times to talk to Spirit about it. He said Maris could come and live with him and Shirley and go to a good school. He would arrange for her to take the entrance exams so she could be admitted to a public school. Spirit said absolutely not. She was adamant that Maris would stay with her on the commune. End of discussion. Fine, said Arthur, she could be bused to Gibsons every day. He knew there was no point arguing with Spirit when she got like this.

Shirley didn't say anything but she was secretly relieved that Maris would not be coming to live with them. She told Arthur, however, that she was very disappointed. She said that she had been looking forward to having a daughter, but she understood why Spirit did not want to let Maris go. She suggested that Arthur increase the children's allowances. It was only fair since they were forced to endure such primitive conditions because their mother had custody.

Arthur provided a tutor so that Maris would pass the high school entrance exams and she started school at Lord Stanley Secondary School in September 1978.

DECEMBER 1923

———

CHAPTER FIVE

Singapore
December 3, 1923

My Dearest Annabelle,
To say "I miss you" is to put into cheap,
inadequate words a longing that surpasses
anything I have ever felt. I am here with
Sutty and we have settled into the Raffles
Hotel and are quite comfortable, except
that half of me is missing because you
are not here. Sutty says that if I don't
stop moping around like a lovesick old
elephant he's going to turn me into a
character in one of his books and have
me die a horrible death. So come to

Singapore, I implore you, and let's be married and fulfill our destiny. Don't abandon me to Sutty's pen.

When I think of you in dreary old London in December my heart breaks anew. The sun shines so brightly here every day that we're forced to shield our eyes. We are like moles who are obliged to live above ground when we have been bred by Mother Nature (as Mr. Darwin said) to exist in a gloomy netherworld called England. We are squinty-eyed and pathetic creatures, our skin turning red wherever it is exposed and our stomachs protesting at the unfamiliar food.

Ah, but I mislead you, my dear. I make this place sound like some kind of hell, when it is only that because you are not here. In fact, it's a glorious place, full of trees and flowers most exotic, and the sun, the sun, is magnificent and warm. And when it rains, it's usually a lovely, warm, soft rain, not like those sharp pellets of filthy water that fall from England's skies.

As for the writing, I have been eking out a word here and there. Nothing like Sutty's proliferation of prose, of course. But then, who else but Sutty can turn the most prosaic encounter into a story of brilliant proportions? He is a true genius while I am but a poor scribbler, aspiring to greatness but always sliding ever backwards because my feet are planted, not so firmly, in the mud. I cannot seem to land on solid ground again like Sutty, because … because … if you were here, you could tell me why.

My Annabelle, my Sweet Annabelle, I long to see you and to hold you in my arms. Come to me, my darling. Sutty wants you to come, too, if only so he can enjoy his beer without hearing me weep.

I love you. I love you.

Your adoring

Francis

Annabelle finished reading Francis's letter and gazed around the dreary sitting room of her father's house. She had grown up in these small, stuffy rooms and it was the only home she had known. Since her mother's death last year, she had been housekeeper and companion to her father, a man once hale and hearty, now suddenly old and broken. "I'll be myself soon enough," he kept telling her. "Don't you worry about me." But how could she leave him and go halfway around the world? And how would Francis support her, with his wanting to be a writer and all? It was all right for Sutty; he had a small income from his grandfather. And people knew him and were buying his books. But Francis hadn't yet made a name for himself. Who would pay good money for a book written by Francis Adolphus Stone when they could buy Edward Sutcliffe Moresby?

Annabelle had begun to worry about such things since her mother's death. She was not yet twenty-four years old but already she felt the burden of life falling on her shoulders like the heavy old woolen cloak her mother had worn when she worked as a nursing sister during the war. Sometimes Annabelle thought she would suffocate just thinking about all the bad things that could happen to a person. She hadn't wanted Francis to go to Singapore with Sutty. The ship would surely sink on the way; he would get a fever and would be buried at sea; or, if he did get to Singapore, there was malaria to worry about and no end to the diseases people were struck down with. She had heard the stories about cemeteries filled with the graves of babies and young women and men who had succumbed to the heat and the brackish water and the contaminated food.

Francis had laughed at her fears. Although Sutty, she noticed, had not. He was a more experienced traveller. He had seen things he didn't like to talk about, but they were in his stories. She was sure he hadn't made them up. She believed that they were basically true, they were so believable. Francis said it was because Sutty was such a good writer. Of course she thought they were true, he told her. You were supposed to believe them. Look at Shakespeare. He wrote about tragedy because people wanted a good cry, and he wrote comedy because people also wanted to laugh. It's all about bums in seats and cash in the till. People wouldn't pay for it if they didn't believe it.

But Francis was an optimist, always seeing the best, and she was a pessimist, although she preferred to think of herself as a realist. The world was not a happy place and life wasn't all happy endings. Even if you worked hard and did all the right things, you could still get run over by one of those beastly automobiles or lorries that seemed to be multiplying like rabbits. Or you could fall off of a bicycle and break your neck. Just last week she'd read about a woman who'd stepped into a lift where she worked and she'd fallen twelve floors to her death because the door had accidentally opened when there was no lift, just empty space. There were lots of words for these events — accidents, bad luck, providence, destiny — but to Annabelle there was only one word: life. Life was dangerous and if you ignored that fact, or chose to believe otherwise, you did so at your peril.

Oh, but she missed Francis and his foolish optimism and his dreams of being a writer. She loved him more than anything because he almost made her believe that life could be good. That she would be safe with him. That because they loved each other, everything would work out, somehow. She wanted to be with him so badly, but in Singapore? It wasn't the last place on earth she wanted to be, but it was nearly the last. China was probably worse, or India, or maybe Russia. Thank God Francis hadn't gone to any of those countries. Or Africa. Singapore didn't seem so bad when you compared it to some of those places. At least there were English people there, but there were English people in India and nothing could induce her to go to India. *Oh, what to do?* she thought.

She knew Francis had no intention of coming back to England, at least not for a long time, and not unless something miraculous happened, like a rich uncle (if only he had one) dying and leaving him a fortune. He had counted up all his money to the last penny and told her, "It's either five months in England or five years in Singapore, including the passage. And what can I write in five months?

Think, Annabelle, think how much I could do in five years. Five whole years, if I'm careful." If I'm careful, he'd said. Not if *we're* careful. So did the five years include a wife or not?

And what about her father? How could she leave him alone to fend for himself? She'd be worried the whole time that he wasn't eating or that he was drinking too much or smoking too many cigarettes. It was an impossible choice.

Maybe what she should do was go down to the P&O office and find out what it would cost for a one-way passage and when the next available ship would be sailing. That way she'd be able to tell Francis that it wasn't possible for her to come. That it was too expensive or there wasn't another ship leaving for four months. Then maybe he'd decide to come back and get a job and they could get married, and maybe even have a family. They could live with her father and they wouldn't have to pay rent.

London
December 20, 1923
Dearest Francis,
I miss you so terribly and wish we could be together. I went to the P&O this week and they told me a one-way fare to Singapore would be fifty pounds, which we simply cannot afford. And the next ship will not be until the beginning of February.

Father is not doing as well as I would like. Of course, he always says he's fine, but I know it's because he doesn't want to be a bother. But since Mother died, he's aged ten years. I want to weep whenever

I look at him. He shuffles about like an old man and falls asleep in his chair in the evening listening to the wireless. It breaks my heart, Francis. He's not even fifty-five years old.

The weather here is nasty, as usual. A miserable chill that pierces to the bone. I envy you your sunshine and heat. The price of beef has gone up again, and soon we'll be reduced to boiling the bones for dinner. As for butter and cream, we've had to cut in half what we usually take.

Francis, I hope you are eating properly and well, and not drinking anything but the boiled water. Always make sure they boil it well, because I've heard that they just take water from the tap and fill the bottles with it. Go into the kitchen, if you must, to be sure. Better to be safe than sorry. And always wear a hat in the sun. It is very common to have sun stroke in the tropics and you don't want that.

Please take care of yourself and write again soon. Tell me everything you're doing. Give my regards to Sutty and tell him I expect him to look out for you. Listen to what he says because he has experience in these things, meaning life in foreign countries, as he's travelled so much.

Please have a happy, happy Christmas, although I shall be missing you every

minute. I miss you and think about you all
the time and dream about you every night.
All my love, your
Annabelle

The next letter, addressed to "Miss Annabelle Sweet,"
arrived in early January and was from Sutty. In it was a
cheque for sixty pounds.

You must come, *it said*, because Francis
is at his wits' end, and so am I, if truth be
told. He's impossible to be with because
all he talks about is you, Annabelle, and
all he wants is you, his "Sweet Annabelle,"
as he calls you. I implore you, Annabelle,
for my sake if not for Francis's, to come
to Singapore. If I could put him on a ship
and send him back, I would. But he is,
quite honestly, better off here. You could
live very well here and Francis could write
something important. It's not forever,
Annabelle, but *for now*. Try to see it that
way and maybe it won't seem so bad to
you. If you don't come, he will waste his
time and his money yearning for you,
and I will go mad listening to him!
Use the money to buy passage on the
next ship, and consider it my wedding gift
to you. No one will be happier to see you
than I (except, of course, Francis Stone!)
and we will both see to it that you are

happy, comfortable, and above all, safe.

I promise. In anticipation of seeing
you soon, I remain,
Yours,
Edward Sutcliffe Moresby

Annabelle embarked on the P&O steamship
Narkunda on February 5, 1924. She had used Sutty's
cheque to pay for her fare, but had debated with herself
long and hard before booking passage. Her father's sister
Ethel, herself recently widowed, had come for Christmas
and had been persuaded to stay on. Her only child, a son,
had taken the Public Services Examination and had been
accepted in the British Indian Civil Service. He had left for
Bombay in November and Ethel had found the loneliness
more than she could bear. Although Annabelle's father
was reluctant to see her go, her aunt had assured her that
he would be fine and that she was looking forward to
keeping house for him. He was her favourite brother, she
said, and it would also help her to have something to do.

So Annabelle had no more excuses for not going to
Singapore, other than the fact that she did not want to go,
but she didn't dare say that to anyone for fear it would get
back to Francis. If she hadn't loved him with all her heart,
she might have found a way out of going. Or she might
have tried to persuade him to come back to England. But
she knew it was his dream to write and, because she had
no dream of her own other than to marry Francis and
have a family, she could not take away his chance to see it
through. They would find a way, as he had said to her so
many times. They would be happy.

The ship was to travel by way of Gibraltar to Port Said and Aden, then on to Bombay, Colombo in Ceylon, Penang Island, and then down the Straits of Malacca to Singapore. It would take about a month to get there and Annabelle fretted that she would be bored and alone the whole time.

Much to her surprise, the trip turned out to be relatively pleasant. After a few days of nausea that came in waves — a description she came to understand firsthand as she experienced the ship's rolling beneath her in perfect harmony with the undulating sea — she found her "sea legs" and was able to take walks on the passenger deck and even enjoyed gazing at the stars in the seemingly endless black night sky. Standing on the ship's deck she could believe that the world was flat, for there was nothing beyond the water and the sky. They came together in the distance like two sheets of paper whose edges were sealed by the unseen hand of God.

She was seated in the dining room with a couple from Brighton who were doing God's work in Borneo. They told her about the history of the Anglican Church mission in Brunei and how the "White Rajah" of Brunei, James Brooke, had invited the first Anglican missionaries in 1848.

"White Rajah?" Annabelle queried. "I must profess my ignorance," she said. "I know nothing about the history of this part of the world."

The Hendersons, a pious young couple who had been married only a few years and who shared a zeal for bringing heathens and cannibals to God, were only too glad to enlighten her.

"James Brooke," Harold Henderson explained, "was originally in the Bengal Army attached to the British East India Company in Calcutta. This would have been around

1818 or 1820. After he resigned from the army, he tried his hand at some Far East trading, but by all accounts he didn't do so well at that. In the 1830s he came into some money — an inheritance from his father — and he bought a ship and sailed for Borneo. Well, when he got there, to a place called Kuching in Sarawak, there was some kind of fighting going on, an uprising against the Sultan by the native Dayaks, who were headhunters and pretty fierce fighters. James Brooke threw in his hand with the Sultan and helped settle things down, and for that, the Sultan made Brooke an official Rajah of Sarawak. Rajah means prince or chief. And he actually ruled the place, too. It wasn't just an empty title."

"My goodness," said Annabelle, a little breathlessly, "that's quite a story." Beryl Henderson, a small woman with thin arms and large hands that reminded Annabelle of a washerwoman's, was nodding in agreement.

"Yes," she said. "Isn't it? It sounds like something out of Kipling, made up, you know. But it's all true."

Harold, a reedy man with narrow shoulders, a thin neck, and hair the colour of an orange tabby cat said, "Yes, absolutely. Every word of it is true. He ruled as Rajah until he died in the late 1860s, and then his nephews inherited his position. One of them, his great-nephew, actually, Vyner Brooke, is the Rajah as we speak. He has been since his father, the second rajah's death."

"And are there still headhunters and cannibals?" asked Annabelle, wondering how far Borneo was from Singapore.

"Well, yes, as a matter of fact there still are, you know, back in the jungle," said Harold. "But we've been making steady progress over the years, and many of our converts among the Dayaks have themselves taken up the cause and have brought many of their heathen brethren to Jesus."

By "we" Annabelle took it to mean that Harold was referring to the Anglican Church, not himself and Beryl. "I'm glad to hear it," she said, although not as glad as she would have been had he told her cannibals no longer existed in that part of the world.

Beryl picked up the thread of the conversation. "Doing God's work is not easy," she said, "but it is rewarding beyond measure. For every soul we are able to bring to Christ, we feel God's presence become ever stronger. He loves us and protects us from harm. You cannot imagine how grateful we are that He has brought us to this place so we can do His work and spread His word. It is its own blessing."

"Indeed it is," said Harold. "Indeed it is."

When she wasn't talking with the Hendersons, Annabelle found herself observing the social mores aboard ship. There seemed to be a lot of single young women like herself on the way to take up married life with a young man who had served his time either in the civil service or in the commercial service with some trading company or other. Most companies forbade their new employees from marrying during the first — and sometimes even the second — five-year term of employment. It often took eight or ten years for a young man to begin earning a salary large enough to accommodate a wife and family.

"Bloody unfair, I say," said Maisie Turner, who was about to celebrate her twenty-ninth birthday. "Why should some rubber company tell me when I can get married?" She and Annabelle had been getting their hair washed in the ship's beauty parlour and had struck up a conversation. Annabelle thought that Maisie was very attractive for her age, but noticed that there were already little pouches forming under her eyes. She could see a varicose vein snaking down Maisie's left calf. *It does seem unfair*, she thought, *to make people wait until they're almost thirty to marry.* But she guessed they had their reasons.

She noticed that there were a lot of handsome unmarried men on the ship, returning from home leave, and Maisie and some of the other girls went dancing every night. There was no shortage of male attention on board the ship. If she had wanted to, Annabelle knew she could probably dance all the way to Singapore, and with a different man every night. But she had no interest in other men, nor did she particularly want to drink cocktails and smoke cigarettes the way Maisie and her chums did. Many nights when she gazed up at the stars, she wished with all her heart that Francis could be there with her. How romantic it all was. In the middle of the ocean you could imagine that time had stopped forever and that the ship would never dock. There might be nothing in the world beyond this ship, and the ship was a tiny speck in a grand universe. *What earthly difference does it make*, she wondered, *if you brought a hundred or a thousand or even ten thousand heathen headhunters to Jesus?* What did anything matter in a universe so infinite?

CHAPTER SIX

Maris had sent an email to her brother Ray telling him her arrival time and asking him to meet her at Vancouver airport. After nearly twenty-four hours of travelling, she was never so glad to see anyone. He stood head and shoulders above everybody else, his fierce blue eyes fixed on the automatic doors as they opened and closed, ejecting three or four people at a time, like a giant Pez dispenser. His dark brown hair was almost black and clipped close to his head, but even so, the unruly curls he had always hated could not be tamed. He looked younger than his thirty-five years, maybe because he was so thin, or maybe because he wore a yellow stretched-out T-shirt with a smiley face on it, under a plaid flannel lumberjack shirt whose sleeves ended an inch above his wrists.

"Ra Baby," she called as she pushed her luggage cart through the gate. "Am I glad to see you."

Ray rolled his eyes. "Are you gonna start that again?"

"Start what?" she said.

"You know I hate that name."

She laughed and threw her arms around him. "Okay, Ra Baby," she said, hugging him so tightly he couldn't escape. "I won't call you Ra Baby any more. I promise."

He smiled and shook his head. "I'm glad to see you haven't grown up yet, Maris. Because if you grow up, that means I have to grow up, too. And I'm not ready."

While Ray went to get the car, Maris thought about what he'd said. Growing up had never been on the agenda while they'd lived on the commune with their mother, Spirit. In fact, the whole idea had been to stay close to the soul of childhood, to embrace innocence, and even to hold on to a kind of unknowing, especially about the outside world. "I want you always to remember how precious and special your life is now," their mother had said. "Don't let anyone take that away from you, not your father, not society, not your lovers when you have them, and not your children when you have them. Promise me?"

Of the three of them, only their sister Terra walked in the shoes of an adult. She had been married for fifteen years to a stockbroker and they had two daughters, Emma and Alison, and a huge, faux-Tudor house with a kitchen that was bigger than Ray's whole apartment. Terra had opted for the comforts of the conventional life, just as their father had, and who could blame her for that? There were things that Terra never had to worry about in this life. Like who she was, how she was going to pay the rent, whether or not she was doing the right thing. Her parents had named her well. Terra's feet were firmly planted. She was the least introspective of the three of them and could make a decision without waffling. "The buck stops with Mom," she always joked about herself. "And Mom always knows best."

Ray, on the other hand, was living in a rooming house in East Vancouver. He was unmarried and still lived like a student. When they got to his place it was Maris's turn to roll her eyes.

"Ray," she said, "you're such a cliché. Look at this place."

"What?" said Ray. "This is my home you're talking about."

"Oh, please," said Maris, shaking her head. "I mean, empty pizza boxes and beer bottles? The unmade bed? And — yuck — green stuff growing in the sink? There's no way I'm opening that fridge." She laughed. "I still love you, but I'm glad I don't have to live with you."

They had hauled her suitcase and the trunk Peter had left her up two flights of stairs. All Maris wanted was something to drink and a place to sleep. "Which is my room?" she asked, looking around.

"Ha ha," said Ray, "very funny. Since there *is* only one room, you can either have the pull-out couch with the dirty sheets or the futon on the floor with the sleeping bag."

"That's a tough one," said Maris. "Uh, can I see the sleeping bag?"

"As it happens," he said, "I actually had it cleaned after my last camping trip. But only because I accidentally made my bed on a pile of bear shit that I didn't see in the dark."

"So bears really do shit in the woods?"

"Yes, indeed they do. Luckily, it was fairly old and fairly dry bear shit, otherwise we might not be talking because I'd be bear shit myself. But I did think it would be a good idea to have the bag cleaned. It was pretty disgusting. I even went for the 'sanitized' option, with deadly chemicals."

"Hmmm," mused Maris. "That almost sounds like the grown-up thing to do. But I'm betting Terra would have burned it and bought a new one. That would be the really grown-up thing to do." They both laughed.

"Dare I ask if you have anything to drink? I'm dying of thirst."

"Well, I have beer … and beer. Which would you like?"

"Uh … I guess I'll have a beer. You mean you don't have any pomegranate juice?"

He pulled two bottles of beer from the fridge and unscrewed the caps. "If you want pomegranate juice, go stay with Spirit. And if you want Perrier, stay with Terra. I'm a beer and pizza guy right down the line. You will not find a single lentil or a Brussels sprout in this house."

"I sure hope you have coffee. I'm going to want some tomorrow, whenever I wake up."

"Ah," he said, "coffee there is. A nice Colombian dark roast, freshly ground today for a French press coffeemaker. My one luxury."

"Ooh la la," said Maris. "I'm impressed."

They drank their beer and Maris told him about her flight. She'd had a three-hour layover at Narita airport in Tokyo and hadn't slept at all. She'd watched three movies and eaten several meals and snacks, all of them tasting the same. Maris had a theory that all airline meals were made out of soybean product, cut into the shapes of various foods, dyed the appropriate colours, and injected with artificial flavours.

"God, I'm tired," she said. "What time is it?"

"It's 11:00 p.m., Pacific Standard Time," he answered. "Time for bed."

Maris slept until ten the next morning. When she woke up — on the futon, on the floor — the place was miraculously tidy — no pizza boxes, no beer bottles, no old newspapers. Even the stainless steel sink was gleaming. Ray had been to the bakery and bought fresh croissants and cheese Danishes. He was sitting at the table reading the newspaper when she stumbled across the room.

"Did you do all this for me?" she asked.

"Of course," he said.

"Okay, okay," she said. "The fun's over. Where's my real brother? Where have you taken him?"

"Contrary to previously observed and incriminating evidence," said Ray, "I'm not actually a complete and total slob. I only have occasional lapses. Coffee?"

"Yes. Absolutely. But let me take a shower first. I feel like I've been on a plane for twenty hours. Come to think of it, I have been on a plane for twenty hours. And why did I dream about bears all night?"

Ray got up to plug in the kettle. "The blue towel is clean," he said.

"And sanitized?"

Ray sighed. "Gee, you're even funnier than I remember. When are you leaving?"

She stuck out her tongue. "How about the day you get married?"

"How about the day *you* get married?" he retaliated.

"Touché," she said. "You're funnier than I remember." She closed the bathroom door. "Oh, wait," she shouted through the door. "I forgot. You're not my real brother. He's been kidnapped by aliens."

Ray smiled as he measured coffee into the French press. He really had missed her.

Maris devoured the croissants and Danishes and savoured the coffee. "Mmmmm," she kept murmuring, until Ray told her to stop.

"You're a hummer," he said. "It's annoying."

"I'm a what?"

"A hummer. You hum, you know, 'mmmmm,' while you eat."

She laughed. "You're kidding. I don't. Do I?"

"You do. And it's not an endearing trait. It's probably why you don't have a boyfriend."

"A boyfriend?"

"Okay, okay," he said. "We won't go there."

"You're right. We won't go there. Not unless you want to talk about your non-existent 'girlfriend.'"

"I only have two words on the subject," he said. "Biological clock." He put up his hands to stop her from responding. "That's all I'm going to say. End of discussion."

She grabbed a section of the newspaper and glared at him. She was definitely not in the mood for this conversation.

After a few minutes of silence he said, "Do you hear something ticking?"

"That's it!" She jumped up and started swatting him with the rolled-up newspaper. "You are such a pig!"

"Ow! Ow! Ow!" he laughed. "I'm just softening you up for Spirit. You know she's gonna want to talk about it. She's on my case all the time. 'You need to have kids, Ra. They'll centre you.' Yeah, I wanna say. Centre me in a deep hole that I can't climb out of."

Maris sat back down. "I know," she sighed. "It's not that I don't want to have kids, it's just that ... well, I'm not sure I want to raise them alone, the way Spirit did. It was rough for her, despite what she says. And I wonder what she might have done with her life if she hadn't been shackled with us."

"What do you mean?"

"I mean, as an artist. She's very creative, you know. Where do you think we get our artistic sense from? Do you think you would have been such a good photographer or I would have been an artist without her encouragement?"

"I notice you didn't say 'good' artist," Ray said. "How's your work going, anyway?"

"Not so good," she said. "Ever since Peter died, I haven't been able to see things in colour, if you know what I mean."

Ray pointed to a wall of framed photographs behind him. They were all black and white. "Yeah," he said, "I know what you mean. But is that a bad thing?"

"It is for me. My art is all about colour. I 'feel' colour; it's a mode of expression for intense emotion, which is what I try and paint."

"But your paintings are so ... so ... almost sterile," said Ray. "And I don't mean that in a pejorative sense. It's just that they're so clean, so precise."

"But that's the point," she said. "I don't want you to be distracted by technique when you look at my paintings.

I want you to respond to the purity … no, that's not the right word … to the …"

"Essentials?"

"Yes," she said. "To the essentials. What all of us share as human beings, beyond all the encumbrances of culture and personality, what we wear and what we eat, what we look like, or what we want to look like. Do you understand?"

"Yes, I do. Maybe that's why I shoot so much in black and white. With photography, you can't control the 'message' in the same way as you can with painting or something you create from scratch. You have to deal with the reality that exists in the frame. I can control the composition and the colour, or lack of it, the shadows, the depth of the perspective, but even that I can control only in a limited way because it's a two-dimensional image. Colour, for me, is distracting. Like you say, a technique. In photography, colour is a technical component. How do I know that the red I'm seeing is the same red you're seeing? The only way I can control that, to show you what I want you to see, is to strip out the colour. That way, maybe we're all looking at the same image. At least to some extent."

"Control," Maris said. "You think art is about controlling the image? Controlling the perception?"

"Yeah, I guess I do. I mean, a writer gets to pick and choose his words. He controls what you're reading. Why can't a visual artist control the elements in his creation?"

"I didn't mean you shouldn't control the elements in a painting or a photograph, as much as you can. That's the art, the craft of it. But you can't control the viewer's perception or their interpretation. That's totally subjective. I mean, maybe it's none of my business how you interpret what you see. Once I hand it off, it's not mine anymore. It belongs to you, and you can see it any way you want to. Hell, you can cut it into little pieces and eat it, for all I should care."

"Ah, but you do care," said Ray.

"Yes, I do. I'm not sure how to get to that place yet."

"Is that the place you want to get to? Not caring?"

"I'm not sure."

"Do you want to talk about Peter?"

She thought for a minute, took another sip of her coffee. "Not today," she said. "But maybe later."

"Okay," he said.

It was early afternoon before Maris thought about opening the trunk. She and Ray had gone out to lunch at a funky diner down the street that served the best grilled cheese sandwiches in the world, according to Ray. The bread was thick-cut from a French stick, and buttered on both sides before it was browned on the grill. The smooth, nutty Gruyère oozed out the sides as it melted. And the fries were cut thick like the bread, done crisp on the outside and moist and firm on the inside. Ray was right. It was the best grilled cheese in the world.

"What's in that thing?" Ray asked as she started to undo the leather straps and locks.

"I don't really know," she answered. "Peter left it to me in his will. I looked through it quickly before I left, but I'm not sure why he wanted me to have it. There are some old books and paintings, and I think I saw a bundle of letters."

"That's weird," said Ray. "Do you think they're valuable?"

"Might be, but he didn't have them in the store, so maybe they aren't. Unless the books are first editions or something." She lifted the lid and they looked inside. She started handing Ray things and he spread them out on the floor around them.

"Edward Sutcliffe Moresby," he said, reading the spine on one of the books. "*Collected Stories*. Who's he? I've never heard of him."

"I've heard of him," Maris said. "I think we read one of his stories in school. He was British but he travelled all over the world, starting before the First World War, I think. Especially to the Far East. I think he wrote some novels, too."

"Yeah," said Ray. "Looks like they're here, too."

Maris looked over his shoulder. "Are they first editions?"

Ray scanned the title page of one of the books. "Could be," he said. "This one's copyrighted and printed in 1921. It's in pretty good condition. Maybe Peter wanted to look after you in your old age."

Maris smiled. "It wouldn't surprise me," she said. "He would do something like that."

"What about the paintings?" asked Ray.

There were several small canvases, each wrapped in brown paper. Maris carefully unwrapped the first one. It was a framed watercolour, about eight inches by ten inches, and covered with glass. The painting was of a young Chinese woman, heavily made up, staring with vacant eyes at something outside and to the left of the frame. There was something very moving about the image. It looked like the woman was gazing into her own past and seeing nothing there. Both Maris and Ray stared at the picture. Neither spoke.

Then Maris said, "Wow. I wonder who the artist is."

"Is it signed?" asked Ray.

Maris examined the bottom of the painting. "It looks like there's something in the corner here, but it's kind of faint. Do you have a magnifying glass?"

"Do I have a magnifying glass?" said Ray. "I'm a photographer. Remember?"

"Just get it, smartass. You can give me your résumé later."

Ray was already on the other side of the room rummaging through the stuff on his work table. "Got it," he said.

Maris turned on a lamp and looked at the signature through the magnifying glass. The initials AS had been inscribed with the tip of a fine brush.

Who was AS? she wondered.

"I wonder who it was," said Ray.

"Don't know. I wonder if they're all by the same person." They unwrapped the rest of the pictures.

"Yup," said Ray. "Looks like it."

"Yes," said Maris, gazing at each of the paintings. "And they're all portraits of Chinese women. How interesting. I wonder who he or she was."

"If we knew the name, we could Google it," Ray said.

"What about Edward Sutcliffe Moresby? Let's Google him," she said.

Ray went over and opened his laptop. "Oh yeah. Plenty about him. Born 1887, died 1965. Hey," he said, "the year you were born. Synchronicity. Cool."

"What else?" she said, reading over his shoulder.

"There's a list of his books. Wow. They're still available on Amazon. That's amazing."

"Great," said Maris. "I can see if any of them are first editions."

They went through the pile of books, checking each one on the Internet. Every one of them was a first edition.

"Amazing," said Ray. "I wonder what they're worth. Must be fifteen or sixteen of them."

"Twenty-five, actually," said Maris.

"Even better."

"Maybe Peter wanted me to read them," she said.

"Maybe. Did he leave any instructions? Like in his will or a letter?"

"No," said Maris. "But his death was sudden and probably a lot sooner than he expected. Maybe he would have done something like that later."

"Yeah," said Ray. "It must have been really horrible. Being with him at the time, and all that."

"It was the most terrifying, sad, depressing experience of my life. I don't think I'll ever get over it."

"No, probably not. I'm the last person to suggest this, but what about counselling? Have you thought about it?"

"I've thought about it but I don't think I could do it."

"You mean you don't want to do it."

"I mean I don't want to do it. I don't want to talk about it with a stranger. I don't even want to talk about it with a friend. I'm afraid that if I start, I don't know where it will end."

"You're afraid it might make you 'normal.'"

"Yeah, something like that. I don't want to mess too much with my psyche. I don't want to over-analyze myself, you know what I mean? If I start explaining what I'm about, maybe all the stuff that I need to do my art will get sanitized." She laughed. "Like your sleeping bag."

"Better to keep all that garbage inside," said Ray. "That what you mean?"

"Yeah, in a way. If I start putting it 'out there,' then it will be objectified. It won't be my shit anymore. It'll just be a bunch of sentences."

Ray laughed. "Believe it or not, I know what you mean. If you untie all the knots, all that will be left is a piece of string. How boring is that?"

"Exactly," she said. "Maybe I can work it out through my art. At least, that's what I keep hoping."

"Yeah," said Ray. "Keep that myth alive: the tortured artist. I have a hair shirt around here somewhere, if you want it."

But she had tears in her eyes, and he knew he had gone too far.

"Sorry, sorry," he said, and put his arms around her. "I'm stupid and a little insensitive. Well, okay, very insensitive. I'd probably be a basket case if I'd been through what you've been through. I wouldn't be able to handle it at all."

"I'm not handling it," she said, drying her eyes on his shirt. "I'm kind of paralyzed by it."

"Well," he said, "you have to start somewhere. Maybe you should read some of these books. Take a break. You can stay here as long as you want."

"Thanks," she said. "I want to go see Spirit at some point, but maybe I'll spend some time at the library. See what I can find out. See if I can figure out why Peter left me this stuff."

Marriage and Love

A Short Story

by

E. Sutcliffe Moresby

It's not often that I'm invited to attend a wedding on my travels, but, occasionally, if I'm in the right place at the right time, an invitation is graciously extended and I usually accept. Weddings are, as a rule, happy occasions and they give one a chance to eat and drink and converse with people who are in a mood to celebrate. And I, once it is revealed that I am a writer, have often been the recipient of a story or two, sometimes divulged after much drink, but usually freely given in conversation by someone who is forced, because of the nature of their occupation, to spend many lonely hours away from the company of people, so talk is a welcome, dare I say it, yearned for pastime.

This particular wedding was, in fact, a very small affair, consisting of the bride (recently out from England), the groom, their two attendants (both male, as it happened), and about a half dozen "guests," including myself. Although it took place in a chapel attached to the Anglican church, there were no flowers and the bride was dressed in a dark blue woolen suit — a bit warm for the intense, steamy climate, but she had only just arrived from England and, I suspect, had nothing else to wear — and a black felt hat pulled down over her hair and framing her face, as was the style *au courant* in the 1920s. I said there were no flowers, but I do recall that she had a small bunch of white jasmine pinned to her jacket that made a simple but attractive complement to her plain white silk blouse.

The groom was someone I had previously met in England, an aspiring writer who had come out to Singapore with his savings in order to produce a book — something he claimed he could not afford to do in England. He had very little money and, as a result, the wedding ring he put on his bride's finger was made of brass. The ring was as shiny and yellow as gold, but before the party celebrating their nuptials ended, it had turned her finger green because of the excessive humidity that is common in that part of the world. I believe shortly thereafter she took to wearing the ring on a gold chain around her neck, the chain having been a gift from her parents on her eighteenth birthday. I felt a little sorry for the poor girl that day. She clearly had not yet adjusted to the heat, nor the exotic surroundings and alien customs of her new life. She seemed nervous and uncomfortable, but now, as I look back these many years later, I realize with some disconsolation that it was the happiest she would be for the rest of her life.

But on that day, when anything was possible, including living blissfully ever after, we were all in a mood to celebrate, so after the formalities were done, we went off to the Raffles Hotel and had a party. The Raffles was the hotel I always stayed at when I was in Singapore. It was opened by the Sarkies brothers from Armenia in the late 1880s. I was also fond of staying at two other Sarkies hotels when I was in Asia, the Eastern & Oriental in Penang and the Strand in Rangoon. They are handsome buildings with well-appointed rooms where one is always made to feel at home. The staff I have found to be exceedingly helpful and polite, and one never has to ask twice for anything.

The two attending witnesses had made arrangements earlier with the hotel staff to discreetly present them with the bill, so as not to stint on the celebrations and not to embarrass the groom. They were both bachelors in the employ of Guthrie and Co., the trading company started by a Scotsman, Alexander Guthrie, around 1821.

I had noticed that one of them, Rodney, seemed more than a little fond of the bride. He had been unable to take his eyes off her during the brief marriage ceremony. I was intrigued by this and decided to have a word with him at some point during the festivities. Maybe there would be an appealing story in it.

As the party progressed, and much food was eaten and much beer and whisky drunk, I was able to glean certain facts about the couple from the various guests, none of whom knew them well, but each of whom seemed to have a piece of the story, as it were. The groom, Thomas Noble, had come out from England about six months earlier, with the grand dream of becoming a famous author. I knew something about the difficulties involved in this kind of endeavour, having once been an aspiring author myself. Being a few years older than the groom, I had already established myself as a writer whose books and stories found a market among the literate and semi-literate of England and those parts of Europe where English books are sought after and read. I wished him well and hoped that he had enough money to support himself for at least five years. Publishing is a hit-and-miss business, and not everyone who writes a book will see it in print, let alone see it sell.

The bride, Adele Simpkins (or Adele Noble, as she would now be known), was no more than twenty-five years of age I was sure, a pretty girl in that classic English way, with a lovely clear complexion, eyes the colour of cornflowers, and soft brown hair that fell in natural waves around her heart-shaped face. Thomas and Adele made an attractive couple. He was several inches taller than her, with wheat-coloured hair and hazel eyes that promised an interesting variety in their children, should they have any. They appeared to be very much in love, but I sensed a degree of self-absorption, common to writers, in Thomas that Adele would have to learn to put up with. Writing is a solitary pursuit, and even though writers want a wife and family like everybody else, they are inclined to live apart from them in some ways. Because they more often inhabit the places of the mind rather than the body, it can be discouraging for those who have to live with them.

I managed to catch up with the young man from Guthrie's who had acted as one of the witnesses to the marriage of Thomas and Adele, and we sat together with a bottle of whisky and swapped stories. He was an intelligent chap, handsome and athletic like most of the young men who came out to that part of the world in those days. A love of competitive sport and a cheerful (verging on jovial) disposition were almost prerequisites for employment with the trading companies and the Malayan Civil Service (or the M.C.S. as it was then called). The workday was long and demanding, the weather often boiling hot, and the climate, to say the least, unhealthy. Marriage was discouraged, in fact often prohibited, by the company for a number of years. Sports and games were considered a healthy outlet for young men's energy. It was also a widely held belief that a man who participated in competitive games was a man you could count on to do a good, honest day's work, and who would do his best for the "team."

Rodney Sewell was just that sort of man. He immediately impressed me as the kind of chap who would lay down his life for king and country if called upon. He was very good looking but in a casual, even indifferent way, and he seemed unaware of his effect on women. His hair was fair and sun-bleached, and his skin was tanned to an agreeable shade that was one part coffee to three parts cream. He sported a handsome blond moustache that precisely framed his top lip.

We sat at a small table in the Long Bar and watched as the wedding guests mixed with the bar's regular patrons. Rodney's arm was casually draped across the back of the unoccupied chair next to him. The afternoon was hot but he looked cool in his white linen suit. I pulled out a handkerchief and wiped my brow. I wanted to ask him how he did it, but instead I thanked him for his generosity to the young couple and offered to pay a share of the bill.

"Very kind," he said, "but not necessary. My mate Archie and I are happy to cover it."

"How long have you known the happy couple?" I asked.

"I met Tommy soon after he got here," he said. "That was about five months ago. He used to come and watch the cricket matches on Sundays. We got to chatting one time and he said he was a writer. I thought that was kind of interesting. Never met a writer before. I started inviting him round to our bungalow — me and Archie share with two other Guthrie's chaps — and we had some grand conversations. He told us all about his girl, Adele, and said she was his fiancée but he couldn't persuade her to come over and get married. He was bound and determined to write a book, and said he couldn't do it in England. Money, he said. He was quite open about the whole thing." Rodney chuckled. "And we could sympathize, I tell you." He poured us both another shot and turned to face me.

"Don't get me wrong," he said. "I love the life here. You know, the adventure, the experience, and all that. Something to remember in my old age, for sure. But you give up a lot when you come here: marriage, family, they all have to wait. Not many women are willing to chuck it all in and take a chance on love in the Far East. And the Company ..." and here he hesitated before continuing, "... frowns, shall we say, on employees marrying before they've been here long enough to save up a nice tidy sum of money. So, female companionship, at least of the English kind," he chuckled again, "is scarce as hen's teeth."

"Come, come," I said. "Are you telling me all of you want to settle down with a wife and children? Because if you are," and I raised a skeptical eyebrow, "I can only conclude you've been spending too much time in the sun without a hat on."

Rodney threw back his head and laughed. "Right," he said. "It does sound a bit daft. I guess it's just that you always want what you can't have. If the place were teeming with available young women, we'd probably ignore them half the time, and complain about their meddling the other half."

"Agreed," I said, and smiled. "I guess it's human nature."

We contemplated for a moment, and I looked over at Rodney. He was watching Adele, who was chatting with the only other female at the party, a thin, matronly woman in a dark green crepe dress with a white collar. Her dull brown hair was severely pulled back into a small knot, and a pair of wire-rimmed spectacles sat on her nose. She looked to be about forty-five, but was probably in her early thirties. She was the wife of the vicar who had married the young couple, and was no doubt giving Adele some sound advice on how to manage married life in Singapore. Adele occasionally nodded her head in agreement and once even laughed at something the vicar's wife said.

"She's lovely, isn't she?" I said to Rodney.

"Yes," he said, "she is."

"Do you think she'll be all right?" I asked. "From what you've told me, it's not much of a life for a woman out here. Especially a young woman, newly married."

"That's right," he said. "She probably won't find too many friends here."

"Why do you say that?"

"Not connected," he said matter-of-factly. "Her husband's not in business and he's not in the M.C.S. His only friends are bachelors like me."

"Ah," I said. "I see the problem."

"It won't be easy for her, that's for sure. I doubt she has any idea what's in store for her. And she's left everything she cares about behind in England. Except for Tommy, of course," he added, almost as an afterthought.

"Yes, of course. Tommy," I said. "Think he'll do right by her?"

Rodney chuckled. "He'd better," he said quietly, "or he'll have to answer to me."

I thought it best not to comment and waited for him to go on.

"Don't get me wrong," he said, pouring more whisky into our glasses. "I like Tommy. He's a good chap. But writing's not a real job, know what I mean?"

I nodded my head. Indeed, I did know what he meant.

"You can't eat dreams. And words and sentences, no matter how brilliant, don't pay the rent." He laughed at this, as if he'd made a joke. But it was an uncomfortable laugh, as if he'd recognized a profounder truth than he'd intended.

"But he has money enough for now, hasn't he?" I asked. For hadn't someone said that Tommy had come to Singapore with a stake that would last him five years?

"Yes," said Rodney, "it's what I've heard. What we all believe. But what if he isn't willing to give up this writing thing if it doesn't pan out? What if one of them gets sick, God forbid, or there's a baby? Then the five years becomes two or three, right? Things don't always work out the way we plan them. Am I right?"

"Yes," I said. "You're right. You can't plan for the unexpected."

"Exactly," he said. "My point exactly. And I wonder if Tommy's thought about that and thought this thing through to all its possible conclusions."

By this time, Rodney and I had consumed a fair amount of the whisky his generosity had provided. We were both a good way into our cups, I must say, and when that happens, one doesn't always think of how wonderful the world is and how lucky we are to be inhabiting it. I'm sure we each imagined a dismal fate for the unsuspecting young couple, who had only been married a few hours at this point. Rodney lifted his right arm and dropped it heavily on my shoulders.

"Just between you and me," he said, focusing his reddening eyes on mine, "I think she's too good for him."

"Ah, yes," I said. "I see."

"She could have any man in this room," he said, waving his left arm in a sweeping motion that took in the small party of seemingly unconnected individuals, including the good Reverend, a few other Guthrie's fellows, and a couple of Chinese waiters. "Any one of them," he repeated.

"I'm sure you're right," I said, "but she's chosen Tommy. For better or for worse."

"Better or worse," he mumbled.

I did not hear how things turned out for Tommy and Adele for many years. By that time I was living in Monte Carlo and was a frequent guest at the salon of Lady Brett Winstone, a woman of exceptional beauty and intelligence who liked the company of writers and artists and who entertained those travellers who passed through the small kingdom of Monaco when heading for eastern and western destinations. At one of these affairs, I found myself chatting amiably with a gentleman who had spent nearly two decades in Malaya in the employ of Guthrie's.

"Guthrie's?" I queried. "I met a chap several years ago in Singapore who was employed at Guthrie's. It was at a wedding, as I recall. At the Raffles Hotel. He and his mate were generously picking up the tab for the young couple. The groom was a writer or, at least, aspired to be a writer."

The man, well into the encumbrances of middle age — paunchy, slightly balding, and of a florid complexion — threw back his head and laughed. "Yes, yes," he said, "that was me. Rodney Sewell, it is, and glad to see you again." We shook hands and I re-introduced myself. "We put away a good amount of whisky that day, didn't we?" he said. "I cursed you the next day, I did. But we were both much younger then, weren't we, old chap?"

Indeed we were, I said, and we chatted amiably for a few minutes, catching up on the years that had intervened between our two encounters.

"By the way," I said, "I've often wondered what became of the young couple who were married that day. Tommy and Adele, wasn't it?"

"Yes, yes," he said. "Tommy and Adele." He reached into his breast pocket and pulled out a cigar. "Do you mind?" he asked. I shook my head and he prepared and lit the end before continuing. Perhaps he needed the time to recollect the events he would relate to me.

"Very sad," he said, finally, slowly shaking his head. "I'm afraid it all ended rather badly."

"Oh, I'm sorry to hear that. I've thought of them over the years and always hoped it had worked out for them."

"Fever," he said. "Poor chap died quite soon after and she was left with very little once she'd paid his debts. He'd told her he had enough money to live on for five years, but that was a lie. He barely had enough for five months. And when that was gone, he'd got himself tangled up with the damnable Chinese moneylenders, and that's a life sentence, let me tell you. But what was she to do? It wasn't five minutes after she buried him that they came after her for the money. She couldn't leave and she couldn't stay. It wasn't as if she could go out and get a job. Poor girl. Poor, poor girl."

I remembered that he'd been half in love with her at the wedding, but I didn't know how to broach the subject. I needn't have worried; he brought it up himself.

"I wanted so badly to help her. I cared for her, you know," he said, looking at me through the smoke of his cigar. "Would have married her myself if I could have.

But the Company, you know, wouldn't allow it. I hadn't finished my two terms yet and they were very strict about that sort of thing. I did what I could," he said, shaking his head, "but it wasn't enough. I couldn't save her."

"What happened?" I asked.

"Drowned herself," he replied. "At least, that's what they said it was. Suicide. But I never believed it. Didn't want to believe it, I guess." He flicked the ash from his cigar into an elaborate Venetian glass ashtray that a footman had placed on a nearby table. "Nearly left Guthrie's over it," he continued. "Blamed them and their stupid, stupid rules. I could have saved her, I believed. Believed it for a long time. But now I'm not so sure. Time and all that, makes a man think differently."

"What do you mean?" I asked.

"Well," he said, looking at me with those same eyes that I had looked into so many years earlier, except this time the redness, I suspected, was from tears.

"She didn't love me, did she?"

Chapter Seven

Maris had no trouble finding information about Edward Sutcliffe Moresby at the public library. Moresby was a British novelist and short story writer who was born in 1887 and died in 1965. He led a fairly peripatetic life due to a small independent income left to him by his grandfather. His travels took him to the Orient, including Thailand, Malaya and Singapore, India, and Ceylon. He eventually settled in Monte Carlo, in a seventeenth-century villa, but never gave up travelling. He wrote twenty-five novels and a hundred short stories that were based on his travels and the people he met. He usually cast himself in the role of narrator and most of his stories were variations on real events in his own life.

His father, a well-known barrister, died when Moresby was nine. He was raised by his mother Maud, with whom he had a close relationship until her death at ninety-one. He never married and, although he had friendships with both men and women, he seems not to have had any lasting attachments except the one with his mother. There was much speculation regarding his sexuality, but no cache of hidden love letters or confessional autobiographies ever settled the matter one way or the other.

Maris recalled reading one of Moresby's novels in high school. It was his most famous and, it was believed, the most autobiographical of his books. *The Heart's Prisoner* was the story of a young man who becomes an Anglican minister like his father because his family pressures him into it. The church was to have been the calling of his elder brother, but that brother died from a weak heart when he was just fourteen. The character becomes involved with a woman of ill repute when he tries to save her from a life of prostitution. She nearly destroys him, but he escapes by deciding to leave the church and leave England. Moresby had studied law at university in an effort to follow in his illustrious father's footsteps and please his mother, but he discovered he hated the profession and didn't have the temperament for law. He wanted to be a writer.

Maris couldn't remember Peter's ever mentioning Moresby or his books, and was no closer to knowing why he'd left her the first editions. Except perhaps because they were first editions and therefore valuable. But still, why did he collect only Moresby's books? Surely there were plenty of more valuable first editions he could have acquired.

Maris could find no connection between Edward Sutcliffe Moresby and someone with the initials AS, which was odd because they were the two sole occupants of the trunk Peter had left her. Why? *There must be a connection*, she thought. But Peter hadn't left any clues. Maybe he would have told her about the bequest if he had lived long enough. He would have thought there was plenty of time for that — and why not? What forty-five-year-old man expects to die suddenly after drinking a glass of his favourite aperitif?

Maris looked around the library. There was hardly anyone there on a Tuesday afternoon and she was overcome by a feeling of loneliness as powerful and frightening as suffocation. She was afraid that if she closed her eyes, someone would push a pillow onto her face and smother her. It was as if something was slowly sucking the air from the room, the way her mother had taught her to use a straw to pull the air out of a plastic freezer bag before sealing the contents. "It needs to be airtight," her mother said, "because nothing lives in a vacuum, including bacteria."

Living in a vacuum. That's what her life felt like right now: an airless, colourless, germ-free void where nothing was happening. Why couldn't she shake this funk that had been gripping her since Peter's death? Shouldn't she have recovered by now? Had Peter's death been such a blow that it could send her to this place of virtual stasis? She thought she was made of sterner stuff than that, thought she was more resilient. Yet when faced with tragedy — it was the first time she had experienced the death of someone she cared about — she had folded in on herself. Granted, it was murder, and a seemingly irrational, unexplainable, and senseless death, so she gave herself that. Her grief had another layer of difficulty piled on top of it, one that robbed her of solace every time she thought of it. Who had the emotional toolkit to deal with the trauma of murder?

Should she talk to a shrink? Ray thought so, and even Dinah had mentioned it before Maris left Singapore. But every part of Maris resisted taking that path. She didn't want to say it was because she was an artist — that seemed so pretentious, like a hoity-toity cop-out. She was who she was and who she was raised to be: a stubborn, independent person who expressed herself creatively through painting. That was central to her existence. Otherwise, what was the point? Without art, what was the point of getting up every morning? Of breathing? It all just seemed like waiting for death. Getting through the day was simply moving closer to death. When had getting through the day become a reason for living?

CHAPTER EIGHT

Francis and Sutty watched as the *NARKUNDA* steamed into the port of Singapore. As always, when a ship arrived from England, there was a sense of excitement on shore that exceeded the anticipations of Christmas morning and the giddiness that resulted from betting on a winning horse at the races. It seemed as if all of British Singapore turned out to welcome the arrival of the ship and everything on it, including the passengers, the crew, and the long-awaited cargo. What if the newspaper headlines were more than a month old? The jams and the tinned puddings and the salted hams would be as fresh as the day they were packed. The young women would be spirited and beautiful, and the wives and soldiers returning from a visit home would be full of stories of family and friends. The break from the monotony of life in a colonial outpost and the drudgery of a strictly regulated military or commercial routine was more welcome than a cool bath at the end of the day and a gin and tonic before dinner at the club.

Francis, who clutched a small bouquet of flowers, had been beside himself for days. While he had been anticipating Annabelle's arrival, at the same time he was dreading that she would be disappointed and would want to turn around and head straight back to England. Sutty had tried everything to keep him distracted from his own thoughts, including playing gin rummy for toothpicks, reading aloud back issues of the *London Times* as well as *David Copperfield*, the only one of his books Francis had professed not to have read. But he couldn't be with him every hour and Francis had turned up for breakfast the last three days looking like he'd been out all night on one of the ubiquitous fishing boats that brought in the night's catch as the sun was rising.

"Can you see her yet?" Francis asked, standing on his toes and craning his neck to add another couple of inches to his height.

"No, not yet," replied Sutty. "But I'm sure she'll be in your arms within the hour." He silently said a prayer that Annabelle was on the ship. It was entirely possible that she had decided at the last minute not to come, and had not written Francis to let him know. She had been so reluctant that Sutty was more surprised than Francis when she had agreed to come. They had both been counting the days since then, Francis because he wanted so much to be with her again, and Sutty because he wanted Francis to finally set aside his disquiet and come back down to earth. He didn't know a man could sustain such a degree of anxiety without succumbing to something worse, like catatonia or fever, or even suicide. *She'd better be on that ship or she'll be hearing from me,* Sutty thought, silently composing the cable he would send straightaway.

"I don't see her," bleated Francis, like a lost sheep. *This must be what the poets meant by "lovesick,"* Sutty thought. Francis was literally sick with love and longing.

"The ship hasn't docked yet," he said, trying to sound patient and reasonable. "Maybe she's finishing her packing and hasn't come up on deck yet. Or maybe she's there and you just haven't spotted her."

But he might as well have saved his breath. Francis wasn't listening and there wasn't anything he wanted to hear from Sutty except: "There she is. I see her now."

The business of docking a ship is a slow one, and Sutty wished he'd delayed their arriving at the port by at least another hour. Standing here with Francis, watching and waiting, was excruciating. It would have been easier to have a tooth pulled.

"Why don't we go and have a drink?" he suggested. "It's going to be a while before they start letting the passengers off, and then there's customs and all that nonsense. No point standing out here in the hot sun."

"No," said Francis. "She'll be expecting to see me and if I'm not here she'll be frightened. I'd better wait. She's never been outside England before, let alone in a place as foreign as this. I mean, it's not like going to France or Germany, is it? She won't know what to make of it."

"All right," said Sutty, giving in to the inevitable. "But let's at least wait in the shade."

They found some shelter from the blazing sun beneath an overhang and watched as the giant passenger ship slowly

slid into port, guided by a couple of stubby-looking tugs.
It was a thing of beauty to see and it brought back to Sutty
the urge to travel that ships and the sea always gave him.
How many passenger ships and freighters had he boarded,
with nothing but a portmanteau and a satchel of books, to
search out some distant outpost in the jungle, some place
he had heard about from captain or crew, where almost
nobody ever went but where there was always a story or two
to be heard from lonely men sent to the outer reaches of
the Empire? If Francis suffered from lovesickness, did Sutty
suffer from wanderlust? *Absolutely*, he thought. Sometimes
he ached from it, longed to be on the move, to feel the miles
moving under him, taking him further away from where he
was and bringing him closer to wherever he was going.

"I think I see her," said Francis, wishing he had
brought a pair of binoculars. "Over there," he told Sutty,
pointing to a section near the ship's stern. "See?" Sutty
couldn't make out anyone, let alone a young woman
travelling alone. But he went along with Francis's sighting
to keep them both occupied.

"I think so," he said. "Bravo."

He followed Francis, who was moving closer to the
landing dock, but the surge of people ahead of them was
almost impenetrable.

"Damn!" said Francis. "I hope she can see me." He
started waving his arms and calling, "Annabelle, Annabelle"
at the top of his voice, but it was an act of futility. The
din was almost deafening, and it escalated with each new
activity from the direction of the ship. When the gangplank
was finally in place, and the first of the passengers began
to descend, Sutty watched Francis's face change expression

from expectant, to joyful, to disappointed, and back to expectant again every time a young woman stepped onto the gangway joining ship to ground.

Sutty closed his eyes and muttered a silent prayer. *Please, please be here.*

Francis, too, was saying his own prayer. For if Annabelle had come and wanted only to turn back, he would be at his wits' end. He would have no solution to offer. He would be beaten, brokenhearted, bottomed out, and buggered. It would mean going back to England, getting a job he would hate, and giving up his dream of being a writer. He couldn't stay on in Singapore without her. He'd learned that much in the few months they'd been apart. He'd made a few friends. There were the boys from Guthrie's he'd met at the weekend cricket matches. They'd had some good times and were a jolly bunch. And there was Sutty, of course, who was always there to pick up the bar tab or pay for the laundry before they brought it up to the room. Sutty, trying to make his, Francis's, life a little easier. And maybe he was also trying to help a struggling young writer, like he had once been. Of course, he hadn't struggled so desperately, so despairingly. Sutty had an income, in perpetuity, so there was no fear of starvation on the horizon. No sense of time running out. No one he loved and couldn't live without. Sutty was a self-contained man of purpose who never seemed to have doubts, although they must have been there in the beginning. All writers have doubts about their ability. Francis knew that. All writers questioned their talent, convinced themselves they had none, and then convinced themselves equally that they had an abundance but nobody appreciated the fact and they would die in obscurity.

But Annabelle believed in him and that was what mattered, even when he didn't believe in himself. Or did she? *I'm a hopeless romantic*, he thought. Nobody wanted him to be a writer, especially Annabelle. Not even Sutty. He was alone in this game — completely and utterly alone. There wasn't another soul in the world who knew the kind of hopelessness he felt when he faced the wall of rejection and tried to scale it without any support, any assistance, any —

"Francis!" He heard his name being called and his mind snapped out of its downward spiralling reverie. At last! She was here, throwing herself into his arms. All was well. The world was set right again and he could breathe a sigh of relief. He could begin to write again.

Sutty breathed a sigh of relief, too, and gave a silent prayer of thanks to whatever gods had granted his first wish. Annabelle had come. *And what a lovely thing she is*, he thought, She was small and slender, with a magnificent head of thick, auburn-coloured hair that reminded him of the sun setting in Somerset. Her skin was exquisitely pale and clear. It, too, reminded him of England, where dewy complexions were often seen and admired. Sutty had no great fondness for the Oriental complexion. Although he could appreciate its beauty on an aesthetic level, it didn't cause his heart to swell or his loins to heat up. He didn't think it was a racial thing, just a male to female preference.

He suddenly understood why Francis couldn't live without Annabelle. He had forgotten how alluring, unpretentious, fresh, and adoring she was. She had flung her arms around Francis's neck and squeezed her eyes shut with relief at finding him waiting for her. He was all that mattered at that moment. She had waited for this moment for months. And all the trauma and turmoil, the worry and indecision, the unknowing that had tormented her since he'd left, melted away as she held him, melted like ice cream on a hot day, leaving only sweetness and delight.

"Francis, Francis," she whispered. "I'm here. At last."

After a few minutes, they unwound their arms from each other and Francis turned to Sutty. "Annabelle," he said, "you remember my good friend, Edward Sutcliffe Moresby? Sutty?"

Sutty smiled and took Annabelle's hand. "Delighted," he said, "to finally see you again. Welcome to Singapore."

Annabelle smiled warmly at Sutty and noted that he had a few white hairs in his well-trimmed beard that hadn't been there before. Otherwise, he was the same. His blue eyes almost twinkled as he shook her hand. He seemed genuinely pleased to see her. Annabelle looked around for the first time and surveyed her surroundings. Sutty noted that her lovely pale complexion was already turning pink from the heat and a light sheen of perspiration covered her face.

"My, it's hot," she said, laughing at her discomfort and fanning her face with her gloved hand. "Is it always like this?"

"Yes, my dear," laughed Francis, "I'm afraid so. It takes some getting used to."

They were married the following week in the chapel of St. Andrew's church, with a small reception dinner in the bar at the Raffles Hotel. The ceremony was attended by Francis's cricket-playing chums from Guthrie's and a couple of Sutty's friends who he played bridge with on Sundays. Sutty was best man and the vicar's wife played matron of honour to the bride. Annabelle wore the same grey wool suit she'd worn on her arrival, along with white gloves because her hands always felt moist in the heat and this embarrassed her. She wore a smart little cloche hat in a shade slightly darker than her suit that was rimmed in white velvet, and she carried a small bunch of white orchids that Sutty had paid for. Her ivory silk stockings and cream-coloured kid leather shoes she had brought from England. She looked lovely but was clearly feeling the effects of the Singapore heat. She frequently dabbed at the beads of perspiration on her forehead with a white linen handkerchief, one of a dozen that her best friend Jean had given her as a wedding present and going-away gift.

Francis was nervous throughout the ceremony and kept tugging at his collar. His Adam's apple bobbed up and down every time he swallowed, and he swallowed deeply each time he spoke. He'd lost weight since coming to Singapore, and there was enough room between his collar and his neck to allow all four of his fingers to rest comfortably.

Fortunately, the vicar kept the service brief and they were soon able to adjourn to the hotel bar for the reception dinner. A sit-down dinner for twelve had been arranged and paid for by Sutty — "Call it a wedding gift," he'd told them — with the Guthrie's men occasionally returning from a trip to the bar with a full bottle of wine or whisky. They ate English-style roast beef with carrots and potatoes and gravy, thick hunks of Yorkshire pudding, and a wedding cake that tasted like coconut with lots of pink-coloured frosting. Francis and Annabelle laughed a lot and listened to speeches that the guests insisted on making as the evening progressed and the bottles emptied. It was a wedding in the spirit of all weddings — a celebration of love and hope. Even the vicar's wife, a dour-looking woman in funereal brown crepe, made a misty-eyed declaration that love and marriage were gifts from God and that two people couldn't be more fortunate than to embrace the Christian values of marriage and family. "Hear, hear" and "Amen" were heard around the table and Francis and Annabelle thanked everyone for sharing their wedding day. The vicar then chimed in with his blessing and all glasses were raised in a toast to the happy couple.

Sutty joined in the festivities but a small part of his heart was heavy and he wasn't sure why. Did he have misgivings about the success of the marriage? Did he wonder if Francis could write his book? Was he fearful for the delicate English bride, Annabelle, who already showed signs of discomfort in her new surroundings? Or was he just being pessimistic in a writerly way, looking too hard and seeing what wasn't really there?

Sutty knew that all things took time. Not everyone adapted to or thrived on change the way he did. He looked around at the young men from Guthrie's who lent the party exuberant energy as only young men can. They shared a camaraderie that encompassed both their joys and their disappointments. These young men had all signed on for an adventure, the experience of a tour of the Far East, hoping it would give them a leg up on the future. They seemed continually to be on the brink of that future, building something that seemed intangible in the present, but that would someday be measurable — wealth, success, property, possessions: the things that came with time and hard work.

Sutty knew that not all of them would achieve this, but that didn't matter now. What mattered was the dream.

When he looked at Ronald and Maurice, his two bridge companions, Sutty saw what some of the Guthrie's boys would become. "Lifers," they would be known as. Men who were mired in the mud of the East and who would never leave until forced to by retirement, when they would return to a drab, dreary life in a one-room bedsit in England. They would realize that the dreams they had had twenty years earlier had not come to be. These men had become drudges, drones in the hive of trade and commerce. Time and opportunity had slipped away with each identical year and they hadn't noticed that they were getting older and their enthusiasm was diminishing along with their energy. They had forgotten to marry somewhere along the line and forgotten about friends and family on the other side of the world. Their companions were other lifers, transients, and Orientals. Some had "gone native," as their more mobile friends liked to say; they'd got stuck in Singapore or Kuala Lumpur or Calcutta.

Sutty shook himself out of his thoughts. This would not be Francis's fate, nor would it be his. They had chosen to document life, not to be swallowed up and trapped in it. As artists, they could soar above the mundane; in fact, they had an obligation to avoid the commonplace at all costs. For a writer to have his feet firmly planted on the ground was a curse on creativity. He hoped Annabelle understood this because if she didn't, she would be waging an uphill battle for the rest of her life. He didn't wish that for Francis, and he especially didn't wish it for the lovely Annabelle.

CHAPTER NINE

"I think I need to go and stay with Spirit for a while," Maris told Ray about a week after she'd arrived in Vancouver. "It's not that I don't like staying here, I do, but I feel trapped. No, that's not the right word. I feel like I could get stuck because it's too easy. Being here. Hanging out with you. Am I saying this really badly?"

"Yes," said Ray, "but I get it. You think that your basic lazy, uninspired, torpid" — *torpid?* thought Maris — "nature will take over and consume you like a giant octopus and you'll be enmeshed in the tentacles of indolence forever. Am I close?"

"Whoa," said Maris. "You're, like, so right on, brother. I'm just blown away by, like, your total clarity. It's awesome, man."

"Shut up. So when are you leaving?"

"In a couple of days, I guess. I've been to every movie, every gallery, and every department store in Vancouver, so I've pretty much covered the local culture. But tomorrow's Thursday and *CSI* is on. It's the second part of a two-parter, so I have to see how it ends."

"Clearly, you have your priorities straight."

"Yes. Speaking of which, I've been here a week and haven't even phoned Spirit. Do you think she'll be offended?"

"Offended?" said Ray, raising his eyebrows as high as he could. "No, Terra will be offended that you didn't call. Mom will be deeply hurt, as only a mother can be, that her firstborn hasn't had the sensitivity, let alone the courtesy, to phone the person who gave her life."

"Since when did Spirit care about courtesy?"

"Okay, maybe I went a bit too far. But she might just wish you had thought to call as soon as your feet touched Canadian soil." He handed her the phone. "Speed dial three," he said.

"What?" she said. "Your mother is number three? Not number one?"

"Shut up and phone her. My private life is none of your business."

Maris hit speed dial and punched in the number three. Her mother answered after four rings.

"Hi, Spirit," said Maris. "It's me."

"Maris? Where are you? Is everything all right?"

"Yes, yes, everything's fine. I'm in Vancouver, staying with Ray. I've been here a couple of days getting over the jet lag." She shot a look at Ray that said, *Don't you ever tell her I've been here for a week ...*

He put up his hands and called out, "Hi, Mom. I'm taking good care of her."

"When are you coming to see me, Maris?" Spirit asked.

"I thought I'd come up in a couple of days, if that's all right. Maybe Friday morning?"

"That's good," said Spirit. "Have you phoned your sister?"

"Um, no, not yet," said Maris. "I'll call her today. Promise."

"Good. See you Friday."

"Okay. Bye." Maris hung up the phone and handed it to Ray. "Whew," she said. "That went well."

"A couple of days," said Ray. "You know there's a special place in hell for people who lie to their mother."

"Get a life," said Maris. "As if you never did."

"Only once," he said, "and that was a long time ago."

"Oh, really," she said. "And that was when you told her what?"

Ray hesitated. He looked down at the ground. "I told her — you promise you won't bring this up again?" Maris nodded. "I told her Dad asked me to live with him and Shirley and I said no."

He looked up at Maris and waited.

"You did not," she said.

"Did so."

"Did not."

"Did so."

"Why?"

"Because I didn't want her to think he hated us."

"But he didn't hate us."

"Spirit thought he did. Well, maybe not hate. But

that he didn't want to be bothered with us anymore. He wanted a new life with Shirley and he wanted us to sort of disappear."

"I think that was Shirley," said Maris. "She never wanted us. But I think Dad was okay with it, at first, at least." Did Ray know that Arthur had tried to get Spirit to let Maris come and live with him and Shirley and go to school? It hadn't happened, of course. Spirit had vetoed it, and so Arthur had started the allowance thing, putting money into bank accounts for the kids' education. Ray had been so young at the time. Maybe he didn't know any of it. *If that's true then it's kind of sad*, Maris thought, *that he'd felt compelled to make up a story like that to tell his mother*. Ray was the only boy. Maybe he'd taken his father's behaviour as rejection.

"Did you really believe that?" she asked him.

"Of course not," he said. "I told you it was a lie."

"So you thought you had to defend Dad. You know how complicated that is, psychologically?"

"You mean, like, youngest child, a boy, at that, is abandoned by same-sex parent at a critical age, therefore sending young male child into a perpetual spiral of negative sense of self, damaging said child's ability to mature and sustain relationships, and resulting in unrealistic expectations and ending in misery, despair, and drug addiction?"

"You forgot the part about homosexuality."

"Oh, yeah. And indulging in homosexual fantasies with unattainable, impossibly beautiful, and hot young men."

"That sounds about right. Are you over yourself yet?"

"Oh, I am so over myself that I don't even look in the mirror anymore."

"Well, I can see why," said Maris.

"Listen. I can't believe we're as well adjusted as we are," he told her.

"We?" she said.

"Well, me and Terra." They both laughed. He handed her the phone again.

Maris looked at him expectantly. "She's not on speed dial?"

Ray scrunched up his face in a pained expression. "I ran out of numbers," he said. "But I've got it written down somewhere." He went over to his desk and started lifting up stacks of paper and books.

"It's okay," she said. "I've got it in my book." She pulled out a red notebook covered in embroidered Chinese silk and started leafing through it. When she found the number, she dialled and waited. "Please be the machine," she said under her breath.

But Ray heard her and shook his head. "Ah, the ties that bind," he said.

She was about to hang up when Terra picked up the phone.

"Hi, Terra. It's me, Maris."

Ray listened as she exchanged pleasantries with their sister for a few minutes then hung up.

"Well?" he said.

"She wanted me to come for a visit but I told her I was going to see Spirit, so she suggested that she organize a family weekend at Spirit's place. She's going to call you about it."

"Sounds like fun," said Ray. "I can't wait."

maris_cousins@yahoo.com
To: dinahstone@hotmail.com
Cc:
Subject: Update from Canada

Hi Dinah,
Just wanted to let you know that I've been in BC
for about a week, staying with my brother and
will probably go and visit my mother for a while.
I've enjoyed being with Ray but I have a feeling I
could just stay and stay — in a kind of vegetative
state — and never get my shit together. He's been
really good, talking about things and helping me
keep them in perspective. A big problem for me is
that I feel like I've lost my "artist's" eye somehow
— that thing I told you about before I left S'pore.
I'm having trouble seeing the colour in things and
that tells me there's something terribly wrong with
me. We're all still reeling from Peter's death (I can't
seem to use the M word) and I'm not sure whether
removing myself, at least physically, is the solution
or not. I only know I had to try it.

Let me know what's happening on your end.
How are you coping? Is the shop still open? And, not
that I really care, but where's Angela? Is she giving
you some room to operate the business?

I miss you, Di. I'll keep you posted.
Maris

dinahstone@hotmail.com
To: maris_cousins@yahoo.com
Cc:
Subject: Re: Update from Canada

Hi Maris,

I miss you too and really wish you were here (no pressure!). I'm managing things okay but am mostly on autopilot a lot of the time. The whole shock thing is a drag — I want it to go away but it just won't. Some days I wake up and feel great and then I remember and I don't feel so great. It's like I'm in a jar and somebody puts the lid back on. Maybe if Peter had died of old age it wouldn't be like this. But I keep thinking he should be here, he wasn't finished whatever it was he was doing with his life. Not fair.

I have hired Lim, a distant cousin, to help me in the shop. Angela wasn't too happy about it but I reminded her I couldn't be in two places at once, i.e., in the back unpacking stuff and in the front selling it, so she gave in. Lim is working out fine. She's a good worker and does most of the packing, shipping, and unpacking. Plus, she's great with a duster. Maybe a little compulsive sometimes, but it's better than the opposite (which I suppose would be lax or lazy — what great words!). She's good company, too, and doesn't mind running errands or making tea. So, lucky for me.

Angela is Angela, and even more so, if that's possible. She's back in Germany but calls me at least fourteen times a week with a million questions and orders, which she calls "requests," but you and I both know Angela doesn't request, she demands.

There is still no result from the police. They assure me the investigation is ongoing, but you wouldn't know it. I guess at a certain point there are no more clues lying around, and they have to hope someone will confess or something will come out of left field. Someone comes into the store every day asking about it, so it never goes away. Peter had a lot of friends and the customers really liked him. How can I replace him? For now the shop runs on reputation and maybe a bit of the "ghoul" factor, but at some point both of those will fade, and then it will either make it or it won't.

A couple of people have been in asking for you — Mr. Choy, do you remember him? He bought *Blood Red Reverie* last year. And Anna Wong said to say hello.

Keep in touch, Maris.

Miss you,

Dinah : - (

CHAPTER TEN

On Friday, Maris took the bus from the Greyhound depot to visit her mother in Roberts Creek. She insisted on taking Peter's trunk with her, so they lugged it by taxi down to the bus station. Ray grumbled but he understood why she wanted to take it. She needed to feel connected and the trunk was full of connections.

"Thanks," she said. "I guess I'll see you soon." The bus was about three-quarters full and would be leaving in a few minutes. "Might as well get on." She gave him a quick hug and climbed into the stale air of the idling bus. She found a seat near the back and sat down beside the window. Ray was still standing on the platform, feet apart so his legs formed an inverted V, his hands jammed in the pockets of his jacket. He'd been doing that since he was a kid, she remembered. Like it was a part of his DNA.

The bus ride took Maris to the Horseshoe Bay ferry terminal and across to Langdale, then along the Sunshine Coast Highway through some of the most spectacular scenery in the world. The forty-minute ferry ride and the scenery kept Maris from thinking about what she would say to her mother when she got to Roberts Creek, but it didn't stop her from thinking about why she was making this trip. She was going for more than a visit, she knew. She was going for some kind of sustenance. There was something she needed, and the combination of her mother's particular view of life and the world, plus the remoteness and physical beauty of her surroundings, drew Maris toward her former home. Growing up in a hippie commune in the sixties and seventies had prepared Maris for some things in life, but had not prepared her for others. She was prepared for the life of an artist, for the isolation, the non-conformity, even the part that involved being judged by people who didn't always understand what she was trying to do. But she was unprepared to grieve her loss. And she knew that was what she was trying to do: grieve for Peter and come to terms with the way he had died.

The commune had been all about celebrating life and oneness with your extended "family," but there had been few real losses during those years. Yes, Arthur had left them, and that had been hard, but Spirit had — at least in the beginning — been able to make it seem like a life-affirming move for them all. Their father, she said, was growing into his potential, his selfhood. It was only right that he be allowed to live his true life, and they, meaning his family, should give him this chance. It would be their gift to him. This was how Spirit had explained it to them, and they were too young to detect the bitterness that his betrayal had spawned. The unfinished part of what she was saying to them was that his "potential," his "selfhood," was really that of a deceitful, uncaring, selfish, self-absorbed piece of shit. Spirit had never forgiven Freedom Man for his duplicity. She had married an ideal and it had been ripped from her in the most inconceivable way. Freedom Man had chosen conventionality, a suit and tie, a car dealership, for God's sake! He had not just rejected the life they had built together, he had stomped on it, pulverized it, and flushed it down the toilet like excrement.

This was the way Spirit had grieved — in resentment and anger that became a festering sore on the inside that she would not let others see — because Freedom Man's actions were not just a reflection of his own shallow, worthless self, but, she believed, a manifestation of his contempt for her and everything she valued.

Maris hadn't known any of this until she was nearly thirty years old. So well had her mother hidden her feelings that it had been a shock to learn that the always serene, even-tempered Spirit had been harbouring a huge reserve of contempt and loathing for the man who had fathered her children. She had revealed it to Maris during a night of drinking Spanish wine, a particularly vicious Rioja, the effects of which lingered for several days. It had drawn things from Spirit's cache of hidden sorrows the way a syringe draws blood from a vein. Maris had listened as the waves of bitterness washed over her mother and wondered how she had never sensed even a fraction of what was there.

This had been her induction into the act of grieving. You hold the pain and the sorrow inside and let it fester for years until, one day, it bursts like a ruptured boil and infects whoever has the misfortune to be nearby. Was this what she was doing now? Internalizing her anger at Peter for dying, burying her sense of betrayal because his life had been taken from him so arbitrarily and so unfairly? Was she eating her grief the way her mother had? Eating it every day but never digesting it? And if she was, why, exactly, was this a bad thing? Spirit had survived, hadn't she? She had made a life for herself, raised her children, become a first-class potter who made a living from her creativity. If there was a downside, Maris couldn't see it. Except that maybe, if this was what it felt like to grieve in such a way, it wasn't a good feeling. In fact, it was achingly unpleasant, like having stomach flu and being forced to stand in the middle of an empty room for the rest of your life.

Maris closed her eyes and tried to focus on the moment. She felt the vibration of the bus's motor from her feet to the top of her head. She listened to the thrum of the tires on the asphalt highway and the soft murmur of conversation around her. The elderly Chinese man sitting next to her ruffled the pages of his newspaper as he turned them. She listened to her own breathing, lengthening her breaths by inhaling deeply and exhaling slowly. As a sense of calm came over her, she turned her head toward the window and slowly opened her eyes. *Just look*, she told herself, *look and absorb, but don't think or analyze. Just be.*

She allowed herself to see only the shapes at first: the spiky pines, the flatness of the highway, the jaggedness of the mountains in the distance, the blooming puffs of cloud overhead. This was the way she had trained herself to see, beginning with the surface and then homing in on the details: the softly fluttering needles on the pines;

the pitted asphalt of the road; the striations of the Rocky Mountains as they climbed above the tree line and into their snowy peaks; the crisp outline of the clouds contrasted against the dense sky.

But when she tried to absorb the concentrated blue of the mountain sky, as she drew her eyes down to the textured green of the trees, the black smoothness of the rock, she felt nothing. That was how Maris needed to perceive colour. Not just with her eyes, but with her gut. And right now, in the midst of the Cosastal Range, truly one of the world's beauty spots, there was no colour for her empty palette. She only saw what everybody else saw: blue sky, green trees, black rock, white snow and clouds. It was not enough for her artist's soul. It left her with nothing to say.

Spirit was waiting at Roberts Creek Road in her 1989 Taurus station wagon. She loved the old car and was reluctant to give it up, even though it had just barely passed its latest emissions test. She justified keeping it by saying that since her environmental footprint was so small on all other counts, she could afford to lose a few points on a car that was a borderline pollutant. Spirit knew this was bullshit, but anything she could afford to buy would not be half as comfortable as the Taurus. Nor would it feel as solid, or be as quiet, at least from the inside.

She saw Maris get off the bus and watched her as she spotted her mother's car across the road. Spirit hadn't seen her daughter in four years and was struck, as if for the first time, by how much she resembled her father. She had always been lanky, and as a child this had translated into awkwardness; she was a kid who was always tripping over her own feet. Now, at nearly forty, Maris carried herself with a kind of grace, as if she'd finally grown into her height and knew how to manage her long legs. She was still lean but not as thin as she once had been. As she watched Maris walk toward her, Spirit noted that her hips were a bit wider and her thighs a bit fuller in the tight blue jeans. Her hair, once a light brown colour, was now streaked with blonde highlights that caught the sun. She had cut it to chin length and it emphasized the square lines of her jaw, the same jaw as Arthur, who had hidden the squareness under a growth of beard when she first knew him.

Maris was waving at her, indicating that her mother should get out of the car and come over to her. She pantomimed carrying luggage and Spirit understood that she needed help with her bags.

She got out of the car and jogged over to her daughter. When they hugged, Maris put her arms around her mother's shoulders and Spirit, shorter by a good six inches, wrapped her arms around Maris's waist. They stood like that for a full minute before Maris disengaged and looked at her mother's face.

"You look great," she said.

"It's the new sixty," said Spirit. "Haven't you heard? Instead of ending, life now begins at sixty."

"Well, it suits you."

Spirit laughed. "You look pretty good yourself. The new forty, eh?"

"Ha ha," said Maris. "No. Still the old thirty-nine for a few more months."

"Okay," said her mother. "I'll let you have that."

They walked back to where her bags were being unloaded. Maris's wheeled suitcase was lying on its side and the trunk was being pulled out of the second compartment. It took some heaving, lugging, and dragging, but they managed to get the bags over to the Taurus and into the back.

"I can't believe you're still driving this old piece of junk," said Maris.

"It's not a piece of junk. It runs just fine."

"I hate to think what it might be spewing into the atmosphere. Aren't you embarrassed?"

Spirit thought about trotting out the footprint argument, but thought better of it. Maris would see it for what it was and she'd be forced to come up with some other feeble explanation for her irrational decision to keep the car long past its sell-by date. It probably didn't even count as a trade-in anymore.

"Your ex-husband owns a car dealership, you know. Maybe he could get you a good deal on a new one."

"Maris," she said, a note of warning in her voice, "he sells BMWs to spoiled rich kids. He's the last person I'd buy a car from, new or used."

"It doesn't have to be personal," Maris pursued, ignoring her mother's tone. "It's just business. Can't you use him to get something you need?"

"No, I can't." By now, Spirit's tone was icy. "I don't want to be beholden to him in any way."

"Mom," said Maris, "it's been nearly thirty years. Can't you let it go?"

Spirit was silent. *No, I can't let it go*, she thought. It wasn't ever going to go away. "I hold grudges," she finally said. "Haven't you noticed?"

Maris laughed. "No, you don't," she said. "You hold one grudge. And nobody cares anymore, so why do you?"

"It's the principle," she said. But she was tired of this conversation already. "Come on. Let's not start your visit with this dead horse. It's been flogged enough times."

"Okay," said Maris. "Truce. I won't mention it again."

"I wish," said her mother. "It's bound to come up a few more times. It always does."

Maris smiled, and Spirit thought once again that her daughter had the warmest green eyes she'd ever seen. They were like the sea, boundless and deep, and maybe a little dangerous, too. Maris only revealed what she wanted to. It came out in her painting, but it also came out in her eyes. It took a long time to be able to read her — and a lot of patience.

"How's your brother?" Spirit asked. "I haven't seen him in months."

"He's still the unconfirmed bachelor, supposedly waiting for Ms. Right to come along, but making no effort to help her find him. He lives like a student, in digs, you know what I mean?"

"I do. Men are not nesters, Maris. They prefer a permanent state of impermanence. The always temporary way of life. That's why women were, unfortunately, put on the same planet. To save men from themselves."

"Ah," said Maris. "A divine plan."

"Well, not so divine for us. But a good deal for them."

"You kill me," said Maris. "Don't ever change."

Her mother's house hadn't changed since the last time Maris had been there, except that there was more stuff, mostly artsy-craftsy knick-knacks, more paintings, mostly by her artist/hippie friends, and pottery, her own and other potters'. Still, Maris had to admit it was comfortable. *My mother is definitely a nester*, she thought, *an über-nester, and it never occurs to her that she could move or move on.* When Spirit dug in, she dug deep. Change was something she was uncomfortable with. Even though her once luxurious chestnut hair was streaked with grey, she still wore it like a hippie, long, parted in the middle, and pulled loosely back in a ponytail at the base of her skull. She saw no reason to dye it or have it cut. It was part of who she was. She still wore jeans and gypsy blouses and ponchos. Long beaded earrings hung from her ears. The glasses that partially obscured her grey eyes were wire-rimmed, not the fashionable little oblongs now in style, but the round granny glasses she had worn for over thirty years. *I suppose I should be comforted*, thought Maris, *that something in this world has stayed the same.*

They had dragged her suitcase and Peter's trunk up the fourteen stairs that were the only way into the house from the driveway. The house had started as a two-room cabin set on the flattest part of the lot. Since the lot rose to 120 metres just beyond the back of the house, the only way to expand was from the front and to the sides. The last thing that had been added to the now six-room dwelling was a wraparound cedar deck that looked out over a rugged and rocky slope that met the road some 60 metres away. Spirit had planted perennial herbs between the rocks, and the sage, chamomile, lavender, rosemary, comfrey, lamb's ear, and tarragon grew in wonderful profusion.

Maris's old room had been dusted and fresh sheets were on the bed. Her books were on the shelves exactly as she had left them — from her Nancy Drews to *Anne of Green Gables* and *Catcher in the Rye*. Drawings and paintings from her teens, that her mother had framed herself, were still hanging on the walls. It was both unsettling and reassuring; it reminded her of who she had been and it told her how far away from that person she had ventured in the last twenty years.

She unpacked while her mother made tea, and tried to centre herself in a present that was so completely suffused with the past. Who was she at this moment? Twelve-year-old Maris who created still-life drawings out of the stuff she found around her, like her mother's utilitarian pottery, her brother's baseball, a few pieces of fruit, and the cat they all called Joan Baez? Or the forty-year-old artist who had found success of sorts in a place halfway around the world? This was yet another disconnect for Maris; it felt like she was holding two extension cords with the same end and had no way of joining them. *I need to slow down*, she told herself. *Things are happening too fast and I'm just not assimilating them. Events are bouncing off me like ping-pong balls. I barely notice them.*

She went into the living room where her mother had set out the tea things. She sat on the old sagging sofa her mother had found in a second-hand shop during what now felt like another lifetime.

"Something's shut down in me since Peter's death," she told her mother as they sipped Earl Grey and munched on butter cookies. "I'm deflecting stuff and I'm not sure how to reverse that." She had called her mother after Peter's murder and they had talked for an hour. But much had happened since then and Spirit could see that Maris was having trouble putting it all together.

"It's only been about four months, Maris. That's not

very long. The grieving process is different for everybody, but most would agree that it takes many months, often years, to work through."

"I haven't been able to paint," said Maris. "I look around and I don't see the colours. I just see shapes and sometimes texture. But I need the colours to paint. I need them to connect to the story I'm telling. I've always been able to see the story in whatever I'm looking at. Do you know what I mean?"

"Yes, I do," said Spirit. "You feel as if you've lost your inspiration. Was Peter a kind of muse to you — if that's the right word?"

"More like a mentor," she said. "He was my biggest supporter, and he made me want to work. I don't mean he forced me or anything; he just always pointed me in a direction I needed to go. He let me find my own way, but I think he was always guiding me."

"That's a big loss," Spirit said. "Of course you're feeling this way. You're kind of untethered right now." She reached over and touched her daughter's hand. "You're like a beautiful animal that's been separated from her herd and you can't find their scent. But you will, Maris. Your instincts will come back, and when they do you'll start to paint again. Right now you need to focus on what you *can* do and not worry about what you can't."

"I want to work," said Maris, "but I can't concentrate. I'm in this beautiful place and nothing speaks to me. It's like, trees, mountains, rivers — so what?"

They looked at each other for a few minutes and then Spirit got up and went into a room she had been using for storage for the past few years. It had once been designated as a future bathroom, but Spirit had decided she really didn't need another bathroom in the house now that everybody had moved out. She rummaged around for a couple of minutes, and when she emerged, she was carrying a large pad of drawing paper and a box of charcoal. She set them down in front of Maris.

"Let's get back to basics," she told her. "If you can't see the colours, then don't look for them. Use charcoal. If all you can see is shapes, then draw shapes. Don't you remember those art classes I sent you to a million years ago? The teacher would set a timer and you had to start drawing something freehand, even before you knew what you wanted to draw. Sometimes it was just shapes, but sometimes it would be something real, like a human figure or a tree or a horse. Remember? You used to come home and tell me how free it made you feel." Maris nodded, remembering the Saturday morning drawing classes. They did make her feel free. The teacher gave them permission to dream, without the pressure of explaining or understanding what they were doing.

"We can get some of those Japanese brushes and black ink, too," Spirit said. "And you can do some of those haiku drawings — you know, fast, strong brush strokes. I used to call them your haiku drawings because they reminded me of Japanese haiku poetry: disciplined and essential; spare and unadorned. They were so contained, but at the same time so open-ended."

Maris smiled. Maybe her mother was on to something. Maybe this was something she could do while she waited for whatever she had lost to come back. She laughed.

"I love you, Mom. You never give up."

"Hey, kiddo," she said, "giving up is not an option."

The Happy Ending

A Short Story

by

E. Sutcliffe Moresby

I happened to be in Singapore during the winter of 1926 and was invited to dine at Government House with the current governor of the Straits Settlements, a man by the unlikely name of Sir Lawrence Nunns Guillemard. I had arrived at the Istana (which is the Malay word for "palace") a few minutes earlier than expected, and took the opportunity to admire the handsome mansion and its surrounding gardens. Typical of the style of buildings designed by the British for their many tropical outposts, it displayed statuesque columns in the Doric, Ionic, and Corinthian modes *(Why have one style when you can have them all?* I thought), and was ideally suited to the hot climate with deep, covered verandahs and louvred windows that promoted cross ventilation and kept the sun's rays from penetrating its many magnificent rooms. Built in the late 1860s on a former nutmeg estate using prison labourers, the sumptuous gardens, or what I could see of them for it was already dark, afforded a splendid view of the sea through the massive trees that must have dated back at least to the time of the estate's construction.

This was to be an evening of "culture and conviviality," as the invitation stated, for Sir Lawrence was reputed to be a great reader. During the course of the evening, I discovered that the governor clearly loved a good yarn, and we were all encouraged to share our stories.

Seated next to me was a medical man, a Dr. Samuels, who, when prevailed upon, told a story that was both moving and, to my mind, tragic. I have remembered it all these years. It concerned a young Englishwoman named Elsie Townsend who had come out to Singapore some years earlier to marry her fiancé, an aspiring writer of limited talent but unbridled hope and ambition. Henry Withrow believed with all his heart that if he could make his meagre savings last five years, he would produce a manuscript worthy of publication and his fortune would be made. Before he left, he told Elsie that he could not do that in England, where the cost of food and lodging was prohibitive. He had decided that Singapore would afford him such an inexpensive existence that could buy his five precious years. Once there he wrote her many letters — pleading, cajoling letters — to persuade her to come to Singapore and marry him. Hadn't Joseph Conrad written *Lord Jim* here? he said. Didn't Rudyard Kipling write wonderfully about the "steam-sweat" heat, and the excellent food (but bad rooms) at the Raffles Hotel? It was a place of writers, and he was a writer, by God, and could be a writer of note if given half a chance.

He begged Elsie to join him, promising her the future — a future filled with their love and his books. But she was understandably reluctant. Singapore was far away; it was, for her, an unexplored and frightening unknown in the middle of the jungle. She also worried about what would become of her widowed father if she left. She would have given anything to have Henry abandon his foolish dream of being a writer, but she, Elsie, knew she could not be the one to make him come to that decision. Henry would have to make it for himself. In her heart of hearts, Elsie knew he would not give up. Finally she relented, but without enthusiasm. It was her deep and abiding love for Henry that prevailed. She could not disappoint him; she could not abandon him at the edge of his dream.

As Samuels told the story of Elsie and Henry, I stole a glance at Sir Lawrence seated at the head of the table. We had just been served the fish course, a quite delectable red snapper that had been steamed with fresh ginger, red chilies, and lime juice. The governor's eyes and attention were fixed on Dr. Samuels. He had scarcely touched the fish.

"They were married within a week of her arriving," continued Dr. Samuels, "as was only proper." Several women at the table solemnly nodded their heads in agreement. The doctor, a portly, balding man with a fringe of fine sandy coloured hair ringing the base of his skull, paused and tasted the fish. Sir Laurence did so, as well. We were all picturing in our minds the wedding of Elsie and Henry. I saw two slim young people, he, several inches taller than her, both nervous, overdressed for the climate in dark (probably wool) suits. She clutching a small bunch of flowers; he nervously pulling his starched collar away from his neck, as if to release the steam that had accumulated inside his shirt. The minister, pious to the expected degree, and his equally pious wife, no doubt required to be witness, would have recited the marriage vows from a well-worn, leather-bound prayer book he had brought with him from England many years earlier.

Elsie hated Singapore, according to Dr. Samuels, especially the steam-sweat heat. The few articles of clothing she had brought were totally inappropriate. She could never have imagined — even if she had laboured in a Chinese laundry, which she had not — the stifling, dripping wet, suffocating hotness of the place. It gave new meaning to the word "sweltering," a word she had heretofore encountered only in books, never in real life. Now she knew all too well what those writers had been referring to. Sweltering meant boiling, like limp, sodden vegetables in a soup pot; it meant steaming, like a clam in its shell; it meant stewing, like meat falling off the bones in thick, unforgiving gravy.

I saw several women dab their foreheads with lace-edged handkerchiefs, even though the room was not hot. A few of the men gulped down ice water. Clearly, the doctor was a master storyteller. We were enthralled.

Initially they stayed at the Raffles Hotel, the doctor went on. But Elsie went out daily, on foot, to look for cheaper lodgings where they could cook their own food and where she could make a home of sorts for them. Living in a hotel was not Elsie's idea of married life.

But they were happy, said the doctor. They were young, he said, shrugging his shoulders and turning up the palms of his hands in the manner of a Frenchman. Several chuckles emanated from the guests and Sir Laurence laughed outright, as if remembering the folly of his own youth. The fish course was cleared and we were served the roast beef, delivered to us on gold-rimmed plates with the governor's crest, along with perfectly prepared Yorkshire pudding, golden roasted potatoes, and boiled green peas. A fine, robust red wine was poured. For a few seconds we could believe we were in an English manor house in the dead of winter.

Eventually Elsie found them rooms at the top of a shophouse owned by a Hindu who sold cloth cut from bolts of silk and cotton in every colour of the rainbow. The Hindu owned several shops and was prosperous enough to be able to rent out the apartments above his shops and keep his family in a large house on Serangoon Road.

The rooms were modest, but furnished adequately with a bed, a table and chairs, a cabinet for dishes and utensils, and a small writing desk and a bookcase, which was what had decided the matter for Elsie. Henry would have a place to write. She would be busy enough with washing their clothes and learning to prepare their meals using a small wood-burning cooker.

Again, Dr. Samuels paused to eat, and we all contemplated a life without the kind of sumptuous meal we were currently enjoying as guests of the governor.

"How awful," murmured one of the women.

"Poor girl," said another. "Living like a native. How she must have hated it."

"Indeed, she did," continued Dr. Samuels. "She had no servant to help her with the heavy washing, and not enough pennies to take it to a washerwoman. It was a hard life for Elsie, what with the crushing heat and all. But Henry was writing, and in the evenings he used to read to her what he had written that day by the light of a kerosene lamp. She told herself it was all worth it. She believed he was a wonderful writer. Alas," said the doctor, as an aside, "nothing remains of his scribbling. At least, not to my knowledge."

The air in the room took on a disquieting heaviness that had not been there before. "But I get ahead of myself," he said. "In due time, in fact, within three months of her arrival, Elsie became pregnant." There was a collective gasp from the assembled company. "Oh, dear Lord," someone murmured. "The poor girl."

"Yes, poor girl, indeed," said Dr. Samuels. "She was not at all well in the early stages of the pregnancy. She lost weight, couldn't keep her food down, and said she felt like she was cooking inside her skin." At this point the dishes were cleared and an assortment of fruit and cheeses was served. The governor asked for the tawny port to be poured. It was a most excellent vintage.

"Go on, go on, Doctor," Sir Lawrence urged. "You have us on the edge of our seats."

The good doctor chewed on a slice of Japanese pear, contemplating his next words. He had our complete and undivided attention.

"Elsie, it seems, was made of sterner stuff than her husband. After three months she started to feel better. She was able to keep her food down and began to put on a little weight. She became stronger as each day passed, and it looked as if she and her baby, both, would survive the ordeal." Again, he paused to eat. We waited, as if for the other shoe to drop.

"But then," he said, and shook his head, "just as things were looking up, Henry came down with fever. And it was bad. Burning up one minute and freezing cold the next. Elsie sent for a doctor but he could do nothing but prescribe some powders to help him sleep. He told her to make sure he drank clean water as often as possible, but, as he told me later, he knew that if the fever did not diminish within forty-eight hours, Henry would most likely die. The fever was malarial, and Henry was exhibiting delirium and experiencing difficulty breathing. Any doctor of tropical medicine knows the signs."

I looked around the table. A couple of the women were dabbing at tears and most of the men were shaking their heads. Tropical malaria is one of the greatest threats to the well-being of the expatriate. Everyone in the room had either experienced its consequences directly or had heard of someone who had expired from it. It was a grim moment.

"And so Henry died on the fourth day," said the doctor. "And Elsie was devastated, as you can imagine. She buried him in the cemetery of the church where they had been married just six months earlier." He sipped his port and looked around the table. We were all silent. None of us knew what to say.

I spoke first. "Whatever happened to her?"

"Yes," said Sir Lawrence. "What became of her? Did she have the child? Did she go back to England?"

"I wish I knew," said Dr. Samuels. "And my friend, the doctor who attended Henry and who told me this distressing tale, never saw her again."

"How strange," said one of the women. "How terribly sad and strange."

"I agree," said the doctor. "But I'm afraid there are only rumours. After she buried Henry, we can't be sure what happened to her."

"Rumours?" I asked. "Tell us what you heard."

"Well," said Samuels, taking another sip of port, "there was a rumour that she had returned to England and had the child there. A boy, I believe."

"That would be the wise choice," said Sir Lawrence, and several of his guests agreed.

"And the other rumours?" I persisted.

"Another story claims she stayed and had the baby here, but no one knows where she went after the birth. Perhaps she remarried, but that seems doubtful. Not many women in her situation find a husband in the East." Samuels pursed his lips and shook his head, as if he were reluctant to relate the final rumour.

We waited expectantly, almost on the edge of our seats.

"The last rumour," he said, his eyes fixed on the glass of port in his hand, "is that the baby was stillborn and that she went mad. Some people say she is still here in Singapore, and that she roams the streets at night, searching for Henry."

"Oh, how dreadful," someone said.

"Yes," Samuels agreed. "Dreadful."

"And which story do you believe, Doctor?" I asked.

He turned to me and took a sip of his port, as if giving himself time to decide. "I prefer to believe in a happy ending," he replied. "That she went back to England and had a healthy baby boy."

"Hear, hear," said Sir Lawrence. "I quite agree. The only sensible conclusion."

"Ah, yes," I said. "The happy ending."

CHAPTER ELEVEN

Maris closed the book of Edward Sutcliffe Moresby's short stories she had been reading. This one, "The Happy Ending," stayed in her mind as she closed her eyes and tried to fall asleep. A tragic love story set in Singapore in the 1920s, it made her wonder if any of it were true. She had been to what was left of the old Christian cemeteries in Singapore and had read the gravestones of people who had probably come to the Far East to find their fortune, but had succumbed to illness and infection within the first year. Many had been soldiers not yet twenty years old. Or young women dying in childbirth, their babies, often unnamed, buried with them. She thought of poor Elsie Townsend and wondered what she would have done in her position.

Would I have come home, as I'm doing now? she wondered. Probably. And what did that say about her?

That she lacked courage? But she had set off for Singapore almost on a whim and without a second thought. Hadn't that taken courage? Or maybe she was an emotional coward, lacking a different kind of courage. The shock and pain of Peter's death had sent her scurrying into a protective hole, a hole like the ones they'd tried to dig to China as children ... only this one led straight back to Canada. Was she looking for the comfort of home, the kind that came with no effort, the kind that didn't require her to stretch herself? Was she looking for the easy way out? She could become like Emily Dickinson, never leaving her room, never taking another risk. Except that Emily Dickinson had a whole world of imagination in her head that she explored fearlessly, brilliantly. *Have I closed my eyes to that world?* she wondered. *Is that why I can't see colours?*

Finally the sleep that had been eluding her came, but it didn't last for long. She woke up well before dawn and her eyes felt dry and scratchy when she opened them. She got out of bed and found the eye drops she always carried in her kit bag. She squeezed two drops into each eye and stood with her eyes closed for a minute. Then she splashed some water on her face and headed back to the bed. But she knew there would be no more sleeping that night. It was a little chilly in the bedroom so she dug around in her still unpacked suitcase and pulled out a dark green sweatshirt and a pair of sweatpants. Her eyes went to the trunk that she and her mother had dragged into the corner of the room. Surely Peter had not planned on an early death, but had he known that his death, whenever it came, might leave her bereft not only of his guiding hand but also of her own confidence in her abilities as an artist? Was that why he had left the contents of the trunk to her in his will rather than giving them to her while he was alive?

She reached over and raised the lid of the trunk. There were the Moresby books, the paintings of Chinese women, and the bundles of letters. What could they mean?

She untied the ribbon around one set of letters and opened the first one. It was dated 1923 and addressed to "Annabelle Sweet" at a London, England, address.

> My dearest Annabelle. I have arrived safely in Singapore and pray that this letter gets to you quickly so that you will not worry one minute longer than you need to. It was what the seasoned passengers called "an uneventful crossing," which I assume means there were no terrifying storms, encounters with pirates, or deadly icebergs. I met an interesting assortment of people, including young, single, or betrothed females heading east to find romance and marriage in the Orient. I can tell you I was never at a loss for a dance partner, although none of them caught my fancy or captured my heart. (Are you jealous? Don't be. You are the only one for me, Annabelle, and I shall continue to say it until you believe it with all of your heart and agree to join me here in S'pore.)
>
> Speaking of Singapore, my God, it's hot here! But don't let that discourage

you — it's a wonderful, bone-warming heat after the chill of England. I love it and so will you. I'm sure of it. But I get ahead of myself.

Sutty was there to meet me when my ship docked, and I was never so glad to see a friend. I had forgotten how tall he is and he stood head and shoulders above everybody else. He looked cool and handsome in his white linen suit and he wore a white straw hat to protect him from the sun. He was every inch the colonial gentleman. The port was tumultuous with noise and activity and I could barely think straight, let alone gather my luggage, get a rickshaw, and find my way to the Raffles Hotel. I suppose, given enough time, I would have accomplished it, but I would have been so much the worse for wear. Sutty, bless his soul, was able to cut through all the chaos and deliver me safe and sound to the Long Bar of the hotel, where I drank cold (yes, cold) beer, and feasted on bangers and mash — seriously! I was able to leap over culture shock with one bound and ease into Oriental life with a full stomach and a fairly clear head.

I will write more about the city in my next letter. I want to get this into the post before it's collected.

I miss you, my Sweet Annabelle,
and begin to count the days until I see
you again.
All my love,
Francis

The next letter was dated three days later and began
"My Sweet Annabelle."

I have settled in a bit now and must tell
you my impressions of Singapore. My first
were seaport impressions of bustle and
noise, heat and salty smells, people calling
out in a strange sounding language:
Chinese? Malay? I heard no English, so
knew I was in a foreign place for the first
time in my life. I felt like a boy in a Conrad
novel who has been thrust into a seafaring
life and arrives at his first port: he could
be anywhere and the new place is full of
promise, for he has seen nothing but the
ugliness of an impoverished childhood,
felt nothing but hunger all his life, and
now he is delivered to a place that could be
the making of him. He sees that anything
is possible. If he has made it this far, he
will only keep moving forward. Life for
him is no longer filled with nothingness. It
is no longer only shades of black and grey.
Life is suddenly filled with possibilities
and colour. It is no longer about who he

must be, but about who he *can* be. This is exhilarating stuff; the stuff of adventure for a boy who was orphaned early or who fled a life of dismal predictability or one of unpredictable violence and danger.

"What lies ahead?" he asks himself, when before he only asked: "When will this misery end?" "I am reborn," he says, when before he only said, "When will I die?" Imagine his excitement, the anticipation, the hope. It is a gift; the first in his life.

No, I am not that boy, but I feel — I live! — his exhilaration. I don't want to close my eyes for a moment. I don't want to miss a thing because any minute can bring something that has never happened before, something that in the blink of an eye may be lost. No, wait, precious moment! I cannot lose you. I must have you. This is how my life begins, my real life, the one I never dared imagine for myself. Now there are no second impressions. Everything is a first impression; everything is new to my eyes. Trees are not just trees but giant monuments of nature that bloom with furious colour and shade with great arching branches of green. A road is not just a road, but a promise of something interesting, something never seen before.

I am inspired, Annabelle, to be something I have only dreamed of being. A writer. A real writer. Someone who lives the life of a writer and gains his inspiration from that life. I don't want to write about what I already know but about what I discover. I don't want to dredge the past; I want to mine the future. I want to move out and up and away from the mundane, to go to a place that most people never get to. I want to be the messenger who brings news of such earth-shattering experience that everyone will want to hear it.

You see how I am flying after only a few days here? This was meant to be, Annabelle, I am sure of it. It is my destiny, and I want it to be our destiny. I want to share it with you because you deserve to experience this kind of wonder at the opportunity that life holds. We can be pioneers, my darling. Singapore is not a new place, but it is new enough. It is barely more than a hundred years since Raffles purchased this island of swamp and rainforest from the Sultan of Johor. One hundred years. Newer even than America. It is still becoming. I am still becoming. *We* are still becoming. This can be our place, yours and mine.

I'm sure I've quite exhausted you, Annabelle, so I will seal this letter with a

tender kiss and write to you again when
I have eaten three meals and slept one
night. Just so you know I am not losing
my mind, but, indeed, finding it. I eat, I
sleep, I dream.

I love you,
Francis

Maris picked up the next letter in the pile. *Who were
these people?* she wondered. Her eyes no longer itched
with fatigue. She wanted to know more of the story that
was unfolding, had unfolded, in Singapore more than
eighty years ago.

Let me tell you about the rain. It can
come without warning and when it
comes it falls in torrents, in sheets, in
great walls of water so that you think
there is an unending supply of water in
the sky. It obliterates whatever view you
might have had of trees, hills, mountains,
tall buildings — anything farther than
ten feet from your eye. There is a
wetness to this rain that surpasses the
wetness of rain anywhere in England.
And England is a wet country. The rain
is often referred to as "the rains," in the
plural, and that is fitting. These rains
pound the surface of the earth as if they
were made of steel instead of water. It

is hard rain — unkind, uncaring, and murderous. I have seen the streets fill with water to the height of a man's knees in less than thirty minutes. Sutty tells me that it rained like that once for five days straight and a hundred people drowned on one street alone.

It is frightening and yet it's thrilling, Annabelle, to see such power in nature. Once I was caught while walking and could only stop and wait under the nearest awning along with everyone else. We were forced to give in because to go forward or to go back was impossible. Mother Nature stole a piece of time from each one of us — a piece of time she had no intention of giving back. We stood and watched as a dead rat floated by. My companions in captivity appeared not to notice but I couldn't take my eyes off the little beast. I use the word "little" in a relative sense. It was a very large rat but it seemed small in the scheme of things. It was no match for the fast moving rush of water that had filled the sewer pipes in seconds. I suddenly realized why the sidewalks are built up so high and the gutters dug so deep. It's all because of the rains.

As Maris read through some of Francis's letters, she realized how he had captured the timelessness of the human struggle with nature. She, too, had witnessed these same blinding, hard rains of Singapore. They were a fact of life, just like the trees, the weeds, the dogs, the babies, and the old men and women who sat in front of shops or in cafés and remembered.

The memory of Singapore's rain was sensory, full of sounds and smells that could still drench you even if you stood in a shelter. It would ricochet off the sidewalk like a hail of bullets and soak you from the ground up. In Singapore you didn't go anywhere without an umbrella between December and March and from June to September. The two distinct monsoon seasons, the first from the northeast and the second from the southwest, kept the land lush and the vegetation profuse. It was a garden city that maintained a tropical rainforest within its urban confines.

She missed it, she realized, and believed she would go back there. But it wasn't time yet: that was an intuition, not a fact. It was just something she knew but couldn't explain. She had come back to British Columbia on intuition, too, because she needed to be refortified, reminded, and restored. Restored to what, she wasn't sure. She could never be the Maris who had left Vancouver nearly five years ago, nor did she want to be. She had grown so much in those years, as an artist, yes, but also as a person. It was Peter who had helped her grow as an artist, and coming to terms with being an artist had helped her discover who she was. But all of that seemed so vague now and seemed to be dissolving the way one scene dissolves into another in a film. She was in the middle of the dissolve, struggling to find a perspective and to hang on to what she knew.

maris_cousins@yahoo.com
CC:
To: dinahstone@hotmail.com
Subject: Can't sleep

Hi Dinah,

It's the middle of the night and I can't sleep, so thought I'd get an email off to you while it's quiet. And I mean quiet. My mother's place is kind of out in the boonies, so there's no traffic, no urban white noise, just the sounds of nature, like chirps and peeps and the occasional screech or howl. I guess the closest thing in S'pore would be the Botanic Gardens, if you were there in the middle of the night. I'm sitting here missing S'pore while right smack in the middle of some of the most beautiful country in the world. Go figure! Maybe I'm just a city girl at heart.

I told you I was brought up on a sixties-style commune and I guess I wouldn't be who I am if I'd been raised otherwise, but I can't help but wonder why the three of us (my brother, my sister, and I) turned out so differently. There's got to be a personality factor in there somewhere. Like we were born with some X-factor that is us, no matter what. I know you and Peter are only half-siblings (the word "only" makes it sound less important, which is not what I mean) and share a father, but I know very little about your upbringings and why you are so different. Is it just personality? Is it culture? Male-female gender stuff? And maybe you're not as different as I think you are.

If I think about my own brother and sister, I wonder if we're more alike than I imagine. My sister has tried the hardest to be "conventional." She married a good man (like, hello, whatever that is!) and has two well-behaved children. Her home is beautiful by magazine decorating standards, and she appears to be "happy." Or maybe "content" is a better word. Because, whereas contentment seems to be a more consistent state, happiness, to me, seems more elusive, more hit and miss. I think you can have happy moments, but to sustain a state of happiness is probably impossible. (Am I writing a self-help book here that will make a million dollars? Wow! I wish...)

You don't have to read this whole rambling mess, Dinah, but I seem to need to keep writing it. I guess, with the time difference, it's the middle of the afternoon for you. You've probably had a busy day and are wishing for a nice cup of sweet, milky tea right now and a chance to put your feet up. This would be about the time Angela will call from Germany and set your teeth on edge with some stupid, petty question or demand. Am I right? Well, at least she's far away and can't show up, like, ten times a day. We can be thankful for small mercies.

I'm not sure what I'll do next, but I know that I have to begin painting again before I can come back to S'pore. And I'm not sure why, but I believe my "inspiration" lies here. Inspiration being a fancy word for jump-start-kick-in-the-ass. I need a jolt of something to get me out of the doldrums. (God, I'm even starting to bore myself — hope this helps you sleep tonight!)

Anyway, my friend, answer when you have time and give me the latest. In the meantime, I'll keep pushing this particular rock up the hill, all the while hoping it doesn't roll back and crush me. (Hmmmm ... forget self-help. I think I'll write a bestselling novel.)

Hahahaha. I'm going back to bed.

Lovya,

Maris

Chapter Twelve

Francis and Annabelle huddled together under an umbrella as the skies opened and the drenching rains began to fall. They were enjoying a brief honeymoon and had decided a day at the Botanic Gardens would be relaxing and recreational at the same time. According to Sutty, the orchid display was worth exploring. Apparently, Singapore's climate was ideal for the natural growth of the graceful and luxurious flowers. It was also a fact that torrential rainfall was a trigger to the flowering of these exotic plants.

"Just think," said Francis, "while we're here getting soaked and cursing the rain, hundreds of orchid flowers are preparing to display their lovely faces."

Annabelle laughed. Francis had told her about the rains in one of his letters, but she hadn't imagined herself standing in the middle of them with only an old umbrella to protect her. *Oh well*, she thought, *it's only rain and not the black plague*. Now that she and Francis were married, they could meet any adversity together and that would make it easier.

There was a shelter about fifty feet away and they debated whether or not to run for it. How much drier would they be if they stood under the open shelter's roof? Running up the pathway and crossing to the other side would be like fording a small stream at this point. However, standing in one place and being pelted on all sides was no better. They decided to run for it, and in minutes they joined about fifteen other drenched comrades to wait out the storm in the garden. It lasted a good twenty minutes, during which time they chatted with one another, mostly about rain and other weather in Singapore and in England. *Weather is such a common ground for people*, thought Annabelle. Everybody experienced it everywhere, and everybody had an opinion about it. It helped to pass the time.

And then, just as suddenly as it had started, the rain stopped. The result was a steamy mist that rose from the well-soaked ground and hung in the air like vapour from a boiling kettle. In time, the sun came out and burned the mist away, leaving the heat just as intense as before the storm.

"Welcome to Singapore," said Francis. "Isn't it lovely?"

"Yes," said his new wife. "It's almost like England, only wetter and hotter."

Francis laughed and believed that Annabelle had just told a joke, which he took to be a good sign. She was in high spirits and had been since their marriage. He guessed it was because she felt more secure now. Her apparently unsettled life was, in fact, more settled. She had a role to play and, as a wife, she had a purpose. She had been stubbornly opposed to his plan for so long, but now that it was a reality, she seemed to accept it as inevitable and was determined to make the best of it. *She has hidden resources of strength*, Francis thought. *She's the picture of English womanhood — delicate as a rose on the outside, but tough and resilient as a leather boot on the inside.* He believed this and he also believed she would be able to handle any adversity that fell into their path. *She'll bend,* he told himself, *but she will not break.*

If Annabelle had known what her husband was thinking, she might have been pleased, or she might have thought, "Pray that we never have to find out, my dear." The last thing she wanted was to deal with more adversity. It was true that she felt more secure being married to Francis, but she would have felt a lot more secure had they been in England. Annabelle preferred the familiar for all that Francis preferred the foreign and exotic. She would let him have his five years — all the while praying that it would be less — and then it would be time to be sensible: back to England, back to reality.

In the meantime, she would look for more suitable lodgings for them. Much as she enjoyed staying at the Raffles Hotel with Francis and Sutty, it was costing too much money and it wasn't really a home. Annabelle wanted a few pieces of her own furniture to polish and a hob where she could do her own cooking. It wasn't much to ask for and she knew Francis would go along with it. She would get him to ask around among the boys who worked at the hotel to see if anyone knew of a place, or even a neighbourhood, where they could look for a place.

They had reached the orchid gardens by now and they turned all their attention to the multihued variety that spread out before them.

"It confirms one's belief in God, doesn't it?" Annabelle asked her husband. "Who else could have designed such a perfect thing?"

They were looking at the *Vanda* Miss Joaquim, which had been discovered by Agnes Joaquim in her garden in Singapore in 1893. She took what she thought might be a new hybrid to the Botanic Gardens' first director, Henry Nicholas Ridley, who confirmed that, indeed, she had discovered a new, natural orchid hybrid. The flower's colouration ranged from pale mauve on its frilly outer petals to rosy violet surrounding a centre of fiery orange. The orchid Agnes Joaquim had discovered was in full flower when Francis and Annabelle saw it.

Later in the rickshaw on the way back from the Botanic Gardens, Annabelle was feeling quite relaxed and almost at home as Francis chatted away about the gardens and how they would go there often and picnic in the years to come. Then, glancing past him, Annabelle saw an elderly Chinese woman lying by the side of the road, apparently dead. Annabelle turned her head and looked back to confirm that she'd actually seen what she thought she had seen. At first it hadn't registered that the woman was dead, if indeed she was, and Annabelle wondered why she would be lying on the road in such a fashion. When it struck her that the woman must have either fainted or died, she thought of her own mother, dying in a hospital surrounded by white sheets and antiseptic, while the nursing sisters bustled about, attending to her needs and telling her she was going to be fine, even though it wasn't true. *Death*, she thought, *doesn't care if you're in a hospital or on the road.* He takes you when he's ready and damns the consequences. The indignity of dying in the road was embarrassing to Annabelle. She wished she hadn't seen the woman and hadn't stared at her in her private moment of humiliation. She couldn't imagine anything worse than dying in the street. *How long will the woman lie there*, she wondered, *before someone takes her away? An hour? A day?*

Annabelle looked at Francis, who apparently had not seen the woman, and a shiver ran down her spine. *I can't protect you*, she thought, *and you can't protect me. What will happen will happen and we will be at the mercy of strangers.*

When they returned to the Raffles, Sutty was in the bar having a whisky. They joined him and Francis ordered a beer while Annabelle asked for tea.

"How was your day?" Sutty asked.

"Splendid," said Francis. "Absolutely beautiful. It is such a lovely, peaceful place that I think it will be our own private sanctuary, even though we'll have to share it with every Johnny, Mary, Chin, and Chan who's also decided it's his own."

Sutty laughed. Francis had been in high form since Annabelle had arrived, and he was glad to see his friend so happy. But Annabelle, he noted, seemed a little distracted, even a little sad, and he wondered why. Maybe it was just the heat that was getting her down, but this seemed more like melancholy than fatigue. He hoped she wasn't regretting her decision to come to Singapore and marry Francis. He had seen it happen before: young women joining their men, filled with enthusiasm and promise, only to slip into a kind of lethargy, sometimes within a few weeks. One such young woman he remembered in particular. Her name was Olive and she had arrived brimming with excitement at the prospect of marrying her long-time fiancé, Ted. She was an attractive girl with a pretty heart-shaped face, dark wavy hair, lovely round hips, and a bosom a man would want to rest his head on. But within weeks she had started losing weight until, after three months, she was as thin as a rail. The colour had gone from her cheeks and her thick, shiny hair was dull and flat.

Ted had taken her to doctors who had given her potions and powders, both to lift her spirits and bring her weight back up, but to no avail. Eventually she became too weak to travel back to England on her own and she was hospitalized. Sutty had visited the distraught Ted, who told him that nobody could figure out what was wrong with Olive: she had just lost the will to stay alive. It was as if something had punctured her surface and the vitality had gradually leaked out. In six months she was dead.

Sutty had seen others simply linger in a state halfway between vigour and exhaustion, slowly and imperceptibly edging toward the latter until, one day, they just gave in or gave up. Some returned to England before it was too late and maintained long-distance marriages with their colonial husbands. He rarely saw couples who shared the same enthusiasm for the expatriate life. One or the other always got the shorter end of the stick, whether it was the woman who was forced to make a home, deal with hostile servants, and raise a family in isolated and unfamiliar conditions, or the man who faced the drudgery of a dreary job in less than ideal circumstances, usually working under a petty tyrant or a mountebank who would never have reached such a position of authority at home.

Whatever the case, it usually started with a dream, a wish, a whim, or a desire for something different, something better in a faraway place filled with the possibility of adventure. How easy when we dream not to include the unpleasant parts: the heat, the unfamiliar food, the waves of loneliness and longing for home, the diseases that wait to infect the unwary, and the fear, always the fear. For Sutty, there was no end to the stories he could tell. And no need to make anything up, it seemed.

Chapter Thirteen

Maris and her mother were weeding the garden after an overnight rain left the ground soft and easy to work. It was a task that took Maris back to her childhood, when Spirit and Freedom Man used to round up the kids and go to the communal garden to spend the morning in shared labour. It had been fun. They were a family within a larger, extended family and it seemed as if it would last forever. That they would never grow up or grow old, and they would always be as happy as they were at that moment. Maris still blamed her father for bringing it all down, but now she realized that blaming him was the path of least resistance. Life was much more complicated than that. She knew very little about her parents' relationship or what had led her father to make such a drastic change in his life. Had her mother seen it coming or had she been just as surprised as their children?

Maris looked over at Spirit, who was concentrating on digging up the root of a large dandelion. "Mom?" she asked.

Spirit grunted. "Hmm? What?"

"What happened?"

Spirit looked up. She frowned. "To what?"

"To us," said Maris. "Our family. What changed it?"

"Oh, that," her mother said, as if Maris had referred to something insignificant. She gave the dandelion one final pull and the root slid out of the ground cleanly. "Hah!" she said, as satisfied as if she'd painlessly extracted a bad tooth.

"Your father," she began, staring at the dandelion root, "is a simple man who thinks he's complicated. I didn't understand that when I first met him. I'll be kind and say he was searching for himself, but in reality he was a poseur. He wasn't so much looking for himself as he was looking for the accoutrements of himself: the wardrobe, the car, the house. It was fashionable in the sixties to wear bell-bottoms and paisley shirts and have long hair. When he put those clothes on, he put on an identity. I found out too late that it had nothing to do with the person inside." She paused and picked up a clod of damp earth, working it between her fingers.

"And I bought it," she said, looking up at Maris. But she wasn't really looking at Maris; she was looking back into the past to a time when the world was changing for women like her. "Freedom Man," she continued, "seemed to be so not my father that it never occurred to me that he might not be what he pretended to be. Maybe pretended isn't the right word. He wasn't pretending as much as he was acting in a play that everybody wanted a part in. He bought into that play the way I bought into him. We needed to believe that the world was changing and that we were changing it.

"A person like your father doesn't think too much about who he really is," she went on. "He got caught up in a vision, an ideal, that excited him for a while, but he eventually lost interest in it." She looked around her, taking in the house and the garden. "I guess, in a way, it was too static for him. It didn't change into anything; it just stayed the same. He got bored with it."

Maris thought about this. "How do you get bored with your own children?" she said.

"Oh, no," said Spirit. "It wasn't you he was bored with. It was the life, and, in part, I think it was me. It was the unchanging nature of it all. Arthur didn't have that much going on inside of him, so he needed a lot of stimulation from the outside. He didn't have the — let me call it *substance* — to make something out of nothing. He's not a curious guy. He's not a creative guy. I guess he didn't realize — and to be fair, none of us did; we were young and inexperienced — that real life is actually about getting up every morning and doing the same thing you did yesterday. It's about maintaining. And I guess when he figured it out, he decided that if he was going to spend his life maintaining something, it was going to be a life that had a lot of distractions, a lot of gadgets. Things that cost money and need to be replaced, with the latest bells and whistles that are better than last year's bells and whistles."

Spirit dug around another weed and worked her fingers into the dirt. Maris didn't say anything. She waited for her mother to speak.

"You know," Spirit said finally, "I never had a problem with who I was. I'm not a complicated person either, but I have instincts — you know what I mean, Maris? — I have something in my gut that acts as a bullshit meter, or maybe a truth meter, and it tells me whether I'm where I'm supposed to be or not. And I trust it. I can't always explain it, but it keeps me centred."

"Then why didn't your bullshit meter go off the charts when you met Freedom Man?" asked Maris. "Didn't you suspect he wasn't sincere?"

"No," she sighed. "I fell for him. He looked the part. He talked the talk. He walked the walk. And I was young. I wanted something different from the life I'd grown up with and Freedom Man was going to take me there. It was heady stuff, Maris. We were reinventing society. We were going to be the living embodiment of everything our parents were not. We were going to prove that people could live together in peace and harmony. We would throw off the shackles of conformity and get back to the basics of human existence. Live off the land. Educate our children at home. Share the labour and share the wealth. We really believed in that."

"And do you still? Believe in that, I mean?"

"I do," said Spirit, "but I also understand now that not everyone wants that. I've come to understand what I call the 'principle of distraction.' Meaning that most people, including your father, don't live by a set of beliefs. They exist. They put in time. They play roles: husband, wife, employee, neighbour, father, grandmother. They move through a series of roles in life and they define themselves by those roles. 'I'm Joe's mother, Anne's sister; I work for Blahblah Corporation; I'm a teacher, a butcher, a banker.'

But it's not enough. We need excitement, so we root for the home team. We need passion, so we have an affair. We need to have fun, so we throw a party. We distract ourselves from the basic ho-hum sameness of our lives."

Maris grimaced at her mother. "You really believe that?"

"Yeah, I do," said Spirit. "I've thought about it a lot. I was angry at your father for a long time. And now I realize I was angrier at myself for being fooled by him. Why didn't I see it? How stupid was I?"

"So you decided that everybody in the world was shallow and lived meaningless lives, pursuing superficial goals? That's how you dealt with it?"

Spirit laughed. "Well, not *everyone*," she said. "Just most people."

"Get out," said Maris. "I don't believe you."

"Okay, okay, maybe I'm exaggerating. I was pretty bitter for a while." Maris snorted. "Okay," said Spirit, "I was bitter for a long time. For years. And I was angry. And you have to understand, Maris, that anger is not an emotion I like to live with. He hurt me. He hurt me bad. I didn't see it coming. And we had three kids we were raising. Raising them the hard way, without societal structures to fall back on. We were winging it, making it up as we went along. I depended on him for fifty percent of everything. We were partners. And then I found out that he didn't have the faith. He wasn't committed to what we had decided — together, I thought — and that nearly killed me. He just walked away."

True to her word, Terra organized a weekend visit to Spirit's place so they could all do the family thing together. They drove up on Saturday morning, Terra, her husband Josh, the two girls, Emma and Alison, and Ray, in a roomy minivan with stereo speakers and little video screens so the girls could watch their favourite movie. They chose *New Moon* because they were both in love with Taylor Lautner. Ray sat in the back and listened to his iPod, watching vampires and werewolves to the music of Coldplay, Amy Winehouse, and Robert Johnson.

Spirit had been cooking for two days. She couldn't quite believe the whole family would be together; it almost never happened. Maris hadn't been home in four years, and the others came only when she put the pressure on. Although Terra was a little more dutiful about bringing the grandchildren around, Ra (she refused to call him Ray) had to be gently reminded by his mother that it was time for a visit. This was special.

Maris had helped her mother prepare everybody's favourite dishes, which meant peach pie for the girls, lasagna for Ray (who brought a bottle of Chianti), salmon grilled on a cedar plank for Terra, and scalloped potatoes for Josh. Spirit had even baked up a batch of her homemade granola — a favourite for breakfast and general munching. Maris and her mother decided to do up a load of mussels in white wine sauce with crusty French bread and an assortment of cheese and fruit for lunch. It was a long way from their days of eating brown rice, millet, and lentils. The weekend would be nothing less than a banquet. Maris thought of one of her favourite movies, *Eat Drink Man Woman*, in which the widowed father of three daughters is a master chef at a top Taipei hotel. Every Sunday he cooks an elaborate Chinese meal for his daughters, who dutifully attend but barely eat a thing. At the end of the meal, they pack all the food in containers and put it away. Each of the daughters has her own problems and the only way the father has of communicating his love is through the food he prepares for them — which they reject. It was the story of a dysfunctional family with a wonderful metaphor at its heart. In a way, Maris saw her own family communicating, or not communicating, through tangible objects, such as food and photographs, which Terra always brought, and furniture, which the kids always complained about and tried to persuade Spirit to replace. But it wasn't about food, photographs, or furniture; it was about the relationships between seven very different personalities and how they acted them out.

"Maris," said Terra, dipping a piece of bread in the mussel sauce, "how have you been? You almost never write, you know. And we worry about you, being so far away and so incommunicado. The girls are always asking about you, aren't you, girls?"

Alison and Emma were spreading thick slabs of butter on their bread, avoiding the mussels and nibbling like little mice on bits of cheese. They nodded and looked at Maris. Please don't ask us to talk, their eyes said. We're not ready to spill our guts at the dinner table. Spirit, who had noticed their reluctance to indulge in the shellfish, had slipped into the kitchen and was making a couple of tuna sandwiches and opening a bag of potato chips.

"Whoa, Terr," said Ray. "I don't believe I heard the part where you say, 'Hey, Maris, it's great to have you back. We missed you.'"

Out of the corner of her eye, Maris caught Josh and the girls ducking their heads and trying not to smile.

"Oh, Ray," said Terra. "Maris knows that. She's my sister. She doesn't need to hear it. Nor do I need to hear her say how glad she is to see me again. And the girls. And Josh. Right, Maris?"

"Right, Terr," said Maris. "We don't need to say it." She mouthed the word "troublemaker" at Ray. Just then Spirit came back into the room with sandwiches for the girls.

"I've made you peach pie for later," she said, "but for now, you can have a nice tuna sandwich."

"Mom always cuts the crusts off," said Emma, the youngest.

"What?" said Spirit. "Terra, you know the crust is the best part." She turned to the girls. "Don't you want curly hair?"

Alison gave her grandmother a strange look. "Curly hair? What's that got to do with bread crusts?"

"Everybody knows," said Spirit, patiently, "that bread crusts give you curly hair."

"Well," said Alison, "you'll definitely have to cut these crusts off, Grandma. I really don't want curly hair. And I especially don't want frizzy hair," she said, looking at Spirit's unruly mop.

"Me, neither," echoed Emma. "No way."

Terra gave her mother a defeated look and reached over to cut the crusts off her daughters' sandwiches.

"Now you know why I wanted to raise you in the woods," said Spirit, "away from all those ridiculous notions. Vanity, vanity, the curse of girls and women," she sighed.

"It's not just girls anymore, Mom," said Terra. "Boys and men are getting facials, dyeing their hair, getting nose jobs, and becoming anorexic in order to be thin. It's an epidemic."

"Blame it on Barbie," said Ray. "She started it, with

that ridiculous body of hers and those impossible boobs."

Alison and Emma giggled. The conversation was getting interesting.

"Well, it's true," said Ray. "Who do you know that looks like that?" he asked them.

"Miss America?" said Emma.

"I mean someone who hasn't been surgically altered. And besides, you don't know Miss America."

"Promise me you won't have breast implants," Spirit said to Emma and Alison. "Promise me."

"Oh, Grandma, of course we won't. Don't be silly."

"Or nose jobs. Or liposuction. People have died from that."

"Spirit," said Maris, looking at her super-slim nieces, "I think we're probably pretty safe with that one."

"You don't know the half of it," Spirit said. "I saw a documentary on plastic surgery that would turn your stomach. There was a woman on *Oprah* who had had something like twenty-five surgeries, and she said she wasn't done yet. She was addicted to plastic surgery. It was horrible."

"I saw that," said Ray. "She started out being a pretty good-looking woman. And she ended up looking like Cher."

"You watch Oprah?" Maris said.

"Once in a while," said Ray. "Someone lent me the video."

"Do you still have it?" said Spirit. "Terra should show it to the girls."

"Enough, Mom," said Terra. "I don't want them getting any ideas."

"Not until they're married," said Josh. "Then their husbands can pay for it."

Chapter Fourteen

THE WEEKEND HAS GOT OFF TO A GOOD START, Spirit thought. Nobody had yelled at anybody or stomped out of the room yet. She was sure that would happen eventually, but she still held out hope that her children had grown up since the last time she'd seen them. She suspected there was no such thing as a serene, mutually respectful, and well-adjusted family, except on TV where father knew best and kids knew father knew best (it was always father, never mother). Spirit had raised her kids, after a point, without a father. Had Freedom Man done more harm than good in the years he was with them? She knew the kids loved him and were devastated when he left. Being kids, they naturally blamed themselves. Ironically, the one who was most angry with her father, Terra, was the one who had turned out most like him. No kid gets raised in a perfect home, Spirit told herself. And what was the point of second-guessing all your decisions? You just ended up waffling and that was worse than being wrong, in a way.

Terra and Josh were good parents, Spirit believed, but Emma and Alison had their own personalities, which could only be controlled — or managed — to a certain extent. In the debate over nature versus nurture, Spirit tended to fall into the nature camp now that she was seeing her own kids as adults. She had thought that by "raising them in the woods" she could isolate them from the big bad influences in the big bad world. But she couldn't protect them from themselves, it turned out. She had armed them with a set of ideas — a belief in themselves, in their abilities, and, she hoped, respect for others and for nature — but had she prepared them for the world they chose to live in? *Look at Ra*, she thought, *still living like a student at thirty-five, with no family, not even a girlfriend.* And Maris seemed lost all of a sudden and without the ballast she needed to work on her art. She believed she had lost everything with Peter's death, even her ability to paint. She had come "home," but was this really her home? Where did she belong? And Terra, seemingly the most stable of the three, sometimes seemed to Spirit to be hanging on for dear life to ... what? A lifestyle? A bunch of stuff in a nice house? An unswerving, and therefore inflexible, faith in the perfectibility of her own family? *God help her*, thought Spirit, *if there's ever a crack in the façade.* If one piece were removed, would the whole thing come tumbling down?

Spirit knew that worrying would not change anything. Life was like a basket of eggs that you had to carry with you everywhere. Sometimes an egg broke and the mess slopped over onto a few other eggs. *Hard-boiled*, she thought. *If you could hard-boil all the eggs, they wouldn't break.* And then she thought, *deviled eggs: I should make some deviled eggs.*

Emma and Alison were up in Maris's room looking through her stuff. Alison, about to turn thirteen and very aware of herself as a girl moving on in life and leaving behind childish things, was tall, as Maris had been, and willowy. She moved with a fluid motion unusual for her age. Where Maris had been awkward, even gawky, Alison was graceful and seemed to know how to make the parts of her body move in unison. In that sense, she was a lot like Terra, including her blonde hair, blue eyes, and straight teeth. *She seems together*, thought Maris, *or as together as a thirteen-year-old could be.* But inside she was probably a jumble of all the parts that went into making her Alison, not quite adding up to a whole person yet. So far she hadn't exhibited any particular talent, as Maris had, but her environment was more sterile than Maris's had been, so maybe it would take her longer to find her creativity, if indeed she had any.

"Maris," she said, "how come you saved all this stuff? It's kid's stuff. Like, what would you want it for?"

"Your grandmother saved it, honey, not me. I guess she needed to hang on to my childhood for some reason. Mothers and grandmothers are like that. Sentimental."

Alison snorted. "You're not kidding. Our mother is always taking pictures of us. 'I don't want to forget these wonderful years when you're growing up so fast,'" she mimicked Terra, using a falsetto voice and rolling her eyes.

"Don't be too hard on her, Alison. She loves you a lot, and you are growing up so fast. She knows that one day you'll both be gone and living your own lives. Right now you are the most important thing in her life."

"How come you don't have children, Maris?" piped in Emma, two years younger and still hanging onto her little-girlness. She was what they now called a "tween," which drove Spirit nuts. "It's all about marketing," she'd say. "Selling these little kids as much junk as they can. Defining them as this little wedge between being a child and being a teenager. A demographic, for God's sake."

"Well, Emma," Maris said, trying to give the right answer, "I guess I haven't been lucky enough to fall in love with the right man who could be the father of my children." *Oh, God*, she thought. *How lame, pathetic, and filled with all kinds of clichéd, socially acceptable mores — equating falling in love with being lucky and finding Mr. Right? How much damage have I just done to Emma's little tween psyche?*

"That's what Mom says," said Emma.

"What?" said Maris, relieved she wasn't the only one doing the damage. "That I haven't been lucky?"

"Yeah. And she says Ray hasn't been lucky either, but he'll have to grow up before any woman will want to marry him."

"And what about me? Will I have to grow up, too?"

"No, she doesn't say that." Emma's honest brown eyes were remembering past conversations. "She says you're artistic and that makes it more difficult for you. Men don't usually fall in love with women who are artists."

"I see," said Maris. "Wow. You guys talk about me a lot, eh?"

Emma laughed. "Yeah, I guess we do. But not all the time." Of the two, Emma was most like Maris, although she resembled her father physically. She was shorter than her sister, but just as slender, with brown hair and eyes that were almost the same colour. Emma was the dreamer while Alison was the pragmatic one. Alison wore outfits that matched and took planning. Emma, on the other hand, threw on some clothes in the morning and, as long as all the essentials were there — top, bottom, socks, shoes — it didn't matter to her whether they were colour-coordinated or not. Alison would have been mortified to step out the front door wearing what Emma usually put on. Of the two of them, Maris was putting her money on Emma to be the more adventurous in life. But maybe it would take one of those earth-shattering, defining moments for either of them to become what they had the potential to become. And what was that? Grown-up maybe? *Nah*, thought Maris, *the most interesting people are never the grown-ups.*

The evening meal went better than Spirit expected. Her family seemed to be enjoying one another's company and it made her feel that all was right with the world, a feeling Spirit seldom had. Any sense of control she might have once had where she made choices in her life and those choices actually happened — like moving to the commune, becoming a potter, having children — was wrenched from her grasp when Freedom Man left. After that there was very little she could control. She suddenly had fewer choices and more imperatives. The kids were growing up fast and the things they wanted or needed were more expensive than the things of childhood. For the next decade, Spirit's life was all about paying the bills, maintaining, and barely keeping up. Then, before she knew it, the kids were gone and she was middle-aged and alone. When she looked around her empty house, she wondered if this was an ending or a beginning. Or both. It was certainly the end of life as she had known it, and she had to convince herself that this wasn't a bad thing. She told herself that in every ending there were the seeds of something new. That "something new" became a more innovative approach to her pottery. Instead of the usual money-makers — coffee mugs, teapots, butter dishes, and serving platters — Spirit started experimenting. She created objects that had no function other than to be beautiful to look at. You could serve cookies on some of the flatter pieces, or put a bunch of flowers into something that would hold water, but Spirit's primary motivation became the creation of form over function. There were plenty of coffee mugs in the world but there could never be too many beautiful objects. It pleased her that two of her children were pursuing a life in art, Maris as a painter and Ra as a photographer. She had tried to teach them the value of self-expression, but only if they had something to say. True art, Spirit believed, was about ideas. And ideas came from watching, listening, learning, and experimenting. Only time would tell if either or both of them would leave their mark.

The usual family skirmish came the next morning after breakfast. In terms of past history, when all three children would get into a shouting match over who was right about something stupid (like whose turn it was to mop the floor), this was a minor conflict, and it occurred when Terra decided Ray wasn't doing his share.

"Have you even so much as lifted a dishtowel since you've been here?" Terra shot at Ray.

"Um, I don't think so, Terr," said Ra in even tones, so as not to appear hostile in any way, "but I believe I have been helpful in other ways." He recognized that tone in Terra's voice. It was like a flashback to the time that was before. The time when they all lived together and Terra was the one who was totally committed to the notion that everyone should pitch in on an equal basis, equality being measured and determined by her alone, it seemed.

"And what other ways would that be?" said Terra.

"Well … I distinctly remember carrying something into the kitchen last night after dinner. It was … wait, it'll come to me … it was … a dinner plate. Yes, definitely a dinner plate. Probably mine. And I'm pretty sure I brought in the cutlery, too."

"You are impossible," said Terra. "Mom, tell him he's impossible. Did you know that you raised a male chauvinist pig for a son?" Terra's anger was escalating as her vocabulary became more aggressive.

"Whoa, hold on there, Terr," said Ray. "How did I get to be a male chauvinist pig all of a sudden? I mean, I'll accept pig, as in slob. I'll even accept filthy pig or lazy pig. But chauvinist?" He looked at Maris and his nieces. "Come on, help me out here, girls. Is Uncle Ray a chauvinist pig?"

"What's a chauvinist pig?" asked Emma.

Terra said, "A male chauvinist pig is a man who thinks men are superior to women, and that housework is beneath him because it is women's work."

Emma and Alison grimaced in a teenage-girl way to indicate they were really not keen on entering the fray.

Maris, on the other hand, was eager to put in her two cents' worth. This was going to be fun.

"I agree with you, Terr. I think Ra Baby has been a closeted chauvinist for well over two decades. I saw it when he was a teenager when he refused even to put his dirty underwear in the washing machine — hell, he wouldn't even put them in the hamper. Expected his mother to pick up after him." She folded her arms in front of her chest, the exact stance Terra had taken.

Josh, a man of few words, was standing a few feet away from Ray.

"You're busted, buddy. No way you can win this one."

Terra shot him a look that said, "Back off, Josh," so he did. He, like the teenage Ray, lived in a household of females. Outnumbered is outnumbered.

Spirit listened to her name being bounced around and her mothering skills being maligned and couldn't decide whether she should speak or not. Her only stand was a defensive one, since she'd, in effect, been accused of being a bad mother. Was this fight worth undertaking? Should she defend Ra, who actually hadn't lifted a finger all weekend, or should she just let it fizzle out? Engagement would lead to escalation, no doubt in her mind. And Terra was clearly annoyed, although Maris appeared to be having fun jibing at her hapless brother.

It was Ray's turn to respond and he was choosing his words carefully because he knew he was, as Josh had said, busted. He had avoided all of the domestic chores that went with a weekend of cooking, eating, and drinking, figuring there were enough women to do the work, and the women, after all, would do the work because they thought it was important. Ray didn't care if the dishes got done or not. That was the tricky part. Was this an issue of duty, responsibility, being a good person, or not giving a shit? Should he just apologize and do some dishes or sweep the floor? Or should he call Terra on her obsessive and skewed sense of justice? *Remember*, he told himself, *you're outnumbered on the gender front. If it comes down to a pitched battle, the women and girls will gang up on you. Of that there is no doubt.*

He looked at Maris. Her face said, "You are so dead." He looked at Spirit. Her face said, "You're my son and I love you, but Terra has a point. You're a lazy pig and you always were." Alison and Emma were a united front: "Ray," they seemed to say, "you're our favourite uncle and we think you're cool, but chauvinist pigs are the enemy." That left Terra, the scary one. Her expression said, "I cannot think of anything that will redeem you at this point. So whatever you say or do right now will probably determine your fate forever." *I'm dead*, thought Ray. Silence filled the room like mist in a horror movie.

"Gee, Terra," Ray finally spoke. Terra raised her eyebrows in expectation. Everybody else watched; a few held their breath. "I was going to surprise you, but I guess I'll have to let the cat out of the bag. Sorry, Josh," he said, giving his brother-in-law a look that was both penitent and pleading. "Got no choice." He turned back to Terra. "Josh and I are making lunch. Right, Josh?" he said, nodding his head up and down. Josh nodded his head up and down.

"Affirmative," Josh said. "We planned it a week ago. Wanted to surprise you."

Terra looked at her brother and her husband. "Great," she said, her voice neutral. "What are we having? Beer and chips?"

Ray and Josh laughed, relief audible in their voices. "Yeah," said Ray. "Among other things. I told you it was a surprise."

"I'll bet," said Terra. "And I'm sure you and Josh are just as surprised as the rest of us."

"Okay," said Ray, rubbing his hands together in a let's-get-down-to-business gesture. "Me and Josh are just going to pop down to Safeway to grab a few things. Anything you need, Mom? Dishwashing liquid, instant mashed potatoes?"

"Go," said Spirit. "Go now."

"Right," said Ray. "We'll be back in a jiff. Call me on my cell if you think of anything." He and Josh backed out of the room, smiling and waving. When they finally heard the car start, all five females started to laugh.

Sunday lunch was hot dogs on the barbecue, with lots of bright yellow mustard and fluorescent green relish. There were chips and nachos, deli potato salad and dill pickles, beer and pop, chocolate brownies, and rocky road ice cream. And all of it was served outside on paper plates with plastic forks and knives. Spirit held her tongue and Terra realized she couldn't remember the last time her family had had so much fun. Mustard stains be damned; it was worth it. Maris ate three hot dogs, drank three beers, and thanked Ray and Josh for the exquisite meal. She felt good. And she still had room for brownies and ice cream.

When the meal was over, Josh and Ray cleaned up. Everything went into a big green garbage bag, which they stuffed into Spirit's trash can, but not before she made them separate the beer bottles and plastic utensils for recycling.

Terra, Josh, Ray, and the girls headed back to the city at five o'clock, and Maris and Spirit opened a chilled bottle of late harvest Riesling from the Okanagan Valley.

"This is nice," said Maris.

"And well-earned," Spirit sighed. "What a weekend."

"Yeah," said Maris. "It had everything: lots of good food, lots of fun, a little bit of tension to spice it up, and a fine finish."

Spirit laughed. "If you can call hot dogs on paper plates a fine finish."

"Well, I think we can," said Maris. "After all, we didn't have to lift a finger."

"That's true," said Spirit. "But I'll have to drop that green garbage bag full of toxic waste at the dump in the dead of night." She took a sip of wine. "My own son," she said. "Where did I go so wrong?"

Maris laughed. "Nobody's perfect, Mom. Not even your children."

"I'm not asking for perfection, Maris, but how about …" She tilted her head in thought. "Is there even a word for what I want?"

Maris looked at her mother and shook her head.

"Do you think Ra will ever find someone?" Spirit asked. "I worry so much about the two of you. Being alone. Maybe not having children."

Maris thought, *I really don't want to have that conversation right now.* "I'm not going there tonight, Spirit," she said.

"Okay. Maybe another time."

"Yeah. Another time."

CHAPTER FIFTEEN

Instead, they talked about Peter. As they drank the wine, Maris thought about how he would have liked it. He would have said it was aromatic, expressing ripe pear and apple flavours. He would talk about the structure and texture and the finish, and she would agree with him, taking it in and remembering it for next time. She was always learning from Peter, and now that he was gone, she felt unfinished. Where was she ever going to find that other half of herself?

She told Spirit about the first time she met Peter. She had walked into the gallery on Stamford Road and immediately known she was in a special place. "That gallery was Peter and Peter was the gallery," she said. "He had such an eye for detail. And he knew exactly where to put things, and how far apart to space them. He gave you just the right amount of time to walk out of one headspace and into another. He just knew. He knew how to maximize a natural light source and he knew how to present a piece from all angles. He was a genius in his own way."

She told Spirit about the time a wealthy Chinese woman had come into the shop. "She told Peter she wanted to see the 'best piece in the gallery.' Peter told her everything in the gallery was the best. Did that mean she wanted to buy everything he had?" Maris chuckled as she remembered the episode. "Needless to say, she was not amused by what she considered Peter's mocking tone, and told him he would quickly go out of business if he wasn't more respectful of his customers' wishes. Peter knew exactly what he was dealing with — he'd seen every kind of customer in Singapore — and suggested that he visit the woman in her home so he could best advise her which pieces to buy. Well, to make a long story short, she agreed and he ended up selling her a lot of stuff over the years. She became one of his most loyal clients and sent all of her wealthy friends to him, too. He was amazing."

"Were you in love with him?" asked Spirit.

"No," said Maris. "It was nothing like that. But I loved him and respected him for who he was. And I trusted him, too, I guess, which is why when he told me I was a good painter, I became more confident and bolder in my work." Maris wondered once again what she would do without Peter's support and advice. "Peter always told the truth," she said. "But he didn't fling it at you like he was a know-it-all and you should listen to him. And truth can be relative, subjective, and situational, all at once. He had a way of somehow getting you to see for yourself that what he said made sense." She laughed. "I'm making him sound like some kind of televangelist preacher, but he was definitely not a preacher. Maybe that was his secret. He never insisted or forced an issue; he just kind of gently led you in the right direction and let you see for yourself."

"He sounds like a rare individual," said Spirit.

"I think he was," said Maris. "I think I'm a different person for having known him. I don't think I would have found my own way without him."

"You don't give yourself enough credit," said Spirit. "You were the one who got on that plane and went to Singapore. At the time I thought you were being a little impulsive, but it ended up being the best thing you could have done."

"Well, it was that proverbial fork-in-the-road thing for me." Maris poured the rest of the Riesling into their glasses. She laughed.

"What's so funny?" asked Spirit.

"I just thought of that old joke. You know, 'If you come to a fork in the road, take it.' Well, I took it."

Spirit laughed. "Of course, that begs the question of the road not taken. Who knows what might have happened if you hadn't gotten on that plane. Or if I hadn't met your father and if he hadn't left me. And on, and on."

Maris thought for a moment. "I think my world, my life, would have been smaller if I hadn't gone to Singapore," she said. "It got me out of myself, if you know what I mean." Spirit nodded. "It kind of put my ideas on a spectrum, so that I could examine them in a larger context. Before, I would be kind of blinkered when I got an idea. I wouldn't question myself or my thinking so much. I'd just say, 'That's an interesting idea.' But now I say, 'That's an idea worth exploring.'" She sipped her wine and, when Spirit didn't say anything, she continued. "Maybe I would have grown into that way of thinking in time, with experience, but I guess I accelerated the process in a way and made a giant leap. Am I sounding pretentious?"

Spirit smiled. "No, not pretentious. Maybe just a little bit wise." She raised her glass to Maris in a kind of salute. "I think it's time to open another bottle, don't you?"

"I'm on it," said Maris. "And maybe a little snack, too." She returned in a few minutes with another bottle of Riesling and a tray with all the odds and ends from the weekend — a chunk of lasagna warmed up in the microwave, a couple of slices of salmon, some cheese, olives, and assorted crackers, and the last slice of peach pie.

"I can't believe I'm hungry again," said Spirit, digging into the lasagna.

"It happens," said Maris, "like clockwork." She slathered some creamy French brie onto a cracker.

"I've been thinking about what you said," Spirit mumbled through a mouthful of food, "about accelerating the process. I had a fork in the road, too. In fact I had a couple of them. One was when your father walked out on me, and the other was when all three of you were gone and I became an empty nester. Except, when I compare my life to yours, I can see that you were much more proactive in your choices. I was directed more by forces outside of myself. I had to make changes kind of against my will. I mean, I didn't want things to change, but they did. And once Humpty Dumpty breaks into a thousand pieces, nothing can put him back together again. I had no choice but to move forward."

"Yes," said Maris, "but we were both desperate in a way."

"What do you mean by desperate?"

"Well, we were both caught in circumstances that we knew we had to get out of. I was trapped in a kind of stasis — kind of like I am now, if you think about it — and you were faced with situations maybe not of your making but that you found unbearable or, at least, not to your liking."

Spirit laughed. "Not to my liking. That's good. I'll have to remember that."

"Maybe it's the wine talking," said Maris.

"Very smart and articulate wine, I must say."

"Anyway, I think it's about survival. Call it survival of the soul, if I'm going to be high-minded. Somewhere we both had instincts that told us our very survival was at stake."

"That certainly sounds desperate. I don't think I would have thought so at the time, but looking back, maybe it's true. But it wasn't just my survival or my soul I had to think about. I had responsibilities. At least, I did when your father left."

"Yes, and I can't imagine what that's like. I've never had any responsibilities other than to myself. It's a kind of freedom, I guess, but — what was it you said about me? — that I was untethered?" Spirit nodded. "Well, I don't think anyone really wants to be untethered. I think of it as an astronaut on a space walk coming unhooked from the mother ship and being sucked into the void or a black hole. Everybody needs to be connected to something."

"Or someone," said Spirit.

"Hmmm," said Maris. "I'm not sure that's possible. Those kinds of connections break all the time. You can't count on someone else to keep you grounded."

"Maybe that's where I went wrong," said Spirit. "I attached myself to someone called Freedom Man and thought that was all I needed. I think if I hadn't had you three children when he left, I might have become seriously untethered."

"Now you're underestimating yourself," Maris said, sliding her fork under a piece of salmon. "You have a very powerful belief system that involves how people should treat one another, what constitutes art and beauty, a commitment to nature and the environment — except for that stupid car, of course — and a real set of priorities that are very clear to you and always have been."

"Yes, it's true," said Spirit. "And I've never lost sight of those things, no matter how bad things got. Although there's always the argument that I held onto those things so fiercely just to spite your father and make him see himself as the narrow-minded weasel he really was. And is."

"That could very well be true," said Maris, smiling. "And it's probably why you hang onto that damned Taurus, too. Just to rub it in his face. I'm sure he loses sleep over it. Not."

Spirit laughed. "I know, I know," she said. "But nobody's perfect."

"No, but this peach pie sure is," said Maris.

"It took me years to perfect it."

"No, it didn't. Your peach pie was always incredible."

"It helps to be so close to the Okanagan Valley, plus my mother made fabulous pies. Let me know if you're ever interested, and I'll pass on some secrets to you."

"Better write them down," said Maris. "I can't see myself baking pies any time soon."

The next morning over granola, Maris told Spirit about

her life in Singapore. Once you adjust to the extreme heat and humidity, she said, there's lots to see and do.

"A few of the traditions are being preserved, almost like tourist sites or museum pieces, but a lot of things are being sacrificed in the name of so-called progress, which means the pursuit of expensive stuff — cars, designer fashions, stainless steel appliances, whatever money can buy." Maris got up to pour them some more coffee. "After World War II," she continued, "Singapore was still part of Malaya and was very poor. Now it's one of the richest countries in the world. In fifty years, it built itself up into a well-organized free-market economy, but it's also a kind of authoritarian state. It's a lot like Canada in the sense that the state provides a lot for its citizens, but in Singapore there are serious penalties for almost everything. Like spitting in the street and chewing gum, if you can believe it, and minor traffic violations. And they're enforced. Do you remember reading about that American kid who got a caning for spray-painting graffiti on cars?" Spirit nodded. "Plus he was fined and sentenced to four months in jail. He denied he did it but that he'd confessed because he thought they'd go easier on him.

"Singapore is a very organized place. Living there is like defragging your brain every day."

Spirit put up her hand to stop Maris. "Like what?" she said.

Maris laughed. "Oh, I forgot. You're still living in a pre-technology world." She thought for a minute. "A computer stores data in a kind of grid. Think of it as a honeycomb. As the little wells randomly get filled up with honey, the bees have to search for empty ones here and there. When you defrag your computer, it takes all the filled pieces of the grid and lines them up in an orderly fashion, so that the empty ones are then joined up and easier for the computer to find. When you're in Singapore, everything is so well-ordered that it feels like your brain cells are also realigned to work more efficiently. It's only when you leave that you realize that chaos does not exist in Singapore. It's not allowed."

"How can that be a good place for an artist to live and create?" Spirit asked. "I mean, it sounds a bit sterile."

"It is," said Maris, "but it's still Asia, which means there are lots of exciting and exotic things bubbling under the surface. It's colourful. Never drab. Nature is all-consuming and relentless, as it can only be in a hot, tropical country. If you let your guard down for a minute, you will be overwhelmed by heat and bugs and vegetation. Orderliness is almost part of the culture now, but there are still enough rogue elements around — like superstition, outside influences, New Age religion — to threaten it. Think of the legs of a table. If one of them is hollow or warps, well, the table becomes unstable." They both laughed.

"Now that definitely is not the wine talking," said Spirit. "And I did not put anything psychedelic into the granola."

"Stop," said Maris, in a fit of giggles. "I feel a rhyming couplet coming on."

"Oh, no," groaned Spirit. "You mean like, 'There once was a lady from London ...'"

"Whose clothing was always coming undone ..."

"She went to a tailor, who she hoped wouldn't fail her ..."

"And said, 'Please fix this because it is no fun.'" Maris couldn't remember the last time she'd laughed so hard. And over something so stupid.

"I think," said Spirit, after she'd stopped laughing, "if I'm not mistaken, that was a limerick."

"Indeed it was," said Maris. "And a damn fine one, too."

"We've definitely had either too much granola or too much coffee."

"It's the granola. Waaaay too healthy. And what are those little green crunchy things?"

"That's dry-roasted edamame. Soybeans. I'm surprised you haven't had them before, living in Asia."

"So that's what those things are. I always wondered but I never tried them. They sell them as snack food."

"Right. And you can buy them fresh and steam them, too. Loaded with protein. I've got some in the freezer. We can have them later. They're great with a bottle of beer."

"Well, you sold me. And just when you had me believing you were stuck in the twentieth century."

"Hey," said Spirit. "I do my best."

CHAPTER SIXTEEN

maris_cousins@yahoo.com
To: dinahstone@hotmail.com
Cc:
Subject: Update from Canada

Hi Dinah,
Just thought I'd touch base. I'm still at my
mother's and we've just had a family weekend.
It's amazing how little has changed since I left.
Most things are about the same, only a little more
so, if you know what I mean. Which reminds me,
I'll have to talk to my mother about sending you
some of her pottery. She's doing some incredible
stuff. I'd buy it!

Still not painting, although I'm working in black and white, sketching mostly, and it might lead somewhere.

I've been telling my mother about living in Singapore and now I miss the place. Especially the food! Remember all those wonderful lunches you and Peter and I used to have at Lau Pa Sat market? God, I love that place. Not just all the fantastic hawker food, but the beautiful structure itself, all that gorgeous Victorian filigree ironwork. They don't build them like that anymore, unfortunately. Right now, I'd give anything for some wonton mee or some char kway teow. Mind you, we had some pretty good food here over the weekend, including a mess of hot dogs my brother and brother-in-law cooked up on the barbecue. You can't beat a good hot dog with mustard and relish.

All this talk of food just reminded me — we never cleaned out Peter's fridge. Oh well, I guess someone else got to do it.

Let me know how you're doing. I miss you.

Love,

Maris

---

dinahstone@hotmail.com
To: maris_cousins@yahoo.com
Cc:
Subject: Re: Update from Canada

Hi, Maris,

I cleaned out the fridge. I went over one day by myself because I knew you wouldn't be able to handle looking at that fish. I have to admit, it was harder than I thought it would be. The last supper that never was.

Angela is driving me crazy. She calls a minimum of twelve times a week. And she never even asks how I am. Just starts right in with her "requests," which we both know are not requests but orders. Sometimes I have to bite my tongue because I want to just swear at her and call her names. One of these days I just might. And then you'll be meeting me at Vancouver airport and putting me up in the spare room! I'm looking forward to meeting your mother and the rest of your family … just kidding (about swearing at Angela, not about your family).

Business has actually been pretty good, although a lot of people have come by just to ask about Peter. Still no results from the investigation. I just can't imagine who would have done this to Peter. He really didn't have an enemy in the world. I miss him a lot. And I miss you, too, Maris. Any chance of your coming back to Singapore? I'll buy the hawker food for a year — anything you want!
Love,
Dinah

maris_cousins@yahoo.com
To: dinahstone@hotmail.com
CC:
Subject: Re: Update from Canada

D.
Ooooh, tempting. But you'll have to give me a job.
No tickee, no washee. Remember?
M.

To: maris_cousins@yahoo.com
CC:
Subject: Re: Update from Canada

M.
You're hired!
D.
:-)

Chapter Seventeen

Annabelle found rooms for them over a silk shop on Desker Road off Jalan Besar. It wasn't much, but it would do. Two rooms: one for sleeping and the other for cooking and eating. The second room had a solid wooden table and chairs that Francis could use for writing. And there were two wood and rattan chairs for sitting and reading or thinking. Annabelle was happy because it was theirs, hers and Francis's. Their first home.

Sutty helped them move the few things they had by rickshaw. Then Annabelle made tea and served cakes she had purchased from a little bakery two blocks over. She had discovered a shop that sold dry goods, and another that sold hardware items like brooms and buckets. In time she would find a morning market where she could get fresh vegetables and fruits in season and another where she could buy meat, although she made sure to get there early while it was at its freshest and before too many flies found it. *As long as I cook it well*, she thought, *it will be fine*. After all, the meat she got at the butcher's in London wasn't that much more appealing just because there was a roof on the shop and a door that was usually, but not always closed.

Francis had been perfectly happy living at the Raffles, but he knew Annabelle was right, that it was too expensive and they could live much more cheaply in rooms of their own. And once they had moved, he could see that she was much happier in her own little nest, even though it was shabby and less than attractive on first sight. But she had scrubbed and rubbed and wiped away other people's dirt and the marks on the walls, and it suddenly had appeared a lot brighter. "It won't even need a coat of paint," she said, admiring the results of her hard work. "A saving right there."

"You're a gem," said Francis, taking her in his arms. "I married the best wife a man could have." He'd almost said "poor man" but caught himself in time. No point in shining a light on that. Annabelle was frugal enough for both of them, and if anybody could make their money last five years, she could. If she hadn't come to Singapore and married him, Francis knew the money would have been gone much sooner. He would have stayed at the Raffles, eating and drinking there, no doubt, and squandering his savings on things a married man could do without.

Life soon settled into a comfortable routine with Annabelle doing the marketing in the morning then the washing and cooking, and Francis sitting at his kitchen desk, pen in hand, blank page waiting for his imprint.

They ate a lot of boiled cabbage with onions and salt, and sometimes a bit of bacon or sausage and boiled eggs, which were always fresh because the shells still had bits of wet chicken dirt stuck to them. Annabelle had no idea how to cook some of the exotic vegetables she saw in the market. They were mostly green and leafy, but like nothing she'd ever seen before. There was also lots of garlic and ginger, and about a dozen different kinds of peppers that she dared not try because she was pretty sure they were all chili peppers of some sort or other. If the butcher had mutton bones or chicken backs and necks, she would make a pot of soup, splurging on a potato and a carrot to go with the cabbage and onions.

Every Sunday Sutty invited them to the hotel for dinner and they gladly accepted. He made it quite plain that he invited them for the company, and that since they were struggling and he was not, it was a good deal all round. He made sure they had plenty of roast beef with gravy, Yorkshire pudding, potatoes, and custard or trifle for dessert. And whatever was left over, he insisted the kitchen pack it up for them to take home. He would hear no protest from either of them. He insisted, saying that when Francis was a successful writer with an income to match, they would not only have to feed him every week, but let him come for tea whenever he wanted. It wasn't charity he was offering them, but a helping hand from a friend while the road was bumpy.

"And you shall name your first-born after me," he said, jokingly.

"What?" said Francis, feigning horror. "Edward Sutcliffe Stone? Sounds like something out of *Wuthering Heights*."

"Yes, it does, doesn't it?" said Sutty. "Well, all right, then. I'll settle for Edward. He must be Edward something or something Edward. That's fair."

"Francis Edward," said Annabelle. "Francis Edward Stone. It has a certain dignity, don't you think?"

"Indeed," said Sutty. "It does."

"Done," said Francis. "He shall be Francis Edward." And they all laughed.

In 1819, an official with the East India Company, Sir Thomas Stamford Raffles, bought the island of Singapore from the Sultan of Johor. It was almost two hundred and seventy square miles of swamp and forest but it provided a natural harbour in a strategic position for English merchants travelling to and from India, Australia, and China. At the time, it was nothing but a fishing village on the south end of the island on what would become the Singapore River, peopled by less than two hundred Orang Laut, ethnic Malay "sea gypsies" who plied the coastal waters of the Malay Archipelago and more often lived on boats than on land.

That had been more than a hundred years before Francis, Annabelle, and Sutty came to the island, and in that time, Singapore's growth had been haphazard. Living conditions ranged from the basic shanties of the very poor to opulent homes of the wealthy, mostly Chinese and British. In between were the shophouses with their five-foot overhangs that allowed one to walk shaded from the scorching sun and protected from the monsoon rains. Sir Stamford Raffles had decreed that these buildings be made of brick to reduce the risk of fire. Raffles had also decreed that the plan of the town be divided along ethnic lines, which created a Chinatown, Kampong Glam for the Malays, and Kampong Chulia for Indian immigrants, of which there would be many. By the 1920s, the population of Singapore, in all its ethnicities, had grown in leaps and bounds through both immigration and rising birth rates. The colony that Francis, Annabelle, and Sutty inhabited was now a busy, congested place. Its English rulers occupied the area north of the Singapore River known as the Colonial District, which also included the neoclassical-styled Parliament House, Town Hall, and the Victoria Concert Hall. Adjoining these was the Padang, the grassy playing field where cricket had been played for a century by young men in the service of government and commerce.

For Annabelle and Francis, just walking through the colonial district on a Sunday morning after church and before they met Sutty for their once-a-week meal, was the most peaceful and serene part of their week. They would attend services at St. Andrew's and then take a leisurely walk over to the Padang to see what games were up. Then they might walk down to the river, past the concert hall and Parliament House, and take a boat ride from the site where Sir Stamford Raffles had first landed in Singapore, appropriately known as Raffles Landing.

Sometimes they splurged on a rickshaw and rode out to Goodwood Hill where the well-heeled — colonial officials and important businessmen and their families — lived in stylish "black and whites," Tudor-style bungalows on a quiet, tree-lined street that Annabelle loved to imagine herself in. "Elegant," she would say to Francis.

And she meant not only the stately homes, but also the people who inhabited them. She could only dream of such a life, and so she did. Dreams were free, after all.

Three months after she married Francis, Annabelle began to feel tired and ill, especially in the morning. Even the thought of a piece of bread or a cup of tea before nine o'clock made her nauseous. At first, she feared the worst, but there was no fever accompanying her other symptoms, so she began to think she might be pregnant. She kept her suspicion to herself, however, because she didn't think Francis was ready to think about having a baby. She would have to wait a while before telling him, and she hoped she would know the right moment to do so. In the meantime, she blamed the heat when he asked if she was feeling ill, because she often looked quite pale. But, luckily, Francis was absorbed in his work and often didn't notice if she didn't eat in the morning or took a nap in the afternoon.

The prospect of having a baby in Singapore did not appeal to Annabelle. In fact, it terrified her. Was there a hospital nearby with a doctor who spoke English? Would they be able to afford to go to a proper hospital where the doctors not only spoke English but *were* English? Maybe she would ask the vicar's wife when the time came. *Plenty of time for that*, she thought. At least seven months, she was pretty sure: Time for her to get used to the idea; time for her to figure out when and how to tell Francis.

The Phantom Sophie

A Short Story

by

E. Sutcliffe Moresby

C.K. Manners was a writer of some repute, known mainly for his short stories and a few well-crafted novels. But nothing he wrote ever paralleled the events of his own remarkable life. Born into a well-to-do barrister's family, he was raised mostly by nannies and tutors, but the dominant figure in C.K.'s life was without a doubt his mother, Emmaline. A stern, intelligent woman, who grew up during the heart of Queen Victoria's reign, Emmaline loved her only son with the ferocity of a lioness and communicated that love in the only way she knew how: by noting and criticizing his every mistake so that he would become the person she believed he was capable of becoming. When he chose to roam the world and write stories about what he saw and the extraordinary characters he met and consorted with instead of following in his father's footsteps, Emmaline was faced with a difficult choice. She could either reject him as a failure or accept him for what he had become: a man who made up stories for a living. She chose the latter and became his most valued and demanding critic. She would not allow so much as a misplaced comma to go unattended.

C.K. was often away for months at a time, usually on a sea voyage on some kind of rusty old tub that carried freight and that took him to parts of the world Emmaline preferred not to think about. Judging from his stories, he encountered the kind of people she would not want to keep company with, the kind who frequently made her fear for her only son's safety. C.K. kept up a steady correspondence with his mother, but luckily his letters arrived long after his latest adventure had ended and she could only sigh with relief that he had survived.

She didn't mind so much when he went to Europe, say, Italy, France, or Spain, though she never failed to warn him about everything from the food to the water to the toilets. But when he went to the Far East — usually for months at a time, with nothing but a valise and a bag of books — she despaired. There was nothing to be done but wait and worry. This was where the real degenerates went: the merchant sailors, the remittance men, the dancing girls and prostitutes who had lost their appeal. At least, according to his stories, those were the unsavoury types who ended up in the jungles of Malaya and Burma and Thailand.

So when C.K. arrived home one day after a long sojourn in the East, carrying a child in his arms, Emmaline did not know what to think. The baby, a boy, was no more than one year old. His skin was white, thank God, but who was his mother? And was C.K. his father? What on earth had he been up to?

"Charles Kenneth," she said, "you need to explain this."

"I know, Mother," he replied. "And there is an explanation. But it's a long story."

"Begin at the beginning," she said. "I'm all ears."

The child was the unfortunate offspring of a writer of C.K.'s acquaintance, who had died rather suddenly in Singapore. He had been set upon by thugs one night, during one of his "thinking" walks. He liked to wander the streets after dark on those nights when he had trouble sleeping. Unfortunately, he occasionally strayed onto those back streets where derelicts and undesirables went to find a scrap to eat and a corner to sleep in. He was less than a mile from home when the thieves struck. The sad thing was that he had less than the equivalent of half a pound on him at the time of his death. Being a writer, he was a poor man, not the wealthy planter the thieves took him for. His wife was three months pregnant at the time of his death, and it drove her mad, losing him like that. When C.K. tried to take her away, she had refused to leave Singapore, even though she hated the place.

"You see," C.K. told his mother, "I think the balance of her mind was affected. She couldn't bear to stay but she couldn't bear to go. She believed her husband's soul was still in Singapore and she could not bring herself to leave him behind."

C.K. gazed at the child while he spoke of its mother. He was a beautiful boy with a head of soft, curly, flaxen hair, bright eyes the colour of a summer sky, and skin as smooth as fresh cream.

"Six months after Alexander's death, Sophie gave birth to her son, and named me godfather. We had always joked, the three of us, that they would name their first-born after me because I had been like an older brother to both of them." He smiled, remembering the good times and conversations they had shared over a meal that C.K. usually insisted on paying for. "You shall name your first-born after me," he'd told them. "You will be giving me the gift of immortality. That's thanks enough for me." When the baby was born, Sophie had kept their promise. The boy was named Alexander for his dead father, and Charles for his godfather.

Alexander Charles made a sound like water flushing through a drainpipe. It was his happy sound, C.K. explained to his mother. He was a happy child, despite the tragedy of his beginnings.

"When Alec was killed," C.K. told his mother, "I stayed on in Singapore and called on Sophie every day. She had very little money and I usually stopped at the market and bought fruit and vegetables for her, and tea and biscuits from a shop run by an Englishman who knew Sophie's story and often added a few extras to the order, like a tin of beef or a small jar of jam. 'Can't you get her to go back to England?' he'd ask me, almost every day. 'I'm trying,' I'd say, 'but she won't have it. She insists Alec would want her to stay.' We agreed it didn't make any sense, but it wasn't as if we could bundle her into a steamer trunk and put her on a ship against her will.

"After Alexander was born," C.K. continued, "Sophie seemed to lose whatever fortitude she had, both physical and mental. It was as if she had put everything she had into this child giving him life, and there was nothing left over for her. She was as thin as a sapling, while he was robust and strong. I know she loved the boy with all her heart, but he reminded her daily of her beloved husband who had not lived to see his child born, and her grief seemed only to intensify.

"I didn't know what to do," he said. "I could only stand by and watch events unfold. I felt as useless as I've ever felt in my life."

Emmaline reached out and patted her son's arm. He was a sensitive man, and she realized that he would not have succeeded had he become a barrister. He would have wanted to compensate every victim by reaching into his own pocket. His heart would have broken on a regular basis as he witnessed injustice, cruelty, and evil.

"How very sad," she murmured, wondering what was to become of this beautiful, unfortunate child.

"I lived in constant fear that something terrible would happen to her or the child, or both of them. She was determined to raise him herself in an alien land with few friends and little money. Such was the condition of her mind that she thought it was possible to do so. I contacted her landlord and arranged to pay the rent every month, and I left money in a jar every now and then, so she would find it and think she had put it there. I didn't want her to think it was charity. Luckily, young Alexander flourished, in spite of everything that might predict the opposite. Sometimes I took him to the park for the afternoon so Sophie could have a sleep — she was always too afraid to sleep at night after her husband's murder. Is it any wonder? She had terrible nightmares and would often sit up all night watching over the child.

"Then one day I went over to take her and Alexander out for lunch, and she wasn't there. The boy was in his crib and, luckily, had not climbed out. He's a placid, good-natured child and he was happily playing with a pile of wooden blocks I had given him. I searched the rooms again — there were only two — and my heart sank as I realized she was definitely not there. I would rather have found her in a dead faint than not at all. Where could she be?

"I ran downstairs to the bookshop below and asked if anyone had seen her. They had not. By then I was frantically worried. She would never leave Alexander on his own. I was certain of that. But clearly something had taken her away. Had she been gone five minutes or an hour? No way of knowing. The baby's nappy was dry, so I assumed she hadn't been gone that long. I went back up and got

Alexander and went back outside to look for Sophie. 'But which way to go?' I asked myself. Left or right?

"I chose right simply because it was the direction to the cemetery and I thought maybe she had got a notion to visit Alec's grave. She did that frequently, but she always took the boy with her. I didn't really think she'd gone there, but I had no other ideas."

At this point, Alexander started to speak, rhythmically repeating one word, "MumMumMum," as if he knew his mother was being talked about. C.K. smiled at him with affection, but the smile fell from his lips as he remembered what had happened.

"She wasn't at the cemetery, although there were fresh flowers on Alec's grave, so I knew she had been there recently. Then I just started wandering, with Alexander in my arms, hoping I would see her on the street somewhere. Eventually, I hailed a rickshaw and told him to drive up and down the narrow streets of Chinatown and Little India, hoping against hope she would be there for some unimaginable reason. Finally, as it began to get dark, I took Alexander back to the rooms over the bookshop, thinking that if she had returned, she must be worried sick to discover him gone. I realized the poor little fellow hadn't eaten a thing all day. He was getting cranky — and rightly so. We stopped and had some soup and rice, which I couldn't feed him fast enough, and then proceeded back to Sophie's rooms. We arrived there by about seven o'clock. But she wasn't there."

C.K. stopped talking at this point, and Emmaline saw that there were tears in his eyes. She dreaded hearing the rest of the story because she knew what he was going to tell her.

"Why don't we have tea," she said in as gentle a voice as she could muster. "I'm sure little Alexander is hungry. I'll just go and tell Jane to fix us something."

C.K. nodded and took the boy in his arms. He tried to get Alec to sit on his lap, but the child was too interested in his new surroundings to sit still for long. He preferred to climb on the furniture that C.K. himself had climbed on as a child. The chairs were high and well stuffed, which made them great fun to climb on top of or hide underneath.

When Emmaline returned, she noted that Charles's eyes were red, and she wondered just how fond of this Sophie person he had been. As a boy, he had cried easily, and his father had frequently scolded him, telling him he was behaving like a baby, or worse, a girl. Emmaline tried not to interfere, but it distressed her to see that as her son grew, he developed a stammer when in the presence of his father. Finally she insisted that he leave the boy alone and not be so hard on him. Emmaline didn't know anything about psychology, but she knew cause and effect when she saw it. Charles responded better to kindness.

They had their tea and the boy drank warm milk with honey. C.K. was patient and gentle with the child, and Alexander appeared to be very fond of him. Charles resumed his story.

"I didn't find her," he said, his voice heavy with sorrow. "I searched for a week. I even went to the police, but they had no record of finding a woman of Sophie's description. Nor of her body." Again, he wiped the tears from his eyes.

"And so, finally, after a month, I decided to come home. I brought Alexander with me because there seemed no other choice. He is my godson, after all." Alexander looked up at the mention of his name and smiled at C.K., who smiled back and said, "Aren't you, my boy?"

Emmaline sighed. Then she smiled. "I was beginning to think I'd never be a grandmother."

The boy grew and flourished. He had been too young to remember his mother, and loved his godfather and his grandmother as the only family he knew. He was the centre of their lives and when he went away to school, they missed him and couldn't wait for his return.

C.K. returned to Singapore four times over the next ten years. Each time he searched for Sophie, hoping against hope he would find her. The first time, he could find no trace of her. He asked shopkeepers and people passing by on the street, showing a small photograph of her that had belonged to Alec. After a few months, he gave up, leaving money with the manager of the Raffles Hotel, a friend of his, with the instruction to give it to her if she should return. And to tell her that her son was safe and well in England with his godfather.

The second trip, he scoured the streets of Chinatown because he heard that an Englishwoman had been seen from time to time among the Chinese prostitutes. No one knew her name, only that she was small and thin, and sometimes drew pictures of the prostitutes. But still he could not find her.

On the third trip, he went back to Chinatown and searched again. He heard further reports of the Englishwoman who painted pictures of the Chinese prostitutes, but none of the women he talked to could tell him anything. Or wouldn't. He wasn't sure. They seemed reticent, as if they were protecting something, or someone. Because he wanted to believe she was alive, he convinced himself that this, indeed, must be Sophie.

Finally, on his fourth trip to Singapore, he found one of the paintings. It was in a small gallery and had been purchased by the gallery owner from a young Chinese woman, the subject of the painting. He told C.K. he thought she was a drug addict and needed the money. The picture was a portrait of despondency, the young woman's eyes cast down and to the side. It moved him to tears. He bought the painting after seeing the initials S.C. in the corner. Sophie Crawford.

He then went to every bordello and cathouse he could find, showing the picture to everyone and asking if any of them had one like it. He offered a lot of money and managed to buy eight more paintings, all with the initials S.C. in the corner.

But of the phantom Sophie he never found a trace.

Chapter Eighteen

Maris closed the book of stories and put it on the bedside table. She thought of the woman, Sophie, in the story she had just read, and how the circumstances of her life had apparently driven her mad. She wondered if such a woman had really existed, and, if so, what had really happened to her. Surely Moresby had based his stories on things he had heard or seen in his travels. The story was written eighty years ago and Maris wondered if the same thing could happen today. Although the physical hardship was no longer there, the emotional devastation of a woman losing her husband and then her child, and in a foreign country at that, would still be almost unbearable: enough to drive one over the edge into madness.

Maris got out of bed and pulled the trunk Peter had left her out of the cupboard. The story had reminded her of something and now she knew what it was. The paintings. The series of small paintings of Chinese women that she hadn't given much thought to, except to wonder why Peter had kept them and then left them to her. She picked up one of the pictures and looked at the face of the young Chinese woman, no more than a girl really. Her eyes were cast down to one side, a gesture that conveyed sadness, shame, and defeat. Her skin was as pale as her hair was dark, and her full, sensuous lips were painted as red as blood. Was she a prostitute like in the story?

Why hadn't Peter left her a letter or something explaining what this strange collection of artifacts meant? Was she meant to figure it out for herself, or had he intended to do it but died before he could? *Maddening*, she thought. *He's left me a mystery. Two mysteries*, she reminded herself. *There's still the one about who killed him.* And according to Dinah, the police were no nearer to a solution than when she'd left Singapore.

The following morning, Maris hiked up one of the nearby hills to do some sketching. After a couple of hours, she looked at what she had done. Then she looked around at the glorious landscape surrounding her, not even two kilometres from her mother's house. Somehow she had rendered its magnificence in charcoal but without the colour that truly defined it. *Doesn't say a thing*, she thought, *except that whoever's drawn it lacks imagination and passion. Maybe I should try portraits, like AS. Maybe that's the way out of this hole I've fallen into.* But no, faces weren't her language; she knew that much. She had to find her way back into the world of colour, to the language she knew so well and spoke so fluently. Or, at least, had at one time. Without that vocabulary, she was no artist; she was mute. And if she couldn't find it in the splendour of British Columbia, where could she find it?

Inside myself, she realized, *not in what I'm looking at. I have to fix whatever's broken inside myself.*

"Maybe this would be a good time to think about having a baby," said Spirit.

Maris stared at her mother. "Do you have any idea how unrealistic that is?" she said.

"No more unrealistic than packing up a few things and heading to Singapore without knowing what you'd find there."

"A slight difference," said Maris. "I only had to worry about myself. I didn't have another human being depending on me for its very life, which is what a child would be."

"That's not the way to look at it," said Spirit. "If you think about it in those terms, you'll scare yourself away from the idea every time."

"I can't believe you're saying this. A child is a living, breathing human being that would die without constant care. How am I supposed to do that when I can barely take care of myself?"

"Maybe that's why you need to have something or someone needier than yourself to think about. Maybe you're too hung up on yourself, too self-absorbed, and that's part of the problem."

"Oh, yeah, what a great idea. Bring a child into the world and see if it will jolt me out of my self-absorption."

Maris shook her head. "And what if it doesn't? What happens to the child? Are you going to take it off my hands?"

"Maris," sighed her mother, "you think too much. Having a child is natural and fulfilling. You'll find dimensions to yourself you never knew existed. Yes, a child complicates your life, and maybe that's too overwhelming to contemplate right now. But I want you to listen to your heart and not dismiss the idea because it looks too difficult. A child is more than difficulty and complications. A child is joy and renewal and hope: all things that are lacking in your life."

"I'm not ready," said Maris.

"Okay," said Spirit. "I just had to say it."

---

maris_cousins@yahoo.com
To: rayc@gmail.com
CC:
Subject: The you-know-what conversation

Hey Ray,
Well, we finally had it — the baby conversation. Spirit thinks it's the answer to all my problems. As if. I told her I wasn't ready, and besides, it would be just my luck that it would look like you. She understood.

Thought you'd like to know. You could be next.
Love,
m.

---

rayc@gmail.com
To: maris_cousins@yahoo.com
CC:
Subject: Re: The you-know-what conversation

hey little mama,

you know me, always agree with big mama. it's better that way. besides, I think this family could use another Me.

lol

r

---

maris_cousins@yahoo.com
To: dinahstone@hotmail.com
CC:
Subject: Update from Canada

Hi Dinah,

Been in a bit of a funk lately and can't seem to shake it. I've been doing some sketching but nothing I'm proud of. My mother, in her wisdom, thinks I should have a baby. Now, there's a solution! If you can't create a painting, create a human being instead. Why didn't I think of that??

How are things at your end? Still getting beaten up by Angela on a regular basis? I know — why don't you have a baby?! That's sure to throw her off.

Sorry, I just needed to vent. I don't know whether to laugh or to cry, actually. Give me some-

thing else to think about....
Love,
Maris

---

dinahstone@hotmail.com
To: maris_cousins@yahoo.com
CC:
Subject: Re: Update from Canada

Hey!
You're kidding, right? She didn't really suggest
having a baby — did she? Well ... it could be fun
... NOT. Any mention of a father for this baby? Just
asking....

As for here ... no fun at all. Angela was here
for a few days and by the time she left I felt like
a pile of ripped-up rags. I mean, she didn't leave
me alone for a minute. Why was I doing this? Why
wasn't I doing that? Where was this? Where was
that? She really tore me into strips. Not once did
she say anything nice like, "You're doing a great
job holding things together, Dinah, since *your
brother died* and the police haven't been able to
come up with any answers. I know it's been hard
for you, and I appreciate everything you're doing,
and you can count on me for support. Anything.
Just ask."

There. I can vent, too.

Actually, to be fair, I have been making a few
small changes, and maybe that threw her off. Not

deliberately, you understand, but nobody can do things the way Peter did, so things are bound to be a little different, right? I actually enjoy setting up the displays. It's the most fun I have these days. Peter and I used to do it together — he decided and I did the grunt work, but I learned a lot from him. It's been a challenge, but we still have customers — and not all of them are ghouls coming in to see how things have changed. After all, we have great stuff, and I have to give Angela credit for collecting some fabulous pieces. She really has the touch. No wonder she and Peter were such great business partners; they had similar instincts about what would sell.

Anyway, she keeps sending it, and I keep setting it up and selling it. So what's her problem? In a word, CONTROL. She's a control freak and she can't stand anyone else making decisions. That's why their marriage didn't work. I'm sure of it. She's a bully. Really. And he got tired of her constantly demanding to be on top (excuse the expression). I don't know how they got together in the first place. I was too young to notice.

Hmmmm … I just had a thought. Maybe Angela needs to have a baby. Do you think you could get your mother to talk to her?

I'm SERIOUS!

Love,

Dinah

maris_cousins@yahoo.com
To: dinahstone@hotmail.com
CC:
Subject: You're seriously damaged

Hi, Dinah:
You need therapy.
Love you, miss you.
M (is NOT for Mother).

General Secretariat

Interpol
Lyon, France

2010

CHAPTER NINETEEN

Axel Thorssen skimmed the file on illegal trade in wildlife and animal parts for the third time. For two years he had been part of a team that had been trying to unravel the complicated smuggling operation that moved some of the most sought-after animal parts used in Chinese medicines sold around the world. Operation Oracle was an international effort conducted with the co-operation of the U.S. Customs Agency, the U.S. Food and Wildlife Service, the German Attorney General's office, the Royal Canadian Mounted Police, the Singapore Police, and Interpol.

Thorssen had been seconded to Interpol as a liaison officer from Sweden's National Criminal Investigation Department (NCID). Because he had an advanced degree in biology from Lund University, he had been chosen to gather and coordinate criminal intelligence in the area of environmental crimes, especially those involving the smuggling of endangered animal parts. Axel Thorssen's character consisted of a dogged sense of purpose combined with inspired, outside-the-box thinking. His research methods were meticulous. All the while he was compiling information, however, a part of his brain was looking for connections that to some might seem unorthodox or even preposterous. He was the one who saw a possible link with Singapore while everyone else was concentrating on the North American connection. Even though it made more sense to route contraband through Canada and Europe to China, Thorssen could see the logic in diverting shipments through Singapore, even though it had extremely stringent customs regulations and searches. If a way could be found to traffic animal parts through Singapore, he reasoned, a smuggling operation could be extremely successful because an international agency like Interpol would discount it as being non-viable. Everyone knew that the Singapore government had a tight rein on anything coming into or going out of the country. That's what made it so perfect. And that was why Axel Thorssen had decided to go to Singapore himself and see what he could find out.

What he already knew was that the trade was controlled by organized crime. They could seize $200,000 worth of bear paws, tiger bones, and rhino horns, and it would be a drop in the bucket. It was like the drug trade; the hierarchy of crime organizations meant that it was very hard to get to the kingpin. There was always another "newbie" who wanted in and who was willing to step up when a grunt got taken down.

What he also knew was that the trade was driven by demand for live exotic animals — snakes, monkeys, Chinese crocodile lizards, Bengal monitor lizards, and Komodo dragons from Indonesia — or animal parts used in traditional Asian medicine, especially bear gallbladders and tiger bones. But to undo the intricate chain that linked the many bottom feeders to the few at the top was a gargantuan task, one that had yet to be accomplished. But Axel Thorssen thought he might be able to take out a big chunk of the middle of the trade and cripple a good part of it, at least for a short time. If he could do that, then maybe, just maybe, some of the big players would be more vulnerable.

Axel had never been farther south than Genoa or farther east than Athens, and he was looking forward to his visit to Singapore. He had had to write a lengthy researched report to get permission to mount an operation there, but he had managed to convince his superiors that he knew what he was doing, and they had agreed to let him go ahead. He would be there with the knowledge of the Singapore police, who were to avail him of their services when needed. But mainly he was on a fact-finding mission, not a catch-and-kill-the-bad-guys mission. That was for others to do. He would merely pass on the information he had gathered and the local police would follow through.

He knew that smuggling operations usually went through local pet sellers, the ones who set up stalls in the markets that could easily be dismantled before the police arrived. Like the woman in Ho Chi Minh City who smuggled tens of thousands of dollars worth of animal parts before police caught her. According to the report, the haul included eight dead lorises, two kilos of tiger skins, twenty-five tiger claws, eight tiger fangs, sixty panther claws, a kilo of panther skins, a kilo of panther bones, twenty kilos of elephant tusks, nearly three kilos of rhinoceros horn, and parts of several other wild animals. She reportedly sold her rhinoceros horn for more than fifteen hundred dollars per hundred grams.

Axel had a feeling the smuggling ring Operation Oracle was trying to crack was a much larger, more sophisticated, and more lucrative production than Mrs. Hu's in Vietnam. But being a systematic, careful operator, he would begin his search at the bottom, visiting pet stores and markets and asking discreet questions and following up every lead. And while he was at it, he'd check out restaurants and hawker stalls for some of the best food in the world. He would also stay at Raffles, he decided, because it had an intriguing history and he wanted to soak up the atmosphere of Singapore from days gone by.

Axel flew into Singapore a week later, business class with an open return. His first impression, as the plane descended toward Changi International Airport, was of a set of dominoes because that's what the rows and rows of seemingly identical high-rise apartments reminded him of; dominoes set up in perfect sequence, ready to topple in a perfect wave once the first one was tipped into motion. The modern city state of Singapore was situated on a densely packed island where one of the few available directions was up. As well, a number of land reclamation projects had expanded the original boundaries of the main island. Singaporeans were nothing if not resourceful, making the most of the island's seven hundred square kilometres.

Raffles Hotel, located on Beach Road, was no longer facing the sea as it had when it originally opened in 1887 in a bungalow known as the Beach House. It was now located in the heart of the business district, minutes from upscale shopping centres, city hall, and the airport. It had been beautifully restored a few years earlier and still retained most of its colonial charm. Axel was not disappointed when he saw it. It was, in fact, much larger than he had expected. But he reminded himself that the Raffles Hotel in his imagination had taken shape through the stories of a British writer, E. Sutcliffe Moresby, which Axel had read in English many years ago.

The Long Bar no longer pulsated with the boisterous chatter of planters and plantation managers come in from the jungles of Malaya for a break from the unrelenting heat and drudgery of their lives. Not that Singapore wasn't hot, but the hotel provided cool showers and clean sheets, and fans that beat the steamy air twenty-four hours a day. It provided roast beef dinners and steak and kidney pie, mashed potatoes and carrots, steamed pudding with sticky sweet sauce, and rich coffee with real cream. And there was more than one kind of ale, more than one kind of whisky. And more important than all that, it provided the company of other lonely, overworked men who were far from home and family, and who wanted nothing more than a chance to blow off steam.

The Long Bar Axel walked into after unpacking his bags was much the same in its leather and bamboo decor, but the people chugging down beer and Singapore Slings were mainly tourists from Europe and America who would go home after their holiday and tell their friends, "We stayed at Raffles Hotel and had drinks in the Long Bar every afternoon." When he saw how crowded it was, Axel opted for a drink in the quiet luxury of the Writer's Bar in a corner of the main lobby. There was something very conducive to contemplation in the dark rattan-backed armchairs and the polished mahogany tables and cabinets. Axel thought he might be spending a lot of time there at day's end.

Chapter Twenty

The fever took Francis in four days. It started with just a headache and then, within a few hours, he felt chilled, so Annabelle wrapped him in a blanket and fed him hot soup and tea. Then a few hours later, he was burning up, sweating and vomiting the soup and tea. The first fever lasted six hours and then he slept. When he woke up, the fever was gone, but he said he ached all over. Annabelle was just relieved that the fever had passed, so she gave him more soup and rubbed his joints with camphor. The fever returned on the third day and Sutty came with a doctor, but it was too late. Early on the morning of the fourth day, Francis had a convulsion and went into a coma. He was dead before the sun went down.

Annabelle wept until she vomited and Sutty briefly feared she might have the fever herself, but she didn't. Her skin was cold and clammy to the touch, and he could feel the bones in her back when he held her, trying to comfort her, but she was inconsolable. She was blind with grief and fear and rage. She wanted to lie beside Francis on the bed, hold him, keep his body warm with her own, as if she could bring him back to life with the heat of her own flesh. What was she going to do without Francis? How was she going to survive? How was she going to have this baby that he would never see?

Sutty, for his part, felt completely helpless. He could not console Annabelle; he could not bring Francis back. He could only pay the doctor and contact the authorities, see to the removal of Francis's body to a funeral home, and pay whatever had to be paid for. Annabelle would not allow anyone to touch Francis's body, and so it was only at dawn, when she was exhausted from crying and screaming at anyone other than Sutty who came into the room, that they were able to wrap Francis in a sheet and take him down the stairs to the removal wagon.

Sutty could see that Annabelle was mad with grief and he tried to get her to come with him to the Raffles, but she refused, saying she had to be near Francis, that she couldn't leave in case it was all a mistake. How would Francis find her if she left? So Sutty went out and got some buns and some milk and came back and made tea and tried to get Annabelle to eat something. She drank the tea and took a couple of bites of the bun, but food was the last thing she wanted. Sutty sat with her until she finally fell asleep, around midnight of the fifth day. He had gotten some powders from the chemist and put them in her tea, hoping they would calm her down and help her sleep. They did, eventually, and she slept for several hours without moving.

Sutty sat in Francis's armchair and dozed fitfully, waking every hour or two to check on Annabelle. He had never seen such grief in his life and it frightened him. When his father had died, his mother had not shown her tears to anyone, not even her son. They were shed in private, if they were shed at all, although Sutty couldn't imagine that she hadn't cried for her husband of so many years. They had had an amicable relationship and were fond of each other. He had no doubt of that. Maybe it was because they had been together for so long that she could more readily accept his death. They had lived their life, a good life, and the passing of one of them was inevitable. Perhaps because Annabelle had been married to Francis for so short a time, the shock and unfairness of his sudden death was so much harder to bear. Shock and grief: they left one emptied out. Frightened, even. Annabelle had lost her anchor; she had come untethered, and he could only imagine how terrifying that must be for her.

Sutty decided that when this was all over, when Francis was buried, he would persuade Annabelle to come back to England with him. He would accompany her because he couldn't see her making the journey alone. He would not have to rearrange much; he lived an open-ended life and could come and go at will. *How lucky I am*, he thought, *to be able to do this*. But Sutty had always believed that life was short and sometimes brutal — he had witnessed the shortness and brutality often enough — and he didn't believe in putting things off. That's why he had admired Francis for his determination to make the most of what he had and to risk everything for a dream. And he had to admire Annabelle for leaving everything behind to come to Francis and be by his side while he chased the dream.

It had been an act of faith, an act of love. She hadn't wanted to come; she didn't have Francis's ambition. But she had understood that he had to do this thing, and that it could be an adventure, one that they would tell their grandchildren about from the security of England once Francis had achieved the dream and they were set for life.

Sutty began to weep for the cruel fate that had befallen them, two young people with all the love in the world to keep them going. Two people who had taken a chance on a future they would never see together. They had accepted the hardship and acquiesced to the necessary economies. They hadn't yet reached a point where it might all be too much sacrifice for too little gain. That was still a long way off. And now it would never happen. Nor would Francis's book happen, and the children, and the grandchildren, and all the rest of it.

His heart broke for them and he wept.

It was almost a month before Annabelle told Sutty about the baby she was expecting. During the weeks after Francis's death, Sutty had tried to persuade Annabelle to leave the dingy little flat and come stay with him at the Raffles, or at another hotel if she chose, because there were so many memories, happy memories, starting with their wedding, that being at the Raffles would bring back. Annabelle wasn't ready for that. She was still too immersed in her grief to begin reminiscing.

"A baby?" said Sutty. It took a minute for the enormity of it to sink in. A baby. What was Annabelle going to do with a baby? How would she cope? She could barely look after herself. She was so thin; the bones in her shoulders were visible through her light cotton dress. She barely slept at night and there were dark circles under her eyes. He had tried everything to get her to eat, to move, to leave Singapore and go back to England with him, but she was having none of it. She kept saying she needed to be near Francis. Near his spirit, she said.

They had buried Francis in the church cemetery, and Sutty had had a stone made and engraved with:

Francis Adolphus Stone
1890–1924
Beloved Husband of Annabelle.

Annabelle went there every day and sat on Francis's grave. Sutty went with her a few times, but stopped going because he couldn't bear to see her wretchedness.

"Yes, a baby," she told Sutty. "I hadn't even told Francis yet. It was too soon and I wanted to make sure everything would be all right."

"But when?" said Sutty. "How long?"

"When is it due?" she asked. "In about five months." She put her hand on her stomach and Sutty could see the slight roundness of her belly, despite the fact that she was so thin. "It's still hanging on," she said, "in spite of everything."

"Yes," said Sutty. "Stubborn, I guess, and tenacious." *Like his father*, he thought, but didn't say it in case it upset Annabelle.

She looked up at Sutty. She knew what he meant. This was Francis's baby she was carrying, and this baby would not let go.

"I haven't really thought much about it lately," she said. And she sighed deeply, a sigh filled with every emotion she had been feeling since Francis's death. "I'm so tired."

"Why don't you try to sleep, Annabelle? I'll stay with you and read, if that will make you feel better."

"Thank you, Sutty. You've been such a good friend to us. To me. I don't think I can ever thank you for what you've done."

"I'll do whatever you need me to do." He was embarrassed by the rawness of her feelings and by the sentiment. "Now," he said, clearing his throat, "you go lie down and I'll bring you a cup of tea."

She did as he said. By the time the tea was ready, she was asleep, lying on her side with one hand on her belly, as if she were holding her unborn baby.

Chapter Twenty-One

In the three months he had been in Singapore, Axel Thorssen had scoured the markets and pet shops looking for possible dealers in animal contraband. He had even set up a small office in a glass and steel tower near Orchard Road and taken on a couple of people to help him. Charles Ong was a young Chinese police officer with a college degree in anthropology and excellent investigative skills. He had been born in Singapore and knew his way around, plus he spoke English, Mandarin, and Hokkien, a local dialect. His second assistant was Satya Das, an Indian police cadet who spoke fluent English, as well as Hindi and Tamil. She was almost as tall as Charles and nearly as thin. She told Axel her name meant "truth"; she was meticulous and thorough and usually ended up writing most of the reports, or correcting the reports that Axel and Charles wrote. Her computer skills were well beyond the two men's. While they did a lot of the legwork, Satya scoured the Internet and worked the phones and Skype.

It was a good team, and Axel enjoyed the added bonus of access to the best Chinese and Indian food for lunch every day. Except for the heat, Axel liked being in Singapore. It suited his orderly mind and his punctilious temperament. Things worked in Singapore; the people were hard-working and law-abiding, much like the Swedes. He tried not to pay too much attention to some of the overzealous laws — no chewing gum on the street, no spitting (although Axel wasn't a spitter, it seemed to him that not spitting was a matter of courtesy, not of law, and that chewing gum wasn't the problem, but spitting the gum out on the street was) — and he knew that taxes were high, but Sweden's taxes were among the highest in the world; it was the price you paid for everything from free medical care and education to clean streets and public transit systems.

Axel's efforts had led him to believe that the major trafficking ring he was trying to break did not do its business at the street level of markets and pet shops. He had no doubt that the trade in endangered species and animal parts existed at that level, and even flourished, making some small-time players relatively wealthy. But it was much more of a one-on-one trade — individual seller to individual shopkeeper/buyer. He wanted the bigger players, those with international connections, who could transport and ship in quantity the rarest and most sought-after goods.

Where to look next? It was a question Axel and his team pondered at various times over dim sum, fried Hokkien mee, dumplings, fish head curry, biryani, and tandoori chicken. Today it was dim sum.

"I'm thinking we should look into import-export businesses that trade in items that can camouflage some of this stuff," said Charles Ong one day. "Like maybe furniture, you know, like, big stuff."

"That stuff gets scrutinized pretty tightly by customs, precisely for that reason," countered Satya Das. "I mean, they look for any number of things, such as gems, drugs, even gold. So don't you think they would have discovered if animal parts were being shipped?"

"You think it's too obvious?" said Charles.

"Yes," said Satya. "I think these guys are smarter than that." She glanced at Charles to see if she might have offended him by implying that he wasn't smart enough to see that. Charles had just popped another shrimp har gow into his mouth and smiled at her. She shook her head. He was either really, really smart or really, really not smart. She couldn't decide which.

"I think we can assume they're very clever," said Axel. "We've been looking for them for three months and we still can't figure out how they're doing it. Unless, of course, they're not doing it from Singapore. But I'm still pretty sure they are."

"So am I, Boss," said Charles, who like calling Axel "Boss" and Satya "Sat." It was his "cool" factor, at least in his own eyes, Satya had decided. Which made him pretty uncool, in fact. But cute.

Satya and Axel watched Charles suck the meat off a chicken foot, a delicacy, he said. Satya masked her disgust by biting into a steamed bun with black bean paste in the middle: one of her favourites. Axel was partial to the steamed pork meatballs wrapped in thin pastry.

"I think we need to brainstorm a list," said Satya. "And then systematically try and eliminate each possibility until we have a core list of real possibles."

Axel was nodding his head. "Good idea," he said. "Anything that involves shipping, mailing, international couriers, travel, but on a fairly large scale with regular shipments in and out of the country."

"I suggest we go on an alphabetical basis," said Satya, and Charles rolled his eyes. But Axel liked the idea. It was systematic rather than random, and that suited him. While Charles liked to let his mind roam and make hit-and-miss connections, Axel and Satya were definitely systematic thinkers. They liked to apply a method to a task, rope it in, and control it. Axel knew Charles would not stick to the ABC method, but that was all right. They'd still come up with a pretty comprehensive list.

"Okay. A," said Satya, pulling out a spiral-bound notebook and pen from her bag.

"Antiques," said Axel. "Alcohol."

"Musical instruments," said Charles. Satya frowned and shook her head. She flipped over a few pages and started a column for M.

"Animal skins," she said. "Legitimate ones like fur and leather — you could hide the contraband in plain sight, so to speak."

"Aircraft parts," said Axel. "Do they make them here?"

"I don't think so but I'll check."

"Armadillo," said Charles.

"What?" said Axel and Satya in unison.

"It was the only A-word I could think of," he said. "So shoot me."

CHAPTER TWENTY-TWO

What Sutty didn't know was that Annabelle had taken to roaming the streets after dark. During the day she rarely went out, except to the local shops if she was hungry. She seemed to be sleeping most of the day, because whenever Sutty came over, she would be in bed, whether it was at eleven o'clock in the morning or four in the afternoon. He thought she was probably depressed, but it didn't occur to him that she wasn't sleeping at night.

She couldn't sleep at night because that was when she missed Francis the most. She felt like she was in a tomb. The flat was stifling and she could barely breathe. She could feel Francis's presence around her, but it was the memory of his last days and hours that still haunted her, and she couldn't close her eyes without seeing his pale face, the beads of sweat running into his eyes, his hair matted to his skull, and the cracked skin of his dry lips as he tried to drink from a cup of water. During the day, at least, she could ward off some of the worst memories simply because of the sunlight and the street noises, which interrupted her thoughts and allowed her to close her eyes long enough to fall into an exhausted sleep.

Strangely enough, she felt no fear as she wandered the streets at night. After the first time, when she simply couldn't stand being in the flat another minute and had fled as if escaping from prison, she didn't care if there was danger. She almost wished someone would knock her down and kill her, then the pain would be over and maybe she'd find peace. She would walk for hours because she couldn't be still. Her eyes devoured everything she saw, whether it was a café full of late-night diners, or a shop that stayed open hoping to pick up some business from those same late-night diners on their way home. She passed bars and fruit stalls, nightclubs and the occasional cinema, temples, and bakeries. Often she came upon a night market and she would wander around, gazing at all the items for sale: dried mushrooms and herbs, fresh vegetables, bolts of cloth, cigarettes, hairnets, shoes, and cooking utensils. It was all a distraction from the thoughts she didn't want to think, the images she didn't want to see. Singapore was alive at night because after the sun went down, the temperature dropped a few degrees and it was so much more pleasant to eat and shop when the sun wasn't beating down on your head.

Occasionally she wandered into a district populated by prostitutes and opium addicts. Opium dens were a fact of life in Singapore, Annabelle knew that, and she knew that prostitution existed everywhere in the world. But she had never been exposed to it before. She became fascinated by the women and men who populated this world. They didn't seem to notice her, or more likely they didn't care, so she sometimes looked right at their faces to see what they might tell her. Would she find pain like her own, suffering, loneliness, boredom, despair, bitterness? She wanted to know what kept these people going, because surely they were worse off than her. They could not have been here by choice. Or could they? Was this a life someone would choose? And if so, why? She could only imagine that they had been forced by circumstances to turn to drugs and prostitution to stay alive. Or was it the other way around? They stayed alive, despite turning to drugs and prostitution.

Annabelle could almost understand that. She knew what it felt like not to want to be alive, yet to wake up every day and still be breathing, heart beating, mouth dry and wanting to drink, stomach empty and needing to eat. It was not of her choosing. It just was. This was how it was when you didn't care anymore. You couldn't feel anything so it didn't matter what happened to you. Prostitution and opium addiction were passive occupations requiring only that you acquiesce. Still, she shuddered to think of being one of those women who stood in doorways or on street corners and went with any man who approached them.

It was their faces that fascinated her the most. They were painted on like masks with black eyebrows, white powder, and red lipstick. Their eyes were evasive, dark and lifeless, and inscrutable. Or else they looked straight at you, cold and glaring. That was when she started to notice that each girl was different in her own way and that they had personalities, even if they didn't express them there on the street at night.

Annabelle began to fantasize about their lives, to write

little stories about them in her head. She even gave them names: Elsie and Angel and Kitty. She imagined the tragic circumstances of their lives that had led them to this: losing a husband, losing a child, losing a lover. Always it was some loss, some unbearable loss.

One morning when she returned to the flat, Annabelle picked up a piece of paper — Francis's writing paper — and a pencil and began to draw some of the faces she remembered. "This one is Elsie," she said, remembering the story she had imagined, "and she is only twenty years old. She had a baby, a little boy, because she was raped by her uncle when she was only fifteen. Elsie's father had died and his younger brother had taken in Elsie and her mother, making a big show of it in the village so he would look like a good man. But he wasn't a good man, of course. He was a monster. And then Elsie became pregnant and her uncle threw her out of the house. The people in the village shunned her, and Elsie was forced to go to the city and beg for food. And all the time, her baby was growing inside her. She tried desperately to find a home for herself and her baby, but she had no money. She was only sixteen. Nobody took pity on her; nobody helped her. Occasionally she was able to scrounge scraps of food from hawkers and restaurants, but mostly they threw the waste food to the dogs because it was just slop. Elsie ate it anyway because she didn't want her baby to die. When she finally had the baby, in an alley behind a row of shophouses, it was born dead with the cord wrapped around its neck. Elsie nearly bled to death as she lay in the alley for two days. Then an old man found her and brought her to his room. He gave her tea and bread and brought her water so she could wash herself. She stayed with him for a week and forced herself to leave because she knew she was eating half his food and he had barely enough for himself. That's when she knew what she would have to do to survive.

Annabelle somehow managed to infuse her drawing with all the misfortune and misery that "Elsie" had suffered in her short life. It was in the eyes, mainly, and in the angle of the head. They said, "I am alive, but I do not live," because that was what Annabelle saw and sensed. Elsie existed, as she, Annabelle, did, but nothing more. Gone were joy and passion; gone forever was meaning and significance.

Sutty had been trying to persuade her to go back to England with him, but Annabelle could not even contemplate leaving Singapore because it meant she would be leaving Francis. Whatever real happiness they had known had been here. Their first home together was here. Their child had been conceived here. Much as she had been loath to come to Singapore, Annabelle was now loath to leave.

"But don't you want to have your baby at home?" Sutty had asked her.

"I don't know that England is my home any longer," she said. "If I go back there, I will be leaving our home, mine and Francis's. And I can't bear the thought of doing that. It would be like abandoning him. While I'm here, he still exists. I'm afraid that if I leave, he won't go with me."

Sutty didn't know how to respond to this. *It's a kind of madness*, he thought, *brought on by grief.* His only hope was that, given time, Annabelle might come through this phase of her anguish and come to her senses. He fervently wished it would happen before the baby was born. He couldn't let her have the child here; it was much too dangerous. He knew women had babies every day in Singapore, and most of them survived, but he knew the risks were greater. With the heat, contaminated water, mosquitoes and other vermin, all that could go wrong was too horrible to contemplate.

As the months passed and Annabelle did not change her mind, Sutty began to look for a doctor and a hospital for her to have the baby in. He knew that most women had their babies at home but that was out of the question. The General Hospital had a maternity wing, he discovered, but Kandang Kerbau Hospital (referred to as KK Hospital or "Tek Kah") was more convenient. It had recently been converted into a free maternity hospital with thirty beds. The head of obstetrics was Dr. Thomas Ashford, and Sutty set up an appointment to see what could be done for Annabelle.

"I should like to see the young woman before her term is up," said Dr. Ashford. "It's important to know if there might be complications on the day."

"Of course," said Sutty. "I understand. But, uh, she doesn't know I've contacted you or that I'm making arrangements for the baby's birth in the hospital. It's a delicate situation and I shall have to find a way to persuade her to come in." Sutty shifted uncomfortably in his chair. The doctor must surely think this a very odd case, but his face didn't reveal what he was thinking. "There's still time, of course, about three or four months, I think."

"Try not to wait too much longer," said Dr. Ashford. "If she's malnourished and underweight, as you've suggested, then it's imperative that she be checked."

"Yes, I understand," said Sutty. "I will do my best. I don't want her to lose this baby. It could put her over the edge."

"It sounds like she may already be over the edge, if not close to it," the doctor said. "See what you can do."

CHAPTER TWENTY-THREE

After six months in Canada, Maris decided to go back to Singapore. Whatever she had expected to happen hadn't, but she acknowledged that some baby steps had been taken in another direction. She had been drawing but not painting. *It was a beginning*, she told herself. Or a "new" beginning, as people referred to it, as if there was such a thing as an "old" beginning. She was caught now in a no man's land between life in Canada and life in Singapore: neither in one nor the other. It was like the time she decided to stop using sugar in her coffee. She tried it for a month but did not enjoy coffee without sugar. So she decided to start adding sugar to her coffee again, and discovered that she didn't like it with sugar either. So she stopped using sugar again and persisted until she began to enjoy coffee without it. It did not occur to Maris to give up coffee, just like it did not occur to her to give up painting. She understood that it was about process, a necessary progression in stages from one state of being or activity to another. Process took time and often seemed unproductive, but when you looked back over a period of time, you realized that many things had, indeed, changed, and usually, although not always, for the better. She recognized that she was in the middle of some kind of change of state and she needed to trust both herself and the process to complete the transition.

Just making the decision to go back seemed to energize her and Maris felt a sense of excitement she hadn't felt since Peter's death. The police had been unable to solve his murder and, after six months, the case remained open but no new evidence had come to light. Maris wondered if it would ever be solved. It wasn't like television or the movies where there was always a resolution at the end. Life wasn't like that. Some murders were never solved. They still didn't know for certain who Jack the Ripper was, even after more than a hundred years. *How do you live with something like that?* she wondered. Never knowing. She didn't believe there was such a thing as closure, but Maris did think that knowing was better than not knowing, even if the truth was horrible. *You can live with certainty*, she thought. *It's uncertainty that can drive you crazy.* Certainty you could file away, bury, do whatever, and try and move on. But uncertainty kept returning, popping up to disturb whatever thin veneer you had covered it with. Uncertainty was like a sink hole that could never be filled, no matter how many truckloads of gravel and dirt you poured into it.

Her mother was disappointed, of course, because she wanted Maris to be closer to home. "Do you have to go so far away?" she asked. "Can't you just go to California or Mexico?"

"It's not about the distance," she told Spirit. "It's about my connection to the place. I don't know what it is. A past life, maybe?" Maris said it in jest, but she knew Spirit believed in those things.

"It's possible," she said. "Maybe you're looking for a home — a physical home and a spiritual home. How can I stop you from doing that? It's what I would want. What I've always wanted, I suppose." She thought about it for a moment. They were sharing a bottle of wine again, this time a New Zealand Sauvignon Blanc with wonderful undertones of lime, grapefruit, and a zinger of lemongrass. *I'm going to miss this*, thought Spirit. *Drinking wine with my daughter.* But Spirit had learned you can't hold on to your children. God knows her own parents had disapproved of her marriage to Freedom Man. "Just trust me," she had wanted to say to them.

---

maris_cousins@yahoo.com
To: dinahstone@hotmail.com
CC:
Subject: Back to Singapore

Hi Dinah,
I'm coming back — don't try to stop me! I'm pretty sure that whatever I needed to find isn't here, although I needed to be here to realize that. I'm

not the same person I was when I left Canada (well, duh), and whoever I've become or am becoming in my life's journey, I'm not ready to get off the train yet. For a while there, I honestly thought the journey was over. I now know it's not and I'm glad. Peter's death (still can't use the M-word) threw me off course and I'm sure I would have been further ahead had he still been here. But he's not and I have to keep going.

Are you sick of the metaphor yet? Because I am.

I'm going to Vancouver to spend a bit more time with my brother and my nieces before I leave, but will send you info as soon as my travel plans are confirmed. Trying to get a cheap flight but Air Canada and Singapore Airlines are not co-operating. The pigs.

Love,

Maris

---

dinahstone@hotmail.com
To: maris_cousins@yahoo.com
CC:
Subject: Re: Back to Singapore

Maris,
Yahoo! I cannot wait to see you again. Should I tell Angela?
Dinah

maris_cousins@yahoo.com
To: dinahstone@hotmail.com
CC:
Subject: Re: Back to Singapore

No, let's surprise her. Would she really give a flying bleep?
    I wonder if she'd give me a job …

dinahstone@hotmail.com
To: maris_cousins@yahoo.com
CC:
Subject: Re: Back to Singapore

Okay, no, and probably not. (I'm so excited!)

Maris arrived in Singapore a month later and took a taxi with her stuff — including Peter's trunk — straight to Dinah's apartment in Yew Tee. It was northwest of the business district and had access to the MRT public transit. It still cost a fortune, even though just a couple of decades before farmers were raising chickens and ducks in what was a bustling village of three hundred inhabitants. There were no cheap apartments in Singapore.

Dinah had bought new sheets for the guest bedroom and prepared a five-course meal of all of Maris's favourite foods. Even though Maris had been travelling for twenty-four hours, Dinah wouldn't let her go to bed until well after dark. "It will help with the jet lag," she said. "Your internal clock won't be so turned around if you manage to sleep through the night and wake up in the daylight."

Exhausted as she was, Maris obeyed and slept through the night, waking only once in the dark, and getting up at ten the next morning. Dinah had already left for the gallery, but there was fresh fruit in the kitchen and the coffeemaker was ready to be turned on whenever Maris got up.

Maris felt a little fuzzy headed, but did not feel like sleeping all day, which would have been a sure sign of jet lag. She turned on the coffeemaker and took a shower, then took her coffee, some fruit, and a custard-filled bun out onto Dinah's postage-stamp balcony. Breathing in the steamy, slightly salty air, she thought, *I don't know why, but this feels like home.*

A Talent for Painting

A Short Story
by
E. Sutcliffe Moresby

I had occasion to be back in Singapore after spending a very pleasant summer in Monte Carlo with the Countess Adessa daVinci. She introduced me to an old friend of hers who had lived in Singapore for many years and was the chief officer of a company trading in tea and spices. He and his wife were returning to Singapore in a month's time on the P&O and he asked if I'd be interested in travelling with them. They would be happy to put me up in Singapore, he said, for as long as I wanted to stay. As I had no pressing reason to stay in Europe, and winter was coming, I gladly accepted his offer and booked passage.

The journey was pleasant with remarkably calm seas most of the way, except for a brief storm early on near Port Said. As my hosts had a first-class cabin, we often took drinks there before dinner. We swapped stories of Singapore and Malaya and discovered we had a few mutual friends, among them an enterprising young man who had told my host an intriguing story about a British woman who was sometimes seen wandering the streets of Chinatown late at night and who often drew portraits of the prostitutes.

"You know," I said, "I think I've heard of this woman. She had a child, I believe."

"So they say," my host replied, "but nobody recalls seeing the child, and apparently she asks everyone she encounters if they know where her little boy is. It's most strange."

"And disturbing," I said. "What if there really was a child? What could have happened to him?"

"I don't know. Some say he died at birth. Others that he was taken back to England by a friend of the woman's husband."

"There was a husband?"

"Apparently. But he died before the child was born."

I was intrigued enough by this tale that I determined I would look for this woman once I was in Singapore, and try to get her story. And there was a part of me, knowing the perils that can befall one in Asia, that wondered if I could help her, although it was easy to think that in the comfort of a first-class cabin on an ocean liner. When one is at sea, one may as well be in a time capsule twenty thousand leagues under the sea. You will see nothing for weeks except the sea, the sky, and the occasional school of playful dolphins or flying fish. It is easy to imagine a perfect world where there are no wars, no parliaments, no disagreeable people, and no poverty and despair. What I thought I could do for this woman, if I ever found her, was not an idea that was fully formed. It was a vague, fuzzy-around-the-edges notion of altruism that got fuzzier and more vague with every cocktail I consumed.

Nevertheless, I held firm to my idea of at least finding the woman who had become a phantom of the night to many of the colonial residents of Singapore.

When we disembarked in Singapore, a car was waiting for us and we were driven to the spacious and quite elegant home of my hosts, whom I see I have thus far failed to name. They were Andrew and Edith Anthony-Fairchild, a fortunate couple whose marriage was sound (you learn a lot about people when you observe them for several weeks on a sea voyage) and whose financial stability was assured. They appeared to live a charmed life, and indeed, Edith Anthony-Fairchild confided to me once that she felt blessed in the life she'd been given — that was how she put it, "been given." I queried her use of the verb, especially its passive voice.

"Oh," she said, "I've done nothing to deserve it. I was born to wealthy and caring parents, and I married a wealthy and caring man — and it was virtually an arranged marriage as Andrew is the son of my parents' best friends. All I've ever had to do was show up." She laughed at this and I was reminded again — for she had laughed often on the journey — of the musicality of her laughter and the sunny quality of her disposition. She was a statuesque woman with large shoulders, hands, and feet, and not particularly pretty, but she had a great sense of style, as many French women do but many Englishwomen do not, that made her both attractive and appealing to both men and women. She knew how to dress to advantage and she wore expensive, well-cut clothes. Her husband was not so handsome, either, but he had a slightly shabby casualness that made you comfortable in his company. He was completely unpretentious and, I believe, an honest man.

I confided in Edith at one point that I had been intrigued enough by Andrew's story of the phantom Englishwoman to want to try and find her.

"Oh, how exciting," she said. "I should like to tag along, if I may. If the poor child exists, I wonder if anything can be done for her."

I hesitated for a moment to consider Edith's proposition and she immediately said, "Oh, of course, how rude of me. Here I am, jumping in on your adventure without thinking that you might want to do this on your own. I'm so sorry."

"No," I said, "not at all. In fact, I think it would be a good idea to have a woman along. She might not be willing to speak to a man alone."

"Possibly," said Edith, "but isn't she a prostitute?"

"I hadn't heard that," I said, "but I suppose anything's possible."

"Well, we shall take it one step at a time," said Edith. "What should our first step be?"

I suggested that we go to Chinatown one evening and simply wander around, see what was up and whether there was an Englishwoman to be found among the Chinese girls. So we did this, for several nights, in fact, because we saw no sign of the so-called phantom lady. Andrew thought we were mad but didn't try to interfere. He was used to indulging his wife's whims and as long as a responsible man accompanied her (I took that to be me), then he did not object.

On our fifth night of slumming through the streets of Chinatown, we decided it was time to talk to somebody. We tried a couple of barmen first, asking if they knew of such a woman and if they'd seen her. One of them nodded his head and said, "Yes," but added "she come very late at night so not see much." Whereabouts had he seen her, we asked.

"Not so far," he said. "Maybe two block over, near hotel Ah Chiu." And he pointed over his shoulder to indicate the street behind the bar.

We found the hotel Ah Chiu and strategically positioned ourselves in a café across the street. It was not even midnight, barely eleven o'clock in fact, so we discussed whether we should stay and wait, not knowing what the barman had meant by "very late," or come back another evening after we had had a nap. Edith was game to stay. She was excited that we had come so close and had actually found an eyewitness who confirmed that the phantom existed. I, on the other hand, being an early riser, knew I wouldn't last much past midnight, and suggested we come back the following night. Edith, being the agreeable sort, immediately acquiesced and agreed it would be better if we were well-rested when we confronted the woman. Besides, I was not keen to sit in a café in this part of town for the next two or three hours. There were a few unsavoury-looking types who might start to get interested in us. Edith was wearing her gold wedding ring and I had a pocket watch and a few dollars in my pocket that I preferred to hang on to.

We returned to the café the next evening around midnight, rested and divested of our valuables. We still stood out because there was not another English couple to be seen anywhere around us. But there were a few solitary, sad-looking foreign men, possibly English, possibly Dutch or German; it was hard to tell. They sat quietly consuming one beer after another, more than likely seeking oblivion not company.

"I say," said Edith, "this is the most fun I've had since I've been in Singapore, and we've been here for ten years." She giggled (if a woman such as Edith could actually utter such a sound) and took another sip of her Guinness Stout. I noticed that several rather thin, elderly looking Chinese men were drinking Guinness, and it reminded me that the Chinese believed it promoted virility or male "potency." My tastes tended more toward German beer, and so I drank Tsingtao from a brewery founded in China by German settlers a couple of decades earlier. Expatriates, I reflected, not for the first time, are a resourceful lot.

We waited until nearly two in the morning, but our phantom did not appear. Disappointed but not daunted, we vowed to return, but other commitments kept us away for a week, and it was eight days before we returned to Chinatown and the Ah Chiu vigil. And, miracle of miracles, the phantom appeared just after one in the morning, on the arm of a somewhat inebriated Scotsman — we determined that he was a Scot because he spoke loudly, if incoherently, and he had a head of thick red hair and a moustache to match. They entered the hotel and twenty minutes later the Scotsman emerged and lurched down the street, calling for a taxi. The phantom lady stepped out of the hotel about ten minutes after that.

Edith and I looked at each other, each of us with the same question in our eyes. Now what? We hadn't actually worked out what we would do when we found the woman and now, suddenly, the moment had arrived.

Then Edith got up and walked toward the woman, saying in a loud, clear voice, "Good evening, my dear. Would you care to join us for a drink?" She turned and indicated the table where I was sitting, and so I put on my friendliest, middle-of-the-night smile. The woman looked from Edith to me and back to Edith, and tilted her head to one side, which Edith took to mean yes. She put her hand gently on the phantom's back and walked her over to our table.

I stood and extended my hand. "Good evening," I said. "It's nice to see another English face" — thinking this might make her relax and think we were tourists — "uh, I say, you are English, aren't you?"

She sat in the chair that I pulled out for her and nodded her head. "Yes," she said. "I'm English."

"I'm Edward and this is Edith. Can we buy you a drink?"

"I'll have a gin," she said. "Straight up."

I signalled to the waiter and ordered a gin. "And do you have a name?" I asked, rather a little too coyly, I thought, but too late. She must have been too tired to care, for she told us her name without reacting. "Isabel," she said.

"It's nice to meet you, Isabel," said Edith. "Have you been staying in Singapore long?"

"Yes. Quite some time, in fact."

"Ah, we've only just arrived, you see," Edith lied, "and have had trouble sleeping, so we've sort of taken to wandering about at night. That's why we were so pleased to run into someone who speaks English."

I was impressed with Edith's ability to extemporaneously ad lib a performance we hadn't previously formulated. I took my cue from her.

"Yes," I said, "I hope we didn't seem too forward." I was tempted to say, "Do you come here often?" but caught myself in time. It was almost two in the morning and we were sitting in a Chinese café with a few derelict old men who had nowhere to go.

"Well," she said, perhaps warming up from the gin, "you did surprise me. It's not too safe for foreigners to be walking about here so late at night."

"But you're here," Edith pointed out, "and you're alone."

"Yes," she said, "but I live around here. They know me and they leave me alone."

We weren't sure what to say to that. After a moment, I raised my glass and said, "Well, here's to keeping safe."

She laughed, a little cynically I thought, and said, "No one's safe in this world. You can be struck down in the middle of the day the same as the middle of the night. Maybe just for different reasons or by different means."

I pointed to her glass and she nodded. I waved to the waiter and circled my hand around the table to indicate another round.

When our drinks came, Edith said, "Would you like to join us for dinner tomorrow evening?" She stopped for a moment and laughed. "I guess I mean this evening, don't I."

Isabel lowered her eyes and thought for a moment. "I don't see why not," she said.

"Fine," said Edith. "Shall we say eight o'clock at the Raffles Hotel?"

Isabel hesitated for a moment, and I wondered if she might be uncomfortable with the idea of dining at the Raffles.

"I say," I jumped in, "I'm rather tired of the Raffles. How about we try that place by the river? The one with the big lobster over the door. I've heard they have very good food. And it's not far from here."

Isabel seemed to relax at this suggestion. "I know the one," she said, and agreed to meet us there at eight.

We ended up having a rather pleasant meal, although Isabel was late and we weren't sure she would be coming. She arrived at about twenty past, without apology, wearing a pretty but slightly shabby flowered dress in shades of blue silk. She wore white gloves and carried a worn handbag of black leather. The Singapore climate is not kind to leather, and it showed signs of incipient mildew, a constant problem in such a damp place. However, her hair had been freshly marcelled and she wore lipstick and rouge. Clearly she had wanted to make a good impression.

She ate heartily, which surprised us both, but I supposed she didn't often have the opportunity of a good meal, so she wasn't about to pass up the chance. We were happy to oblige, and the food was quite good, as promised. We ordered gin all around to start with, then an assortment of seafood, including cuttlefish, prawns, and grouper, and some noodles and some sort of greens, all done in the Cantonese style. I ate the least, not because I wasn't hungry, but because my two female companions had the heartier appetites. Edith's love of food didn't surprise me — I'd seen her tuck in many evenings during the sea voyage — but the slender, in fact, waiflike, Isabel must have had what my mother used to call a "hollow leg," because I have no idea where all that food went. Anyway, we did not begrudge her a mouthful, and it helped shave the edges off our guilt at deceiving her. I'm sure she thought we were a well-to-do husband and wife on holiday, for truthfully, only the well-to-do took a holiday in the Far East.

She was not much more forthcoming on that second meeting than she had been on the first. She told us she had been in Singapore for five years, that she had come out to be married, and that her husband had died not long after their marriage. When I asked why she'd chosen to remain, she just looked sad and didn't answer.

"Do you have any family left in England?" asked Edith.

"Not really," she said. "My father died a few years ago, but I do have an aunt and some cousins near Dorset."

"Ah, Dorset," said Edith. "I used to know someone from Dorset. Archie Fellowes. He's been dead for nearly a decade. Perhaps you knew him, or your aunt might have known him."

"I didn't spend much time there," she said. "We weren't very close."

"And your husband?" I ventured. "Any family on that side?"

"No. He was an orphan, I'm afraid."

"Ah, I'm sorry," I said, as if condolences were called for. It was clear to me that the woman bore a deep burden of sorrow, and that this unhappiness had become a part of her personality. She was a very pretty girl, with a heart-shaped face and blue eyes, but she seldom smiled or laughed. I imagined her as a young woman in love, engaged to be married. It was probably the happiest time of her life. And, seemingly, it had all gone wrong. And here she was, barely thirty, and a prostitute in Singapore. It seemed a long way to fall.

Once we finished eating, Isabel lingered for another half-hour listening to our chatter and then said she had an appointment — that's the word she used — and really had to get going. Edith and I expressed polite dismay and said we must do it again sometime. Where could we get hold of her?

"Just leave a message at the café," she said, "and I'll meet you somewhere. That's the easiest way."

"All right," said Edith. "We'll have tea or perhaps dinner again."

We watched her walk away, her body so thin you could see her shoulder blades jutting through the fine silk fabric of her frock. I felt sad for her, and knew she must be going off to some distasteful assignation for a few dollars, probably just enough to pay her rent and buy some cigarettes.

"What can we do?" Edith said in a tone that implied she did not expect an answer. For really, was there an answer? Was there anything we could do for Isabel?

We met a few more times after that, and on one of these occasions, after a few gins and some gentle prodding about why she had chosen to stay on in Singapore, she confided that she had had a child, a boy, and that he had died before his first birthday. His father, she said, had not lived to see him born.

"It's why I can't leave, you see. They're both here, buried in the ground, and I can't leave them. I've nothing else left in the world."

"Oh, my dear," said Edith, on the verge of tears, "that's not true. You're young, and very pretty, and you could find love again. You've known great tragedy in your life, but you can't give up."

"But what can I do?" she said. "I have no money, no skills. You've seen what my life is. I know I haven't fooled you."

"What would you like to do?" I asked. "Perhaps we can help you."

"I'd like a job," she said, "a proper job that pays my rent and buys me food and clothes, and maybe a ticket to the cinema once and a while. That's not a lot to ask, is it?"

"No, my dear, it's not," I said. "But you're unlikely to find that here. Why don't you consider returning to England, starting again?"

She laughed. "How could I get back to England? I have no money."

"I could take you back," I offered. "I travel back and forth frequently, and I would happily buy your passage, if you'd let me. I have many friends in London and I'm confident we could find you a job. I assure you, it's not impossible."

She looked at me for a long moment. Edith saw the virtue in remaining silent and said nothing. Then I watched as large tears began to fall from Isabel's eyes. Her chest heaved and her shoulders began to shake. Great sobs came from her throat. I couldn't remember ever having seen someone cry like that, as if she had taken the sorrows of the whole world inside her.

"Yes," she whispered between sobs. "Yes."

I booked passage the very next day and we returned to England on the first ship. During the course of the voyage, Isabel showed me her drawings and paintings, mostly small, eloquent portraits she had done of the Chinese prostitutes she had befriended. They were, I thought, quite accomplished and I offered to buy them from her. She was astonished that I would consider them worth anything. I told her I thought they were very good — not a lie, for they were — and that it had given me an idea. When we got to London I told her I would contact a friend of mine who had a commercial advertising firm. I was pretty sure he would be willing to take on someone in his art department who had a talent for painting.

Chapter Twenty-Four

Annabelle usually slept until midday and when she woke her first thoughts were of her darling little boy, Frankie. *Francis Edward Stone would be almost three now*, she thought. She hadn't seen him in a year since Sutty had taken him back to England to be raised by his own mother, Maud. Dear little Frankie. How she missed him. The only photograph she had of him, showing his beautiful silky blond curls, was already tattered and stained with tears. In her last letter to Sutty she had asked him to send her a recent picture of the boy so she could see how happy and healthy he was.

The decision to give him up had been the hardest of her life. Sutty had tried so many times to get her to come back to England and give herself and Frankie a chance at a new life. He had offered her the world, and she had turned him down. A part of her knew it didn't make sense, but another part of her realized that she couldn't raise her own child. She had tried for two years, and for two years had been tortured by the fact that every time she looked at Frankie, she felt the loss of his father even more. The boy was so much like Francis that she should have been comforted, but she wasn't. She wished it could be otherwise. In some strange way, she felt it was more important to take care of Francis, who was no longer living, than to take care of Frankie, who was so vital and full of promise.

If truth be told, Annabelle wanted to be dead. She wanted to be in the ground with Francis, and she knew this fact made her unfit to be a mother. After a lot of thought, much of it illogical and driven by grief, she begged Sutty to take the child back to England with him and give him the life and education he deserved. In her heart, Annabelle believed these things would replace a mother's love, especially a mother whose love was buried with her dead husband.

May God forgive me, she thought as she watched the departure of the ship that would take young Frankie and Sutty far away from her. She knew she might never see her son again, but she didn't dwell on that thought. She would watch him grow up through letters and pictures, and maybe, someday, he would come back to her as a young man, a successful lawyer or doctor or teacher — whatever he wanted to be. She knew Sutty would give him that.

Sutty had spoken often of his mother, Maud, for whom he had the highest regard. If Maud had raised a son who admired his mother so much, then she would be a good mother to Frankie, even at her advanced age (Sutty wasn't exactly sure, but he estimated her age to be about seventy). Besides, she was wealthy and there would be servants to help out, most likely a nanny or nurse, maids, a cook. Frankie would be loved and well cared for.

The birth had been difficult. Annabelle had been thin and undernourished, even though Sutty constantly brought her food and fresh milk. "Please try to eat, Annabelle," he would say. "This baby needs you to be strong and healthy. Please give him a chance." Her arms had been like twigs, but she had tried her best, even though she woke up every morning in tears, and fell asleep every night the same way. She seemed to love Francis even more in death, if that was possible. What haunted her was that all of his hopes and dreams and enthusiasm were gone as well, and those things, she realized, had sustained her in the difficult life she endured in Singapore just to be with him. It was so unfair that he should have been wiped from the earth so horribly by a fever so voracious it had eaten him alive in a matter of days. What kind of world was this? What kind of world to bring a child into? Did Annabelle want her baby to die rather than be born into such a world? It was unthinkable, she told herself. But while she didn't want him to die, she didn't seem able to give him a life. There was nothing left in her to give. At least, that's what she believed.

But Francis Edward Stone had been born, in spite of her misgivings and her thinness. He had come into the world, kicking and screaming after a labour that seemed to last for days. She had been in agony for five hours before Sutty came and found her. The shop owner downstairs had heard her cries, and had finally sent for Sutty, who he knew was staying at the Raffles. The pain had started well before dawn, and the shop had not opened until nearly ten in the morning, so there was no one to hear her during those early hours.

They got her to hospital and a bed had been found. She was two weeks earlier than expected. Sutty had persuaded her to see Dr. Ashford and he had estimated the date of birth. There were eighteen more hours of agony before little Frankie arrived. She would never forget it. She had nearly drowned in her own sweat. *Let me die now*, she kept thinking. *Please, let me die now. Cut me in half if you have to and take the child, but let me die now.*

When it was over, they placed the baby in her arms and she wept because it was Francis she saw, and she remembered again how she had lost him.

But Frankie was safe now, in England with Sutty and Maud. And today there was another letter from Sutty telling her he was coming to Singapore in three months time.

> January 12, 1928
> Dearest Annabelle,
> It has been many months since I've seen you, but I look forward to seeing you again on my next visit to Singapore. I am booked to arrive March 10 on the P&O and will look you up as soon as I'm settled. I will be staying, as usual, at the Raffles should you wish to leave me a message.
> Little Frankie is doing exceedingly well and growing like a weed. He is already three and a half feet tall and runs like the wind. He is quite the chatterbox and never tires of asking questions. His

"Grand Maud," as he calls her, adores him and answers each and every one of his questions with patience and wisdom. Grand Maud she truly is, with more stamina than the entire Indian Army.

But I know he misses his mother still and says a prayer for you every night — "God bless Mummy and God bless Daddy, who's in Heaven, and God bless Georgie" (his new Beagle pup, named for the King) "and teach him not to chew everything to bits," after which follows a long list of names, including Grand Maud and me, the cook, Nurse Nancy, the maids, the gardener, and anyone he met that day, and not necessarily in that order. He is a real treasure.

I implore you and will continue to implore you to come back with me to England, Annabelle.

In the meantime, I enclose a recent photo of Frankie.

We send our love and hope this letter finds you well.

Your devoted friend,

Edward

Annabelle looked at the photo of Frankie and saw how he had changed, even in a few short months. He was no longer a baby, but a little boy, and soon he would be going to school. She knew he would miss her less and less as time went on, but she seemed to miss him more. One thing she was certain of was that he would not die of fever the way his father had. And this knowledge sustained her in her loneliest moments.

The path she was on, if it was a path, seemed to be taking her nowhere, and yet ... what? There were the Chinese girls whose portraits she painted, although portrait was too grand a word for the drawings she did. Annabelle drew comfort from being among people whose lives were sadder and more desperate than hers. She couldn't explain this, but that's what it was: a kind of cold comfort. And as time went on and she became more deeply mired in their unhappy lives, it became more difficult for her to think of leaving.

She folded Sutty's letter and put it with the others in a lacquered box he had given her. Too much thinking would do her no good. Besides, it was time to go out and do what she usually did at this time of day: visit Francis's grave. She would tell him about their son and about Sutty's pending visit. On the way, she would pick up fresh flowers for his grave and a steamed bun for her lunch. She would look at the small oval photograph of him embedded in the gravestone and she would pretend he was there with her. It was her favourite part of the day. The cemetery was peaceful and shaded and they would be alone together.

It never occurred to Annabelle that her daily visits to Francis's grave might be morbid or strange. It had become a normal part of her day, like stopping at the greengrocer and picking out the bruised fruit and wilted vegetables that he would give her at a reduced price and then buying a packet of biscuits or tea from the shop two doors down.

She had been doing this for nearly four years now. And in the evening, she would walk over to Chinatown and talk to the prostitutes and persuade them to let her paint their pictures. Sometimes she sold a picture and that would keep her going. Sutty sent her money, too, and although she hated to take it, she knew she couldn't survive without it. He paid her rent in advance so she could stay in the same rooms she had shared with Francis. And the shopkeepers knew that if she couldn't pay, Mr. Edward would pay the next time he came back to Singapore. And he always came back.

Annabelle knew it wasn't much of a life, but it was the one she had made for herself — the one she clung to and the one that connected her to Francis. That was all that mattered.

CHAPTER TWENTY-FIVE

"I never thought I'd enjoy unpacking crates so much," Maris told Dinah. "The last time I did it, Angela gave me shit for being so slow. Remember?"

"I remember," said Dinah. "You got off easy. She's been on my case for months."

"When's she coming back, by the way? Does she let you know or does she just surprise you?"

"She lets me know, thank God. Otherwise I'd be in a constant state of anxiety."

"I don't know why she treats you so badly. You're Peter's sister, after all."

"His half-sister," said Dinah, "by a Chinese mother."

"Meaning you had the same father. But I knew that. Do you remember your father?"

"Oh, yes, I remember him well. He was very much

in love with my mother. She was much younger than him and very beautiful. At least, I thought so. Maybe I imagined the whole thing, but I always thought it was a big love affair between them."

"So he left Peter's mother for her?"

"Oh, no. She was his mistress. You didn't know that?"

"I guess not. I always figured she was his second wife. Silly me," said Maris, making a face.

"It was very common then," said Dinah. "I was born ten years after Peter. His mother, Henny, knew about me, but didn't acknowledge either me or my mother."

"Henny?" said Maris.

"Yes," Dinah laughed. "Henrietta, I think. She and Father were married in England in the fifties. I have Peter's photo albums. We'll sit down sometime and have a look at them."

"I'd love that," said Maris. "It sounds like a fascinating story."

"It is," said Dinah. "Believe me."

Maris had started coming into the gallery every day with Dinah and helping out. There was plenty to do because Angela was always sending a new shipment. She was relentless and was constantly on the move, making new contacts and milking old ones. Sometimes Dinah had instructions to hold shipments until Angela came, in which case they were stored in the back room or in a locker Dinah had leased when the back room filled up.

"I think she doesn't trust me to price it right or display it," said Dinah. "And of course, Peter always called up the customers when he thought there was something they would like. Although I do remember that she didn't trust him to open all the shipments, either."

"Control freak," said Maris.

"Big time."

They sent Dinah's cousin Lim out to get lunch while they continued unpacking, dusting and polishing, discussing the displays, and deciding on pricing. Dinah was grateful for Maris's help with the displays. She seemed to have a good eye for it, the way Peter had, sensing what would show better where and next to what. For her part, Maris found herself enjoying the work. She felt useful for a change and it felt good to carry on with what Peter had been doing. It was like keeping his memory alive. It was still very much his gallery.

Maris liked Lim — she called her "Slim" because she was so tiny, smaller even than Dinah — and Lim thought Maris was wonderful. A real artist. Lim was impressed whenever one of the artists came into the gallery. She would run out to get fresh buns and make their favourite tea, treating the visit as a special occasion.

"She's young," said Maris. "Give her a few years and she'll get over it. Be prepared to pick up the pieces when she discovers we have feet of clay. It could be crushing. I'm thinking nervous breakdown, major depression at the very least."

Dinah laughed. "You know what would be really funny?" Maris shook her head. "If Angela comes back and starts giving you a hard time. I can picture Lim turning into a Rottweiler and letting Angela have it — right between the eyes. Wouldn't that be great?"

"You're scaring me, Dinah," said Maris. "Maybe you need a holiday."

"Actually," Dinah agreed, "I probably do. Now that you're back, maybe I'll just do that."

"All right by me," said Maris. "I'd be happy to manage things for a while. I'm sure Slim and I could do very well. I think we'll try and double sales, just for the fun of it."

"On second thought," said Dinah, "maybe I'll wait. I don't want to be out of a job when I come back."

Maris had been back in Singapore a month when Axel Thorssen walked into the gallery. Dinah spotted him first and thought he was a good-looking guy, but not the usual type of customer to amble in off the street. When Maris came out of the back room carrying a carving of a fertility goddess from Indonesia, Dinah saw her eyes widen when she spotted the tall, fair-haired man. Maris looked over at her and smiled, then mouthed the word "cute."

Dinah went up to him and said, "Can I help you with anything, sir?"

Axel said, "I'm kind of new at this, but I liked what I saw through the window and thought I'd come in and have a closer look."

Maris was listening as she set the fertility goddess on a pedestal. She thought she detected a Scandinavian accent. Either that or German, she wasn't sure.

"Are you interested in something that hangs on the wall, or an object, say, pottery or a carving?" Dinah was saying.

"I think maybe an object would suit me better," said Axel.

"Are you living in Singapore?" said Dinah.

"No, just here on business. I live in Sweden."

Right the first time, thought Maris. Scandinavian. The accent was a little softer, more lilting than German.

"We ship to Sweden," said Dinah. "In fact, we ship all over the world."

"How long have you been here in Singapore? The gallery, I mean."

"A long time," said Dinah. "My brother opened the gallery in 1989."

"That would be Peter Stone, of Peter Stone Gallery? Like the sign says?"

"Yes. Peter Stone."

"Is he around?"

"No, I'm afraid my brother passed away nearly a year ago."

"I'm sorry," said Axel. "I didn't mean to pry."

"It's all right. I'm slowly getting used to it." Dinah smiled. "I'm Dinah, by the way. And this is my associate, Maris Cousins. She's a painter."

"Pleased to meet you both," said Axel. "I'm Axel Thorssen. Future collector, perhaps."

"You've chosen an excellent place to start, Mr. Thorssen," said Maris. "Dinah and I can guide you gently and painlessly through the process."

"I'd like that," said Axel. "And, please, it's Axel."

"Where would you like to begin?" said Dinah. "Should we be talking about age, colour, shape, basic material?"

"Whose?" asked Axel. "Mine or yours?"

They both laughed and Maris smiled. *Sense of humour*, she thought. *Or, at least, trying to be funny.*

"Maybe we should be talking price range," said Axel. "I'm not a wealthy man."

"You don't need to be wealthy to be a collector," said Dinah. "Especially at the beginning."

"And later?"

"Well … if you get the bug …"

"There's a bug? Uh-oh. Then I'm in trouble because I usually catch whatever's going round."

Dinah laughed again. "Would you like some tea, Axel? We have green, oolong, black, and orange pekoe."

"Ah, so we're starting with colour. I'll have green, thank you."

Maris smiled and went back to ask Slim to bring them green tea for three.

When she returned, Dinah was showing Axel the Indonesian fertility goddess. The figure was kneeling with her hands on her large belly; her enormous breasts were shaped like coconuts with the nipples pointing skyward. "This is a relatively new piece," said Dinah, "carved from chinaberry wood from Bali. We have priced it at 125 Singapore dollars, which is around seventy Euros. Not expensive at all."

"It's exquisite," said Axel, picking it up. "It feels solid."

"It is," said Dinah. "Chinaberry is a fairly dense hardwood of very high quality. It's resistant to humidity, which is why the Balinese use it for their carvings. Although it's a coarse wood, when properly finished it has a beautiful smooth texture and interesting grain. Don't you agree?"

"Yes, it's quite remarkable," said Axel. "I think I'm getting the hang of this collecting thing. You see a piece and you have to have it."

Dinah laughed. "You're a collector at heart, Axel. I can feel it."

Just then Lim walked in with the tea, and Dinah invited Axel to sit with her and Maris to talk about some of the finer points of collecting.

"You mean Visa or MasterCard, I imagine," said Axel.

He just gets funnier, thought Maris. *Better not to encourage him.*

"Just kidding," he said. "I'm smarter than I look."

"That's a relief," said Maris and smiled at him. "Just kidding," she added.

"Maris," said Dinah, "Mr. Thorssen is a potential client. Don't be cheeky or we'll lose him."

"Axel," said Axel. "And I think I like the way you do business. The personal touch and all. It's the most fun I've had in weeks. I don't suppose you'd both consider having dinner with me sometime. Maybe even tonight. I'm free, and I'm sure you'll be hungry later."

"Well, that depends," said Dinah.

"On what?"

"On whether you're just interested in us, or in us and our stuff," said Maris.

"Oh, both," said Axel. "Definitely both."

CHAPTER TWENTY-SIX

Axel treated Maris and Dinah to dinner at Raffles. He thought about doing a prowl of the hawker stalls in Chinatown, then decided it would be better the first time to talk to them in a quieter place. He didn't want them to know he'd been in Singapore for several months and thought it seemed more tourist-like to have dinner at the hotel. *Besides, it would be a nice change for them,* he thought. They probably weren't used to such grand dining. The downside, of course, was that they might try to sell him some of the more expensive items in the gallery. Actually, he had liked the Indonesian sculpture and was considering buying it.

Dinah and Maris arrived on time and met him at the cocktail bar of the Courtyard restaurant. Here, under the ornately carved arches, they could order oriental or

Mediterranean-style seafood, al fresco, surrounded by palm trees and potted plants. It had a charming colonial look and feel and was one of Axel's favourite spots in the hotel, mainly because the dress code was more casual. Axel hated being told what to wear to dinner.

They ordered drinks and chatted about things Singaporean in general for the first half hour. Axel told them he was there on business and hadn't had a lot of time to sightsee, but that he was looking forward to a little time off so he could wander around the various districts and maybe do the boat trip on the river.

"It's so hot and humid all the time," he said, "that I walk one block and I have to stop for a cold drink and some air conditioning." He laughed. "I'm not used to this kind of weather. Even in the middle of summer in Stockholm it's never this hot."

"I know," said Maris. "It takes some getting used to. I grew up near the mountains in British Columbia, where it gets cold and it gets hot, but never this extreme. It's the humidity that kills you. I've gotten used to being sort of damp all the time, but Dinah never seems to sweat at all. And she wears long sleeves when it goes below thirty degrees. It drives me nuts."

Axel laughed. "You have my sympathy."

They moved to a table with a large umbrella and the waiter brought their appetizers. They dug into crispy calamari, chicken satay with spicy peanut sauce, and vegetable spring rolls. Axel ordered a New Zealand sauvignon blanc, not the cheapest thing on the menu by any means, but he intended to write it off as a business expense. The wine reminded Maris of her mother and the evenings when they had shared a similar vintage. It seemed like a long time ago now.

"So tell me more about the gallery," said Axel, as they waited for their main course. "I'm interested in where you get your stuff. Do you travel around the world looking for it or do you have agents doing that for you?"

"Well," said Dinah, "my late brother's ex-wife actually owns the business now and she operates mostly out of Germany, where she has agents, but she also travels a fair bit, too. She has a good eye, and I have to admit, she and my brother were a great team, businesswise. They just didn't do as well as husband and wife." Dinah giggled. "Oh dear," she said, "am I being indiscreet? I'm not used to drinking."

"It's okay, Dinah," said Maris. "You haven't revealed the combination to the safe, yet."

"That's a relief," said Dinah taking another sip of wine. "This is very good, Axel. Thank you for treating us so well. But I'm sure it's supposed to be the other way around. We're supposed to be entertaining you so you'll buy our stuff."

Axel laughed. "You're right," he said. "I could always quietly disappear before the bill comes, if you like."

"That's quite all right," said Maris. "We're happy with this arrangement. I don't think Angela would like it if we spent all the profits on one potential customer."

"Angela?" said Axel.

"Yes," said Maris. "Peter's ex. She's a very shrewd businesswoman."

"Well, you seem to have a pretty successful enterprise. You're not a partner, Dinah? Being Peter's sister and all?"

"No," said Dinah. "That might have changed in time, but I don't think Peter intended to die so soon."

"Oh, I'm sorry to bring that up. It must be painful for you. Was he ill?"

Maris and Dinah looked at each other.

Maris said, "He was murdered, Axel, and the case has never been solved."

Axel stared at them in silence. He hadn't expected that and wondered how it had escaped the scrutiny of Satya and Charles.

"I'm sorry to hear that," he said. "Very sorry."

"Thank you," said Dinah.

"It's been hard," said Maris. "Dinah's done her best to carry on, and the clients have been very loyal. But the worst part is not knowing what happened to him and why. I mean, it's not like Peter had enemies. He was so decent and honest, and the gallery was his life. It was his own work of art, if you will."

"You were close to him, too, were you, Maris?" said Axel.

"Yes. He was my mentor in a way. He gave me confidence in my work and sold a lot of my paintings."

"Yes, that's right," said Axel. "Dinah said you were a painter. I'd like to look at your work sometime."

"I haven't done much lately," said Maris. "Not since Peter died. It kind of took the stuffing out of me and I had a bit of a dry period. I even went back to Canada for a while to stay with my family. But I decided I really wanted to be here, and I'm glad I came back. Dinah's been shouldering the whole thing on her own, and I want to help her keep the gallery going. I certainly owe it to Peter, and Dinah's the best friend I've got."

Dinah smiled. "Thanks, Maris," she said, raising her glass of wine.

When they finished their meal, Axel and Maris ordered dessert, but Dinah declined and just had coffee.

"That's another thing I hate about her," said Maris, "besides the fact that she doesn't sweat. She eats only as much as she needs and doesn't stuff herself like a Christmas turkey."

"That's okay," said Axel, signalling for the bill. "Between the two of you, I think I got my money's worth. It's been a pleasure, ladies, and I hope we can do it again sometime."

"I hope so, too," said Dinah. "But it will be our treat next time. We'll do a hawker crawl. You can't be in Singapore and not eat hawker food."

"Absolutely," Maris agreed. "We'll show you the town."

"Sounds fantastic," said Axel. "And will you hold that goddess piece for me, Dinah? I'm giving it very serious consideration."

Dinah smiled. It was a small sale, but maybe they had a real collector in Axel and he'd buy more. Angela would be pleased. A new client was always good news.

The next day when he got to the office, Axel said to Satya, "Get me everything you can on Peter Stone, gallery owner, murdered about a year ago. And I mean everything."

"Okay, Boss," she said. "I'm on it."

Chapter Twenty-Seven

Satya managed to get hold of the police report on Peter's murder. As he read through it, Axel saw that the investigation had been pretty thorough — interviews with all known associates, customers, neighbours, people from both the personal and professional sides of Peter's life — but it had all turned up nothing. Death by poison, inflicted by person or persons unknown. *Strange*, thought Axel. And worth filing away for future reference.

For the last few months, Axel had been working through Satya's alphabetical list of possible smuggling operations, which included his own suggestion of art galleries. There were many in Singapore, and there had been another alphabetical list to work through in that category. Peter Stone's gallery was pretty far down the list, but it was the only one in which the owner had been murdered. Could there be a connection?

He had enjoyed his dinner with Dinah and Maris, and found himself thinking about Maris. She was very attractive: tall, big-boned, but graceful and kind of sexy. She had worn a gauzy blue dress that swirled and clung to her at the same time: very feminine without being girlish. Axel wasn't attracted to thin girls who never seemed to enjoy food and usually smoked to kill their appetite. He'd grown up in Sweden where girls were health-conscious but not to the extreme of working out five times a week and eating only raw foods, or whatever fad diet was current. Maris had enjoyed her food and didn't seem self-conscious about it. She had joked about Dinah being so slim and not overeating, but it had been with affection, not malice or envy.

Axel decided to wait a while, then go back to the gallery, purchase the Indonesian piece, and take them up on their offer of a hawker crawl, as they called it. That way he could see Maris again, and find out more about the workings of Peter Stone Gallery.

Satya's research had revealed that the gallery had opened in May of 1989 and had quickly become successful. Stone's taste and his instincts for what people would like were undisputed, and it hadn't taken long for word of mouth to spread among well-to-do Singaporeans, expats, and tourists. A good part of the business involved distributing artworks (mainly sculpture) from mainland China, Thailand, Burma, Laos, Cambodia, and Vietnam to Europe and America.

Stone had been born in England in 1959 and had moved to Singapore with his parents as a child, where his father worked as a tea exporter. Raised and schooled in Singapore, Peter had met his future wife in Germany where he was taking a fine arts course at Berlin University of the Arts. They had married in 1986 and moved to Singapore. Shortly after that, they set out on a tour of Southeast Asia. Their interests in art and sculpture, especially South and Southeast Asian, had coincided and, during their trip, they had shipped back numerous artifacts, including sculpture, jewellery, paintings, and handicrafts, both modern and ancient.

The decision to open the gallery had been a joint one, and they became equal partners in Peter Stone Gallery in 1989. As time went on, Peter spent more and more time at the gallery and Angela spent more time in Germany, where she contracted a number of agents to travel and buy for the gallery — young, adventurous travellers like she and Peter had been.

Eight years after they married, Peter and Angela divorced, although they remained business partners. Peter's half-sister, Dinah, had been hired in 1993 as Peter's assistant. Dinah also had a degree in fine arts, from the Malaysian Institute of Art. As she had told Axel, she was not a partner in the business, but she had taken over the day-to-day running of the gallery after Peter's death.

Axel finished reading the file and wondered if it could be a front for a smuggling operation. If it was, it seemed doubtful that Dinah knew about it. Although why he thought that, he wasn't sure. He had liked her and had not detected anything of a devious nature in her. She had seemed open and honest and genuine. That didn't mean she was, of course, it only meant she seemed that way. Axel had known very charming and seemingly guileless people who were actually pathological liars and thieves. If you were going to operate in the world of international smuggling, you had to be good to survive and not get caught. Being personable was part of the game. Still, his instincts were telling him that Dinah was not a liar and a thief.

Maris seemed to have no part in the business, other than that her paintings were sold through the gallery. She seemed to have taken Peter's death hard, and it had blocked her from working for several months. Could she be the connection? Was there more at stake for Maris in the gallery's continuing than met the eye? Maybe Peter had been the mastermind all along. And maybe his untimely death had nearly put an end to the whole operation. And what about the ex-wife? Where was she in all this?

He would definitely have to meet her.

CHAPTER TWENTY-EIGHT

On the Tuesday following their dinner with Axel, Angela arrived at the gallery unannounced. Maris thought the gallery was looking wonderful and was quite pleased with the way she and Dinah had displayed the new works but Angela barely noticed and did not comment. She swept into the back room, depositing her umbrella and bag in the space behind Dinah's desk, and demanded that Lim bring her tea and biscuits.

"Welcome back," said Dinah under her breath. *Really*, she thought, *there's no excuse for this kind of rude behaviour.*

Maris, who hadn't seen Angela for months, popped her head around the door and said, "Angela! What a pleasant surprise." Her face was expressionless and her voice flat. Angela didn't seem to notice.

"Hello, Maris," she said absently, as she sifted through a pile of mail. Looking up, she said, "When did you get back?"

"Didn't you get my email?" said Dinah. "I told you Maris was here two months ago."

"Yes, of course you did," said Angela, looking down at the papers on the desk. "I forgot."

Maris looked at Dinah and mimed wiping away tears. Dinah rolled her eyes and thought, *Here we go.* She had learned long ago that it was better to wait until Angela spoke. There was no point being polite or asking questions. Angela would tell you what she wanted you to hear when she was good and ready. Anything else was useless chit-chat.

"Has anyone interesting been in the store lately?" Angela asked, without looking up.

"Interesting how?" said Dinah. "All our customers are interesting."

Angela shot her a scornful look. "I mean unusual, different, asking a lot of questions about how we do business."

"No," said Dinah. "We've had a few new customers. Just last week a man from Sweden was here and purchased an Indonesian fertility goddess. He was a beginner and asked questions about collecting." Dinah didn't mention that she and Maris had gone to dinner with Axel and he had paid.

"Sweden?" said Angela. Dinah nodded. "Hmmmm," murmured Angela.

"What?" said Dinah. "We've had customers from Sweden before."

"Nothing," said Angela. "It's just that there's a rumour going around that Interpol is planning some kind of sting in Singapore, something to do with animal skins or whatever."

"So what's that got to do with us?"

"Nothing. I just don't want anybody snooping around, that's all. You never know who might talk to who about what." Angela was being cryptic and both Maris and Dinah looked baffled.

"Okay," said Dinah. "I never talk about the business to anyone, anyway." She tried to remember if Axel had asked any probing questions. But why would he? They didn't deal in animal skins. She shrugged at Maris and shook her head. When they were alone in the gallery, she said, "See what I mean? She comes in here out of the blue and then comes out with something like that. I think she's paranoid."

"She's probably got permanent jet lag," said Maris.

"Do you think it might be terminal?" said Dinah.

Maris groaned. "Was that a deliberate pun? Like, should I laugh now?"

"Yes, and yes. You see how she spreads darkness and despair whenever she's here? You were in a good mood half an hour ago. So was I. Now look what's happened."

"Hmmmm," said Maris. "And you were funnier half an hour ago. You're right. It's her."

They agreed to keep their heads down and avoid contact with Angela. She'd hunt them down when she wanted something.

"What do you think of this sting thing she's talking about?" said Dinah.

"I don't know. Sounds weird. I know there's a lot of smuggling of exotic animals and birds that goes on, but why would she think we had anything to do with it?"

"Because she's paranoid, that's why."

"We haven't had any strange customers lately, have we? At least, not that I've noticed."

"No," said Dinah. "Things seem pretty normal to me. Look at this," she added, picking up a small framed drawing of a rickshaw. "Isn't it lovely?"

"Yes," said Maris. "It is. Very evocative of another time and another place."

"I wish you'd start painting again, Maris. I really miss seeing your work in the gallery."

"I know. I want to, Dinah. I really do," she said. "Soon. I promise."

"Okay," said Dinah. "I'll hold you to it."

Over the next few days, it became apparent that Angela was going to be around for a while. She was staying in Peter's condo, for which she had continued to pay the maintenance fees. "No point staying in a hotel while I'm here," she'd told Dinah. "It's a perfectly good apartment and a good location. Besides, it's not the right time to sell. The market's down."

If you say so, thought Dinah. There was never any point to arguing with Angela. She did what she wanted. There were still things in Peter's estate that hadn't been settled because of their business arrangement. As far as Angela was concerned, the condo belonged to the business. The paperwork just needed to be completed, which she hadn't gotten around to yet.

Axel called one day to ask about their hawker crawl. Dinah told him the gallery was closed on Mondays, so that would be the best day for her and Maris. Axel agreed to meet them at Raffles and they would go from there. Dinah wasn't keen on Angela finding out about their spending time with Axel — she might want to muscle in and hard-sell him on something expensive — so she waited until Angela was out of the gallery before telling Maris.

"I said we'd meet him at his hotel," Dinah said. "No point arousing Angela's curiosity."

"Agreed," said Maris. "Good idea."

They met at eleven in the morning and Dinah suggested they take the MRT to the Maxwell Road Food Centre. "The nearest station is Tanjong Pagar and then we can walk to the corner of Maxwell Road and South Bridge Road. It's right in the heart of Chinatown," she told Axel. "Don't be fooled by the modest exterior. It's one of the best, if not the best, hawker places in Singapore."

"I'm in," said Axel. "Lead me to it."

They got there in plenty of time before it started to fill up with the lunch crowd.

"You have to try the Guangdong wonton mee," said Maris. "It's my favourite. Noodles with roast pork and wonton."

"And the pork rib soup with rice and the char kway teow," said Dinah. "Sublime."

"Char what?" said Axel.

"Char kway teow," Dinah said. "It's like a national dish, with noodles and soy sauce, and eggs and cockles."

"Cockles?" said Axel. "You mean those little clam things?"

"Yes, that's right," said Dinah.

"I think we should get one more dish," said Maris. "Why don't we order some oyster fritters?"

"Good idea," said Dinah.

"And Tiger beer?" said Axel.

"Tiger beer all round," said Maris. "We don't have to go back to work."

They told Axel about Angela's unannounced arrival and complained that she always criticized whatever they did. He listened attentively and without comment. He had called Satya and Charles that morning and told them he wouldn't be in the office, and that he was going on a hawker crawl with the two women from the Stone gallery.

"Are you sure this is strictly business, Boss?" Charles had asked.

"Of course it's business," said Axel. "What else would it be?"

"Um, let me think," said Charles. "Two attractive females. One Chinese, one Canadian, unattached." He paused. "You're right. What else could it be?"

"Exactly," said Axel.

"I bet they take you to Maxwell Street," said Charles. "If they do, make sure you have the wonton mee. It's exceptional."

"If it's so good," said Axel, "how come you haven't taken me there?"

"It's on the list," said Charles. "Keep me posted."

"About what?"

"The food, of course. I want to know what you eat."

"Goodbye," said Axel.

"Bye," said Charles.

Axel had to agree. The food was exceptional. He didn't let on to Maris and Dinah how long he'd been in Singapore and how he was being educated in the local cuisine by his two assistants. He wondered if there was some way he could find out more about this Angela character. Why she spent so much time in Europe and also why she flew back and forth to Singapore unannounced.

They sat there until almost three o'clock, digesting their food along with another beer. Dinah told him he should come back another time and try the Hainanese chicken rice at Tian Tian, and she pointed out the hawker stall with the blue and white sign so he'd remember. But for tonight, she said, we'll go to Lau Pa Sat Festival Market because there's a night market on Boon Tat Street, and also, he simply had to see the amazing Victorian cast-iron filigree structure that was the old market. It was one of their favourites, and she and Maris went there often. Tonight they would go for satay and the twenty-four-hour dim sum.

"Not to be missed," said Dinah.

"Definitely not to be missed," said Maris.

"You two can eat more than any two women I've ever known," said Axel.

"The secret is to pace yourself," said Maris. "We'll have the satay as a kind of appetizer, maybe with a little more beer, then later, much later, after we've shopped the night market, we'll do the dim sum. It's not far from your hotel," she continued, "so you'll be able to roll yourself back and into bed."

Axel sighed. "Count me in," he said. "Not to be missed is not to be missed."

As the afternoon and evening wore on, and they ate, drank, and shopped their way through Lau Pa Sat and Boon Tat Street, Dinah noticed that Axel became more and more interested in Maris and Maris seemed to get more and more interested in Axel. He bought both of them beaded bracelets at one of the craft stalls. Then he bought a few trinkets for his nieces in Sweden. "My sister's kids," he said. "They tell me I'm their favourite uncle, and I know it's true," he said, laughing, "because I'm their only uncle."

Maris told him she had two nieces, as well, and they were growing up way too fast. She told them the story of her mother begging them not to have breast implants. "Then their father told them to wait until they were married so their husbands could pay for it."

Dinah thought Axel laughed harder than was warranted, but then decided it was because they had drunk a lot of beer and were having such a good time. Besides, she reminded herself, she had no nieces or nephews so maybe the story was funnier than she thought.

They finished their hawker crawl around one in the morning and took Axel back to his hotel, where he put them in a cab and paid the driver to get them home safely.

Back in the apartment, Dinah turned to Maris before going into her bedroom and said, "I think Axel likes you."

Maris yawned and said, "Get out. He was flirting with you all night."

Chapter Twenty-Nine

But it was Maris that Axel was interested in. He couldn't seem to get her out of his mind. She was smart, funny, beautiful, and she had a sense of adventure. He wasn't looking to fall in love, but he knew that when two people were away from home, anything could happen. There always seemed to be a heightened sense of urgency, as if everything would end when the journey was over. People were more impulsive when they travelled, especially when they travelled alone. *Should I take a chance?* he wondered. *Would she reciprocate?*

There was only one way to find out. A week later he asked her out to dinner. Not her and Dinah, just Maris alone. When Maris accepted, Axel made a reservation at Imperial Treasure Super Peking Duck Restaurant. He had been wanting to try the Peking duck, which was reported to be excellent.

Maris met him at the restaurant, in the Paragon Mall on Orchard Road, and they ordered drinks. Maris was nervous but tried not to let it show. She hadn't been on a "date" in years — funny how she hadn't even thought about it until Axel phoned — and it felt like a first-ever date. *Silly*, she told herself. After all, she and Dinah had been out with Axel on a couple of occasions and she hadn't felt the least bit nervous. Maybe because she hadn't thought Axel was interested in her; he had paid her and Dinah equal attention, even though she'd told Dinah otherwise. And maybe this wasn't about dating and Axel's liking her at all. Maybe he wanted something else. Maybe he was going to pump her about the business, confirming Angela's suspicions. She was speculating, she knew, just in case it (whatever "it" was) didn't work out. Just because he was good looking and eligible didn't mean she should fall for him. Nevertheless she had dressed extra carefully, choosing a periwinkle blue shirt with a scoop neck that was very flattering, and pairing it with flared white pants, also flattering. She wore her favourite earrings, long and dangly, in blue and silver, with four silver bangles on her left arm. She decided not to wear her watch. She would not think about time tonight.

While they waited for the Peking duck, they talked about a lot of things. Axel didn't like to talk about his work, she discovered. ("I do nothing but work all day. In the evening I like to forget about work.") So they talked about art (which he said he didn't know much about) and collecting (about which he said he was learning, thanks to her and Dinah), about travel (he was a more experienced traveller than her, but it was mostly for work, so he couldn't claim to be adventurous), and about food (he liked to cook as well as eat).

"Women find it attractive when a man likes to cook," said Maris. "But then you probably already know that." She laughed and so did he.

"Well, I don't always cook for women," he said. "Mostly it's for my pals when we play cards. Then I cook up a big pot of something, like pea soup with pork or maybe some meatballs with potatoes. Swedes love potatoes. We have many potato dishes, like Jansson's Temptation, my specialty."

Maris laughed. "What's Jansson's Temptation?" she asked.

Axel smiled. "It's potatoes and onions baked in cream with sliced herring or anchovies on top. Very delicious. Maybe I'll make it for you sometime."

"Sounds good," she said, but her face said otherwise. "Tempting."

Axel laughed. "Trust me. It's very good. I cook it the way my mother did."

"Your mother was a good cook?"

"Still is," said Axel. "Especially her kåldolmar: cabbage rolls stuffed with beef and pork. Nobody makes them like her."

"My mother's a pretty good cook, too," said Maris. "We never had much money so she had to use her imagination. We grew a lot of our own food, so it was always fresh and wholesome, but there wasn't much variety. We ate a lot of brown rice and vegetables," she laughed. "That's why Singapore is food heaven for me." She told Axel a bit about growing up in British Columbia on a hippie commune, and about how her father had split for another life. "My mother says it shows he doesn't know who he is, but he's been living his 'new' life for almost thirty years, so maybe that's who he really is. A car salesman."

When the duck came, it was perfection. Nice crispy skin with a thin layer of fat between the skin and the meat. It came with shredded green onions, sticks of raw cucumber and hoisin sauce. The pancakes were as thin and delicate as crepes. The rest of the duck meat was taken back to the kitchen and turned into a tasty noodle dish.

"I'm glad I wore loose clothes," said Maris. "I'm stuffed."

"Me, too," said Axel. "I couldn't eat another thing."

"Not even your mother's cabbage rolls?"

"Please, stop," said Axel, holding his stomach. "I may never eat again. Ever."

"All right," said Maris. "Best meal ever. What's yours?"

"That's a tough one," said Axel, "but I think it's got to be a grilled salmon I had once in Norway. It was rubbed with lemon and vodka and some tarragon, and was cooked over a fire on a cedar plank. Exquisite. They told me it was a Norwegian Viking recipe." He laughed.

"Mmmm. Sounds delicious. My sister would love that. I'll have to tell her about it."

"And what about you?" asked Axel. "What's your best meal ever?"

"I had a lobster once in Old Montreal that I actually dreamed about, it was so good."

Axel laughed. "Only women dream about food."

"What do men dream about?"

"Women. Or nothing. I don't think men dream much."

"Everybody dreams," said Maris. "Not everyone remembers their dreams."

"Perhaps. I remember very few dreams."

"Maybe you wake up too fast. I think you have to wake up slowly so the dream doesn't escape your consciousness."

"It's true. I do wake up fast. I open my eyes and that's it. I'm ready for the day."

"Not me," said Maris. "I linger."

At one point during the evening, Axel's mobile rang. He answered with a terse "Hello" and listened for a moment. "Oh, hi," he said, and turned to Maris. "I'll just take this call, if you don't mind. I won't be long."

"No problem," she said.

He got up and walked away from the table, toward the entrance to the restaurant. He seemed to listen more than he talked, nodding and occasionally making a brief comment to the caller. When he came back, he apologized and said it was business. Because of the time zones, he sometimes got calls at odd hours and was obliged to take them.

"I don't mind," said Maris. "Business is business, after all. And that's why you're here. Right?"

"Right," he said, and smiled. "But next time I'll turn the phone off."

"Not on my account," she said. "I really don't mind."

Axel took a sip of his drink. "I'd like to sleep with you," he said.

Maris laughed, startled. "What? Because I don't mind if you take business calls during dinner?" Axel smiled. "It's okay," she said. "You're under no obligation to sleep with me."

"Okay," he said. "But I still want to sleep with you."

She looked at him. "Maybe," she said, "but not tonight. I'll need a little more time."

"How about tomorrow?" he said.

She laughed. "No. But next week is a definite possibility."

"Okay," he said. "I'm not going anywhere."

"Good," she said.

When she told her the next morning what Axel had said, Dinah nearly choked on her coffee.

"Get out," she said. "He didn't."

"He did."

"And what did you say?"

"I said okay. But not till next week."

"Get out. You didn't."

"I did."

"Get out," said Dinah. "That's crazy."

"I know," said Maris. "I have to tell you, that Peking duck was incredible."

In Matters of the Heart

A Short Story
by
E. Sutcliffe Moresby

If there is one thing I have learned in life, it is that it doesn't pay to be dishonest in matters of the heart. Where love is concerned, honesty must be the first principle. Any lie told at the beginning of a relationship, even the smallest lie, and even if it only seems to be a chance meeting, will surely catch up with the teller at some point.

I met a man once on the crossing from Malacca to Calcutta who told me his story. The weather was foul for most of the trip, so there was nothing to do but sit in the bar, drinking beer and swapping stories. As I am something of a collector of stories, I kept him entertained for a short time. But when he began to speak of recent events in his life, I knew he would better me. His tale was far more interesting than any of mine.

He had been living, he told me, for some years in the back of beyond in the Malayan jungle, managing a rubber plantation. It was the most unappealing sort of work that required one to rise at four in the morning, drink a cup of tea, and then make the rounds of the plantation on foot to inspect the trees and select those ready for tapping. This would take a good four hours, at which time he and his men would return to the kampong for a hearty breakfast before resuming the rest of their work. For his part, this involved a lot of paperwork and settling disputes that arose among the Malay workers. By mid-morning the heat would be brutal, murderous, and partnered most effectively by the stinging insects and the poisonous snakes.

He had been doing this for nearly ten years when he decided he would like to experience the companionship of marriage. He was nearly forty and didn't expect to live past sixty, given the hardship of his working life, the fevers he had suffered, and the toll of too much loneliness and too much drinking. The question was, where to find a woman who was willing to share the life of a plantation manager? He had a decent enough house and a couple of servants, but there wasn't a woman around for miles, except for a few natives who cooked and washed for the local workers.

So this chap, George, decided to advertise for a wife in the British newspapers, hoping that some equally lonely woman would respond. He sat up nights trying to write an ad that would be appealing and not too far from the truth. He knew that if he were completely honest, no woman in her right mind would consider his proposal. Finally he settled on the wording: "Single white male, Birmingham-born, age 39, seeks single female of similar age and interests to join him in Malaya, where he is manager of a large rubber plantation. Good income, spacious house, servants provided. Must be someone who enjoys nature and can adapt well to surroundings. Good health, intelligence, a love of reading and music will be reciprocated."

What he neglected to mention was that the climate was beastly, he worked long hours and was usually exhausted at the end of the day, there was no one else around for miles, nothing to do, and it was six hours travel on a bad road to get to the nearest town. Of the insects and snakes, he also remained mum. He hadn't exactly lied, he told himself, he had merely omitted certain facts. If someone was interested and responded to the ad with a list of questions, he would answer them as honestly as he could. But until and unless that happened, he would say no more.

It was two months, in fact, before he had a response: two responses to be exact. One was from a woman named Adelaide from Manchester, who asked if he was a Christian. She had a friend, she said, who was a missionary in Sarawak, and she wondered if she would be far from her friend. He replied that yes, he was a Christian (although he had a feeling he wasn't as devout as Adelaide would have wished) but that Sarawak was several hundred miles away and he doubted she would have a chance to visit her friend very often, as travel in this part of the world was difficult.

The second reply sounded more promising. A woman called Rose wrote from Yorkshire to say that she preferred a warmer climate — she was tired of English winters and would welcome the change — and that she did, indeed, enjoy reading and music and thought they might be compatible. The difficulty, of course, was that she was reluctant to agree to anything as serious as marriage without first meeting him, and since the journey was a very long one and involved some expense, she did not see how they could get to know each other. Would he, by any chance, be returning to England in the near future? She understood that people working overseas were given leave once in a while, and if his was not too far off, perhaps they could wait and meet when he was on British soil.

As it happened, he told me, he was to have a leave of three months before the end of the year. If Rose agreed to wait, they could get to know each other and have a courtship of sorts if she was interested in pursuing the possibility of marriage. She wrote back to say she would wait, and, in fact, she looked forward to meeting George and finding out more about him.

He became quite excited at the prospect of getting together with Rose, and he even pictured them married and returning to Malaya at the end of his leave. In order to keep their expectations of each other realistic, he suggested they exchange photographs so that they might at least know what the other looked like. Rose agreed and sent him a formal portrait of herself taken just six months earlier. It was a good likeness, she said, although she didn't always look so elegant. She had had her hair done before the photo session and they had applied some makeup. She didn't want him to think she was always dressing up and swanning about, but that she could "muck in," as she put it, when required.

The photograph showed a pretty woman with large eyes and a small mouth whose lips were slightly pursed to make them seem plumper. Her nose was long, which kept her from being beautiful, but it added character to her face and she was not unattractive. Her hair appeared to be a medium dark colour and was waved softly around her face. Although it was a head and shoulders portrait, she did not appear to be either overweight or underweight. In fact, she looked quite ordinary, which was a good thing because it meant she would not be vain and foolish and would probably have a fair amount of common sense. As he spoke, I wondered how George had gleaned all this from a posed photograph, but this was the way he described her to me.

She, on the other hand, would have seen a somewhat rugged-looking man with a craggy face, the lines etched deeply from hard work and many years in the sun. He was not exactly handsome but he had a certain manly appeal, being square-jawed and big-boned. She probably thought he was honest, straightforward, and decent, which he was, as far as I could tell.

The day came when George arrived back in England and he immediately took the train to Yorkshire to meet Rose. He would see his mother and sisters later and, if things worked out, he would be able to introduce Rose to them before they married. He was feeling exceedingly optimistic. He and Rose had corresponded during the past five months and had got to know more of each other and their likes and dislikes. Rose liked to cook and, with four brothers, she had been a big help to her mother in the kitchen when she was growing up. Now that she was nearing forty — thirty-six on her last birthday — she, too, was thinking about marriage. She had been working as a teacher for fourteen years and it was well past the time when she might have had her choice of suitors. George's proposal — an exciting one, at that — had seemed just the ticket. She had started to pin her hopes on this new life in Malaya as the wife of a plantation manager.

Rose had good reason to feel optimistic. George was a first-rate letter writer. With a mother and two sisters at home, he had been writing cheerful and glowing letters for ten years. He knew how to turn a phrase and tell a joke. His letters were charming and funny. He didn't want to alarm his aging mother or his sisters, who had led sheltered lives and didn't know much of the world. They were both unmarried, although Frieda, the eldest, had been engaged during the war, but her fiancé had been killed at Ypres. Daphne, the younger, worked part-time at the post office and had never had a beau. Their mother despaired at times but kept quiet. She had been a widow for five years and enjoyed having her two daughters living with her. She still hoped that her only son would marry and perhaps someday have children.

At last the day came when George and Rose were to meet. He knew as soon as he saw her that she was the one for him. She was taller than he expected, which was fine because he stood a good six feet. Her hair, which had been a medium dark colour in the black and white photo, was auburn and her skin was fair. Even before she said a word (in a voice that was low and warm and even intimate) he was swept off his feet. And it would only get better as he got to know her. Her chatty letters had not revealed what a wonderful throaty laugh she had, and how she enjoyed a good joke. Being raised with boys and having been a tomboy as a child, Rose was comfortable in the company of men. George thought this was a good thing because there were no other women around in his part of the Malayan jungle. But George didn't mention this. Plenty of time for that later.

Rose was equally impressed with George but she kept her feelings in reserve. She had told herself she would not be silly about him when she met him, and she would take her time and decide whether or not to marry him based on his character. Was he the kind of man she could spend her life with? At her age, she had to be practical. After all, she was not a foolish young girl, but a woman who had worked for a living and knew a thing or two about life. People often rushed into marriage for the flimsiest of reasons and came to regret it. Rose would not be like that. They didn't have a long time to get to know each other and make the most important decision of their lives, but she intended to do it properly, with care and sound thinking.

Nevertheless, she came very quickly to relish the sound of his voice and the endearing way he had of bending his head closer to her when she spoke. She asked him if he was hard of hearing — she was determined not to be blind to his faults — and he assured her he wasn't. He simply enjoyed the sound of her voice, he said. Her heart beat a little faster when he said this, and it occurred to her that no man had ever uttered those words to her before.

"Don't think you can charm me with that kind of talk," she told him, but she said it with a smile, and he knew he had charmed her. It meant he had a chance. He was staying at a small inn in the village, but he spent most of his time with Rose and her family. He liked her brothers, two of whom were married, one was still a bachelor, and the youngest lived at home with his parents. They were a rowdy lot, but down to earth and kind hearted. They teased him about Rose but he took it all in stride. Nobody asked him any pointed questions about his life in Malaya, other than to ask if he liked it, and to comment on how exciting it must be. George didn't disabuse them of this notion, and just laughed and nodded his head when they said things like that. He chose not to remind them that if Rose married him, they would not see her for quite a long time. Or that letters often took several weeks to arrive, or that news, good and bad, also travelled slowly. *All in good time*, he thought. If they were not concerned about these things, he would not burden them.

Only one thing remained, and that was for Rose to meet George's mother and sisters. They took the train to Birmingham and both of them were nervous during the trip. George was absolutely certain they would love Rose, but he wanted Rose to love them, too. Rose, on the other hand, was prepared to like them and hoped they would like her. Her family had embraced George as one of their own and had high hopes for their marriage. It would be perfect if George's family felt the same.

She wasn't disappointed. Although George's mother and sisters would probably have accepted anyone he brought home because they wanted so badly for him to have a wife and family, they couldn't have been happier with Rose. She was ideal, they thought, and the two of them made a very handsome couple. So it was settled. George proposed and Rose accepted and the marriage date was set for a week before his scheduled return to Malaya. He booked a second ticket, requesting a larger cabin, and plans for the wedding were undertaken. For his part, George left it to the women. He agreed with whatever they wanted, including the colour of his tie. He was prepared to stand on his head and walk on his hands if that was what Rose wanted. Anything, just to be happily married to her at last.

The wedding day arrived and the wedding took place at Rose's village church, going off without a hitch. The men were all scrubbed and stuffed into their best clothes, and the women were glowing with happiness, especially Rose. Rose's father gave the bride away and her brothers acted as groomsmen. The bridesmaids had known Rose all her life and treated her like a queen on her wedding day. Everything was perfect. Birds sang gloriously; flowers bloomed in profusion; people laughed heartily and wiped away tears of joy. The dinner was a sumptuous banquet and the liquor flowed like a river.

Rose and George set off for a week's honeymoon in Brighton before boarding the ship at Southampton that would take them "home" to Malaya. Rose's excitement was palpable; she had a husband and would soon have her own home to take care of. In time, she hoped, there would be children. George had never been happier.

And then, as if copied straight from a Victorian melodrama, it all came crashing down. They arrived during the monsoon when flooding was at its worst. Rose's luggage, containing all her worldly goods, including her carefully packed trousseau, was soaked on the pier and didn't dry out properly for weeks. Rose herself was soaked to the skin from her first day on Malayan soil. But there could be no waiting it out. George had to get back to the plantation and his job. They would need to travel for days in torrential rains, enduring muddy roads and gloomy skies. A heavy grey pall hung over them. Water ran down hillsides in buckets, often washing out the road. At times, they would be forced to wait in the car, or sit it out in a café if there was one nearby. It seemed to Rose there wasn't a dry place in all of Malaya.

"At least it's not freezing cold. In Yorkshire there would be hailstones," she said, in an attempt to remain positive and cheerful in the face of such disaster. "I said I wanted to live in a warmer climate, didn't I?"

"Well, you got your wish," said George, who would have given anything to change all of it in a single stroke.

He didn't tell her that it would be much, much hotter after the monsoon rain stopped and the sun came out.

Rose's auburn hair hung damply around her face, the lovely waves of her portrait washed away. "It'll be better once we get home," she said, imagining clean sheets and dry towels. George knew better, but he remained silent. *She'll adapt*, he thought. She was game.

But Rose wasn't game enough. When she saw the cramped and gloomy bungalow that was to be home, she tried to hide her disappointment. Dreary on the sunniest of days, it was plain and lackluster in the rain. "It's not as spacious as I thought it would be," she said, surveying its smallness.

"We can add on some rooms," George said. "It might take a bit of time, and we'll have to wait for the rain to end, but it can be done." He was nothing if not optimistic.

"Yes. That's a good idea." Rose was looking at the lumpy bed that took up most of the space in the main bedroom. There was a wardrobe that held what few articles of clothing George possessed, and a wooden rung-back chair. There were sheets on the bed, and they were dry, but the mattress beneath felt damp.

George sensed that things were not going well. "Cheer up," he said, putting his arm around her shoulders. "It won't rain forever. When the sun comes out, you'll forget all about the wet."

She smiled in an effort to appear unfazed. "You're right," she said. "It won't rain forever."

But it continued to rain for several more weeks. When the clouds parted and the sun came out, it was only briefly, and not long enough for anything to dry.

Rose could see mildew beginning to appear on her leather shoes and handbag. And there was a musty smell to everything, including the furniture — what there was of it. *All of this can be changed*, she told herself. *I can make this into a comfortable home, as soon as it stops raining.* But in the back of her mind, a little voice kept saying: *It rains like this every year, and maybe twice a year. I guess I'll just have to get used to it.*

The problem was that she truly loved George and wanted to be married to him. But as the days went on, each seemingly wetter than the previous one, Rose began to feel that she had been deceived. Still, she tried to give him the benefit of the doubt. Perhaps she just hadn't been listening properly. Although she had vowed not to be "silly" about George, maybe she had been. Surely it was her own fault that she was disappointed. She blamed herself for having inflated the whole thing in her mind into a blissful tropical paradise. *It's only rain*, she reminded herself. *It's not the end of the world.* She told herself she would just have to get on with it. If you don't like something, make an effort to change it. That had always been her motto. She would buy new furniture and sew curtains. She would meet other women and find out how they coped. There were plenty of things she could do.

But one by one, Rose's ideas and plans were flattened. There were worms in the flour; the butter and oil were rancid; the water needed boiling, even to wash the clothes; the mosquitoes were horrendous — small and silent, they struck without warning, leaving red, itchy welts on the skin. There seemed to be test after test of Rose's resilience. Yet time and again she bounced back with another idea, another plan. And then, one day, the rains stopped as suddenly as they had begun, and the sun came out. The relentless, scorching sun. Rose's fair skin burned and blistered; she was constantly thirsty but daren't drink anything unless the water had been boiled for half an hour. And she didn't trust the servants to tell the truth, so she monitored the boiling of it herself. She felt her energy draining away as the temperature rose. And then there was the humidity, the stupefying humidity that poured sweat into her eyes and onto her blisters.

By this time, Rose had come to understand that there were no neighbours, no other women she could commiserate with. There was no one and nothing that was less than half a day's journey away. She had brought books with her, but she found it difficult to focus her mind on them. The days became long and stultifying. She barely saw George most days, and when she did, he was too exhausted to give her much attention. The servants all spoke a foreign language or their English was limited and often incorrect. She spent her whole day trying to communicate simple things. She longed for real conversation.

Then, finally, when she couldn't hold it in any longer, it all came pouring out. Why hadn't George told her, warned her even, that it would be like this? What had possessed him to think she could be happy here? That she would come to like it? How many lies of omission had there been? At first, she said, she'd thought it was her fault that she was miserable. But in time she came to realize that he had deceived her. She had been mightily deceived. She had been brought here under false pretences. He had known and he hadn't told her. It was unforgivable. He had no right. She wanted to go home. It was over. She had loved him once but now it was over.

"I'll never trust you again," she said. Her expression was stony, unyielding; she was long past tears by now. Her mind was made up.

"And so," George told me these many years later, "I had to let her go back. I couldn't hold her. I couldn't ask her to give it more time. She had changed and there was no going back to the old Rose that I had fallen in love with."

"Do you wish now," I said, "that you had been more truthful?"

"I do," he said, "but who's to say she wouldn't have been scared off sooner? Who's to say she would have come at all if I had been more truthful?"

"Ah," I said. "Yes. Who's to say?"

CHAPTER THIRTY

In 1928 Sutty made yet another trip to Singapore to see Annabelle. He found her greatly changed from the year before. Whereas the previous year she had been "herself," this year she wasn't. It was as if the part of her that was Annabelle, the core of her, had shifted a few degrees off its axis. Something had slipped out of place and she wasn't quite Annabelle anymore.

She had gradually become nocturnal, which Sutty already knew. Her nighttime wanderings in Chinatown had extended further and further into the night until she was coming home at daybreak. She had begun to spend more time with the prostitutes and their clients (or maybe they were pimps; Sutty didn't know) and now she was smoking cigarettes and drinking whisky, something she had never done before. It troubled him greatly.

"Annabelle," he said, "what are you doing?" It had taken him a long time to find her, and when he did find her, it was four in the morning and she was in an all-night bar with a young man she called Dicky.

"What does it look like I'm doing, Sutty?" she said. She seemed to speak more slowly than she had in the past. "I'm having a drink with my pal Dicky."

Her pal Dicky was well past the point of sobriety, and although he was probably only about twenty-eight, he looked forty. He had a round baby face that was attractive in a young man but didn't age well. His eyes were puffy and bloodshot, his jaw was already slackening, with little pouches at the corners, and his pale brown hair was thinning.

"Hello," he said, standing up unsteadily and extending his hand. "My name's Dicky. Who are you?"

"This is Sutty," said Annabelle. "An old friend of mine. From before."

"Oh," said Dicky. "How do you do?"

"How do you do," said Sutty, shaking the man's limp, damp hand. He pulled up a chair and sat, signalling the barman for a drink. It didn't look like anybody was ready to leave yet.

"How have you been, Annabelle?" he asked her because he couldn't think of anything else to say.

She looked at him. "You know," she told him. "It doesn't get better." She lit another cigarette. "How's my little Frankie?"

Sutty didn't want to talk about Frankie in that place and in that company, but he said, "Frankie's wonderful, Annabelle. Full of mischief. A right little devil he is, into everything. He's going to be four soon."

"I know," said Annabelle. "I remember."

"Of course you do," said Sutty.

He remembered the time he had searched all day for Annabelle with little Frankie in his arms. She had disappeared from the flat, leaving the baby alone. Sutty had been frantically worried, imagining the worst. He had finally brought the baby back, put him to bed, and waited for her to return. She did finally and couldn't, or wouldn't, account for her absence. She just said she'd been walking. He told her he'd looked everywhere for her. She said she was sorry but she just had to be alone for a while.

"But you left the baby alone, Annabelle. What if I hadn't come along?"

"But you did," she said. "Besides, someone would have heard him. He would have been all right."

That's when Sutty had realized that he couldn't leave little Frankie with her if she continued to refuse to return to England. There was no choice but to take the boy back with him. He, Sutty, and his mother could raise him, and little Frankie would be safe and secure. The boy would have an education. Whenever Annabelle agreed to come home, she would naturally take him back. But for now, while she was in this frame of mind, there was no other solution.

He was surprised that she agreed to his plan so quickly. And now little Frankie was almost four years old. He hadn't seen his mother in three-and-a-half years. He thought of Sutty's mother, Maud, as his mother, and his nurse Nancy, whom he called "Nanny," was more of a mother to him than anyone.

As the days went by, Sutty had a now-or-never sense about Annabelle. He believed that if he didn't extricate her from the life she was leading in Singapore this time — he had failed so many times in the past to get her to return — that she would never go back. She was on a slippery slope right now and soon she wouldn't have the strength to pull herself up. He feared it might be too late even now.

Every time he had tried to persuade her to go back to England with him, she had refused, saying she couldn't leave Francis, that he was here, his soul, his spirit, whatever you wanted to call it. But Francis had been dead for over four years now and Annabelle was more concerned about the dead than the living, namely her own child.

As he came to see more of how she was living now — especially her dubious relationship with the wretched Dicky — the more he despaired. It was as if Frankie didn't exist for her anymore as a real person. He was more than a memory, but less than a presence, whereas his dead father, Francis, was a constant and real being to Annabelle. She still spoke to his grave as if he were there. Because of this, Sutty decided that firm and even extreme measures were called for. He would get Annabelle onto a ship, come hell or high water.

The next P&O passenger ship would be leaving Singapore for England in fourteen days. Sutty booked two cabins. For the next two weeks, he kept close tabs on Annabelle, watching her, spending time with her, talking to her. Yet he never once mentioned the ship or the two tickets, or his intention of taking her with him. If you had asked him during those two weeks if he had a plan to get Annabelle onto the ship, he would have said no. He had no idea, short of knocking her over the head and carrying her, how he would do it. But he had fourteen days to figure something out.

If Dicky had been half a man, he could have enlisted his help, appealing to his better nature (if he had one) and persuading him that Annabelle would be in peril if she stayed in Singapore. But Dicky was a moron, a word Sutty was loath to use but he could think of no other that described him better. Dicky couldn't save himself if his hat was on fire, let alone help another human being. Besides, Sutty suspected that Annabelle was buying Dicky's drinks from her own meagre allowance, one that Sutty provided.

With only three days left before the ship's departure, Sutty came up with a plan. On the day of embarkation, he would meet her at Francis's grave to bid farewell to his friend (until next time) and then ask her to accompany him in the cab to the pier. Once there, he would invite her to his cabin for a drink. But he would take her to the cabin that was designated to be hers, and lock her in until the ship left. He would deal with the consequences later. The important thing was to get her on the ship. Once they were underway, she might come to see the rightness of his decision. She would begin to focus on seeing her little Frankie and would soon understand that she hadn't really left Francis behind, that his spirit would be with her wherever she went.

Sutty believed there was no other way and that it must be done.

If Dicky suspected something was afoot, he didn't show it. And Sutty didn't think he had the wherewithal to figure it out. Dicky was soused during most of his waking hours. Thinking wasn't an activity he engaged in.

Sutty barely slept the three remaining nights. He told Annabelle he would be leaving and, on the last night, asked if she would meet him at Francis's grave the next day at one o'clock so he could say goodbye. She agreed, and as far as Sutty could tell, she suspected nothing. He slept fitfully that night, waking several times. He had left her at three in the morning at a café where she was drinking, as usual, with Dicky and a few other less than desirable companions. It was no different from any other night, except that this night he had pulled out the recent photographs of Frankie and shown them to her again.

"He's so beautiful," she said. "He's like an angel."

"He looks like an angel," said Sutty, "but he's a little rascal. And smart as a whip."

"Like his father," said Annabelle.

"Yes, a lot like his father."

She went to put the photos in her handbag. "You don't mind if I keep these copies, too, do you, Sutty? I want a set to carry around and a set to keep at home."

"No, of course I don't mind, Annabelle. He's your son and he always will be. Maud and I are only temporary guardians."

She had smiled wistfully and said nothing.

The next day she did not appear at Francis's grave. Sutty waited an hour but Annabelle did not come. He went round to her flat in a taxi, with his luggage on the back seat, but she wasn't there either. He cursed himself for not knowing where Dicky lived, if indeed he lived anywhere but in bars and cafés, or occasionally bedding down in Annabelle's flat when he had nowhere else to go.

Where could she be? And why hadn't she shown up? Had she discovered Sutty's plan? But that was impossible because he hadn't said a word to anyone about the second cabin.

Reminded of the last time he had spent the day searching for Annabelle (that time with the baby Frankie in his arms), Sutty told the cabbie to drive around slowly so he could look on both sides of the street and into the open-fronted restaurants and bars. Surely he would spot one of them, either Annabelle or Dicky. But they were nowhere to be found and this presented Sutty with a conundrum. The ship was departing at 6:00 p.m. Should he be on it or should he stay behind and try and get some of his money back from P&O? What if Annabelle were ill or hurt? He couldn't just abandon her.

Sutty retraced his steps and checked the flat again. Maybe she had forgotten that he was leaving today. But Annabelle was not at the flat. He went back to the cemetery to Francis's grave hoping to find her waiting there for him. But she wasn't there either. As a last resort, he told the driver to take him to the pier. Maybe she had gone there directly, knowing she had missed their meeting at the cemetery. He told the cab driver to wait with his bags while he checked passenger waiting rooms and the ticket office. Then, finally, he boarded the ship and found the purser, who told him the lady had not come aboard the ship. He was positive.

By this time it was after four o'clock and Sutty had to make a decision: stay in Singapore or go. He decided to stay. There would not be another ship for three weeks, but that couldn't be helped. He had to find out if Annabelle was all right. He took the cab back to the Raffles and checked in again. The desk clerk was puzzled; he had known Mr. Sutcliffe Moresby for many years as a regular guest at the hotel and he had never done such a thing before. But Sutty did not explain; he merely went to his room and lay down on the bed to rest and to think. A little later he heard the ship's horn as it pulled away from the dock.

Sutty slept for a few hours, then decided to look for Annabelle again. Maybe she would show up at one of her haunts later that night. And surely he would find Dicky hanging around, cadging drinks from someone. Dicky would know where Annabelle was; he was never far away from her. Annabelle had never explained her relationship to Dicky and Sutty had been reluctant to ask. Annabelle didn't seem to have any real friends in Singapore, just people she met up with at various cafés. Not friends by any stretch of the imagination. Dicky was the closest thing, and he wasn't someone you would rely on if you were in a situation. Maybe they were lovers, but Sutty found that hard to fathom given Annabelle's continuing obsession with her dead husband.

Sutty set out at midnight on foot and walked to Chinatown. Most of the bars and restaurants were still going strong. Food was still being cooked in cast iron woks over hot fires — noodles, rice, prawns, pork, cuttlefish — because Singaporeans seemed to eat round the clock. It was a national pastime, and one Sutty didn't really understand; he preferred to eat his meals at regular times — breakfast in the morning, luncheon at midday, then tea, followed by supper later in the day. That made sense to him. But who was he to criticize? Every country was entitled to its culture. This was a different climate, a different race of people. The Chinese had been cooking and eating like this for centuries. Maybe Annabelle had gone native and that's why she preferred to go out late at night. But he knew that wasn't true as soon as he thought it. Annabelle had not gone native; she had gone a little mad. She had never recovered from the shock of Francis's illness and death. She had never really recovered from the shock of arriving in Singapore, marrying shortly after, becoming pregnant, and losing her husband, all within a matter of months. Sutty understood that it had all been too much, which was why he had stuck by her and tried to help her. But now he feared she was truly lost, possibly beyond redemption.

As he prowled around looking for Annabelle, Sutty recognized and was recognized by some of the people he had encountered while he'd been out with her. None of them had seen her that night and none of them seemed concerned that they hadn't seen her.

"She'll show up," one of them said. "She's gone missing before and she always turns up eventually. Don't worry."

But Sutty was worried. She had never failed to show up for an arranged meeting with him. This was not like the Annabelle he knew, no matter what her local acquaintances said. Annabelle would not do this to him.

CHAPTER THIRTY-ONE

For their fourth date, Maris invited Axel to the Jurong Bird Park. It was one of her favourite places in Singapore and she wanted to share it with him. They had been out to dinner a couple of more times and each time had been better than the last. Something had clicked between them and they were both being cautious, as if whatever this thing was, it was fragile and they didn't want to drop it.

"This bird park," she told him, "is truly one of the wonders of the world. You can't spend time in Singapore and not go see it."

"Okay," he agreed. "I can't argue with that kind of logic."

"This isn't logic," she said, "it's passion, pure and simple. I love this place."

"If you love it, then I'll love it," he said.

That's what she liked about him. Axel was always willing to go along. And his enthusiasm wasn't faked. He was genuinely interested in what she said, what she liked, and what she wanted to do. How often did a man like that come along? Even Dinah agreed: you didn't meet a man who shared your interests every day.

And Axel was encouraging her to paint again. He suggested she bring her sketchbook along to the bird park. Maybe she'd be inspired by all the magnificent plumage to express herself with colour again.

The day started out bright and sunny but by midday the whole of Singapore was under heavy cloud. The threatened rain arrived a few hours later with a familiar force. There was nothing to do but run for cover. Even the birds headed for shelter. But at least Maris and Axel had seen the best the park had to offer: almost a hundred species of the gregarious parrot, including colourful parakeets, macaws, and cockatoos, exotic birds of paradise, elegant (and screeching) peacocks, playful hornbills and toucans, odd-looking pelicans and penguins, and even the graceful black and white swans.

And she had been inspired. One bird had caught her eye — a scarlet macaw — and it was as if a light had gone on. He was magnificent; his plumage was blazing at her in red and yellow and blue. She did several sketches of the bird and couldn't wait to paint him in oils where the true intensity of his colours could come through. It was the first time since Peter's death that she'd felt this kind of excitement. It was as if some dormant part of her had been wakened. She had forgotten what it was like to feel this urge — no, it was more than an urge, it was a surge — and she sparkled. Axel was moved to comment on the sudden change.

"My God," he said. "I didn't realize that you were operating on such a low battery all this time. I thought you were luminous before, but now you're positively incandescent."

Maris laughed. She felt incandescent. She had been switched on after months of living in a gloomy half-light of depression and loss. That's what she had been experiencing, she realized, a huge sense of loss that nothing could replace. Peter had been irreplaceable in her life. And now Axel was here ... and the magnificent scarlet macaw to re-inspire her. Life was good again.

That night she and Axel had made love for the first time. Even though they had talked about it on their first date, it was spontaneous, the two of them going to his room at Raffles for a drink after a day of bird-watching, drenching rain, the excitement of Maris's new-found creative vision, and plates of hawker noodles. As Maris later told Dinah, it just happened, even though it had been all around them for weeks, the anticipation of it, the knowing it would happen.

For Maris, that day had been like the end of one road and the beginning of another. Her direction had changed in a matter of hours and it felt right. Everything about it felt meant to be. She wouldn't have used the word destiny, but what Maris felt that day amounted to a sense of destiny — that somehow this was fated. She was meant to go back to Singapore, to meet Axel, to go to the bird park on that day and see the macaw. It wasn't something she would say to just anyone, but Peter would have understood. He believed she had a destiny; it was why he had never given up on her, why he had encouraged her to work and grow and find herself artistically.

She spent the night with Axel, and even though he got one of his awkward business calls and went out into the corridor to take it so as not to disturb her, her happiness was uninterrupted. She would always think of this as her "night of nights." Corny, she knew, but Maris believed you did not get many days and nights like this in one lifetime.

Chapter Thirty-Two

On the morning of the third day, Sutty came down to breakfast and saw Dicky sitting in the hotel lobby. He looked haggard; his skin was grey and he had dark pouches under his eyes. He looked as if he hadn't slept in days. When he saw Sutty, he stood immediately and rushed toward him.

"What's happened?" said Sutty, fearing the worst. "Where is she?"

"She's in hospital," said Dicky. "She's all right but it's been touch and go. She tried to drown herself."

Sutty felt his knees go weak and put his hand on Dicky's shoulder. It felt hard and bulbous, like a doorknob. Dicky was like a skeleton and he reeked of alcohol. He told Sutty he had barely slept the past two nights. Annabelle had been unconscious when they found her and had remained in a coma. Luckily someone had seen her go into the river, but it had taken the boat some time to get to her. She had been drunk and very, very upset, Dicky said.

"But she didn't say a word," he told Sutty. "I had no idea she was going to do such a thing. I swear. No idea." He seemed bewildered and kept looking at his hands, as if the explanation had just slipped through his fingers.

"I was terrified," he said, suddenly burying his face in his hands and weeping. "I thought she was going to die," he sobbed.

Sutty continued to hold on to Dicky's shoulder while the man shuddered and tried to compose himself. He felt sick at the thought of Annabelle lying in a hospital while he had searched for her and cursed her for hiding from him. He hadn't allowed himself to think of the worst and now he realized he should have. Why hadn't he checked the hospitals?

"Why didn't you come sooner?" he asked Dicky. "Why did you wait so long?"

"I thought you had left," said Dicky. "You were leaving on the P&O. You said so." He reached into his pocket for a handkerchief and wiped his red-rimmed eyes. "Then someone told me you'd been around asking for Annabelle, and I decided to come here and see if you had stayed behind."

"Come on," said Sutty, pushing Dicky toward to door. "Take me to her."

She was in the women's ward of the General Hospital. Her skin was the colour of the bed sheet, a grey-tinged white.

She looked small and fragile, as limp as a rag doll. Sutty was suddenly so angry with her that he shocked himself. She was helpless, unconscious, and he wanted to shake her and scream at her to wake up and listen to him. She should have been on the ship with him, sailing for England and her son. Not lying in a hospital bed after trying to kill herself. How could she do this to him? To Frankie? What right had she to give up on her own son? Years of outrage came to the surface and Sutty had to back away from the sight of her before he lost control of himself. He knew this was the wrong reaction, but there it was. He would have to pull himself together and figure out what to do next. Annabelle must have been at the end of her rope to do such a thing, and so, he realized, was he. After all he had tried to do to bring her and Frankie back together, to give them a life together, and this was what it had come to.

He left Dicky to stay by Annabelle's bedside and went outside for a walk to calm himself. *What now?* he wondered. If she lived, could he somehow force her to come back to England with him? If she died ... but he didn't want to think about that. She would live.

Annabelle regained consciousness sometime during the night. Dicky had fallen asleep on the floor beside her bed and Sutty was sitting in a chair, awake but exhausted. The doctor had said it could go either way; there was no telling with cases like this. A lot depended on the patient and whether there was the will to live. Annabelle would probably need treatment, a long rest with fresh air and good food. She would be depressed and might even attempt suicide again, so she would have to be watched. Best to put her in a sanatorium where she would be supervised.

Sutty was composing a letter in his mind to his mother when Annabelle opened her eyes. "Sutty?" she whispered. "Is that you?"

"Yes," he said, moving to sit on the bed so she could see him better.

"Where's Dicky?" she said.

"He's sleeping," said Sutty, "under the bed."

"Oh," she said, and closed her eyes. "That's good."

In a minute, she opened her eyes again and said, "What happened?"

"You tried to drown yourself," said Sutty. "Do you remember?"

She looked puzzled. Then she turned her head away. "Yes," she said, in a voice that was barely audible.

Sutty took her hand. It was small and cold and he shivered because it felt like the hand of a dead person.

"I was very angry at you earlier," he said, "but I'm not anymore. Now I'm just very sad."

"I don't blame you for being angry," she said. "You've been so kind to me and to little Frankie. What would I have done without you?"

"I keep feeling I should have done more."

"No," she said. "You couldn't have done more. No one could have done more than you, Sutty." She turned to face him. "I'm so sorry," she said.

He nodded.

"Can you forgive me?"

He looked at her for a long moment. "I'll try," he said.

"Don't say that, Sutty. Say you'll forgive me."

"All right," he said, patting her hand. "I'll forgive you. But please don't ever do it again."

"I won't," she said.

"Promise?"

"Promise."

Chapter Thirty-Three

Maris had set up an easel in the utility room of Dinah's apartment. It was supposed to be used for drying laundry, but Dinah preferred to hang the clothes on the balcony where the sun shone in the morning. The utility room had a good light for painting and there was just enough room between the washing machine and the storage shelves for Maris to work.

Axel had surprised her one day by dropping by when she was working on a painting. It was a Monday and the gallery was closed, but Dinah had decided to go in and do some paperwork.

"How did you know I was here?" she asked him.

"I called the gallery and a little bird called Dinah told me."

"And you were just in the neighbourhood...."

"Well, not exactly," he said. "Let's just say I was out exploring Singapore."

Maris started to clean her brush but Axel stopped her. "No," he said. "Don't stop working. Can I watch for a while?"

Maris wasn't sure she could work with someone watching, but she said, "Okay. I'll try to pretend you're not here."

"I'll sit in the kitchen and be quiet as a mouse."

She was painting the scarlet macaw, or at least her version of the bird, which was more about colour than replicating the detail of every feather. She was immersed in the red part, her favourite colour, and felt confident for the first time in months that she knew what she was doing.

Axel watched her, fascinated by her intense concentration, and also by the way her shoulder and back muscles moved as she applied the paint. Her movements were sure and fluid, without hesitation. She was working with an electrifying red colour and applied the paint thickly in short, broad strokes. He recognized the macaw they had seen at the bird park and realized that she was turning it into something else. It was the bird but it was much more than the bird. Then he remembered that she had told him that art was about ideas, not just lines and colours. Good art conveyed much more. As she worked, he understood that she was painting the idea of a bird, and that he, the onlooker, could take this idea from the painting and see anything he wanted. He could make it his, absorb it into himself, and not just admire it from afar.

I think I'm falling in love with this woman, he realized. *I love her passion, her intensity, her intelligence, and the way she puts them all together and creates something original, startling, and beautiful. I've never known anyone like her. What am I going to do?*

Maris worked for another half-hour, then wiped her hands and announced, "Time for coffee."

Axel exhaled and realized that he had been on the edge of his chair, barely breathing, and totally focused on Maris and the painting. "Good idea," he said. "I'm exhausted."

She laughed. "Well, I can understand that," she said. "You've been working hard."

"No," he said, "I've been watching you work hard. I can't believe how brilliant your work is. I mean, it's stunning. And you're amazing."

She kissed the end of his nose and then he pulled her close and kissed her on the mouth. "I mean it," he said. "You're wonderful."

Her breath caught in her throat and she couldn't speak for a minute. "You're not so bad yourself," she said, kissing him again.

"Do you really want coffee this minute?" he asked.

"Well ..." she said. "Maybe later."

Two hours later, Maris went back into the kitchen and made coffee and a couple of sandwiches. They ate sitting on the bed and talked about many things. They spoke about their childhoods, how different and how similar they had been. They touched briefly on past relationships, boyfriends and girlfriends, and why they hadn't lasted: "We were too different." "The sex was great but…." "He played around." "She wanted to get married and have kids right away. I wasn't ready. We weren't ready." "I wanted to travel. He didn't." "I wanted to travel but she didn't."

How long did Axel think he'd be in Singapore? He couldn't say for sure. Would he go back to Sweden when his job was finished? Probably for a while. But then he might be given another assignment somewhere else. Was Maris going to stay in Singapore now that she was painting again?

"It feels like home to me," she told him. "I don't know why exactly. It's not anything like the place I grew up in. We lived in a small town, a village really, in one of the most beautiful places in the world. I wouldn't exactly call Singapore beautiful, certainly not in the sense that British Columbia is beautiful, but there's an energy here that I haven't found anywhere else. And it's not like I'm crazy about all the glass and steel office towers and the rows and rows of high-rise apartments," she said. "But the trees and the gardens are wonderful and restorative and they feed my soul. I feel free here." She laughed and shook her head. "In a place where it's against the law to chew gum."

"Maybe it's because you're so far away from everything you grew up with," said Axel. "That can be liberating. I always feel a little bit freer when I'm away from home. Nobody knows me, and they can't point to the man and see the boy he once was. I can shed that skin and be whoever I want to be."

"Does that mean you're not really the man you seem to be?" she said, looking at his naked body.

He laughed and pulled the sheet up. "Ask me no questions and I'll tell you no lies," he said, reaching for her. "What you see is what you get."

Later, much later, they took a taxi to Clarke Quay for something to eat. It was one of Maris's favourite places in Singapore, especially at night when all the little cafés and bistros were lit up and full of people. The former colonial row houses were brightly painted, the patrons were young and eagerly enjoying their food and friends, and former fishing boats went up and down the river with tourists and locals out for a night of entertainment.

Sitting opposite Axel, drinking a glass of wine, Maris tried to imagine them growing old together. Maybe they would be in a place like this, talking about their children, or even their grandchildren, or a trip to Greece they might take in the spring. They would share memories, finish each other's sentences, taste each other's food, and walk home arm in arm. They would be content.

Silly, she thought. *Nothing lasts forever.* She watched the boats on the Singapore River, their twinkling lights reflected in the water. *But then again*, she thought, *some things do last a lifetime.*

CHAPTER THIRTY-FOUR

Maris continued to be obsessed with the contents of Peter's trunk. She had dragged it halfway around the world and back again and still had not figured out what it meant. Whenever she had a chance, she read the stories by E. Sutcliffe Moresby, she studied the paintings of Chinese women by the mysterious AS, and she read the letters that were tied in bundles with blue ribbon.

It still baffled her why Peter had left these things for her. She picked up one of the first editions and started riffling through the pages. It was pristine, as if it had never been read. She picked up another and another; they were equally immaculate. Then she noticed one that appeared less perfect. She picked it up and turned it over in her hand. It was *The Severed Edge*, a book she had read years ago in school and one that Peter clearly had also read. She opened the book to Chapter 1 and an envelope fell out. It was addressed to her and contained a single sheet of paper. Peter's stationery was instantly recognizable by its colour, a deep taupe, and its heavy, linen-like texture. The note was in his handwriting.

Dear Maris, she read, *If you're reading this letter, it's probably because I'm not around anymore. I have bequeathed you this trunk and its contents in my will, which I hope will not be read for a very long time.* (Maris looked at the date on the letter; it was written just two months before Peter's death.)

I have made a disturbing discovery, he continued, and I'm not sure what to do. When I was unpacking a shipment the other day, I accidentally dropped a ceramic jug from China — one with a lid, traditionally used to hold herbs and dried medicines — and discovered that it was not empty, as I would have expected, but contained several dried artifacts. They appeared to be small animal parts: paws with the fur still on and possibly organs or dried snake meat. I'm pretty sure they're not ancient, like the jug, but fairly recently dried.

I spoke to Angela about it and suggested that she talk to her supplier. He (or she, Angela doesn't tell me who her contacts are) may not be aware that contraband is being shipped along with antiquities. He (or she) could be in a lot of trouble if these were discovered somewhere en route.

Angela thought it would be a bad idea to alert him (she admitted it was a man). She said it was probably a mistake and had been meant for another shipment. She felt it would be best to leave it alone and say nothing. She didn't want her supplier to know that she knew he was dealing in contraband. Or, if it was a mistake and had happened further up the chain, she didn't want to get her supplier into trouble. These were dangerous waters (her words) and it was best not to swim with sharks.

I have been uneasy ever since the discovery, and have decided to write it all down for someone else's eyes (yours, in fact) should anything untoward (meaning, not favourable, adverse, or unseemly) happen to me. Not meaning to be morbid, but just cautious.

By the way, if you're eighty years old and reading this, ignore all of the above.

With much love and affection, and many thanks for a true friendship (in case I forgot to tell you), I remain
Yours,
Peter

Trust Peter to be funny when he was obviously upset and disturbed by his discovery. It seemed that Angela's warning about a possible Interpol investigation was not unfounded. But she hadn't mentioned anything about her conversation with Peter. Well, that wasn't surprising. Angela never told her or Dinah anything related to the business end of things. It was typical of her to keep something like this to herself.

Maris's first impulse was to show the letter to Dinah and see what she wanted to do. It would have given her a lot of satisfaction to show it to Angela and watch her reaction, but somehow this didn't seem like the wisest choice. Angela would probably want to destroy the letter, while Maris wanted to keep it. It was personal, in a way, and it was between Peter and her. Did it have any connection to his death? Should she show it to the police? Doing that would definitely involve the gallery in some kind of investigation — not something she relished, and nor would Dinah and Angela, she was certain. Peter hadn't named any names in the letter and the police would surely want to know who the supplier was, at the very least. She knew this would infuriate Angela.

The next morning she took the letter into the gallery and showed it to Dinah. She watched as Dinah read the letter then closed her eyes to hold back her tears. When she opened them again, her lashes were wet, and she wiped them with the back of her hand.

"Well," said Maris, "what do you think?"

Dinah thought for a moment, read the letter again, and said, "I think we should go to the police."

"Really?" said Maris. "Seriously?"

"Yes, seriously."

"But that would mean an investigation and Angela will be furious."

"Too bad," said Dinah. "I don't care if Angela bursts into flames. This letter might help solve Peter's murder. It could be a clue."

"I agree. It could be a clue, but it's pretty vague. I mean, he doesn't name names and obviously the jug is long gone, as, I'm sure, are the contents. It's pretty flimsy evidence. They could say that Peter was just being paranoid."

"They could," said Dinah, "but Angela knows who the supplier is. She would have to reveal him. It's a start."

"So I guess that means you want to show the letter to Angela."

"I sure do," said Dinah. "And I can't wait to see her expression."

"Wow," said Maris. "You're one tough cookie. I'd have bet money you'd want to keep the letter secret."

Dinah looked at her. "I want to find out what happened to Peter," she said. "And if someone killed him, I want them punished." She paused for a moment. "Don't you want justice for Peter?"

"Of course I do," said Maris. "But I don't want to see the gallery destroyed in the process. This gallery is your future, and possibly mine as well. It's not about Angela; it's about you and me."

"No," said Dinah. "It's about Peter."

They showed the letter to Angela with predictable results. She was dead set against going to the police.

"No, absolutely not," she said. "That letter must be destroyed. Don't you understand what it would do to my reputation and the reputation of the gallery? Just the mention of contraband animal parts and the stink will hang around us. We'll always be suspect. My contacts will refuse to deal with me. We'd have to close the gallery. No," she repeated, shaking her head. "Destroy the letter. Right now, in front of me."

"It's my letter," said Maris, "and I'll decide what to do with it." Even though she knew Angela was right and she didn't want to see the gallery destroyed, it annoyed her that Angela was being so imperious. She didn't like being told what to do, especially by Angela.

Dinah, on the other hand, disagreed with Angela for different reasons. She held to her belief that this was an important clue to Peter's murder and that they owed it to him to find out who killed him.

"The police have been useless," said Angela, "and this letter won't make them any more efficient. Besides," she said, "they can pull my fingernails out and I won't tell them who my supplier is."

"Don't be so melodramatic," said Dinah. "The police don't have to resort to torture; they can probably arrest you for obstruction of justice or something and you'll have to testify at your trial." Secretly, though, she wouldn't have minded if they tortured Angela. She was fed up with her management style. Angela had no right to tell them what to do.

Ultimately the choice had to be Maris's. The letter was addressed to her. Peter had relinquished the information to her because he expected her to do the right thing. He could not have known what the future held, although clearly he feared that something might happen to him as a result of his discovery.

Maris thought about showing the letter to Axel. They had become intimate and she trusted him. She valued his opinion and would have liked his advice in the matter. But she wasn't sure this was the right time to introduce something this emotionally upsetting into their relationship. On the one hand, it would test Axel's commitment to her, but on the other hand, it could also drive him away. They were still in the early courtship phase of their relationship, she figured. Not the time for a big ordeal.

So what should she do? *When in doubt*, she thought, *wait*. Nothing was going to bring Peter back. There were a lot of things to consider and her decision would have consequences for all of them and the gallery. Would Peter have wanted her to bring about the end of the gallery? Something that had been his life's work? Was there a way she could do this and not have it ruin the gallery? Was there any way to separate Peter's life — and death — from the gallery?

Chapter Thirty-Five

That evening, Maris decided to show the contents of the trunk to Dinah. She thought it might help her make a decision about the letter. Since opening the trunk with Ray, she hadn't wanted to share the contents with anybody else, but she thought it was time and Dinah was the right person.

"You know Peter left me this trunk of stuff," she said, "and I want you to see what he left me. Maybe you can help me understand why he left it to me."

She opened the trunk and began to remove the items, starting with the books by E. Sutcliffe Moresby. "I've been reading my way through them, starting with the stories. I only found Peter's letter by accident when I opened the cover of this book and it fell out. Otherwise I don't know how long it would have taken me to find it."

"Maybe that's why he left you this stuff," said Dinah, "so you'd find the letter."

"He was taking a chance," said Maris. "I might not have found it for years."

Dinah laughed. "He probably knew curiosity would get the better of you and you'd comb through the whole thing looking for answers."

"Maybe you're right," said Maris. "But it's a strange collection of stuff and I can't figure out the connection."

Next she pulled out the portraits of the Chinese women and showed Dinah the initials AS in the corner of each of them. "They're quite beautiful, aren't they?" she said. "I'm fascinated by them. I mean, who's AS, why did she paint them, and why did Peter leave them to me?"

"I think they're wonderful," said Dinah. "Those faces are so expressive on the one hand, and yet so hidden on the other. They reveal everything and nothing, if that's possible."

"I agree," said Maris. "In trying to hide themselves, they actually seem to be telling us a lot. I think they were probably prostitutes, don't you?"

"Yes, probably," agreed Dinah. "Just from the amount of makeup. And also, there's a kind of hardness in the faces, even though they look terribly young. A pampered young woman might wear makeup but she would have a softness that these women lack."

"But why only prostitutes? And why only faces?"

Dinah shook her head. "And was the painter a man or a woman?"

"Ah," said Maris. "I think AS was a woman. There are two packets of letters, as well, and they're addressed to Annabelle Sweet. At least, the ones I've looked at are written to Annabelle Sweet from Francis something."

Dinah looked at her and her eyes widened. "Annabelle Sweet and Francis Stone?" she said. "Those were my grandparents. Peter's and mine. Our father's parents." .

"Stone," said Maris. "Of course. I wondered about the name when I first saw the letters, but then I completely forgot about it. I figured if he was related, Peter would have left them to you. I guess I just put it out of my mind. That was when I was back in Canada, so I didn't follow up on it at the time. Well, duh. How stupid am I?"

Dinah was shaking her head. "I didn't even know Peter had this stuff. He never showed it to me."

"Tell me about your father."

"What I know is that he was taken to England as an infant by a writer who was a friend of his father, my grandfather. He, my grandfather, died of fever before my father was born, and his mother, Annabelle, refused to leave Singapore. I think she went a little crazy," said Dinah, "after her husband died. Anyway, she was terrified that her baby would die of fever like his father, and she let this writer — who I now realize is probably this guy, E. Sutcliffe Moresby — take him to England to be raised by his mother.

"They — the Moresbys, I guess — had money and he received a public school education. Then he joined the air force during World War II. After the war, between about 1945 and 1955, he spent time in India and Ceylon, learning the tea trade. He became a successful tea merchant and married Henny in 1955 in England. I have pictures of them in an album Peter gave me.

"Peter was born in 1959 in England, but the family came to Singapore in 1960, after Malayan independence."

Dinah paused as if considering whether she should elaborate on this, then continued. "A few years later, my father took a Chinese mistress and I was born in 1969."

"I never knew any of this," said Maris. "I don't recall Peter ever talking about his parents. For that matter, neither did you."

"Our father, Peter's and mine, was like two different men," said Dinah. "The father Peter knew was married to an Englishwoman, Henny, who spoke her mind and took what came her way with a stubborn kind of courage and tenacity. I never knew her, of course, but I remember seeing her a few times. She was very tall and slender. Kind of like Lady Mountbatten — remember her?"

Maris nodded. "Yes, I've seen films of her and Lord Mountbatten in India before the partition."

"Yes," said Dinah, "very elegant and aristocratic. Although what I remember of Henny — and don't forget, I was a very young Chinese kid who was raised by a Chinese mother — Henny was cool, you know, cold. Not friendly or approachable, like Lady Mountbatten seemed to be.

"The father I knew lived with a Chinese woman, my mother, a nameless, faceless nonentity who bowed to his will and was subservient in every way. Because her family disowned her, she had even less of an identity — no ancestors to worship, no parents or parents-in-law to serve. I had very mixed feelings toward my mother," said Dinah. "I didn't like the way she kowtowed to my father and kind of shrank from people, never speaking unless spoken to, that kind of thing. But in many ways we were very close. She didn't have any friends and neither did I.

We were kind of shunned and that pulled us together. I felt very loyal to her, and protective, too.

"I think my father didn't really like women or their company. He didn't really leave Henny so much as withdraw from her. He forgot she was a person with feelings. He never considered her pain or her humiliation over what he did to her. Even though I didn't know her, I believed that what had happened had been my father's fault. I never heard my mother speak against Henny or demand that my father divorce her. She wouldn't have dared."

"Your father probably did it — you know, held on to everything—because he could," said Maris. "That generation of men felt entitled. He had the best of both worlds."

"Yes," said Dinah. "And in Singapore, it was common for a man to have a mistress, especially if he could afford it. I think the only woman who ever meant anything to him was Moresby's mother, the one who raised him. But because she was always old to him, he never really comprehended young women's passion or their vitality. Never saw them as creators and sources of life. I think that comes from never having a mother or possibly from being abandoned by his mother, which he was, in a way. She gave him up, after all, gave him away to Moresby. That probably left some scars."

"So this Annabelle Sweet was his mother and she stayed behind in Singapore?"

"As far as I know, she never left."

"That's very strange," said Maris, "because the letters from Francis were written while she was still in England and he was begging her to come out and marry him. I got the impression she didn't want to come. He kept telling her they could live a lot more cheaply in Singapore and he could write a book, which is what he wanted to do. If he went back to England, he would have to give up his dream of writing."

"What I gathered from my father, who didn't say much about her, believe me, was that she went mad after his father died. According to this writer Moresby, she kept saying she had to stay in Singapore because Francis was there. She cared more about her dead husband than she did about her baby. I don't understand how she could give up her baby, but apparently she could. Which maybe says a lot about her state of mind."

"So he never saw her again?" asked Maris.

"Not as far as I know. I'm pretty sure she died while he was still a child."

"Maybe the other letters will tell us something. I think they're from Moresby to her."

It was past midnight so they agreed to go through the letters another time. Maris was seeing Axel the next night, so it would have to wait a couple of days.

CHAPTER THIRTY-SIX

Maris and Dinah pulled out the trunk a couple of nights later to read the letters Moresby had written to Annabelle. They had opened a bottle of Chardonnay and were prepared to make an evening of it. Maris had been with Axel the previous evening and had not arrived home until the early hours of the morning, just enough time to shower and change her clothes for a day at the gallery. She wasn't being paid for her time, but Dinah was giving her free room and board and that was fine with Maris. And Dinah didn't seem to mind that Maris was spending a lot of time with Axel. She thought they were a good couple, and she was especially pleased that Axel was encouraging Maris to paint again.

"I've barely slept the last two nights, I've been so excited about this stuff of my grandmother's," said Dinah. "I wish I knew why Peter never showed it to me."

"Well, you know," said Maris, "he probably hadn't looked at it or thought about it for a long time, and then came across it when he decided to put his affairs in order. He was probably going to show it to you, but then he was murdered." Maris realized this was the second time she had used the word "murdered" when referring to Peter. The first was when she had told Axel about Peter's death.

"How shall we do this?" said Dinah.

"Let's put them in order first and see what dates they cover." They untied the bundle and checked the postmarks. All had been sent from England, between 1928 and 1931. There appeared to be three or four letters a year.

"Let's start with 1928 and read them in order," said Maris. "We'll single out anything unusual that isn't just letter chit-chat."

"Okay," said Dinah, and slipped the first letter out of the envelope. In a couple of minutes, she said, "You should read this one."

> August 12, 1928
>
> Dearest Annabelle,
>
> I arrived home a few days ago and can report that Frankie is in fine form. He painted me a picture of himself standing in front of his pony, which he has named Dulcie. Don't ask me where he got that from!
>
> I was reluctant to leave you, Annabelle, after all that happened recently, but Dicky assured me he would keep a close eye on you. I hope you will not

forget your promise not to do anything like that again. Suicide is not an answer to anything, and your death would break many hearts, mine and Frankie's uppermost.

I will never stop asking you to return to England. If you ever change your mind, let me know immediately and a ticket will be on its way.

As ever, with great affection,
Sutty

"Suicide?" said Maris. "Did you know anything about this?"

"No," said Dinah. "I wonder if Peter ever read these letters."

"I guess we'll never know," said Maris. "This next one is pretty straightforward."

November 26, 1928
Dearest Annabelle,
I was so pleased to receive a letter from you this month. Of course I'll send you the painting by Frankie. In fact, I'll get him to paint one especially for you. He asks about you all the time, but I fear you are moving further and further away from him as time goes by. I don't say this to make you feel guilty — never, never — but only so you'll know how much you mean to your dear son.

He does not forget you. You remain in
his heart.
We send our love.
Sutty

The letters from 1929 and 1930 were in a similar vein
with Sutty replying to letters from Annabelle, but not
always. Occasionally he would drop a note to say he hadn't
heard from her in a while and he hoped she was all right. A
couple of times he asked if she needed more money. Once
he wrote: I hope you're not giving the extra money to Dicky
because I fear he will only drink it away. I appreciate that he
looks after you to some extent and that he is a friend, but I
worry that he will inadvertently leave you with not enough
for yourself. Do be careful, Annabelle. There are some who
might want to take advantage of you. You have heard the
expression "fair-weather friends," I am sure. I'm not saying
this is Dicky, just that someone attached to Dicky might
not be so reliable. Sorry, I don't mean to lecture.

Toward the end of 1930, the tone of the letters began to
change, indicating that all might not be well with Annabelle.

December 8, 1930
Dearest Annabelle,
I am concerned about the note of
dismay in your letter. I won't say
despair, because I truly hope it is not
that. People often feel out of sorts
at this time of year, with Christmas

coming. Especially people who have suffered loss such as you have. Please assure me in your next letter that this is a temporary mood and that you are in fact feeling better.

As to your question whether I would be coming to Singapore in the next year, I had no plan to, but if you would like me to come, I certainly will.

Frankie is looking forward to Santa's visit and has submitted a long list of suggestions in case Santa's elves can't think of anything to bring him. His Grand Maud cannot say no to the boy, and I fear he is becoming spoiled. But he is a boy like no other and life would now be so dreary without him.

Wishing you a good Christmas, Annabelle and, dare I say, a happy one. I am enclosing a few extra pounds for you to buy yourself something special.

Please be well and don't wait too long to respond.

Yours, as ever,

Sutty

"Well," said Maris, "for a writer, he's not the most sensitive guy. I mean, if she was suicidal at one point, and now he senses dismay, shouldn't his warning bells be going off?"

"Maybe they were," said Dinah, "but he knew he couldn't do anything about it. I mean, what was he supposed to do? Jump on the next ship and spend two months getting there, only to find she had PMS that day?"

"I suppose," said Maris. "It must have been tough being in touch only by letter. No instant communication like now. People might die between letters and you wouldn't know it for weeks, even months. I guess there was a level of acceptance I find hard to understand."

"Listen to this," said Dinah.

> April 20, 1931
> Dearest, dearest Annabelle,
> Your last letter truly frightened me. You tell me you spent a few days in hospital, but you don't really tell me why. Was it fever? Did you meet with an accident? I wish you would be more forthcoming in your letters. I'm afraid my imagination runs away with me at times and I imagine the unimaginable. You know what writers are like. We are always making things up, especially if we don't have all the facts.
>
> Anyway, I'm glad you're feeling better and that whatever was the matter no longer troubles you. But next time you write, be more explicit. Please. If it was "female troubles," you don't have to give me details. Heaven forbid. But better that than what my uneasy mind can conjure.
>
> Sorry to be an old nag.
>
> Frankie, Grand Maud, and I send our love. And I also enclose a new

photograph of Frankie. See how fast he's
growing up! Before we know it, he'll be
in cap and gown.
Sutty

"Another suicide attempt?" said Maris.

"If that were the case, she probably wouldn't say
anything. I wouldn't, anyway. I think I'd want to hide the
fact from him. Unless, of course, she wanted him to come
right away. It could have been a ploy, but he didn't bite."

"Strange relationship they had," said Maris. "He
obviously cared about her, but she didn't seem to care
about anybody. Except her dead husband, of course."

"And maybe this Dicky character," said Dinah. "The
one Sutty doesn't trust but has to trust because he's the
only one around."

The last two letters appeared not to be replies to
Annabelle's letters, but pleas from Sutty to write to him
immediately.

October 23, 1931
Dear, dear Annabelle,
What has happened to you? I have heard
nothing for months and am frantic with
worry. I have booked passage on the
P&O leaving next week and will arrive
in Singapore the last week of December.
Please, I beg you, contact me as soon as
possible. I am forfeiting Christmas with
Frankie because I am so worried. If he
were a few years older, I would bring

him with me so we could ring in the New Year together.

This time you must return with me to England. I will not take no for an answer. It's time you were reunited with your son. He needs you, and I believe you need him.

I am not happy playing this authoritarian role, but you leave me no choice. I am losing patience, but remain Your affectionate, devoted friend,
Sutty

CHAPTER THIRTY-SEVEN

Maris showed Dinah some of the stories Sutty had written. "Read these," she said, "and tell me what you think."

Dinah read the stories and didn't say anything for a few minutes. "Wow," she said softly. "It's all there."

"That's what I thought," said Maris. "All of these stories seem to follow the same path, but they all end differently."

"I don't know the real ending," said Dinah. "I'm not sure how my grandmother died, but I'm sure she died a long time ago. My father told me he never saw her again after he was taken to England."

"It's almost as if the writer, Sutty, was trying to find a better ending. Like he couldn't accept the real one, whatever that was."

"I wish Peter were here," said Dinah. "He might have the answer. Maybe our father told him things he didn't tell me."

"Your father might not have known the real story either. Only Sutty knew and he chose to muddy the waters. He never wrote an autobiography, did he?"

"Not that I'm aware of. But there's been a lot written about him. Some biographers even suggested he was homosexual because he never married and had such a close relationship with his mother."

"Another possibility," said Maris.

"All we know is that he never had a long relationship with anybody — except my grandparents."

"Maybe he was in love with both of them," said Maris.

Dinah smiled. "Maybe," she said.

Later that evening, Dinah said, "I have an idea. Why don't we look for their graves? There's a cemetery adjacent to the church they were married in. Maybe they're buried there."

They decided to go to the cemetery on Monday when the gallery was closed. Again, Maris considered telling Axel and inviting him to join them, but then she thought better of it. Dinah might not appreciate an outsider tagging along.

As they rode the MRT to the City Hall stop, Dinah explained to Maris that there weren't many old cemeteries left in Singapore. Because of the scarcity of land, most of them had been closed, cleared, or relocated.

"They actually exhumed over a hundred thousand graves," she said. "The cemeteries board, or whatever it's called, managed to cremate and relocate a lot of the remains to Choa Chu Kang Columbarium, in one of the few existing cemeteries today. Most of the old cemeteries were closed in the late 1800s or the early 1900s. Or, once they were full, they were not allowed to expand and had to close."

"So the graves might not exist at all," said Maris.

"They might not," said Dinah. "At first, I thought they might be buried at the Fort Canning cemetery, but then I found out that it was closed in the 1860s. I think our best bet is the little graveyard next to St. Andrew's chapel, where they were married. Not all the churches have graveyards, either. One of the few is the Armenian Church, and that's not really a graveyard but a memorial garden. When one of the cemeteries, I think it was Bukit Timah, was closed in the late eighties, they sent the remains of some of the more famous Armenians there."

Maris smiled. "Famous Armenians in Singapore?"

"You'd be surprised," said Dinah. "Did you know that the four brothers who built Raffles, the E&O in Penang, and one other famous hotel — I think it was in Rangoon — were Armenian? The Sarkies brothers, but don't ask me their first names."

"I'm impressed you know that much," said Maris.

"And," said Dinah, "Agnes Joaquim, an Armenian who discovered the first hybrid orchid here, *Vanda* Miss Joaquim, which was named Singapore's national flower, is also buried there."

"Get out," said Maris, "now you're showing off."

"Seriously. We learned all this in school," said Dinah. "We even had a field trip to the church. It's the first one built in Singapore. And there's another famous Armenian, too. The guy who founded *The Straits Times* newspaper. He sold it after a year because he thought it wouldn't be profitable."

Maris laughed. "Good instincts, bad judgment," she said.

The chapel that Francis and Annabelle were married in

was part of St. Andrew's Cathedral, designed in the early
English Gothic architectural style and built by Indian
convicts. The existing cathedral was actually the second
structure built on the site. The first was erected in 1835
(during which time much jungle had to be cleared) and
demolished in 1855 after being struck twice by lightning.
The second building was begun in 1856 and consecrated
in 1862. Dinah insisted on reading this information from
the pamphlet provided at the entrance to the church.

"The spire rises 207 feet (63 metres)," she read. "Housed
in the spire are the Cathedral's eight bells, the largest being
equal in weight to No. 8 in the peal of St. Paul's Cathedral,
London. Given in memory of Captain JSM Fraser,
HEICS, they were cast by Taylor of Loughborough. After
installation it was discovered that the foundation of the
tower would not stand the strain of ringing. The bells were
then permanently fixed, their clappers tied, and they were
struck with hammers instead, so that they still 'chimed.'"

"That's lovely," said Maris. "Now, can we get on with it?"

"In a minute," said Dinah. "There's more: 'The small
graveyard that lies adjacent to the chapel was originally
a walled garden intended for meditation and prayer. But
as cemeteries in Singapore began to close in the latter
part of the nineteenth century due to the shortage of
land, the Bishop of Singapore decreed in 1910 that the
remains of church members and clergy could be buried on
consecrated ground within the meditation garden. This
practice continued until 1942 when the cathedral was
used as an emergency hospital before the fall of Singapore.'

"So chances are good that they're both here," said
Dinah. "Let's have a look."

The cemetery was still well maintained, even though it had effectively been closed for more than six decades. Many of the stones, however, had not held up well to time and climate. As they wandered among the graves looking for Francis and Annabelle, Maris and Dinah stopped to read a few of the gravestones.

"Some of them are so sad," said Dinah. "Look at this one. 'Here Lies Amy McCall, Age 19, Dearest Wife and Mother, With Her Beloved Infant Daughter, Mary, Age 3 Months. In Heaven with the Angels.'"

"Over here," said Maris, pointing to a granite headstone. "Three little boys, brothers, age three, five, and six. How dreadful."

Very few of the stones marked the graves of elderly people. Most were children or adults between twenty and forty-five years old. Many were "Beloved," "Cherished," or "Precious."

Maris was two rows away reading the headstone of a "Dearly Loved Daughter Taken Too Soon" when she heard Dinah say, "I found them." Maris turned and walked over to join her. They looked at the two stone markers set side by side:

Francis Adolphus Stone
1890–1924
Beloved Husband of Annabelle
and
Annabelle Sweet Stone
Dearly Loved Wife & Mother
1900–1931
She Died of a Broken Heart

Chapter Thirty-Eight

A few days after their visit to the cemetery, Maris made her decision about Peter's letter. She would show it to the police. She realized that Peter would not have left the letter for her if he didn't intend her to do something about it. And if his discovery of the animal parts had led to his death, she owed it to him to get to the bottom of it. She decided she would not tell Dinah — and she certainly would not tell Angela — that she was going to the police. The time for debate had passed. She had made up her mind.

She left the gallery early, telling Dinah she was going to the dentist. She didn't feel good about lying, but decided she would come clean later and tell Dinah the truth after she had spoken to the police. She took the 197 bus to Neil Road and then walked to New Bridge

Road where the Criminal Investigation Department was located. She asked to see a senior officer in the major crimes division. She wasn't going to tell her story to five different people as she ascended the hierarchy. The police officer at the information desk had to be persuaded that she was reporting a serious crime. It wouldn't have been worth his job to send her upstairs with a nuisance complaint. Maris refused to budge and he finally phoned someone who instructed him to send her up. An irate foreign lady could make a lot of noise if she wanted to.

A young female police officer took Maris to Block C, Room 304. The nameplate on the door said Inspector Simon Lam. The officer knocked on the door, opened it, and listened for a moment. She then told Maris to sit and wait for a few minutes. Maris obliged and sat on a yellow plastic chair bolted to a bar along with several other yellow plastic chairs. She was the only one waiting.

After a while, Maris looked at her watch and saw that ten minutes had passed. It felt like half an hour. There were no magazines to read, no piped-in music to listen to, just the sounds of phones ringing and people talking in the distance. There was a time, she thought, when there would have been the clacking of typewriters, but no more.

Another ten minutes passed and Maris realized she was tapping her foot in impatience. She reminded herself that she didn't have an appointment and that the inspector was probably a busy man. She thought of Peter and reminded herself why she was here.

After a few more minutes the door to Inspector

Lam's office opened and a man walked out. At first his head was turned toward the occupant of the office as he said goodbye, but when he turned toward Maris, she recognized him immediately. It was Axel. He saw her at the exact moment she saw him.

"Axel," she said. "What are you doing here?"

He didn't say anything for a moment. Obviously, he hadn't expected to see her. *Was he trying to think up a story?* she wondered.

"Maris," he said. "What are you doing here?"

"I asked you first," she said.

"Oh," he replied. "I, uh, was consulting Inspector Lam on a matter of personal business."

"But this is the major crimes division," she said.

"Yes," said Axel. "Yes, it is."

She looked at him and raised her eyebrows.

"Why don't we meet later and I'll tell you all about it," he said. "Come to my hotel when you're done and we'll have a drink."

"Okay," she said. "I will."

Axel left and Maris stood up as a tall Chinese man in a grey suit opened the door to his office and signalled for her to enter. He pointed to a chair and she sat. The office was not large and seemed even smaller because of the file cabinets lined up along two of the walls. There were files stacked on top of the cabinets, and more files piled on Inspector Lam's desk. The chair she sat in was upholstered in a woolly brown fabric and had wooden arms. Lam sat behind a large wooden desk half-covered with a green blotter. He had very short black hair, high cheekbones, and black eyes that revealed nothing.

"I'm Inspector Simon Lam," he said. "What can I do for you?"

"My name is Maris Cousins," she said, "and I have evidence in a murder case."

This got his attention and he raised his eyebrows, which were like two straight black lines that had been painted on with a brush, the kind used in Chinese calligraphy.

"A murder," he repeated. It wasn't a question.

"Yes," said Maris, reaching into her handbag for Peter's letter. "I recently found this letter in a trunk that was left to me by Peter Stone. He was a friend of mine. He owned an art gallery until his untimely death. I'm an artist and he used to sell my paintings there."

"I see," said Lam, reaching for the letter. He put on a pair of wire-rimmed glasses and read the letter. He appeared to read it twice. His face revealed very little, but he seemed to be considering what he read very carefully.

"And you think he was murdered," he said.

"He was murdered," said Maris. "I was there when he died. It's an unsolved crime. Look it up."

Lam sighed and turned toward a computer that was sitting on the side of his desk. He punched a few keys and read what Maris assumed was the file on Peter's death.

"You're right," he said. "It's an unsolved homicide."

"Do you think this letter might be a clue?"

Lam looked at her and said, "Leave it with me. I'll look into it."

"I'll want it back," she said. "Can't you take a copy?"

Lam shook his head. "No, but I'll see that you get it back." He reached into a drawer and pulled out a plastic bag with a zip top. He dropped the letter in and wrote something on the front of the bag. "It's evidence," he said.

As soon as she walked out of Inspector Lam's office, Maris remembered Axel. What had he been doing here? Did it have something to do with his job? When she thought about it, she realized she knew very little about what Axel did for a living and why he was in Singapore. Whenever she asked, he put her off by saying it wasn't very interesting or he didn't want to talk about work while he was with her. "It's just a job," he said. "I work for a company with international interests and I sometimes have to go in and re-organize things. I'm kind of a troubleshooter. I solve problems."

It sounded kind of interesting to Maris. "What kind of problems?" she asked.

"You know," he said, with a dismissive wave of his hand. "Low productivity, bad management, that kind of thing. Boring stuff. And you're making me talk about it."

"Okay," she said, giving in. "But if it's so boring, why do you do it?"

"The paycheque," he said. "It pays well, and I get to go to exotic places and meet exotic women like you."

"I'll bet you're good at it," she said.

"What? Meeting exotic women?"

"No. Troubleshooting. I'll bet you don't give up until you solve the problem."

"You're right about that," he said. "That's why they pay me so well. I get results."

"But I'll bet you don't make many friends."

"Friends?" he said. "What are they?"

She laughed. "We're friends, aren't we?"

"Am I missing something here?" he said. "I thought we were more than friends."

She smiled. "Just checking," she said.

Now Maris wondered how a major crimes inspector could be part of Axel's troubleshooting job. Or had he said it was personal business? That was even harder to fathom. He could have discovered some sort of crime in the workplace; that would be understandable. But personal business? What could that mean? Was he in some kind of trouble?

Maris was back on the 197 bus heading for Raffles. Then she realized Axel would probably want to know why she was seeing Inspector Lam. They would be playing "You Show Me Yours and I'll Show You Mine." But she would make him talk first.

Axel was waiting for her in the Writer's Bar in the lobby of the hotel. He stood up when he saw her and said, "Let's go out to the Courtyard. Less chance of being overheard." She was glad, in a way, that he hadn't invited her up to his room for a drink, but she thought it was strange. Was he afraid she'd make a scene?

They ordered a pitcher of Tiger beer and Maris said, "What's up?"

Axel didn't answer right away. "I've been debating all afternoon whether I should come clean with you," he finally said.

Come clean? Was this going to be some kind of confession?

"What do you have to come clean about?" she said. "Aren't you who you say you are?"

"Yes," he said. "I'm Axel Thorssen and I'm from Sweden. But I'm not a businessman. I'm a police officer and I've been seconded to Interpol to investigate a crime." He waited while she absorbed this. "I'm working with the Singapore police to track down an international smuggling operation."

She smiled. "You're kidding, right?"

"No, I'm not, Maris. I didn't want to tell you because I didn't want to jeopardize the investigation."

"How could telling me jeopardize your investigation? Don't you trust me?"

Axel poured more Tiger into his glass. Maris had barely touched her beer. "Of course I trust you," he said. "But it's more complicated than that."

"I don't understand," she said.

"I'm investigating the gallery. I was undercover when I met you. That's why I didn't identify myself."

"Are you investigating Peter's murder?"

"No, not exactly. But Simon Lam called me after you left and told me about the letter. I'm investigating the smuggling of animal parts, endangered animals that are being killed for those body parts. It's a huge, billion dollar industry and it involves a number of countries. Peter Stone stumbled onto something that probably got him killed. These people don't fool around."

"So you got chummy with me and Dinah to find out what we knew?"

"No, it wasn't like that. The gallery was on a list of places I was checking out. We didn't know how the stuff was being transported, and one of the possibilities was through the shipment of artifacts. Galleries came up as a possible conduit. I had no idea when I walked in that there was anything going on. I got curious when I found out that Peter's ex-wife spent a lot of time in Germany and shipped stuff from there on a regular basis."

"Angela?" she said. "You think she's involved?"

"I don't know. I just know that there are complex networks set up to throw us off the track. These shipments go through Europe and North America and most of them end up in China and other parts of Asia, where the demand is high. I thought Singapore might be a link in the chain, mainly because it was so unlikely. Regulations here are so strict that it would be hard to get stuff in and out. But in a way that made it perfect. If they could circumvent all those regulations, they'd be home free. They could ship anywhere. And what better front than a gallery like Peter's?"

"But Peter couldn't have had anything to do with it," she said. "I know he couldn't."

"No, you don't know that," said Axel. "Not for sure. He and Angela might have had a lucrative sideline that you knew nothing about."

"But the letter," said Maris. "Why would he write the letter?"

"I don't know," said Axel. "That's something Lam and I are going to have to look into."

Maris felt like she was talking to a stranger. Axel wasn't the man she thought he was. She had fallen in love with the other Axel. Was she in love with this one, too? Could she love someone who might destroy everything that mattered to her?

"I don't know who you are," she said.

"Yes, you do," he said. "I'm Axel. I'm still the same man I was before."

"No, you're not," she said. "You're a man with secrets; you must have lied to me. You were thinking things about my friends that could destroy them."

"No," he said. "I wouldn't do that."

"Are you going to arrest Angela?"

"Look," he said, opening his hands in a gesture of surrender, "I don't have any evidence yet connecting Angela or Peter to the smugglers. But I have to look into it, especially now that we have the letter. I have no choice."

Maris shook her head. "Am I in some kind of alternate universe?" she said. "I feel like my whole world has just been turned upside down and I have no control over anything. Do you know what that feels like?"

Axel shook his head. "No, not really. But I'm trying to understand."

"You're trying to understand?" she said. "I don't think so. You're just doing your job, isn't that right? And nothing's going to get in your way."

"Please, Maris. I've already said too much. This is an ongoing investigation and I shouldn't be talking about it. I just wanted you to know the truth. For me it's a relief to be able to tell you, but I can understand that for you it's a terrible revelation. I do understand. These are your friends. I'm sorry it had to happen this way. There's no way I could have known."

"Will you tell me what happens next?"

"I don't know what happens next. Obviously we'll have to talk to Angela and to Dinah. Something was delivered to the gallery that shouldn't have been. We have to find out how that happened."

"Oh, so now Dinah's involved, too, is she?"

"Please, Maris. If they haven't done anything, it will be a non-issue."

"If?" said Maris. "If they haven't done anything? It sounds like they're already prime suspects."

"Just let me do my job, Maris. I'm sure we can clear this up quickly."

Maris stood up to go. "Yes," she said. "Clear it up quickly and then we'll examine the wreckage."

He looked at her and understood her anger. "I have to ask you for one favour," he said quietly. "Please don't say anything to Angela and Dinah. Will you promise me? Just for the next few days. Please."

"Fine," she said. "Whatever."

CHAPTER THIRTY-NINE

Maris was angry when she left the hotel. Angry and hurt. Axel had lied to her from the beginning and now he was asking her to lie to Dinah and Angela. He was a policeman, of all things. She went back over some of their conversations and wondered if she had said anything that might put the gallery in a bad light. No, of course she hadn't. Because there was nothing wrong. The gallery had a reputation that Peter — okay, and Angela; give her some credit — had painstakingly built over the years. The gallery did well. Why would they be involved in smuggling?

The artifact that Peter had broken must have been sent by mistake. But would they be able to prove it? Or would there be a permanent shadow cast on the gallery because she had gone to the police with Peter's letter. She felt guilty, and then she was angry at herself for feeling guilty. None of this was her fault, but had she been stupid to trust Axel? Should she have seen something, a sign that told her he wasn't who he said he was? But she hadn't. She had fallen in love with him, which meant she had fallen in love with a lie. Did that mean he wasn't in love with her? Maybe this wasn't any easier for him. He was in the middle of an Interpol investigation that had led him to Peter's gallery. He had either used her and Dinah to get information — although she couldn't think what information they had given him — or he had fallen for her and everything he'd said was true. Fifty-fifty. Which was it?

Maris didn't go back to the gallery but took the bus to Dinah's apartment so she could be alone for a while. Dinah wouldn't be home for a couple of hours. Maris decided to pick something up for dinner so they wouldn't have to cook. She stopped at the food court near the apartment and got some fish sambal and rice. They could re-heat it in the microwave if Dinah was late. She also bought some beer at the 7-Eleven and some ice cream. Then she got a video — something called *The Bourne Ultimatum* with Matt Damon. Dinah loved Matt Damon. Maris figured the more they were eating, drinking, and watching the movie, the less they would be talking. And the less they talked, the fewer lies she would have to tell.

She hated the idea of lying to Dinah. True, she had told a lie when she said she was going to the dentist, but she had intended to confess and tell Dinah where she really had gone and why. But now she wouldn't be doing that. She would be continuing the lie, dragging it out, compounding it. She felt a little sick.

The following Monday, Angela told Maris and Dinah to unpack a shipment that had come from Frankfurt ten days before Angela arrived back in Singapore. It was one of the shipments she had instructed them to hold. Now she was supervising the unpacking and repacking of items to be shipped out to customers, or "clients," as Angela liked to call them.

Most of the items were very old or antique — pots, jugs, small statues, carved boxes inlaid with ivory, hand-painted dishes, and various spice jars and perfume bottles. Angela had a list of clients and their addresses, many of them in Singapore, but some in Japan, Taiwan, Canada, the United States, and South America, especially Argentina. Maris and Dinah were told which items were to be sent where, and how they should be packed. Wrapping them involved cotton batting, aluminum foil, bubble wrap, newspaper, and waxed butcher paper. Angela filled out the shipping and customs forms, as well as the address labels, and affixed them herself to each of the packages. Some items were being shipped to other galleries, but most went to individual clients. Lim was put to work cutting paper, tape, and string, occasionally stopping to make tea or go out for food. Angela wanted the work done in one day while the gallery was closed. She didn't want to have to stop for customers because she didn't want any mistakes made. She was a taskmaster and wouldn't even let them listen to music while they worked. No distractions, she said. They had to concentrate.

Maris and Dinah found the work tedious and a little mind-numbing, especially since Angela discouraged conversation, so they took frequent breaks just to annoy her, and also to alleviate the boredom. Eventually, though, they could see the pile of wrapped packages exceeding the pile of unwrapped ones. Angela, however, did not relax. "Remember," she said, "the first nine miles of a ten-mile journey is only halfway." They looked at her and shook their heads. *What had Peter ever seen in her?* Maris wondered. It certainly hadn't been her sense of humour that had attracted him. But Maris knew what it was. Angela's shrewd business sense had been a perfect fit with Peter's excellent taste and his savvy way with clients. They had been a team and the partnership had outlasted the marriage.

Just after three o'clock, when they were tying up the last of the parcels, someone started pounding — not knocking — at the front door of the gallery. They all stopped and looked at one another. The closed sign was squarely in the middle of the door, so no one could mistake the fact that the gallery wasn't open. The pounding persisted and Dinah finally went to see who it was, even though Angela told her to ignore it.

After a minute, Dinah came back with Axel, Simon Lam, and two uniformed police officers. Axel looked at Maris with an expression that seemed to ask for understanding. But Maris didn't understand. He had led her to believe things would move more slowly.

"Angela Stone, Dinah Stone, you're under arrest on suspicion of smuggling endangered animal parts into Singapore and attempting to export them illegally." It was Simon Lam who spoke. "Confiscate everything in this room," he told the two officers. "I'm sorry," he said, "but this gallery is closed until further notice."

Maris knew her mouth had fallen open but she made no attempt to close it. "Axel," she said, "what's going on?" His expression was grim as he turned away from her and signalled to Angela that she should go with him. Lam took Dinah's arm and began to lead her out through the gallery.

"Axel," said Maris, annoyance, anger, and frustration all collecting in her voice to make it sound harsh. "What are you doing? I told you nothing was going on."

Axel just shook his head and said, "I'm sorry, Maris, but I'm afraid you're wrong."

Dinah turned to Maris and said, "I don't understand. Did you know this was going to happen?"

Maris shook her head. "No. Dinah, I swear I didn't know. I'm sure this is some kind of mistake." She looked at Axel, but he was already putting Angela into the back of a police car. Simon Lam was leading Dinah to a second car. Maris looked back at Angela. Her head was down and she hadn't said a word. Had she known this was going to happen?

CHAPTER FORTY

Maris went to Axel's hotel later that night. She had waited for him to call but he hadn't. She had stayed in the back room of the gallery trying to figure out what to do. Finally she had called Peter's lawyer, Henry Fong, the one who had read the will and given her the trunk of Peter's things. He was as shocked as she was about what had happened. "I don't believe Peter would have been involved in such a thing," he said. "I'll see what I can do."

He called her back in a couple of hours and said they were holding Angela and Dinah for questioning and would not be releasing them for at least forty-eight hours.

"Can they do that?" she asked.

"Apparently, they can," he said. "This case involves Interpol and so there are a lot of players outside the Singapore police. I'll do what I can, but for the moment, that doesn't seem to be much."

"Can I see them?"

"Not tonight," he said. "Maybe tomorrow."

When Axel didn't call or answer when she called, she locked up the gallery and headed for Raffles. She would not leave until he told her what was going on.

Axel was in his room and appeared to be expecting her. He had ordered room service, and there was food and a bottle of wine on a cart that was covered with a white tablecloth.

"Come and eat something first," he said. "And have a glass of wine. This has been a terrible day for both of us and I think we need to step back for a minute before either of us says something we might regret."

"Are you going to tell me you were just doing your job?" she said.

He didn't answer her but started to uncork the wine. He poured her a glass and handed it to her. She took it but her hand was shaking and she had to put it down. He removed the silver covers from the plates of food and she saw that he had ordered sandwiches. She realized she was hungry; she hadn't eaten since lunch. She had sent Lim home right after the arrests and had asked her not to say anything, although she knew that word would have spread pretty fast already. The police had not been discreet; they had taken Dinah and Angela out the front door and put them in police cars in full view of everybody.

"I actually don't know what to say to you," Axel finally said, "except that the investigation led right to the gallery and we had to act fast. Obviously, I couldn't warn you. We had to have the element of surprise on our side."

"You mean the element of shock, don't you?"

"Look," he said. "We did it as quickly and as quietly as we could."

Just then, Axel's mobile rang. He looked at the call display and said, "I have to take this. Excuse me." He went out into the corridor, closing the door behind him. Maris picked up a sandwich and took a bite. It was roast beef with horseradish, but it might as well have been sawdust.

Axel returned after ten minutes, turning off his phone. "I'm sorry," he said. "We won't be disturbed again."

"Who calls you at this time of night?" she said.

"My boss," he said. "There's a time difference and he waits until the end of his day. I had to give him an update."

"Why don't you just call him instead?"

"He's hard to reach. And it's easier this way. Besides, he's the boss." He smiled a half-hearted smile and shrugged. "How are the sandwiches?" he said, taking one.

"Fine," she said. "Why are you holding Dinah and Angela?"

"It's necessary," he said, taking a bite of his sandwich. Maris understood that chewing on the sandwich made it impossible for him to say anything. It gave him a chance to think up a plausible answer. "Look," he said, "this is a serious crime. We've been trying to crack this ring for two years now. We think Angela, and maybe Dinah, might be able to tell us something that can lead us to the bad guys."

"And for this you had to arrest them?"

"It's more complicated than that," he said, taking another bite of his sandwich. Maris sighed and took a big gulp of her wine. This was going to take a while.

"They're being held for questioning. If they're involved — and I'm not saying they are — then they could be a flight risk. We have to hold them."

"Where would they go?" she said. "I don't even think Dinah has a passport."

"She does," said Axel. "And Angela has lots of places to go."

"You think she'd take Dinah with her?"

"It's possible."

"You're nuts," she said. "Angela wouldn't do that. Not even if Dinah's life depended on it."

"We don't know that."

"Well, I know it," she said, defiance creeping into her voice. "Dinah's my friend and I know she doesn't have anything to do with this."

"And what about Angela?" he said.

"Angela is not my friend, but I've known her a long time. She's not the nicest person in the world, but I can't imagine she'd be involved in a crime."

"See, that's something you can't know," said Axel. "If she is involved, then she's good at keeping secrets and being circumspect. Of course you wouldn't know."

"But Peter …"

"Yes, Peter," he said. "Peter may have suspected but, unfortunately, he didn't say that. It might be what got him killed — this whole secret operation."

"So you don't think he was involved?"

"I can't say for sure, but he was killed for a reason, and it was probably connected to this. It all depends on who killed him. And we may never know that."

"Gee," Maris said, sarcastically, "maybe Dinah did it.

His own sister. Or Angela, his ex-wife. Or maybe they did it together."

"Don't, Maris. Don't make light of this. I'll do everything I can to find out what really happened. And if Dinah and Angela are cleared, I'll be the first one to break open the champagne. I don't want this to be happening any more than you do."

"Why do I have trouble believing that?" she said. "It would be a real feather in your cap to break up this smuggling ring. This is the perfect solution to the crime."

"Please, Maris, don't do this," he said. "I don't want this to destroy what we have."

"And just what do we have?" she said.

"I love you," he said. "I would have given anything for this to turn out differently."

Maris didn't say anything. She wanted to believe him but there was just too much stacked up against him. Obviously, his job came first. And, apparently, he didn't trust her enough to tell her there would be a raid on the gallery.

"If I had told you," he said, as if reading her mind, "would you have kept quiet and not told Angela and Dinah? Can you honestly say that?"

She took another drink of her wine. "I don't know," she said, finally. "I really don't know."

"Then maybe you can understand how torn I was about this. I wanted to tell you, but the policeman part of me knew it wouldn't be wise. None of us knows what we'd do in such a situation. What is right? To tell your friends or to do as the police say? Where does our loyalty ultimately lie?" He shook his head as she stood to go. "I never wanted to come between you and your friends."

A Comfortable Marriage

A Short Story
by
E. Sutcliffe Moresby

This is a tale of infidelity and betrayal, something that none of us would openly condone. Yet, who among us can say that, faced with these circumstances, we would not have done the same?

It is the story of a married man, a happily married man, in fact. I will call him Robert, but that is not his real name. The events of this story happened a long time ago and were told to me by Robert's wife, whom I will call Grace. Robert and Grace had been married for ten years when they decided to go to France for a holiday. They chose Nice because it was a pretty place and affordable. They would go for three weeks because that's what their budget allowed. If they had gone for two weeks, they could have lived quite well; four weeks would have meant they had to be extremely frugal; so they settled for three weeks, which would allow them to eat out and drink wine every day, and to stay in a nice hotel with a shared bath. They agreed it was a reasonable compromise. They could not know it would change their lives.

Robert and Grace considered themselves collectors of art on a small scale. They enjoyed discovering young artists who had not yet made a name for themselves. They would buy a painting or two and fancied they were patrons, helping out a struggling artist whose work they might not be able to afford some day in the future. They never thought of selling the art they purchased, for they were true collectors. No collector willingly gives up the things he collects. One of the reasons they had decided on Nice for their holiday was that there were a lot of painters in Nice and you could buy their pictures from them right on the street, no need for a middle man. That way, Robert and Grace knew that the artist got all the money. They felt good about that.

As soon as they arrived and checked into their hotel, Grace and Robert went out to look for the painters. It was a Sunday, so they knew the streets would be lined with artists displaying their pictures. It was a feast for an art lover, and the prices were extremely reasonable. Robert and Grace could buy anything they wanted. They felt like millionaires.

One artist whose work they particularly admired was a young woman named Celeste. She was very young, probably twenty-four or -five, with long, straight black hair, pale skin, with a seductive mouth and wide hips (remember, it was Grace who related the story to me). Celeste had talent and a passion for her work. "She had an inner fire," said Grace, "and she smouldered, all the time. I've never seen such energy. You could feel it coming off her, the heat of it."

Predictably, Robert felt it more than Grace. Grace knew it was there, but she didn't succumb to the ardent charm of it the way Robert did. Grace didn't know it at the time, but Robert was falling in love with Celeste. "She was everything I'm not," said Grace, "and I guess that appealed to him. I don't know. Who knows how men think in these situations?"

I suggested that perhaps they didn't think. Or they thought with something other than the brain. She nodded. She had never inspired such thinking in Robert, even though they had a happy, comfortable marriage. They certainly loved each other and had everything in common. But Robert must have been missing something. He didn't know what he was missing until he recognized it in Celeste.

Grace wasn't suspicious at first. Robert often went out walking at night by himself. She preferred to put her feet up and read a book or write a letter. They were comfortable with each other and didn't mind sometimes doing things separately.

"You must think me awfully naive," she said to me. "I should have guessed something was going on, but I hadn't a clue. I trusted him completely. We were happily married. I thought that was enough." But clearly, she admitted, it wasn't enough.

The affair came to light two days before they were to leave Nice. Grace had been wrapping and packing their acquisitions — they always brought an empty suitcase to carry them in — and she noticed that Robert was unusually pensive.

"What is it, dear?" she said. "Are you feeling all right?"

When he looked up, she saw tears in his eyes. "Robert," she said. "What on earth is the matter?"

"I'm so very sorry, Grace," he said, choking back a sob. "But I've fallen in love."

"In love?" she said. "With whom?"

"With Celeste," he said. "I'm mad about her."

It took Grace a moment to remember who Celeste was. They had encountered her on their first day in Nice, and had gone back a couple of more times to view her paintings, but that was over two weeks ago. Then Grace remembered. The long black hair, the pale skin, the smouldering brown eyes, the luscious red lips. (I think perhaps Grace may have embellished her memory for my benefit, knowing I was probably going to use it in a story some day.)

What were they to do? Although at first she was stunned, Grace soon had the presence of mind to suggest that perhaps this was just an infatuation and that Robert would get over it in time. These things happened to men in middle age in strange countries, except not usually when their wives were along. Grace was certain their marriage was strong enough to withstand Celeste's charms. It never occurred to her that Robert might have other ideas.

"Grace, dearest Grace," he said and she suddenly knew what was coming. *Don't*, she thought, *please don't say it. Please*. But say it he did. "I can't bear the thought of leaving her. She's ... she's ... I don't even have the words to describe what she means to me."

Grace had a few words in mind but she kept them to herself. As she was telling me the story some years after the fact, she was able to inject an irony and lightness of tone into it that I'm sure she did not feel at the time. I occasionally caught a glimpse of her sorrow as she related the events to me.

Robert did not return to England with Grace. He didn't want to deprive her of anything, he said. She was the best wife a man could have and she shouldn't blame herself for anything. She could divorce him if she wished. Grace couldn't believe he was saying such things. She was still certain that this was a middle-aged fling, an infatuation, and she had no intention of doing anything permanent. She would not divorce him.

Robert returned briefly to England to resign from his position as office manager for a shoe manufacturer. He called Grace and asked if she would pack a few of his things for him. He would stop by and pick up the suitcase when she wasn't there. He supposed she wouldn't want to see him. Grace was relieved. She wasn't ready to see him yet. Although she had convinced herself he would be back, Grace was hurting badly. She spent most of her days in a kind of fog. Her own reality was running parallel to the rest of the world's. She wasn't quite connected.

Robert, for his part, was living a bohemian life in Nice.

It was all crusty bread and smelly cheese and red wine. And sex. Celeste was a voracious woman, deeply passionate, and endlessly needy. Her artistic self was volatile and unstructured. One day she would be wildly ecstatic, the next deeply despairing. Robert had never known such a woman, except perhaps for his mother. But she did not have an artistic temperament; she had merely been moody and unstable.

What neither Robert nor Grace had considered was that Celeste would become pregnant. When she gave Robert the news, he knew he should feel joy, but instead he felt a tiny pang of distress in the pit of his stomach. What had begun as a wild ride into an open-ended future was now turning into a four-walled structure with a roof on it; something that felt a lot like a cell or a cage. Suddenly Celeste's passionate nature didn't seem so carefree and thrilling to him. The other thing was that Grace had refused to divorce him and Celeste was starting to talk about marriage, about being a family. She was demanding things of him. Material things: a decent place to live, furniture and clothes for the baby. Her needs were different now, she said.

So Robert panicked and did a runner. He went back to England and to Grace. He was ashamed of himself, he admitted, but he couldn't face a future with Celeste and a child. He just wanted it all to go away. But when Grace heard about the child, she wasn't so keen to take Robert back. Like Celeste, all she could think about was the baby: what it would need, how it would be looked after. She told Robert to go back to Celeste and face up to the life he had chosen. She would give him a divorce so he could make an honest woman of Celeste and give his baby a name. Grace said she could never live with a man who had abandoned his child. That was the end of it. She could manage without him. Celeste and the child could not.

Now it was Robert's turn to be stunned. Go back? Marry Celeste? Be a father? He hadn't asked for any of this. Celeste was being unreasonable and Grace was being unfair. It was as if nobody cared about him, about how he felt. It was all too much.

Grace went with him on the train and put him on the ferry at Dover. She wished him luck and told him she was sorry it had ended this way for them, but he had a responsibility to Celeste and the child and he must face up to it.

"It was the hardest thing I ever did," she told me. "I knew he was going to be deeply unhappy, that he wasn't suited to being a parent (nor was Celeste, for that matter), but it had to be done. I went straight home and took all the paintings we had bought and burned them in the backyard. I couldn't bear to have them around any longer."

Two weeks later she learned that although Robert had got on the ferry — she had watched him walk on and he had stood by the railing watching her as the ship backed away — he never got off at Calais. It wasn't until his body washed up on the beach in France that anybody even realized he was missing.

Grace took their life savings out of the bank (because she could not collect Robert's insurance after his death was declared a suicide) and went to Nice. She found Celeste and gave her the money. "It was all I could do," she told me. "I've never been back to Nice since, and I never shall go again. I hate the place."

CHAPTER FORTY-ONE

"I never wanted to come between you and your friends," Axel had said as she left his hotel room. She would give him the benefit of the doubt on that one, she decided. How could he have known things would work out this way? But to get so close to her and not to give her the slightest inkling of what he was up to? He had come into the gallery looking for smugglers. That's essentially what he'd said. They were on a list and he was checking everybody on the list. His interest in collecting had been a ruse so he had a reason to come back. He was good, she conceded. They hadn't had a clue.

But what about those mysterious phone calls he was always getting that he took in private? He said they were business. Now she knew they were probably police business. Interpol business. That annoyed her when she thought about it because it meant he was conspiring against her — against the gallery, at least — in front of her. Damn! The more she thought about it, the angrier she got. His behaviour was totally duplicitous. Had he been honest about anything? He had been conducting an investigation, not forging a relationship. They had been at cross purposes the whole time.

He had said he loved her. Should she demand he prove it? Should she call his bluff? Find out for once and for all? Either he loved her and wanted to be with her, or he had been using her and would find a way out. One way or the other, she needed to know.

But first she had to see what she could do about Dinah and Angela. They were being held, but had not yet been charged. Henry Fong, the lawyer who Maris had called, told her they were in a detention centre near the Polo Club. He could arrange bail, he said, but they could be held for forty-eight hours without charges being laid, so there wasn't much he could do until then. If charges were not laid after forty-eight hours, they would be let go. Best to wait, he said. In the meantime, he had arranged a visitor's pass for Maris so she could talk to them, but not both of them at the same time. Maris said she wanted to see Dinah first, then Angela.

Dinah was a mess. She knew enough about the Singapore prison system to be afraid. She told Maris not to be surprised if they locked her up and threw away the key. "And I haven't even done anything," she said.

"I know," said Maris, "and Henry's doing everything he can to get you out of here. Just try not to go crazy. We'll get you out."

"How could Axel have done this to us?" she said. "I thought he was our friend. I thought you and he were ... you know ... close."

"So did I," said Maris. "I don't know what to think now. I keep going over everything in my mind until I'm more confused than ever. The bottom line is that he's a cop, Dinah, and duty comes first. He told me he'd been working on this case for a couple of years. He didn't know anything about the gallery, just that it was on a list of possibilities that he was checking." She was shaking her head. "I just can't believe that this is happening."

"Believe it," said Dinah. "And be glad you're on that side of the Plexiglas."

Maris smiled. "I'd trade places with you if I could," she said. "You shouldn't be here."

"Have you talked to Angela yet?"

"No. I'm seeing her next," said Maris. "Do you think she knows anything about this?"

"I have no idea," said Dinah. "For all I know, she's the mastermind behind the whole thing. You know Angela, which means, I suppose, that neither of us knows anything about Angela. She comes and she goes. The shipments come in and the shipments go out. Your guess is as good as mine."

"Don't worry, Dinah. You'll be released. They won't find anything and they won't be able to hold you."

Dinah nodded but she looked defeated. "I hope I can stand another twenty-four hours of this. They keep asking me the same questions, over and over. And I keep giving them the same answers: I don't know anything. I don't know what they're talking about. I didn't see anything."

"Hang in," said Maris. She couldn't think of anything else to say.

Angela was cool and calm when Maris saw her. Even her hair was neatly combed, whereas Dinah looked like she hadn't slept or eaten. Angela looked the same as she had when Axel had taken her in for questioning. Her clothes weren't even wrinkled. She didn't say anything to Maris at first; she just watched and listened.

"Henry's doing everything he can to get you and Dinah out of here," she said. "They only have forty-eight hours to charge you, then they have to let you go."

Angela nodded. "Dinah didn't know anything about it," she said. "They have to let her go."

Maris stared at her. "What are you saying?"

Angela looked straight at her. "If they charge me," she said, "I will say nothing. It will be up to them to prove their case. And that will be difficult."

"Are you saying you knew about this?" said Maris.

"I'm not saying one way or the other. But Dinah definitely knew nothing about this. Don't let them railroad her, Maris. Talk to your friend" — she emphasized the word *friend* — "and tell him they have to let her go."

"I don't understand," said Maris. "You knew about the smuggling?"

"I'm not saying I did and I'm not saying I didn't. All I will say is that there are some very powerful people behind it and it's unlikely they'll be caught. It's unfortunate that Peter discovered what he did."

"So Peter didn't know anything about it," said Maris.

"Peter didn't know anything about it."

"Thank you, Angela. I needed to know that. But it got him killed, didn't it?"

Angela nodded.

"Why are you telling me this?" Maris said.

Angela shrugged. "A moment of weakness," she said. "It won't happen again."

Maris closed her eyes. She felt dizzy and knew if she stood up, she would probably pass out. She took a deep breath and opened her eyes. Angela was still looking at her with the same unreadable expression. In that moment, she realized that Axel had been right. And the letter from Peter that she had given to Simon Lam had merely confirmed his suspicions and sped up the investigation. Had she made a terrible mistake or would things have turned out the same way without the letter? She would probably never know.

Maris took a taxi back to Dinah's apartment. There was nothing to do but wait.

Why? Why had Angela done it? Why had she risked everything, including Peter's life, as it turned out? The money? Had it been worth it? She thought of a hundred questions she wanted to ask Angela, but it was too late. She wouldn't be able to ask them now. Angela had probably said all she was going to say. And why had she said it to Maris? That was one of the hundred questions. *Why me?*

Maris managed to sleep a few hours that night but she was awake at dawn pacing the apartment and drinking coffee. Her insides were in a knot and she threw up the coffee, which made her feel even worse. She found some cooked rice in Dinah's fridge and heated it in the microwave. She poured some milk over it and ate a couple of spoonfuls. Coffee on an empty stomach; she should have known better.

At ten o'clock, Henry Fong called. "They've released Dinah," he said, "but Angela's been charged with smuggling illegal contraband into and out of the country, and as a possible accessory in Peter's murder. They know she's not the big fish, but she's not talking. It's probably not worth her life," he said.

A few hours later, Axel brought Dinah home. She hugged Maris and burst into tears. "Come on," said Maris. "Get out of those filthy clothes and I'll run you a nice, hot bath." While the bath was running, Maris put the kettle on and made a chicken sandwich for Dinah. She asked Axel if he wanted a sandwich and he said, no, but he wouldn't mind a cup of tea.

While Dinah soaked in the tub, Axel and Maris sat in the living room not saying much. Then Axel's phone rang and he left the apartment to take the call.

Maris crept over and opened the door a crack to listen to the conversation. "I can't come home yet," she heard him say. "We've made an arrest in the case and I have to stay to tie up all the loose ends." Then he said, "I miss you, too." Maris quietly closed the door.

When he came back into the living room, she said, "You're married, aren't you?"

Axel hesitated, not knowing how to respond. Then he nodded. "Yes," he said.

"You were speaking English."

"Yes," he said. "My wife is from England. We met while I was attending a series of lectures at Oxford. Five years ago."

"So all those calls you took, those business calls at night ... they were from her?"

Axel nodded. "I'm sorry," he said. "I'm really sorry."

"Not as sorry as I am," she said.

He started to speak and she put up her hand. "Don't," she said. "Don't bother."

CHAPTER FORTY-TWO

The gallery remained closed for two weeks while Dinah and Maris decided what to do. Dinah had been shaken to the core by her experience with the police and with Angela's arrest. Maris had persuaded her to see a doctor and he had prescribed an anti-anxiety drug for six weeks to help her filter out the extreme feelings of stress and to help her sleep at night. Since she had no previous experience of stress brought on by trauma, or even mood swings, he decided against prescribing an antidepressant, and Maris was relieved. Dinah just needed a little time, some rest, and to have her confidence in the future restored.

She and Maris had many talks about the past and the future, but not much discussion of the present. The shock of what had happened to Peter hit them all over again now that they realized Angela had been involved.

"Do you think Angela might have poisoned him herself?" said Dinah. "She's capable of it."

"She might have," said Maris, "but she may have been acting on orders from some gangster and afraid for her life."

Dinah shook her head. "But to kill Peter? I just can't get my head around it."

"I know," said Maris. "I guess she was in too deep to get out. But we don't really know she did it."

"I don't care," said Dinah. "At this point, all I know is that what she did got him killed. It's the same thing."

"Well, maybe something will come out at the trial, but I doubt it." Maris hadn't told Dinah much about her conversation with Angela, except to say that Angela knew Dinah hadn't been involved. "She definitely did not want you to be charged."

"That makes me feel so much better," said Dinah. "I won't be blamed for killing my own brother. Thanks, Angela."

There are some wounds that don't heal, Maris thought. And this was one of them. They both believed that Angela should pay for what she did. But in Singapore, that probably meant the death penalty. At the very least, it meant a long stay in prison. Angela's life was effectively over. She believed they wouldn't be able to prove the charges, but Maris was pretty sure they could. There would be a trail somewhere. And Axel and Interpol were after the big fish. They wouldn't stop until they caught them.

Maris had thought long and hard about whether she should tell Axel about her conversation with Angela, but now that Dinah was free, she saw no reason to. Nothing would bring Peter back. They knew the truth now, even if they didn't know all the names. Peter had been killed because he'd accidentally stumbled on the evidence of wrongdoing. If he had just written the letter to Maris and not said anything to Angela, maybe he'd still be alive. But his mistake had been to assume that Angela knew nothing about it. His mistake had been to trust her.

Axel had called twice since Dinah's release. Once he had spoken to Dinah to make sure she was all right. And the second time he had talked to Maris, to apologize again and to try to explain.

"Just go back to your wife, Axel," she said. "Whatever we had is over. I could never trust you again. Let's just move on."

Move on. That was a laugh, she thought. What did moving on mean, anyway? You just forget it happened? You pretend it didn't happen? You draw a line, step over it, and never look back? It was easy to say, but not so easy to do. She thought about Axel most of the time, especially last thing at night and first thing in the morning. He was just there, in her thoughts, all the time. She truly had fallen in love with him. It wasn't so easy to let that go. And then, of course, there was the baby. She was sure now, but she hadn't said anything to anyone. Pretty hard to move on when you were going to have a baby.

She wanted the baby; it hadn't taken long for her to decide to keep it. What took longer was deciding whether to tell Axel about it. But finally she decided not to. Maybe someday, for the child's sake, she'd say something. But that was a long way off. Right now, the important thing was to have a healthy baby and to raise her child.

So for now, she concentrated on getting the gallery going again. She told Dinah she wanted them to run it together. Technically, the gallery belonged to Dinah. Angela had agreed to sign the necessary papers so that Dinah had sole ownership. Nobody could take it away from her. That was ultimately what pulled Dinah out of her funk. The gallery was hers and she could keep Peter's memory alive in it.

"Maris, are you sure you want to stay and help me?" she said. "I'd understand if you didn't."

Maris told her she was sure. She would tell Dinah about the child soon. But first they would make plans for the gallery.

"I'm going to get my brother Ray to come here," she told Dinah. "I want us to give his photography a show. I promise you he's good enough."

Dinah smiled. "I'm sure he is," she said. "If he's half as talented as you, he'll be very good."

"And next year, we'll have a show for me. I promise."

"I'll hold you to it."

"I'm serious. I want to paint again, and I will. I've already started."

"I know," said Dinah. "I love what you've been doing."

"You peeked?" said Maris.

"I peeked." Dinah hesitated. They hadn't talked about Axel, but it was Axel who had told her that Maris was working again. She had begun soon after their visit to the bird park. She had been inspired to paint by the brilliantly coloured parrots, lorikeets, peacocks, and, especially, the scarlet macaw. The macaw's magnificent plumage, starting with the vibrant red head and shoulders, moving into a ring of molten yellow around the middle, and extending into a stunning cerulean blue on the lower body and tail, had grabbed Maris's heart and hadn't let go. The bird was an explosion of colour that reminded, re-minded her, of why she painted.

It was then that she had known that life was full of colour and possibilities.

HISTORICAL NOTE

There is no graveyard attached to St. Andrew's Cathedral in Singapore. For story purposes I had to invent one because most of the old cemeteries in Singapore (including the Fort Canning Cemetery, which is also referred to) were dug up to make room for urban development. Records from 1952 show that there were 229 registered burial grounds in the rapidly growing metropolis. As these cemeteries were closed, the bones were exhumed and cremated. Whenever possible, the cremated remains were moved to the Choa Chu Kang Columbarium, part of the only cemetery in Singapore still open for burials. The terms and conditions of the Choa Chu Kang Cemetery state that after fifteen years, a body shall be exhumed for reburial or cremation.

A Cold Season in Shanghai
978-1894917797
$19.95

In this searing historical novel set amid the turmoil of early twentieth century Shanghai, three women, one Russian, one Chinese, and one French, determine the tragic fate of a young piano prodigy. Which of them is really responsible? *A Cold Season In Shanghai* is set against the backdrop of revolution in China, when decadent Shanghai was like no other place on earth. The narrator is Tatiana, a Russian woman brought up in a wealthy family. Looking back on her actions thirty years later from her new life in Toronto, she recalls the complex relationships between the three women and the effect they had on each other's lives. She suspects she may have been the catalyst for a series of devastating events that caused havoc in the lives of her friends. Tormented by the aftermath of her decision, she chooses to live a life of careless abandon, turning her back on her family and, ultimately, her friends.

DUNDURN

Visit us at
Definingcanada.ca
@dundurnpress
Facebook.com/dundurnpress